The Girl In Room 16

A Darcy Hunt FBI Mystery Suspense Thriller
Book 1

EVA SPARKS

Prologue

An orange flame flickered atop a solitary candle perched in the middle of the stone floor. The muted glow animated eerie shadows that danced across the greystone walls, dark sheets of gyrating motion that looked like evil spirits conspiring to step into the room.

The girl huddled her ten-year-old body into the corner as tightly as she could, trying to use what little warmth she was generating to insulate her younger sister against the cold.

"I can't feel my toes," Lila said.

"Me neither," she replied. "It won't be much longer."

"I'm scared."

I am too.

But she didn't say it out loud. She had to be strong for Lila, which meant that she had to keep her own fear and terror locked tightly inside. On the other side of the steel door, she could hear

1

the chanting getting louder. She tugged at the hem of her nightgown again, drawing it back down to her bare ankles. Her teeth began to chatter.

"Whatever happens," she said, "I'll protect you. I promise."

"I miss Mommy."

"Mommy is looking for us right now. So is Daddy. They'll find us."

The chanting was almost feverish now, its cadence rising and falling with an unearthly energy that brought muted sobs from Lila's little body. "What do they want with us?" she cried.

I don't know.

"They won't hurt us," she reassured her little sister. "They'll just..."

The chanting stopped, and everything became eerily quiet. High above them, a narrow horizontal opening in the wall whistled in a flurry of snow that drifted to the floor like frozen tears.

The silence was shattered by the heavy bolt in the iron door sliding back. It echoed across the stone floor and walls, not fully dissipating before the door was thrown open. Lila screamed as a hooded figure stepped into the room. Her sister gathered her close as it moved toward them and stopped not three feet away. When it spoke, the deep resonance of the voice caused a haunted shiver to run through both girls.

He extended his arm and then, slowly, a finger. It was directed at Lila. "You. It's time."

The man was clothed in a dark flowing robe, the contours of his face hidden beneath the sprawl of a thick hood. The robe drifted along the floor, and the oversized sleeves rested below his wrists.

"No..." Lila's sister said, and then with a sudden surge of

panic, "*No!*"

The man in the hooded robe reached out and snatched at Lila. Like a terrified rodent with no place to run, Lila huddled closer to her sister, who then snapped at the man: "Take me. What—whatever you want with her, mister... *please*, take me."

"All in the proper order." The man took a step back and raised an arm high above his head. Moments later, soft footsteps sounded on the floor behind him. Two more figures similarly clothed stepped in beside him. He pointed down at Lila again. "Her."

With swift, ghoulish movements, the two figures swooped in and grabbed Lila, quickly pulling her from her sister's grasp.

She screamed as Lila was yanked from her. "*Nooo!*" She scrambled to her feet and reached for the little girl. One of the figures stepped forward and shoved her back. Her shoulder blades slammed into the wall just before the back of her head smacked against it with a hollow crack. Dazed, she fell to the floor and watched through blurry vision as the three shadows disappeared through the door with her sister. She wildly screamed Lila's name again and again, begging for help as she was carried away.

The door slammed shut, and the bolt was secured. Soon, the sound of her sister's cries drifted away. "Lila... Lila..." she muttered through a state of half awareness. "I'll protect you... I promise."

She swam in and out of consciousness. High above her, snow continued to swirl in and drift down, dusting her in a powdery film. Too cold to even shiver and too dazed to tug her gown across her bare legs, she lay there, unmoving and unthinking, hardly able to feel the horror of what was happening, but wondering deep inside why anyone would do something like this to two young girls.

Time slipped by. The candle went out. Somewhere she could smell smoke. The next thing she was aware of was a loud thud that jolted her back into a semi-conscious state. It sounded again, and she heard anxious voices coming from the other side of the door. Too weak to move her lips, she tried to squeak out the only thing screaming to get out of her chest. "*Help.*" But the word miscarried in her throat. She couldn't speak.

The thud came again, louder this time, and then again. The door clattered off its hinges and crashed with an ear-splitting clang to the floor. A rush of footsteps entered the room, accompanied by an assembly of worried voices.

One of the voices called her name. It was gentle, not hard and commanding like the voice of the man who had taken her sister.

She tried to speak, but her voice would not obey.

"It's okay, Sweetheart. Just a minute. We're going to get you out of here."

She felt the soft fibers of a blanket draped over her, and the cold slowly retreated beneath it. Minutes passed and she was laid on a stretcher and carried out of the room. Flashlight beams cut across the walls, but she could make nothing out. Nothing but cold, gray stone.

Swallowing, she focused all her energy on uttering a single word. "Lila."

A long pause, and then another gentle voice, different from the first, said, "Just relax. You're safe now."

As they carried her to safety, she felt the unrelenting grip of sleep pulling her back under. Just before she closed her eyes and drifted off, her lips traced the words: "I'll protect you. I promise."

Chapter One

Present Day
Delfax County, NY

"Do you think he's dead?" Skylar's fingers squeeze my forearm while her other hand covers her mouth and concerned eyes bulge toward the scene of the accident.

"I don't know," I say. "He hit his head pretty hard. He'll be lucky to walk away with just a concussion."

We're standing behind a temporary railing designed to keep spectators off the road and out of the path of the cyclists. Twenty yards away, golden bales of hay stand along the verge where the country road enters a hairpin turn, some of them overturned now and hay strewn across the asphalt.

"Or walk away at all." Her voice is pitched and filled with concern. "How was his helmet not on?" Skylar is still speaking from behind her hand. Because I prefer the feeling of blood flowing through my arm, I slowly peel her iron grip off me as medical personnel and training staff hurry to the scene of the crash.

"When the bicycle flipped, one of the handlebars snagged the back of his helmet and ripped it off," I reply.

We arrived in the New York countryside last night from Albany to watch a regional cycling race. Cycling is Skylar's preferred sport of choice, and she regularly travels around the region to watch and participate in races. Although I prefer tennis, the race was a perfect opportunity to get away and get in some much-needed girl time with my best friend. Work has kept me busy lately as I focus on catching the unsubs that are still running free throughout my city.

I have hardly seen Skylar at all these last few months. She is a special agent in the FBI's Rochester field office, on the other side of the state, which means that we don't get to spend nearly as much time together as we would like. One of us usually tries to make the trip to see the other every few weeks, but even that has been hard to do lately, as I haven't had a single moment for myself, opting for short catnaps at my desk or on a couch at the office. At one point, I didn't even return to my apartment for three days, only doing so when my ASAC ordered me to under threat of transferring the case to another agent. I finally conceded and returned home for a shower and a change of clothes. After sleeping for several hours in the comfort of my own bed, I made a protein shake in the kitchen before making a beeline back to the office.

All my diligence finally paid off when we caught the Night Knocker Killer four days ago. For over a year now, he had plagued northeastern New York. His MO was simple enough: at exactly midnight, he would knock on the front door of a single woman's home. After making sure that he woke them, he would leave. The next night, they would be dead in their beds, strangled to death. Seven victims had fallen prey to his hands when he finally grew bolder and started to increase his frequency. Instead of one victim a month, he moved to one a week.

The Night Knocker was growing thirstier, looking for a fresh kick of endorphins and a rush of adrenaline that, for him, accompanied the violent taking of an innocent life. My ASAC finally let me get involved with the case when the number of victims had risen to double digits and no clear leads had been established. For six weeks, the Night Knocker struck every week without fail. Four of the final six victims had even gone to stay with relatives or friends away from the city after receiving a midnight knock on their door. But it hadn't helped. The killer still managed to find them the next night, slipping in and out of the homes without being detected.

And that had been why I couldn't sleep, why I couldn't allow myself to get back to normal life. Every week that went by meant another innocent woman whose life would be taken from her. If my office couldn't stop the Night Knocker, then he would only continue to prowl and breed terror in the community that I love and have sworn to protect. That meant sleep and going to visit Skylar for the weekend was a luxury I couldn't allow myself.

The break in the case finally came when a piece of evidence from the most recent murder connected with another detail I had found tucked away in an ME's report. We scrambled a SWAT team to a house on the outskirts of the city and arrested James Chalmers as he sat on his couch watching *Taxi Driver*. His kitchen table was littered with the names, photos, and addresses of his next five victims. He had it all planned out.

My office presented me with an award for breaking the case, even going so far as to order cake and bring in balloons. I really hate that kind of attention. Being in the spotlight is just not my thing, and knowing the names and faces of the very women whose lives we had saved was reward enough.

I didn't join the FBI because I knew the work would be easy or because I could put in my forty hours and then go home without thinking about work until Monday morning. I became a federal law enforcement officer because, more than ever, dedicated people are in demand, men and women who expect to put in long hours with average pay, but who feel a strong sense of purpose knowing that they are a necessary arm of justice.

Don't get me wrong. Some days I catch myself wondering if there are other lines of work that I might enjoy more. It's usually when Bureau politics somehow hinder the forward progress of one of my investigations that I start to wonder. I have friends who love being lawyers, flight attendants, and small business owners. But no matter how much political garbage I have to navigate in the workplace, I remain committed to my work as a special agent. The FBI isn't just a career for me. It's a calling, and nothing else will make me feel truly fulfilled.

"Look," Skylar says. "They're putting him on a stretcher."

We watch as the medical staff wrap the cyclist's neck in a cervical collar and then slip a stretcher beneath him.

"It might be a good thing that you didn't race this morning," I said. "That's a hard turn in the road. I can't believe he has been the only one to bite it so far."

The women's race had been held earlier this morning. Normally, Skylar would have entered it and placed somewhere in the top ten, but a recent knee injury kept her out this time around.

"It was a freak accident," she says. "It could have happened to anyone."

"My point exactly."

"You sound like my mother right now. Stop sounding like my mother." She shoots me a wily grin.

"Fine, but looking at that cyclist and thinking of it being you—"

"Well, it's not," she interrupts. "And everything worth doing comes with its risks."

"All I'm saying is that you have a kid to think about. If you wipe out, then I'm the one who will have to bring Reuben to the hospital and watch him see you like that. Anyway, I'm not telling you not to get back on the seat after your knee heals."

"Darcy," she says. "I'll always be careful. I promise."

"I know," I sigh. "And I'm sorry. I don't mean to sound like your mother."

Her mouth curves upward into a smile. "I know you don't. And I'm just teasing you. I know why you watch out for me like that."

"Thanks." I take in a deep breath of fresh, country air. "I'm glad I came with you. I didn't realize how much I needed the time away."

As soon as we arrived last night, Skylar and I immediately found the nearest—and possibly the only—foot spa. After getting full pedicures, we crossed the street, settled into a booth at the steakhouse, and ordered steaks and drinks. With our stomachs full, we returned to our hotel room and watched a movie with Kate Winslet in the lead role. Exhausted from a rigorous work schedule, I fell asleep halfway through, leaving Skylar to finish it by herself. But this morning, I woke up feeling refreshed and ready for a relaxing day in the countryside.

The sun is climbing higher into the sky, and I can feel the heat warming my face a little too much. Reaching into my handbag, I bring out a ball cap, pull my long hair back, and thread it through the hole in the back of the cap before settling it onto my head.

"You need to come in this week and let me give you a cut," Skylar says. She runs her fingers down the length of my chestnut brown hair. "It's way too long."

"I like it," I contend. "It's not even halfway down my back."

"But it needs more style—layers. Not many. Just enough to give it a little more charm."

Skylar has been styling hair ever since we were in high school. Even though she's a top-notch FBI agent during the week, in her spare time, she works magic with her scissors and hair dyes on a few clients every weekend. She has gained a reputation for turning bland into bravo and gets paid well for it, too.

Her sunflower blonde hair contrasts sharply with mine, her bright blue eyes with my hazel, and she stands an inch taller than my five-foot-seven frame. We couldn't look more different, but we couldn't get along better; I'm lucky to have her as a best friend. At twenty-nine, she's a year older than me and has a beautiful nine-year-old boy, Reuben.

Skylar keeps me balanced. She's always pushing for me to get away, cut loose, or just find a way to relax. I really don't know what I would do without her. I would probably be a workaholic on my way to complete burnout. There are plenty of good agents who can put the job behind them when they go home to their families at night. I'm not one of them. For one, I don't have a family to go home to. And second, I feel the weight of solving each and every case I work on. The victims deserve it. At the Academy, they teach new agents to leave work at work whenever possible. It's their attempt at making sure that their agents stay fresh and don't go looking for a new line of work a few years into their new career. But what never leaves me is the knowledge that if I don't solve a case, then the odds are it will never get solved. Other agents have their own cases to deal with. They don't have time to pick one up that I can't solve. Even if they did, it would only be added to a stack of other cases they're currently working on. Eventually, it would get placed into a cold case folder and the victims' relatives would never know peace. I know something about not getting closure, about going to bed every night wondering... I don't want that for anyone else.

Skylar is shooting me a look.

"What?" I ask.

"You didn't answer me."

"About what?"

"Your hair. You need to let me style it."

I gave her the same answer I do every time she brings it up. "Maybe. We'll see."

"Mhm."

It's not that I don't care about adding a little more style to my look; it's more that I like it the way it is. My hair is naturally shiny and easy to throw into a ponytail, something essential when you're pouring over a thick file or inspecting a crime scene. I know Skylar and she'll want to layer it, which means that half the ponytail will probably try to slip out of whatever hair tie I throw it up in.

Skylar glances at her watch. "It's not noon yet," she says. "Once they get the road cleared, the race should be over in another half hour. We should have time to peruse some of the boutiques in town before we head back to the city. Want to?"

Just as I begin to form an answer, we're interrupted by my phone ringing.

Chapter Two

County Road 58
Delfax County, NY

"You're getting a signal out here?" Skylar asks.

I draw my phone out of my pocket and glance at the screen. It only shows one service bar, but that's not what I'm paying attention to. Skylar must have seen a change in my demeanor because she quickly says, "It's not your office, is it? Tell me it's not work."

"It's work," I sigh. "Hold on. Maybe they just have a quick question."

"And maybe I was in the race this morning," she mutters as I walk off for some privacy.

The collective attention of more than a hundred spectators remains riveted to the crash area as I answer my phone and set it to my ear. "This is Darcy."

"Hunt, I'm sorry to bother you on the weekend. Are you still at the race?"

It's Ted Kemper, the SAC of the Albany field office. I was expecting a fellow field agent to be calling with a question about a case. But Kemper calling doesn't give me much hope that my weekend will continue uninterrupted.

"Yes, sir. The men's race is going on now."

"And that's in Delfax County, right?"

I don't know how he got that information. I didn't make a public announcement to the office where I was going this weekend. "Yes, sir. That's right."

A dead silence takes up the next several seconds. I assume Kemper is thinking, trying to come to a decision. I don't have to wait long for an explanation.

"Here's the deal, Hunt. I know you have been working both ends of the candle with the Chalmers case. And now that you finally got that wrapped up, I'm sure you are enjoying a Saturday in the sun."

I can see the remainder of my relaxing weekend with Skylar fading away. "Actually, sir. That's exactly what I'm doing."

"Then I hate to be the one to send you back out, but a township not too far from you is requesting our help. It's the next county over... Cascade County."

Hearing the name of the county makes my insides bristle. "They're asking for our help?" I say. "That's unusual."

Generally speaking, law enforcement prefers to keep local cases in-house, as it were. Procedures and transmission of case information tend to get off balance when more than one agency is involved. Bringing in an outside agency like the FBI is basically an admission that their guys aren't able to do something on their own. It also creates a clash of egos, with both sides wanting to assert authority and the locals generally losing that battle to the

Feds. "It is unusual," Kemper agrees. "But they have an unusual situation on their hands."

Something had started eating at me the moment Kemper told me the name of the county. I recall that Cascade County is large and boasts several townships. I say a silent prayer that this is not fate about to mock me. Speaking through pursed lips, I say, "What town?"

Kemper doesn't miss a beat, and when he answers, I immediately feel like the bruised and broken cyclist laying on the stretcher ahead of me. "Miller's Grove."

I close my eyes and my knuckles turn white as I tighten my grip on the phone.

"Hunt?"

"I'm here," I say, and take a deep, quiet breath. "What is the situation they need help with? You said it's unusual?"

"Someone found a body at a local motel. Normally, their local PD could handle it, but of their two detectives they have, one is on an Alaskan cruise and the other is in ICU recovering from a car accident. Since we're the closest FBI field office, they called to see if we had someone to send out. I figured since you're probably not fifty miles from there, you could pick it up."

"What about a county detective?" I ask. I know bringing up other possibilities won't stop me from having to go; Kemper wouldn't have called if there was another solution. But I want to get a fuller picture before I have to bring my relaxing weekend to an abrupt conclusion.

The crowd of spectators lets out a happy cheer as the cyclist, still lying on the pavement with race personnel huddled over him, slowly raises an arm into the air.

"County detectives are swamped making sense of a fertilizer

plant explosion on the other side of the county," Kemper explains. "The Miller's Grove police chief has already asked them. They don't have anyone to send out."

In my three years with the Bureau, I've heard horror stories from special agents all over the country who work for ASACs and SACs that make their life a living hell, forcing their agents to use unnecessary procedures, micromanaging, and overall making it difficult to do their jobs. I've been lucky to have a boss like Kemper. He's always pushing me to know my limits, to take time off, and to enjoy life. I'm usually the agent who opens up shop every morning and closes it down long after everyone has gone home. There have been times when Kemper has stood over my shoulder until I stand up out of my chair and leave the office with him, ensuring that I go home and take a night off. And I'm not the only one in the office who respects him. Across the Bureau, he's built a solid reputation for taking care of his agents and clearing the way to get them whatever they need to help them close out a successful case. So I know he wouldn't be making this call unless it was absolutely necessary.

"Okay," I say, trying to keep the frustration from my voice. "Send me the details and I'll head over there."

"I appreciate this, Darcy. I'll make it up to you."

Thinking through the logistics of getting there, I remember that I came with Skylar in her car. "And sir. I don't have a vehicle."

"I figured as much. I've already spoken to the Cascade County Sheriff's Office. They're going to drop off an unmarked cruiser for you at Dixie's Theater. Does that work?"

Dixie's Theater is just down the street from our hotel. "That's fine," I reply.

16

"Good. I'll email you the details now. Call me tonight after you make sense of things."

"Will do, sir." He thanks me a final time and we hang up.

Crossing my arms, I stare vacantly at the small crowd in front of me. Inside, I am reeling, suddenly feeling like Frodo being sent into Mordor. Except I don't have anything I'm trying to take in. I've spent my entire life trying to smuggle every part of me out of that town, trying to forget, wishing the past could be re-written. I know it can't be, but that doesn't make the desire go away.

Out near the torn bales of hay, the medical team lifts the stretcher and stands up. The crowd starts clapping as they carry the cyclist off the road and into the shade of a refreshment tent. In the distance, the high-pitched sound of an ambulance siren cuts through the air. I walked back to Skylar, who is still leaning against the temporary railing.

"If I had a hundred dollars for every time I've seen that look on your face," she says, and then releases a heavy sigh. "Well, at least it was fun while it lasted."

"I'm sorry."

She offers a genuine, albeit disappointed, smile. "I know you are." Digging into the pocket of her denim shorts, she comes out with her keys. "Where am I taking you?"

"Just back into town. They'll have a cruiser waiting for me."

"They?"

"There's been a murder in the next county. Basically, they are dealing with a shortage in investigators and asked if the Bureau could help out."

She studies me for a moment. "That's right up your alley. So why do I get the feeling that you don't want to go? It's because you're having a great time out here and don't want to leave... that's it, isn't it?" She grins as she throws me a wink.

A makeshift parking lot had been constructed for the race's spectators in a fallow field. We start walking toward it. "Oh, the joys of working for the FBI," Skylar says with a grin. "The bad guys never take our vacation plans into account, do they? You think at least once they would call in to the station and ask if anyone has plans for the weekend?"

That gets a short chuckle out of me. "Don't I wish."

Reaching her car, we get in and buckle up. She starts the engine and follows a dirt path for a mile to where the main road reaches out past the racing zone. I watch the tall trees rush by as she picks up speed, wishing Kemper had never called me.

"I had a good time," I say. "Thanks for planning it and making it happen. I needed this more than I realized."

"You'll always be able to count on me being the crowbar that gets you away from your desk. Life is more than just solving crimes, you know?"

I do know that. But bringing a case to a successful conclusion is the engine that keeps me going each and every day. Maybe one day I will have a husband or a family to go home to each night. But in the meantime, working on behalf of the victims and their families is what I live for. If their file is on my desk, I'm the only one fighting for them. If I don't find a way to bring the truth into the light, then who will?

We arrive at the hotel, and I stop by the room to grab my small suitcase. After that, we make our way down the street to Dixie's, a marquee-style theater that features black-and-white classics every Friday and Saturday night. Parked among several other vehicles is a black Crown Victoria. The front door is unlocked, and I find the keys beneath the floor mat. After tossing my suitcase onto the back seat, I smile at Skylar. "Thanks again," I say. "Let's do something like this again soon."

"Absolutely we will. I say next time we take a weekend and go out to the Finger Lakes. One of my hair clients has a cabin up there and said I can use it anytime I want. I just have to let her know."

"That sounds amazing."

"It does, but only if you leave your work phone at home." She raises her brows at me, and a grin plays at her lips. "I leave my work phone at home."

"And you're not supposed to," I remind her. "I'll tell you what. If you get me a free weekend at the Finger Lakes, then I promise to find a way to leave my phone behind."

"That's what I'm talking about."

We hug goodbye, and I get into the car, pulling out of the parking lot as Skylar waves. I know she understands—we have the same job after all—but I really do hate to leave her like this. But it's the nature of the job. I can't say no when duty calls. Turning at the only traffic light in town, Skylar disappears from my rearview mirror and my thoughts quickly shift to the task Kemper has put in front of me.

This isn't the first time our office has gotten a call from a regional municipality asking for our help because their resources are spread thin. Kemper has tried to build a reputation for helping local law enforcement while not stepping on their toes in the process. At the end of the day, we're all on the same team, and if the FBI can bring their federal resources to help at the local level, we're happy to do that as we can.

I put the town behind me and take another county road west

into farm country. Soon I see a sign that makes my stomach turn: *Miller's Grove - 78 miles.* Instinctively, I tighten my grip on the steering wheel.

There isn't one person in the world who doesn't have their own demons to fight. The only difference is that some demons choose to grab hold of us when we are younger, some as we get older. It doesn't matter when they decide to hitch a ride with you; what matters is that you keep fighting them, that you decide you're going to beat them after all, no matter how long it takes.

This is the guiding principle of my life. There have been too many times where I've almost given in and let the pain of the past drive me to ruin. But I know that if I do that, then they've won, and I'm no longer in control of my life. Order has always come out of chaos, light out of darkness. It takes a great deal of courage to face down your fears and your pain, to tell them resolutely that they will not own you. That they *don't* own you. But taking control and not remaining the victim is the first step, and doing that is a choice I still have to make at the start of each new day.

That is why I can do this now. It's why I didn't tell Kemper that I wouldn't go, that he had to find someone else. I will always stand up to the darkness and refuse to let it dominate my life.

This is what I remind myself as I drive the road back to Miller's Grove, and to the pain.

Chapter Three

The Diamond Palace Inn
Miller's Grove, NY

The address Kemper provided in his email directs me to a motel on the outskirts of town. I slow down to match the changing speed limit and pass a sign welcoming me to Miller's Grove.

A sign ahead peeks out from the trees and comes into full view as I draw nearer: *The Diamond Palace Inn.* I turn into the cracked and sunbleached parking lot, where three police cruisers and a CSI van are parked haphazardly behind a cordon of yellow crime scene tape. The front door of a black SUV is stenciled with a mark that identifies it as belonging to the Cascade County Medical Examiner.

The motel is two stories, painted a dirty white color, the trim and railings a dull red, like they let a blind man select the palette. A small crowd is gathered near the office door, some looking like curious residents and others like disheveled patrons who have been temporarily expelled from their rooms.

A door is open on the second floor. A uniformed officer is standing at the railing. A series of bright flashes blink inside the room behind him. I park beside the ME's vehicle, and after taking a deep breath to ground myself, I step out.

The Diamond Palace Inn is about as seedy as they come and looks like the kind of place that women turning tricks frequent when they need twenty minutes alone with their client of the hour.

It has always amused me that rundown motels take on names that completely belie reality. Just because you give your pet pig a pretty name doesn't mean it stops being a pig. But I suppose it's better for business to endow itself with a fanciful name instead of something more truthful, like *Best Roach Motel* or *The Bed Bug Inn*.

I make my way across the parking lot to the outdoor stairs and take them up to the second-floor landing. The police officer at the open door takes notice of me and starts to raise his hand as if to ask me to go back down. But before he can speak, I have my badge out and take note of his name as I quickly introduce myself. "Officer Dobbs, I'm Special Agent Darcy Hunt with the FBI. Your chief requested that I stop by."

His demeanor immediately relaxes, and he offers me a warm smile. "Of course. Thank you for responding so quickly. We're running low on detectives at the moment." Dobbs is a few inches taller than me—closer to six feet—and has a shiny bald head and a round babyface. His eyes are kind but look troubled. He offers me a meaty hand, and after we shake, he leans into the room and yells out, "Chief! FBI is here."

Another series of flashes light up the room as a tall, broad-shouldered man steps across the threshold. Looking to be in his early sixties, he has a handsome, weathered face and piercing green eyes. A well-trimmed mustache adorns his upper lip, giving him a Tom Selleck-like appearance. Instead of a Stetson on his head, I'm surprised to see him wearing a worn gray ball cap with the New York Jets logo stitched above the bill.

I introduce myself, and we shake hands. "Jim Bancroft," he says. "Your SAC told me you were in the general area. I know it's the weekend. Hope I didn't take you away from anything." His voice is deep but has a slow, relaxed drawl.

"Not at all," I lie. "I'm happy to help. What are we dealing with?"

The chief sighs and hitches up his gun belt. "A young lady. Late teens or early twenties. The cleaning crew found her a couple hours ago. Come on in, I'll show you."

He hands me a couple of nitrile gloves and a pair of disposable shoe covers. I quickly don them, and then Bancroft leads me into room 16.

Four other people are inside: two crime scene techs, another officer, and the medical examiner. "Crime scene is just wrapping up," Bancroft says as one of the techs returns a camera to a hardshell case.

The room has a small pressboard table near the window and two worn chairs beside it. On top of a low rise dresser sits a small flat screen TV that's chained to a bolt in the wall. The carpet is threadbare and stained, and the room smells of musk, old fried food, and stale cigarettes.

I take in the gruesome scene that I've been sent to see. On the bed lies the body of a young lady wearing a navy blue spaghetti strap dress and no shoes. Her toenails are perfectly polished, as if she's recently had a pedicure. What strikes me is that she appears staged. Her head is on a pillow, her feet straight out toward the end of the bed. The bed is made, and she is lying on top of the bedspread. Her blonde hair looks brushed out, and her arms are crossed over her chest. The ME has already bagged her hands.

I step farther into the room so the crime scene techs can slip out. Bancroft appears beside me and calls out to the ME, who is standing on the far side of the bed staring thoughtfully at the body.

"Kyle!"

The ME snaps out of it and looks at Bancroft, then smiles politely as he takes note of me. He looks only a few years older than I am. Slender, with short dark hair, searching blue eyes, and a well-trimmed beard, he is subtly handsome.

"This is Special Agent Hunt. Hunt, this is Kyle Connely."

He raises a hand in greeting but doesn't move from his spot. "Come on over here and I'll show you what we're dealing with."

Stepping past the body, I join him on the other side of the bed. He reaches out and extends a finger, pulling the lady's hair away from her neck. "I can't say for certain until I get the autopsy done and the toxicology labs come back, but right now, this certainly appears to be the cause of death."

As the hair is pulled back, I see a narrow bruise encircling her neck, the mark of a wire or thin rope.

"Strangled?" I ask.

"Looks like it. I have the time of death around midnight. If she's been lying here for half a day, then her core temp will already match the ambient temp." He glances at his wristwatch. "As it is right now, based on the stiffness in the muscles, I'd put

TOD between ten and fifteen hours. Although..." Kyle reaches out again and gently grabs her forearm, extending it slightly. Because of the onset of rigor, the muscles cause the arm to move unnaturally.

On the inside of her arm, there are clear puncture marks. "She was a junky," I finish for him.

"Maybe." He returns the arm to her chest. "Or the killer could have pumped her with something. Although the marks look older. But if she was using, then it could have caused rigor to set in faster."

Some drugs can elevate the body temperature, which must be taken into account when determining an estimated time of death. "When did the cleaning crew find her?"

"Two hours ago," Bancroft answers.

"And she was just like this? The cleaning crew didn't touch her?" I ask.

"I spoke with the maid," Bancroft says. "She's a small, grand-motherly type. I thought she was going to have a heart attack just telling me what she saw. Couldn't get her to stop crying. She came by earlier in the morning and knocked. When she didn't get an answer, she opened the door and saw this lady lying on the bed. So she excused herself and quickly shut the door."

"And when she came back later, she saw that the body hadn't moved," I say.

"Precisely. She returned around lunch and was about to shut the door when she remembered that the room had only been booked for one night. So she called out to let this lady know it's time to vacate. When she didn't respond, the maid tried again and got a feeling that something wasn't right. When she stepped into the room, she saw the color of the body and ran out."

"I assume that someone paid cash for the room?" I ask.

Bancroft nods. "The desk clerk says that the lady came in alone, around nine, and paid cash. Because of the nature of the clientele in a place like this, they don't typically get names. They just mark down that the room is occupied and hand off the key. We didn't find any ID in the room, and all the cars outside are accounted for by other guests."

"Come look at this," Kyle tells me. I step back and he walks over to the sink. The scuffed formica counter it's mounted into is clean, except for a large triangle painted with blood. A small section, no wider than a finger, is rubbed off the upper right part of the triangle. What makes a chill run down my lower back is that inside the triangle is a number, also painted in blood: **16**.

"The crime scene guys took a sample of the blood," Kyle says. "Obviously, I haven't examined the body yet, but from a glance, I don't see any cuts or lacerations that have manifested any blood. Unless the killer drew it out through one of the needle marks in her arms."

"Did the crime scene techs find anything else?"

"As you can imagine, this room is a Petri dish all to itself. They found several semen stains on the carpet, two of which were fresh enough to grab a sample of. Between those, hair, and fingerprint samples, I wouldn't be surprised if they don't end up with fifty different people. Hopefully, I can find some DNA on the body that doesn't belong to the victim."

I return to the foot of the bed. The staged body and the cryptic message left in blood are a neon sign that this was no typical murder. The marks on her neck are not from a wild killer choking her out in a sudden rage of anger. It's a single clean mark fully encircling the front of her neck, clearly made antemortem.

And the number on the counter written in blood, matching the number of the room... The killer is drawing our attention to it.

"So the killer takes her purse or wallet as well as her shoes," I say out loud, looking at her bare feet, "and stages her body. Chief, have there been any other recent murders similar to this?"

"No." He sighs, removes his ball cap, and runs a hand through his graying hair as he shakes his head. "The last murder in Miller's Grove was four months ago, and that one was pretty cut and dry. Sam Calhoun got fired from his job at the steel yard in Pine Bluff. He suspected it was because of a running dispute between him and Vic Nader. So after getting fired, he went straight home, grabbed his .45, and then drove to Vic's auto shop. He put six holes into Vic's head before turning the gun on himself." He shrugs. "The one before that was last year when a hitchhiker came through and killed the clerk at the corner store for less than a hundred bucks in the till. My detectives mostly spend their time with domestic abuse or petty burglary." Bancroft slides his cap back on and stares wistfully at the body. "I don't think she was from around here. No one has reported her missing yet. I've lived here for seven years. I would probably recognize most all the high schoolers by face. If she graduated from Miller's Grove in the last few years, I'd recognize her."

"Did you notice anything under her fingernails before you bagged them?" I ask Kyle.

His reply sends a chill down my back. "I didn't bag them."

And yet I'm staring at both her hands, which are hidden beneath paper bags that are tied at the wrist. The bags are the exact kind used by every medical examiner and forensic team in the country. Paper is used so as not to create moisture problems that can contaminate potential evidence on the hands. "Then who did?" I ask.

"The killer must have. The maid found her exactly like this."

I pinch the bridge of my nose and try to fight off an unwanted feeling that my time in Miller's Grove is going to be much longer than I had hoped.

"Let me work on getting the body out of here," Kyle said. "Agent Hunt, if you'll give me your number, I'll give you a call as soon as I finish the examination."

"Thank you. And please, call me Darcy." I looked toward Bancroft. "Both of you."

"Fair enough," the chief says.

I hand Kyle my card, and then Bancroft and I step out of the room. I follow him downstairs to the parking lot, where we stop beside his cruiser. "I know I already said it, but I really appreciate you coming out," he says. "Crimes like this are something we rarely deal with around here."

You don't know the half of it. But I keep that to myself. If Bancroft has only been in Miller's Grove for seven years, he may not be fully up to speed on the events of the past. Small towns have a way of locking their skeletons in a vault before shoving it into a closet far out of reach.

"Like I said, I'm glad to help," I say. "Any chance you could email me the reports from the interviews your team did on site before I got here? I'd like to look them over."

"Sure thing. I'll see if they can't get them completed by the end of the day. If I'm honest with you, seeing that young lady up there like that has me feeling a little creeped out and angry all at the same time. My department will do anything we can to help you. Whatever you need, you just let me know. I've already got my staff working down the list of registered sex offenders."

I thank him and then, scanning the outside of *The Diamond Palace Inn*, ask where I can find a good place to sleep.

After stepping out of the room, Bancroft had put his sunglasses on. Now he looks at me through two black mirrors as he considers my question. He scratches his chin and nods, seeming to come to a conclusion. "Tell you what. Follow me down the road. I know just the place."

I want to press him for a little more detail but don't. Whatever he has in mind has to be better than this place. I'm certainly not a snob, but I'll probably have to find arrangements of my own if the hotel he's thinking of isn't a whole lot better than where we are now. "Okay," I tell him. "If you don't mind, give me a few minutes. I need to check over some emails before we leave."

"Take your time. Just pull around behind me when you're ready. The place we're heading to is just ten minutes down the road."

Returning to my car, I shut the door. I sit behind the wheel and set my hands on the steering wheel before closing my eyes and drawing in a deep breath. What I said to Bancroft wasn't entirely truthful. I don't need to check any emails. I actually need a few moments to myself, a little time to perform a brief custom of sorts. Some might even call it a ritual. I do it at the very beginning of every case I'm handed. It's meaningful and serves to remind me why I do what I do. It gives me fresh focus to treat every case with the care and attention that it deserves.

I recall the scene up in room sixteen. The way the young lady's body lay and the horrific way in which she met her end. My mind sketches a placeholder of what the killer might look like. Then I pledge to get him, to find him no matter what it takes. I can't bring the girl in that motel room back to life. But I can vow to catch who did it so that no one else has to suffer the same fate as she. I protect the next victim by catching their future killer.

It doesn't always shake out the way that I hope. Sometimes the killer strikes again, and just like the very first time I made the vow, it falls flat and meaningless. But I need to feel the resolve deep inside me. I need to feel the gravity of what I've been brought here to do.

And so my lips trace out the promise from all those years ago, the solemn words that I spoke to my little sister as she was forcefully pulled from my arms: "I'll protect you. I promise."

Chapter Four

Bancroft Vacation Chalet
Miller's Grove, NY

"So what do you think?"

I'm standing in front of a beautiful chalet deep in the woods on the east side of town. The driveway is at least a hundred yards off the main county road, and all I can hear is the whisper of the breeze high in the trees and the chirp of a distant bird.

"It's beautiful," I say. "Is this your place?"

"Sure is. My wife and I bought it when the kids were little. We used to vacation out here."

"Chief, I couldn't impose on you two. I'm sure you're both used to having your space."

His chest heaves as he utters a laugh. "Oh, we don't live here, Darcy. It's a second home of sorts. We use it as a rental property. Use that website... forget what it's called at the moment."

"AirBnB?"

He snaps his fingers. "That's the one. Folks rent it out for a weekend or a couple weeks. Mostly couples and small families from New York City or Boston looking to get away from the city for a bit. That's how we used it when we lived in the city and the kids were young. But it's available right now. Don't think anyone has it booked until next month."

The dirt drive terminates in a roundabout near the front. The main roofline rises into a tall A-frame, and the two wings on either side are formed mostly of floor-to-ceiling glass—a fishbowl to see out into the beautiful nature surrounding the home. In front of the wide front steps is a bed of yellow and purple flowers. "Chief. Really, I couldn't stay here."

He brushes me off. "Nonsense. You have everything you need right here. The pantry is stocked with water and canned foods, and please have whatever you want out of the deep freezer in the garage. You'll probably want to make a run to the market in town to get some fresh items. But the place has good internet and an oversized bathtub if you need something to relax you. I know how much cases like this can wear on a person." Taking his keys, he begins to work one off of the ring. "I'll let you show yourself around if you don't mind. I need to get back and make sure the interview reports are getting done. Just make yourself at home." He tosses me the key, and I grab it out of the air.

"This is very kind," I say. "Thank you."

"My pleasure. Like I said, we'd be up a creek if you hadn't come out. I'm a bit of an also-ran when it comes to investigations. In this stage of life, I'm more suited to making sure everyone is in the proper place doing the proper job."

"I understand."

"There's a diner in town. Maybelle's. Why don't we meet up

there for breakfast in the morning and figure out how to move this case forward?"

The idea of spending any time at all in Miller's Grove didn't appeal to me in the least. But if I was going to be here for a while, then I might as well grit my teeth and deal with it.

"That would be fine. See you there at, say, seven?"

He chuckled. "Seven it is. I half expected you to say eight or nine. Figured you city folk get started a little later than we do out here."

"Not me," I smile. "I love charging the day." He wasn't completely wrong, though. Skylar is a slow riser, and plenty of agents in my office typically roll in well after eight-thirty each morning.

"All right then. I'll leave you to it." He gets back in his cruiser, and I give him a quick wave as he pulls away. A minute later, he's disappeared down the lane and I'm left in serene silence. I take a deep breath and actually find that I'm looking forward to being alone in the quiet tonight. It will help me think through the facts of the case and orient myself to the best way to move forward.

Grabbing my suitcase from the back of the car, I take the front steps to the covered porch and unlock the door. It smells faintly of cedar and cinnamon, and I see a bowl of potpourri on a side table. Leaving my suitcase by the door, I tour the inside.

The front hallway leads me past a bedroom and down the center of the chalet, bringing me into a large open room with a high, vaulted ceiling. Naturescapes of Swiss or German Alps hang on several walls, and mounted above a massive stone fireplace is the head of a brown bear, its mouth frozen in an open snarl. The dining table and kitchen are across the room and the entire space is filled with light coming in through the high, curtainless windows. A thick forest of maple and birch trees surrounds the cottage like a womb. Looking out the window, I see a narrow path leading away from the back porch and disappearing into the woods.

I can see why a place like this would be so attractive to people in the city who need a quiet place to get away and relax. Right now, I feel like I'm the only person in the world. I could walk out the front door and not see anyone for miles. As cities go, Albany isn't very big, but it's certainly not the serene and secluded small town that Miller's Grove is. I'm glad that Bancroft offered for me to stay here. It will be the perfect place to work on the case and to think without interruption.

My phone rings, startling me out of my relaxed mood.

"Hey," Skylar says, "did you get there okay?"

"I did. And you're not going to believe this. The police chief put me up in his chalet. I've got it all to myself."

"What?" she exclaimed. "You're joking! Are you soaking in the bathtub right now?"

"I just got here. But a bath doesn't sound like a bad idea. I don't have much to go on until some reports get finalized."

"Hey…" Her voice takes on a conspiratorial tone. "The race is over now. You want me to come out there? That cabin has got to be too big for just one person."

"I'm sure you'd like that," I laugh. "But seeing that this isn't my place, I can't just invite you to stay. Besides, this isn't a vacation. Most of my time will be out in the field. I need to stay focused on the case."

"Okay, fine." she sighs. "It was worth a shot. How long do you think you'll be gone?"

"I wish I could say. Your guess is as good as mine."

What I don't tell her is that this isn't a typical murder. The number on the bathroom sink, written in blood, and the fact that the victim's hands were wrapped make me think that I'm about to play cat and mouse with the killer. He wants us to know something, and that probably means following his clues until we reach his pot of gold. Except in this scenario, it's probably more like a pot of gore.

"What's the name of the town you're in again?" Skylar asks.

"If I tell you, you have to promise not to come. I mean it."

"I promise I won't come. I just want to know where you are."

"It's called Miller's Grove."

The line goes quiet for a few moments. "Holy hell, Darcy. Why didn't you tell me? Hell, why didn't you tell Kemper? You don't need to be out there."

"I'm fine. Really. I promise."

"No, you're not. You've said for as long as I've known you that you would never set foot in that town for as long as you live."

"Sometimes people have to grow up. I was given a job to do. My feelings don't need to get in the way of that."

Skylar lets out a frustrated growl. "You are so stubborn, Darcy. Kemper could have sent someone else out there."

"No," I remind her. "I was the closest agent by at least two hours. It had to be me."

"I don't like it."

"If it makes you feel better, I don't like it either," I tell her. "But it's how things shook out. I'll figure out what happened, get the bastard who did it, and be out of here before we know it."

"You'd better be right. Geez, it's like you pissed off one of the gods or something. What are the odds?"

"I don't know. But I can't think about all that right now. I have a job to do and that's what needs to have my attention."

"You're so much tougher than I am. I really respect you for sticking with it."

"Just cross your fingers I can close this out fast."

"Absolutely I will."

I don't talk about the past anyway, and speaking vaguely about it even now is discomforting. The last person I spoke with about it was during my onboarding process with the Bureau several years ago. The pain of losing my sister has never left, but I've had to move on, to decide that the event no longer defines me.

Skylar tells me that she's rooting for me and we hang up. I take out my notebook and pull out a chair at the kitchen table, then start to write down everything I saw at the motel, making sure the details are fully set in my mind. Sometimes the difference between solving a case and it remaining open/unsolved is a single detail that the investigative agent failed to connect to the broader facts. It's essential that I have a clear mental picture of what was in the hotel room.

A young lady's life has just been severed. Had a cruel monster not carried out his wicked intentions on her, she may have grown up and had a wonderful career, or children and even grandchildren. But now the one life she was given was cut short far too soon. Thoughts roll through my mind like restless waves. Who was she, and why hasn't anyone reported her missing yet? Did she know the killer? Her nails were freshly painted, her makeup done, and she was wearing a pretty dress. She didn't seem like the regular kind of rabble that would stay in a motel like that.

The sun is starting to drift below the trees when I finally close my notebook and stand up. I'm famished and go to the deep freezer in the garage, coming away with a frozen pot pie. I throw it in the microwave and peruse the chalet while I wait for it to cook.

Pictures of Chief Bancroft and his family punctuate many of the shelves and tables. The early pictures show a pretty blonde wife and two children, his son a little older than his daughter. There are photos of the family at the Statue of Liberty, the beach, and standing together in their snowsuits at the base of a ski slope. As the children move out of their teens, I notice the son is no longer in any of the pictures. The smiles are still there, but there is a subtle heaviness in each of their eyes. I can't find any other pictures that include his son over the age of seventeen or eighteen.

It appears that Chief Bancroft knows what it's like to lose someone, too.

Chapter Five

Bancroft Vacation Chalet
Miller's Grove, NY

I wake the next morning and quickly don a tank top and a pair of shorts before lacing up my sneakers and stepping outside. The blue glow of early dawn fills the sky, and the forest is alive with the chirping of birds and squirrels bounding through trees. Walking down the front steps, I stop in the grass and lie down on my back. It's slightly damp from the dew, but I don't mind.

Over time, stress can do terrible things to our bodies. And in my line of work, it can seem like all I ever deal with is stress. When I was accepted into the FBI, I made a commitment to take care of myself, to go easy on the wine after a hard day, and to keep physically strong and fit. And most nights, instead of falling asleep to a TV show, I transition out of the day by listening to relaxing meditation that helps me drift away.

I start my workout by performing a series of crunches and leg lifts, then move into jumping jacks, pushups, and burpees, taking a brief rest after completing each exercise. For fifteen minutes, I push myself to the limit, keeping my heart rate up and giving my body a chance to melt away the tension that can so easily build up inside it.

By the time I finish, I'm dripping in sweat and my heart is racing like a jackhammer, my face flushed. I walk around the front yard several times to cool down and then get into a cold shower that wakes me up better than any cup of coffee ever could.

I'll need to find a department store where I can buy some clothes. Skylar and I had only planned to stay away for two nights, and I'm down to my last change of clothes. There is a washer and dryer in the garage that I will use, but since I don't know how long I'll be here, I don't want to wear the same two outfits everywhere I go.

Finished with the shower, I change, head outside to the car, and start down the driveway. Being out here is so quiet and relaxing, and yet I can't help but feel the tension growing inside me the closer I get to town. My shoulders tighten and I focus on breathing deeply and slowly, forcing myself to relax my grip on the steering wheel.

Being sent here on assignment feels like some kind of cosmic joke. Never in a million years did I think I would ever come here again. Miller's Grove holds everything that nearly destroyed me, and everything that did destroy my family. The events of that weekend sent a jagged brick crashing into the pristine mirror of our lives. We never recovered.

Even so, as I pass up *The Diamond Palace Inn*, I remind myself that I'm not here to relive the past, or to let it consume me again. I'm here for the girl in room 16. That's why I entered the Bureau to begin with—to help others get the answers that I never did. I know what it's like to lose everything you hold dear because of evil monsters who think that they have a right to destroy the lives of others. Skylar has called me a monster hunter more than once—a fitting moniker, I suppose.

Entering the small town, I pass by the hardware store, a lumber yard, and a two-pump gas station. A sign up ahead catches my attention: the outline of a frying pan with the word "Maybelle's" scrolled in the center. I turn in, and since all the parking spaces at the front of the diner are full, I park on the side of the building between two trucks.

Inside is a din of lively conversation amid forks and knives clinking against plates. My stomach grumbles as I take in the delicious smell of bacon, sausage, and biscuits. Chief Bancroft is already in a corner booth. He waves me over, and I slip into the seat across from him.

"Mornin'," he says. "You look bright-eyed and bushy-tailed. You must have gotten some good sleep."

I nod. "The bed was very comfortable. I really appreciate you letting me stay there."

"It's my pleasure. There's only two other hotels in town. Certainly nicer than the Diamond Palace, which I know isn't saying much. But I'm glad you can use the cabin. My wife and I enjoy going out there some weekends if it's not rented out."

A wide lady with red puffy cheeks appears holding a coffee pot. She's wearing a nondescript food service dress, and her gray hair is rolled into a large bun on the back of her head. She gives me a once-over and then an inquisitive smile. "You're not from around here. What's your name, hun?"

The Chief answers for me. "Ruth, this here is Special Agent Darcy Hunt with the FBI."

Understanding dawns in her eyes. "Oh, you're here about that murder at the Diamond Palace?"

"Yes, ma'am."

She lowers her voice and leans in conspiratorially. "I hear they cut that poor girl's feet off. Is that true?"

Bancroft rolls his eyes. "No one got their feet cut off, Ruth. Who did you hear that from?"

"Now you know I can't say that, Jim." Looking at me, she said, "Agent Hunt, what can I get started for you?"

"A cup of coffee would be great."

"I'll have it right out." Then she heads toward the kitchen, pausing to refill a few coffee cups on her way.

"I swear," Bancroft says, shaking his head. "Eleanor Riggins... Ruth and her friends believe every damn thing that lady says. If she said the girl in the hotel room was abducted by aliens, they would have believed her."

"I guess she keeps things interesting around here," I laugh.

"You've got that right."

I scan the menu, and when Ruth comes back with my coffee, I order a classic breakfast: fried eggs, bacon, and hash browns. Bancroft orders the same but adds sausage and grits. When we're alone again, he asks me for my first impressions from the crime scene last night.

I assemble my thoughts as I take a sip of coffee. "I'll be direct with you, Chief. I think whoever killed that girl is going to kill again."

His face curves into a frown. "How do you figure?"

"The number on the counter, written in blood. The bagged

hands. I'd be willing to bet that when Kyle does the autopsy, he'll find something unique under her nails."

"Unique? What do you mean?"

"I've worked on a lot of cases over the last three years, but I've never seen the killer bag his victim's hands. Sometimes the killer might leave behind a photo or even a note of some kind. But in this situation, he's trying to draw our attention to her hands. Whatever we find there will be exactly what the killer wants us to find."

"But Kyle would have examined the hands and fingers regardless," Bancroft says.

"Which is why I think the killer is trying to send us a message. And a large percentage of the time, when a message is left behind, it's because the killer isn't done. It's a game for them, and the first one is them just getting started."

"Okay. I can get on board with that," he nods. "But what about the number? He kills her in a hotel room and then writes that number in the room. In blood, no less."

I take another sip of my coffee before answering. "Now that I'm not sure of. But there's no doubt in my mind that it's a puzzle piece. If I do my job right, I'll find a way to fit it into the greater whole."

Bancroft sighs and looks into his half-empty mug. "I don't like the idea of some nut job running around my town, Darcy. These are good folks. This kind of thing, it unsettles them."

"That's why I'm here, Chief. We'll get him. I promise you."

The front door opens, and after a glance at the person shuffling through the door, Bancroft rolls his eyes and looks away, nearly giving off the impression that he would hide under the table if he thought he could get away with it. "Oh, great."

"What?" I ask. "Who is it?"

"Eleanor Riggins herself. Before supper time, this whole town is going to think that you and I are dating and that I'm cheating on Linda."

I nearly choke on my coffee as I assess the tiny, wizened lady standing just inside the glass door. She can't be more than five feet tall and is wearing white slacks and a turquoise blouse. Her hair is completely white, permed into tiny curls, and I can't help but think of a cotton ball glued to her scalp. Her eyes scan the diner, and as soon as they fall on the chief, she brightens like a cat who just caught sight of a fallen bird.

"She's coming over," I whisper through unmoving lips, and Bancroft groans.

"Chief Bancroft," she purrs. "How lovely to see you."

When the chief turns to look at the town gossip, he's wearing a pleasant smile. It's wide and even reaches to his eyes, almost convincing me that he's actually happy to see her.

"Eleanor, you're looking as lovely as ever. Did you do something to your hair?"

The older lady blushes slightly and smiles proudly. "Well, thank you, Jim. And yes. Yes, I did get my hair done." Then she rolls her eyes and lowers her voice. "But Irene spent almost three hours on it. *Three hours.* Can you believe that? I'll tell you what, I just..." Her voice trails away as she looks at me, seeming to realize that we haven't yet met.

"Oh, sweetheart, I'm sorry. I haven't introduced myself." She pauses to give me a once over, but her gaze falters for a moment and I think I see a frown trying to form. But then a full smile returns. "I'm Eleanor Riggins," she says with an edge of pride.

"Darcy Hunt," I nod.

"Are you new in town?"

"I'm working with the chief on the murder from last night."

Her eyes widen slightly. "Oh, yes. I heard about that. Such a shame. And in our quiet little town?" Eleanor gives a small shudder. "I just hate that. Does anyone know who it was?"

Clearly, she is pressing for information. Bancroft gives her what I imagine is his most patient smile. "Eleanor, you know I can't say anything about it right now. We don't want to compromise the investigation."

As if she didn't hear him at all, she says, "So she was a local girl, then? Oh, that's terrible."

"Now, Eleanor, that's not what I said. And I think it might be time for you to find a table of your own."

"Of course." Her gaze moved back to me, and her thin brows crinkle into a frown. "I'm sorry, sweetheart, but do I know you from somewhere?"

My stomach tightens and I force a smile. "I don't believe so."

"Have you ever been to Miller's Grove before?"

My answer stalls on my lips as I hesitate.

"Now, Eleanor. Leave the poor lady alone," Bancroft interjects. "If she had any interest in getting grilled by the locals, she would have shown up at the Bingo parlor last night."

"I'm sorry," she says. "You're right. Darcy, it was nice meeting you. And Chief." She nods at him and then shuffles off to a long table at the other end of the diner where a gathering of older women are sitting.

When she's gone, Bancroft says, "She's a sweet lady, but her tongue is more forked than a serpent's. Sometimes it feels like I spend half my time squashing rumors that she's started."

Ruth brings our breakfast and sets it in front of us. It smells delicious, making me aware of just how hungry I am. We dig in and I quickly discover that everything tastes as good as it smells. The bacon is crispy, and the eggs are cooked just right. Soon enough, between the energy in the food and the caffeine in the coffee, I feel ready to take on the day.

"So," Bancroft says around a mouthful, "you've been with the Bureau for four years? Been in Albany all that time?"

I swallow and nod as I blot my mouth with a napkin. "Yes. As field offices go, ours is quieter than those in the larger cities. But because we handle a wide region of the state, I find myself in small towns like this fairly often."

I'll be working with Bancroft until I bring this case to a conclusion, so I find myself wanting to know more about him, too. "You said last night that you've lived in Miller's Grove for seven years. How long have you been chief?"

"Seven years. Linda and I both grew up in small towns in Georgia, but our careers took us into the Big Apple. I was with the NYPD for many years. But one day, we both decided we missed our roots. We had bought the chalet about twenty years earlier and vacationed here with the kids a few times a year. Just as I was retiring from the NYPD, Miller's Grove was looking for a new chief of police. So it worked out. We're stepping into our golden years being able to see the stars at night and hear the wind in the grass." He shrugs. "So that's how we ended up here."

"I noticed some of your family photos in the chalet last night," I say. "You have a beautiful family."

"Thank you. The kids got their good looks from their mother. Vicki, she's out in California pursuing an acting career. And Timmy, he..." Bancroft trails off and hurriedly shovels his last bite of food into his mouth. He shakes his head as he swallows and gets a faraway look in his eyes. "Sorry," he said. "Probably best if I don't talk about that over breakfast."

"Of course."

His phone is sitting beside the salt and pepper shakers. It rings several times before he answers. "Bancroft." He doesn't say much, but I'm eating my final forkful when he hangs up and tosses his napkin on his plate. "That was Kyle. He's just finished the autopsy."

Chapter Six

City Morgue
Miller's Grove, NY

The Miller's Grove morgue is located in a back wing of the police station, on the other end of town from the diner, near the water tower and city hall. After following the chief to the station and going inside, he leads me through a set of double stainless steel doors. This area of the station is quiet; the only noise is the cadence of my shoes and the chief's boots.

A door opens down the hall, and Kyle steps out. "There you are. I was starting to wonder if you two were dead."

I eye him. "Is that an ME joke?"

"Yeah," he sighs. "They never land the way I want them to."

"That's because they're terrible," Bancroft grins. "I think the county would do well to invest in a new joke book for you."

"Are you coming in with us?" Kyle asks him.

"Always do."

Kyle looks at me. "You ready?"

"Let's do it."

I never enjoy viewing the body of a victim. The dead bodies themselves don't bother me; it's the fact that the body used to be someone's home. I always feel a deep sense of respect when looking at someone whose life has just been taken. But I can't let it affect me too much. If I did, I wouldn't be able to do my job properly. I'm trained to find killers, not to add another name to the list of the grieving.

I'll never forget one of my fellow trainees at Quantico, who ended up dropping out after a day trip to the morgue. After being in there for less than a minute, he darted out and threw up his lunch into a trash bin. He tried coming back in a little later but ended up with the same results. For him, it wasn't just the novelty of seeing a dead body. It was that he felt deeply for the person who had died. The idea of solving crimes had appealed to him, but somehow he hadn't considered part of the job was examining grisly crime scenes and visiting morgues. One of the advisors at Quantico suggested that he might be a better fit as a priest or a pastor. And that's exactly what he ended up doing. He dropped out of the program and went to seminary. The last time I heard, he was a minister at a small church in Oklahoma. Apparently, he can handle an open casket at a funeral much better than a cold, stiff body on an examination table.

Kyle leads Bancroft and me into the morgue and into his small examination room, which is like every other one I've ever been in: a bare, concrete floor with a drain in the center, stark white walls with an apron of white porcelain tile, bright halogens above.

"Okay," Kyle begins, snapping on a pair of gloves. "I was up late last night trying to get a jump on this autopsy. Agent Hunt, I know you want to get things moving as quickly as possible."

"Darcy," I correct him. "And thank you."

We're standing before the stainless steel examination table now. The girl's body is laid across it, and a sheet is draped across her. Since the body arrived here, Kyle would have spent hours probing and measuring it, cutting and sawing on it. Even so, draping a sheet over it is another form of respect for the girl who lived in it.

I appreciate Kyle's willingness to move quickly with the autopsy. I've worked with small town and big city MEs. Not all of them are alike. Most of the time, they work on their own clocks and have more than one agent or detective standing over their shoulder seeking lightning-fast results. They get to yours when they can. I recall what Bancroft said last night, that, other than a murder-suicide a few months ago, this had been the first murder in town in over a year. Even though Kyle's territory as an ME extends well beyond Miller's Grove, I can tell he is anxious to do his part in giving us any clues that might lead us one step closer to the killer.

"Okay," he says as he pinches the edge of the sheet. "Here we are."

He pulls the sheet away from her face and folds it down across her breasts. A large Y-shaped incision runs between the shoulders and down the sternum. Beneath her chin, a dark bruise runs around to the other side of her neck, showing the area where she had been strangled even more starkly than last night.

"I wish I could give you more, but the time of death I estimated last night hasn't changed. I'm putting it between nine o'clock, when she arrived at the motel, and midnight." He indicates the mark around her neck. "Cause of death was asphyxiation by strangling. Based on the markings on her skin and the bruising in the muscles, I can say that she was strangled with a braided steel rope. One-sixteenth-inch rope to be exact." Kyle pulls the sheet back over her face and then lifts it over to the side. He gently takes her wrist and lifts her fingers. "There is a reddish dirt-like residue beneath her fingernails and no biological material. No skin that would indicate that she scratched her attacker."

That was strange. It's a natural reaction for a victim of strangling to claw at their attacker, especially in the final seconds. In this case, the attacker must have been wearing a long-sleeved shirt or even a ski mask. "What about chipped or broken nails?" I asked. "If she was clawing for her life, then a nail could have snagged on his clothing."

"No. Look." He turns her wrist for a better view of the nails. They, like her toenails, are perfectly painted. There are no chips in the nails or the paint. "The red residue beneath the nails was not deep, and there is no residue on the tips of her fingers," Kyle continues. "I hate to say it, but it's as if someone placed the dirt, if that's what it is, under her nails after she was killed."

Bancroft removes his hat and blots his forehead with a handkerchief. "I am not fully up to speed on fingernail painting and such, but what you're saying sounds to me like she didn't put up a fight."

"You're right," Kyle replies. He lays the hand down and points to a tiny mark in the crook of her arm. "The killer did inject her with something. I'll have to wait for the lab results, but it was probably a muscle inhibitor that prevented her from having full control of her movement. That would explain her apparent lack of fight."

"Any indication of sexual trauma?" I ask.

"No. None at all."

Bancroft and I exchange a glance. Most murders involving young, pretty ladies generally involve some kind of sexual molestation. The killer uses her to play out a twisted fantasy and then moves to cover his tracks; a girl who's dead is a girl who can't talk. But the staged body, the room number written in blood on the sink, the painted nails with red dirt beneath them, no indication of sexual trauma... It could only mean that we were dealing with a different type of killer. One who is methodical and rational, who did not murder in the heat of the moment.

I set my hands on my hips. "I think a demon just entered your town, Chief."

His broad chest heaves a deep sigh.

"This murder was a message," I say. "And we're going to have to find out what it is."

"Kyle," Bancroft says, "do we know this young lady's identity yet?"

"Yes." He reaches over and grabs a clipboard from the counter beside him, then flips over the top page. "Kayla Hanover. Seventeen years old. No identifying markings on her body except for a scar on her left forearm from a bicycle accident years ago."

"Where is she from?" I ask.

"Pine Bluff. About half an hour west of here. She fractured her right femur three years ago and received treatment for it at Larns Memorial Hospital. The ER records indicate that it was from playing soccer. Since I'm just the ME, I didn't do much digging on her. But a preliminary search revealed that she had been in the foster care system since she was five years old. Other than that, I don't have anything else. I'll let you know when I get the labs back on the material under her nails as well as her blood work." I ask him if he can email his report to me. "Sure. I have to make some final notes, but I should have it to you within a couple of hours."

"Perfect."

Kyle looks down at Kayla Hanover's stone gray face. "They tell you in training not to take things personally. But my baby sister is seventeen. This one hits pretty close to home." He looks back at me. "Whatever I can do to help you find the bastard who did this, I'll do it."

"Thanks, Kyle."

Bancroft and I take turns shaking Kyle's hand and then make our way back to the front of the station. "This is some real pile of horse manure," Bancroft says. "I can skin a deer with my eyes closed, and I have no problem looking at bodies like we saw back there. But I'd be lying if I said that this whole thing doesn't give me the willies. I don't like the idea of some murderous master-mind playing footsie with my town."

"Chief," I reply, "I'm going to do everything in my power to find the person who did this. We're going to catch him."

I don't offer my promise to Bancroft as a professional means to placate him. It's not conceived out of some false pretense that I will bring this case to a satisfactory conclusion. Instead, it stems from the deepest parts of who I am.

The FBI was not my first choice for a career. In fact, neither was any aspect of law enforcement. From the time I was a small girl, I knew I wanted to be a veterinarian. I loved animals of every kind, and my mother was eternally patient when she would find turtles in her kitchen sink, lizards in her Tupperware, or the kitten in my closet. Once I even found a baby raccoon and put it in her bathtub for safekeeping. Later that afternoon, a scream from her bathroom reminded me that I had forgotten to tell her about my new friend.

After high school, I flew the nest and went to college at the University at Albany. After getting a bachelor's degree, I still had four more years of veterinary school before I would become a Doctor of Veterinary Medicine. I started to feel like my life was finally back on track. A lifelong dream was coming true, and I was excited for what the future held.

But a year into veterinary school, something happened that would permanently alter my career choice. Returning home from school one night, I switched on the news to see the local news broadcasting a picture of six-year-old Tessa Edwards, who had been snatched out of her front yard earlier that afternoon. She had been playing with a soccer ball while her father was twenty yards away trimming the hedges when a truck pulled up to the curb and a man grabbed her. By the time her father made it to the sidewalk, the truck had disappeared around the first corner.

Her father and mother's desperate pleas for help were broadcast on all the local syndicates that night. It didn't take long for the national networks to pick up the story, and soon the entire country was hoping for the best for little Tessa. Quiet, upper-class neighborhoods were supposed to be safe. That was the unspoken bargain you made with the universe when you dropped upwards of a million dollars on a house and faithfully paid your exorbitant HOA dues.

Days passed, and local and state law enforcement, for all their best efforts, were unable to find her. When things began to stall, the FBI was brought in to assist. Five agents from the FBI's Behavioral Analysis Unit 3, which specializes in crimes against children, went over every detail, lending fresh eyes and analysis to the known facts while extrapolating everything into a workable profile. The nation held its collective breath as it waited for an outcome that had become dire and hopeless.

Then Tessa was found.

Eight days after being plucked from her front yard, Tessa was safely returned to the arms of her parents. The FBI had found her in a Section 8 apartment on the southern outskirts of the city. The three men connected with her disappearance were arrested.

The entire ordeal surfaced old memories and wounds inside me that I had spent most of my life trying to keep beneath the surface. But it also stirred up something else. Without the FBI's expertise, Tessa may never have come home at all. The idea that I could play a role in families experiencing the joy of being reunited with a loved one was appealing to me. For the next few months, I would often lie in bed at night wrestling with what I should really do with the rest of my life.

One of my fellow students at veterinary school had an uncle who had been part of the team sent out from Quantico. He had been with the FBI for over a decade, and his keen sense of observation and his ability to think outside the box had been instrumental in bringing Tessa home.

He agreed to meet with me and patiently answered all of my questions, graciously offering his two cents on the agency, as well as all the good that agents can do. A week later, I sat down and took the FBI's Phase 1 Entrance Test, a test that seventy percent of applicants do not pass. I ended up being among the thirty percent who did. In under three hours, I had to demonstrate proficiency in logical reasoning, figural reasoning, personality assessment, situational judgment, as well as provide a clear picture of my personal preferences and interests.

Once I was accepted into the Academy, I pulled the plug on veterinary school. I still love animals and always will, but seeing Tessa returned home flipped a switch inside me. My focus shifted, perhaps even becoming a newfound calling.

So when I joined the FBI four years ago, I did so out of the commitment to make this world a safer place for those who live in it. My own childhood was split in two by the horrific actions of evil men. When my sister was taken from me, my parents and I were never the same. Our perfect family, which had only known ballet recitals, school plays, and family vacations, was torn apart at the seams.

At the end of my life, when I'm on my deathbed, I want to be able to look back and know that I made a difference in this world. I want to know that because I was here, others had to suffer a little less, that they received the closure that so many never do. Every year, thousands of families are forced to continue living their lives, not knowing what really happened to the people they loved most in this world. Their loved one's killer still runs free while they suffer in harsh, lonely silence.

Every case that is put into my hands is assigned a number. But to me, the case is far more than that. That number represents a life that has been taken, a person who will never know the joy of seeing another day. So I have given my life to bringing some kind of peace into the heavy wake of pure and unadulterated evil.

Bancroft thanks me for my commitment to get the man who did this. "I'll be honest with you, Darcy. I do feel better knowing that you're here. My detectives aren't trained to handle something like this. Let me see about getting you an office of your own that you can use while you're here."

"Actually," I say, "your chalet is the perfect place to work from. I'll be able to think through the case more clearly there instead of in a cramped office. If I could just get a laptop, then I'll be squared away."

"Sure thing. Let me see what I can scrounge up for you."

He takes me down a narrow hallway, through the squad room, and into the administrative area, where several desks are pushed together. On the door of a windowed office in the corner, I see his name. After introducing me to several officers and support staff, he finally locates a working laptop and brings it to me.

"If this doesn't suit your purposes, then you may want to see if your office can overnight yours. I had Donna look it over. She helps with the technical stuff around here. She removed the login password. I think you can create your own once you get it running."

"I'll see what I can do with it," I say.

Bancroft crosses his arms and scratches his chin. "So, what's your next step?"

"I need to see what I can find on Kayla Hanover. If I'm lucky, the police in Pine Bluff already have a missing persons report on her. If not, then it will probably take me some time to start connecting the dots. Either way, I'll need to go over there and speak with her foster parents."

"You've got my number," Bancroft says. "If there's anything you need, anything at all, you let me know."

Chapter Seven

Main Street
Miller's Grove, NY

When I walk out of the Miller's Grove police station, the town is fully awake; Main Street is bustling with people arriving for another day's work. The neon "Open" sign in a small boutique window blinks on; a barber approaches his shop and unlocks the door; a garbage truck rumbles by.

I stand beside my car and closely observe the faces of the residents. They are all drawn and filled with concern. No doubt the news of yesterday's murder has spread through this small community like wildfire. It's easy to see that people who generally feel safe and secure will be locking their doors at night and throwing sideways glances at their neighbors until the killer is identified and captured. Until then, playgrounds will sit empty of laughter as mothers keep their little ones safe inside. Teenagers will be given earlier curfews as their parents expect them home well before dark.

Returning to the chalet, I set the laptop on the kitchen table before preparing myself a pot of coffee, something I can't function properly without. Skylar is always chastening me for drinking too much of it and even convinced me several months ago to try to wean myself off of it for a while. I still don't know how I let her talk me into such a looney idea, but it lasted for only two days before the headaches and the muddled way my brain was processing information convinced me that a life without coffee is not a life worth living.

But I have learned not to drink as much of it as I was before. Instead of six or eight cups a day, I now only drink three or four. Too much of anything can be a problem, and it's important to me that I take care of myself, making sure that I'm alert enough to do this job properly without being overly dependent on caffeine to bring each case across the finish line.

The coffee pot finishes brewing and I pour a steaming cup, adding a little half-and-half from a carton that I pull from the door of the refrigerator. Taking a seat at the table, I create a new profile to gain access to the laptop and then log in with my FBI access via the web portal.

A quick search across the nationwide database used by local precincts reveals that Kayla Hanover has not been reported missing. I can find no indication that anyone is worried as to her whereabouts. It's been a day and a half since she was killed—two full nights—and yet no one close to her seems to know what happened.

That in itself doesn't mean much. It could be that her family expected her to be gone for a while. They could have given her permission to go on a trip with friends, or maybe she had been left at home alone while her family went away for a short trip.

I locate Kayla's CPS file and quickly learn that she had been in nine foster homes over the last twelve years. Her parents died in a boating accident when she was five years old, leaving her alone with no other family to raise her and love her.

Searching deeper, I come across a file on her with the Pine Bluff Police Department. Sixteen months ago, Kayla was arrested for possession of marijuana. As a first offender, they had been lenient and had only given her a few hours of community service. The file also details two separate runaway attempts over the last year.

The first time, she had hitched a ride with a friend who had taken their parent's car without permission. A broken taillight had gotten them pulled over not twenty miles down the road.

The second runaway attempt was nearly successful. Kayla hitched rides all the way across state lines, through Pennsylvania and into Ohio. She was missing for a full three weeks before someone reported her panhandling at a truck stop.

That was only a month ago. It could be that she tried to run away again and got tangled up with the wrong person. It was a likely scenario.

If there's anything I've learned during my time at the Bureau, it's that there are always monsters watching from the shadows. They lurk and prowl, watching grocery store aisles, highway underpasses, and neighborhood playgrounds, waiting for the perfect chance to grab up their next prey. They don't think like the rest of us. Instead of looking out for their neighbors, they are actively looking for ways to inflict harm and pain.

It wouldn't have been difficult for Kayla to run off again only to find herself in the hands of someone with malintent. A pretty seventeen-year-old girl on the shoulder of the road with her thumb out makes the perfect target for anyone wanting to take advantage of the situation. She would be scared and vulnerable, willing to trust anyone nice enough to pull over and offer her a ride.

Looking further into her file, I discover that Kayla's foster parents have fostered for almost twenty years. They have no children of their own and currently have three other children that the state gave them to watch over and care for.

Kayla running away doesn't necessarily speak to the quality of life that existed in her final home. Sometimes foster parents create a wonderful home environment for the children that come to them. They make home-cooked meals, enroll them in sports, and attend all of their practices and games. They make the children feel loved. And then some take full advantage of the system, taking in foster kids only so they can get a monthly check to spend on themselves. I won't know which kind of home Kayla was in until I speak with the foster parents.

Picking up my phone from the table, I dial the number listed for her foster parents. It rings out and then I try again. Still, there is no answer, not even a voicemail recording inviting me to leave a message. I'm unable to find any other phone numbers in her file.

Standing up, I rummage through the cabinets until I find a tumbler, then take it to the table and pour my coffee into it before fastening the lid. Then I grab my keys from the counter and head out the door.

THE ROAD to Pine Bluff slaloms back and forth through the trees, hairpinning tightly every couple of miles before winding across the forest again. I can't help but wonder what the planners were thinking when they drew up the road. They clearly had to deal with topographical considerations like watersheds, ravines, even private property and the exercise of eminent domain. But this particular route makes me wish that I had taken a Dramamine before getting on it. I've always been an easy target for motion sickness; when I was younger, I learned the hard way that deep sea fishing and circuitous routes through the mountains are not my cup of tea.

Slowing my speed, I prepare for yet another sharp turn and roll down the windows, enjoying the fresh piney scent of the country as it passes through the car. The radio is switched off, and I continue the drive in silence. This case is going to require my complete focus. I don't want to risk the familiar associations that a song could bring up, old memories that might send my mind wandering down some rabbit hole from my past. I can't allow any distractions. A savage psychopath remains on the loose, sending cryptic messages to a small town via the murder of a young lady. Whoever he is, he's smart, and if I'm not careful, if I'm not completely focused on finding him, he'll stay one step ahead of me the entire time.

A sign on my right announces that the town of Pine Bluff is two miles ahead. Following the GPS, I slow my speed and turn off the county road onto a dirt lane with a patch of grass running down the center. Tall trees slide by on either side of the car as I drive deeper into the woods. The occasional dirt driveway asserts itself, winding back into the woods and toward homes or hunting cabins tucked out of view of the road.

Finally, I arrive at a plastic mailbox perched atop a wooden post that leans steeply away from the road. A large dent in the side and a smudge of blue paint reveal that it had been hit by a vehicle and not yet righted. The numbers on the side are easy to read and inform me that I'm at the right place, so I turn down the potholed dirt drive and jounce in my seat while doing my best to avoid the muddy holes laid out before me.

The driveway terminates on a double wide mobile home whose corrugated metal apron is dented all over, the bottom fringed with lacy spots of rust. The yard is overgrown, as if it hasn't been cared for in weeks, and children's toys stick out among the long green blades of grass.

I park beside an old car that looks as well cared for as the house. A short flight of wooden stairs takes me to a small landing littered with cigarette butts. Through the door, I can hear the whine of an old television along with what sounds like an audience cheering on a game show contestant. I knock, take a step back, and wait. When no one answers, I try again, louder this time. After a moment, the sounds of the game show are gone, but the high-pitched whine persists.

From somewhere inside, a woman bellows. "Who is it?"

I offer my name without designating my agency. Experience has shown that if I give away that I'm with the FBI too early, then oftentimes people won't come to the door. Even if they haven't done anything wrong, having the FBI knock on your door can be an unsettling experience.

"What do you want?"

"I would like to speak with you about Kayla."

No answer. I'm about to call out again when she finally yells for me to come in.

Wrapping my fingers around the handle, I give it a tenuous turn and gently push the door open. My nostrils are immediately hit with an ungodly concoction of what smells like sour milk, stale smoke, and mildew. I step into a linoleum foyer to see a large woman filling up an easy chair.

"What'd she do this time?" she asks.

It's midday, and she's wearing an oversized nightgown and fuzzy slippers. Her gray hair is cut just above her shoulders and doesn't look like it's been washed in some time. The interior of the home is dark with aluminum foil and dusty brown curtains covering the windows. The only light originates from a small table beside her chair.

"Are you Mrs. Winston?"

"I am." Her voice is as raspy as a newspaper. "What do you want with Kayla? Are you one of her teachers?"

"No. Not her teacher. Is Mr. Winston here as well? I would like to speak with you both if I can."

She looks me over and frowns. Thankfully, she chooses not to give me any pushback and calls out. "Glen! Glen, get out here!"

While I wait, she returns her attention to the muted TV screen, where contestants on *The Price is Right* are throwing out numbers to see who gets the closest to the real price of a new car. After a minute, she appears lost in the show and her husband has yet to appear.

I cough gently into my hand, but she seems to have forgotten that I'm here. "Mrs. Winston?"

She blinks and then turns to me. "Oh. Right. Glen! Glen, get out here! There's someone here who needs to talk with us!"

Another minute rolls by, and I'm relieved to finally hear a door open at the back of the trailer. Footsteps thud down the hall, and a large man, who is nearly the size of his wife, emerges into the living room. He has bushy gray eyebrows and a wide stomach pressing out on a dirty black T-shirt.

He looks me over and puts his hands on his hips. "Who are you?" he growls.

"My name is Darcy Hunt. I'm with the Federal Bureau of Investigation."

Mrs. Winston's eyes widen, and she sounds annoyed when she speaks again. "The FBI? You didn't tell me you were with them."

Mr. Winston seems to freeze in place, more worried than surprised. "What do you want with us?"

"I have some information and some questions about Kayla. Would you like to have a seat?"

"I'll stand." When he doesn't offer me a chair, I continue with the purpose of my visit.

"All right," I say. "I'm sorry to inform you that Kayla was found dead yesterday morning."

I pay close attention to each of their expressions. Right now, I have no reason to think that one of them had anything to do with Kayla's murder. But I also don't have enough information to scratch anyone's name off the list.

"Dead?" Mrs. Winston says quietly. "She's dead?"

"Yes, ma'am. Her body was found at a Miller's Grove motel."

Mr. Winston crosses his arms and huffs. While shaking his head and staring at a spot on the floor in front of him, he says to his wife, "What did I tell you about that girl? I knew this would happen."

She sighs and shakes her head as well. "You did. It's not surprising, I guess."

"So what do we have to do?" he finally asks me. "We have to sign a death certificate or something?"

I find myself repelled by both of their responses. No sense of grief or remorse comes from either one of them. They don't appear shaken in any way.

Technically, I should have notified Kayla's social worker before coming here and giving the foster parents news like this. But I didn't want to waste time waiting, having to coordinate with someone else. Now that I'm here, I don't feel guilty in the least. The social worker, whoever he or she is, should be fired. Now that I'm here, it's not difficult to see why Kayla would have risked running away, if that is, in fact, what she did.

Behind Mr. Winston, I watch a roach skitter past his feet and enter the kitchen.

Ignoring his question, I look at him and ask, "When was the last time you saw Kayla?"

He rubs his chin thoughtfully. "Not sure... Marg, what do you think? I hadn't seen her in a few days."

Mrs. Winston throws a worried glance at me and then looks down at her knees. If I had to guess, it just occurred to her that if she couldn't give me a good answer, then the two of them were going to look negligent. Of course, it could be because she had something to do with the murder, but my instincts tell me that's not the case. This lady just wants to see the government checks keep rolling in.

"Mrs. Winston?" I prompt.

"I... saw her... four days ago. She said she was going to spend a few nights at a friend's house."

I take out my notepad and scratch a few notes. "What is her friend's name?" I ask. She blinks and gives me a blank stare. I'm starting to get the impression that these two know nothing about her life outside this home. "Mrs. Winston?"

"I don't think she said."

"Then I'll need the names of any friends that she spends time with."

"She doesn't have any friends," Mr. Winston barks. "Marg, she lied to you. *Again.*" He rolls his eyes, not seeming to realize that the entire scenario is reflecting more poorly on them than their foster daughter.

"I looked over her file before I came over," I say. "It was noted that she attempted to run away several months ago. The first time, she left with a friend. Melissa Downing. Does she still spend time with her?"

Mr. Winston's shoulders tense and his brows furrow. "No. After that little escapade, we wouldn't let those two spend time together anymore. Besides, that Downing girl moved to Texas a few weeks later."

"Any other friends besides Melissa?" I ask.

"No," he says flatly, giving the impression that he doesn't really know.

"What about a boyfriend?"

Mrs. Winston huffs loudly. "Yeah. Kayla had a boyfriend. They started dating about a year ago. That boy was nothing but trouble. He introduced her to marijuana and then finally got her hooked on the cocaine. And I don't mean the sniffing kind. I'm talkin' the shootin' up kind." She juts out a flabby arm, turns it up, and taps the inside of her forearm with a finger.

That would explain the markings that Kyle found on Kayla's arms. "You mentioned their relationship as past tense," I say. "When did they break up?"

"He got arrested for possession and intent to sell," Mr. Winston says. "Should have been charged with sleeping with a minor, too. Kayla was only sixteen at the time. But she wouldn't admit to the authorities that she'd been dating him. He was twenty-one years old, worked at a convenience store in Pine Bluff until he got arrested."

I ask for his name and then write it down alongside my other notes. "You have three other foster children? Is that right?"

Both of them visibly tense at the question. "Yeah, that's right," he replies.

"Are they here?"

They exchange a brief glance. "No," he says. "They spent the night with some friends. Went camping."

I have to ask for the name of the friends twice before they reluctantly provide it. "What campground are they at?"

"Uh, not sure," he says.

Inside, I'm raging. These people don't care at all that a young lady that has been in their care for over three years has been murdered. They've asked no questions about the circumstances surrounding Kayla's death, and they've clearly dumped the other younger children into someone else's lap.

"Did Kayla have a cell phone?" I ask.

"No," Mrs. Winston says. "None of us has one." She nods her head toward an old landline phone on a side table. "That's the only one we've got."

Even though I don't expect to hear from them, I hand Mr. Winston my card and tell them to call me if they think of anything else I should know.

"We certainly will," he says, but I don't believe him.

I show myself out the door, and before I'm halfway down the

steps, I hear the sounds of the game show again. I want to storm back in there and grab them both by their throats, to shake them and force them to care about Kayla, to get them to give a damn about the other children in their care. But that wouldn't help anything. The Winstons clearly stopped caring for anyone but themselves a long time ago.

Reaching my car, I get in and roll down the windows. The stink of their home still clings to me, and the fresh air is welcome as it whisks some of it away. I follow the driveway back to the dirt lane and return to the county road. My thoughts wind back and forth with the road as I ponder the dilemma that Kayla must have found herself in.

She, like any other girl, would have had dreams for her future. Perhaps she wanted to be a nurse or a doctor. She could have had hopes of being an actress or a competitive athlete. But after bouncing around from foster home to foster home and spending the last three years in a place like the Winstons', I wondered when those dreams had started to die. Had she given up on hope and simply settled for just getting out?

After witnessing the conditions she had been forced to live in for the last three years, I can't blame Kayla for wanting to run away. Anything would be better than living in that squalor with people who care nothing for you at all. Risking oneself to an unknown world would have been a risk worth taking. Unfortunately, Kayla rolled the dice and lost.

Navigating another hairpin curve, I think back to what that clerk at *The Diamond Palace Inn* told the responding police officers. Kayla had come in alone and paid cash for a room. Only a few hours later, she was dead.

It's the fact that she was wearing a dress that leads me to

believe that she was at the hotel to meet someone. She wasn't wearing jeans and a T-shirt. She was dressed nicely and her makeup was done, which tells me that she was expecting to meet someone and hadn't booked the room simply as a place to crash for the night. But how had they met? And how had they communicated before that night?

The road mercifully straightens out in the final stretch leading into Miller's Grove. Up ahead, I see a black F-150 stalled out on my side of the road. A man is standing beside it, and the driver's door is open. I slow my speed and pull up behind it, putting my hazards on before getting out and approaching him cautiously.

"Do you need any help?" I ask.

He's tall and looks to be in his mid-thirties. His full face is clean-shaven, and he looks me up and down with his pale green eyes. "You're that FBI agent, aren't you? The one investigating the murder at the Diamond Palace?"

The way he says it makes me think that he doesn't need any help at all, that he orchestrated this to speak with me.

"Have you been following me?"

"No. But I heard that girl was from Pine Bluff. Figured you went out there to check things out, and I decided to catch you on your way back."

I can feel my face flush with anger. "You parked in the middle of the road so you can talk with me?

"There isn't much traffic between towns this time of day. I waved a couple people past. No big deal."

"If you wanted to speak with me, you could have gone through the proper channels," I snap. "The chief has my number. You could have gotten it from him."

"Look," he drawls. "You need to know something about this place. People don't want you sniffing around here. We have our own police force who can handle an investigation like this just fine."

I narrow my eyes on him. "What exactly are you saying?"

"I'm saying that it would be better if you got back into that car of yours and just kept driving until you're back in whatever big city you've come from. We don't need someone like you around here."

I cross my arms over my chest. "And just who is 'we'?"

"This entire town."

"What's your name?" I ask.

"My name isn't important," he says condescendingly. "What is important is that you hear what it is I'm saying to you." He takes a step closer to me.

"You are way out of your lane," I say. "I didn't come out here to make friends with the locals. I'm here to find out who killed that girl and to stop them from doing the same thing to someone else. To be frank, I don't give a damn what you or anyone else around here thinks. I was asked to come here by your chief of police. And I'll be staying until my investigation is complete."

He runs his tongue along the inside of his lips and then spits near my feet as his glare stabs at me. "All you FBI people are the same. You just stay out of this town's business. We don't need anyone poking around."

"Look," I snap, straightening up and taking a step toward him. "I don't know who you think you are or where you get your information from, but I'm here to help." He opens his mouth to speak, but I raise a hand. "And let me tell you, if you even try something like this again, I'll arrest you for harassing a federal agent. Are we clear on that?" I return his pointed glare and hold it, unblinking. "I asked you a question."

"Yeah... okay. Loud and clear, missy." He takes a step backward, and then another. His features slowly change from militant to concerned as he returns to his truck. Within seconds, he has started the engine and is gunning down the road, heading back into town.

Chapter Eight

Miller's Grove Police Station
Miller's Grove, NY

"That would be Darren," Bancroft says. "Darren Malloy." His voice is threaded with irritation after I call him to let him know that one of his residents accosted me in the middle of the street. "And he blocked the road?"

"He was just sitting there waiting for me."

"Well, I guess I'll drive on over to his place and have a talk with him."

"No," I say. "Don't do that. It wasn't anything I couldn't handle myself. I just thought you should be aware."

I don't need anyone thinking that I called the town's chief of police to complain about an irritating conversation. During my time in the Bureau, I've been shot at, chased down, followed, and threatened by more people than I can count. I don't need the chief talking to Darren on my behalf. It's already an uphill battle for a woman to be taken seriously in this world, especially in law enforcement where the arena has typically been populated by men, many of whom feel threatened by a woman doing their job. I don't need Bancroft taking up for me. I can handle my own problems. And besides, Darren doesn't really concern me.

"Okay," Bancroft concedes. "So you said you were on your way back from Pine Bluff? What did you learn out there?"

As we talk, I drive slowly past the florist's shop and pull into the grocery store parking lot. I sit in the car as I fill him in on my conversation with the Winstons. "You need to call the state and file a complaint against CPS. The caseworker assigned to the Winstons is completely negligent. How anyone would think that even a dog or cat should be assigned to that place is beyond me."

"I'll get right on that," Bancroft says. "I'm sure you know as well as I do, Darcy, that sometimes the foster system gets over-crowded. A lot of the time, there are far more kids to go around than there are families to take them."

"I do know that, Chief. But this situation is completely unacceptable, and someone needs to be held accountable for it." What I don't add is that, had Kayla been placed in a better home, then she may not have ever been in a position for her killer to notice her.

"Sure thing," he agrees.

"Thank you. And I have a couple more things I need to add to that list."

"Fire away."

"Can you have someone call over to Kayla's high school and get in touch with the principal? I want to know if they can identify anyone that Kayla may have spent time with at school. Any friends or just people that she spent time with. There has to be someone who knew her, someone who understood even the vaguest contours of her life. They might be able to tell us if she was hanging around someone else outside of school hours. If she was, I'm sure she wouldn't have told her foster parents."

"Okay. And what else?"

"We need to pull the Winstons' phone records. It's a long shot, but Kayla could have been in contact with the killer over their home phone."

"Good point. I'll let you know when I hear something. Also, it looks like Kayla didn't have any social media accounts. So we won't get any help from that end. What will you be working on the rest of the day?"

"Kyle sent me his full report. I need to comb through that and also analyze how Kayla would have gotten connected to the killer. Without that, we don't have much to go on." Another item is tugging at the back of my mind as I turn off the car and step into the parking lot. "Chief, why would Darren Malloy want to accost me like that? He was warning me off. Does he strike you as the kind of person who could murder a young lady?"

"No," he says quickly, almost defensively. "Darren kill someone? Not a chance. He's a good man, even if a little rough around the edges."

"Then what's his problem with me?"

I hear the chief sigh into the phone. "His family has been through a lot over the years. He's grown up here his whole life. He was a police officer in this very department for a while. But that didn't work out for too long. But he's always seen himself as a protector of the town. He means well, Darcy. I know it doesn't come across that way, but he does. Darren is no murderer, I can tell you that." He promises to get back to me as soon as he has anything else, and we hang up.

I stand beside my car thinking about what he had said. I'm glad he trusts the people in his town. But I'm not from here; I have no allegiance but to the truth. In the chief's mind, Darren might be the furthest person from a suspect. But I don't have such a luxury.

Sometimes, the people we least expect are the ones actually perpetrating heinous crimes: the friendly mail carrier who lives next door harbors a kidnapped harem of women chained in his basement; the peppy leader of the PTA is poisoning her stepchildren; a high school math teacher prowls the streets in the earliest hours of the morning.

Darren Malloy might have the trust of the people in this town, but he hasn't earned mine. If anything, that little stunt he pulled back on the road gives me plenty of reason to think that he's hiding something. If not the murder of Kayla Hanover, then something else that he doesn't want slipping into the light. Like it or not, Darren just had a hand on putting his name on my list.

Stepping away from my car, I make my way across the parking lot and grab a grocery cart before entering the store. Since I don't know how long I'll be here, I want to stock up on a few items at the chalet, mostly fresh items like fruits and vegetables. The freezer meals are fine, but I'll tire of them very fast, and after a while, my body will be crying out for something more nutritious.

Pushing the cart into the produce section, I pick out several apples, bananas, and a bag of mixed leaves to make a salad with. I'm just reaching for a tomato when I hear a familiar voice behind me.

"Well, look what we have here. How are you, sweetheart?"

I turn around to see none other than Eleanor Riggins smiling pointedly at me. She's clutching an empty shopping basket, and her white hair is as perfect and immovable as it was at the diner this morning.

"Eleanor, hello." My reply is lacking enthusiasm; I just want to get back to the chalet where I can continue working in the quiet.

She produces a bright smile as her eyes quickly scan the contents of my cart. "It's Agent Hunt, isn't it?"

"It is."

"My, what a beautiful day it turned out to be, don't you think?"

"It is a pretty day, Eleanor."

She takes a half step toward me and leans in. "You know, I heard that Darren Malloy stopped you down the road. Dear, I just want to apologize for that. He can be so rude sometimes."

Ten minutes. It has been less than ten minutes since Darren got in my face. In that amount of time, Eleanor has managed to hear about it and flag me down. I have to give her credit; so far, she is ranking as the best town gossip I've ever met.

"It wasn't all that bad," I say blandly.

"Oh?"

"He's just watching out for his town."

"Well, I'll tell you what, ever since he was young, he's felt a need to show himself strong around here. And for good reason, too, I suppose."

Her eyes gleam up at mine as she waits for me to take the bait. But I don't. Instead, I glance purposefully down into her shopping basket. "Were you here to purchase anything?"

She immediately picks up on the implication and gives a nervous chuckle. "Oh, yes. I needed to get some... flour. I'm making a cake for... the lady's bridge club tonight. If you'll excuse me."

"Of course."

Without pausing to get flour, she hurries off to the front of the store and starts to make conversation with the lady behind the customer service counter.

I take my time rounding up a few more items—oatmeal, butter, and a bag of coffee beans—and by the time I arrive back at the front, Eleanor, to my relief, is nowhere to be seen.

Eleanor Riggins is a good reminder that I will need to be careful who I share information and opinions about the case with. I'm not back in Albany working with my team in a secure building. There I can freely discuss my cases without fear of the wrong person listening in. But when I'm out in the field for long periods, it's important that I keep everything close to the chest. Even well-meaning persons can spread the right information to the wrong people, or end up twisting the facts until they get completely out of hand.

After checking out, I walk outside with my groceries and place them in the trunk of the car. I then walk next door to a small department store and purchase several pairs of socks, underwear, another pair of pants, and a couple of shirts. I don't have an official FBI polo with me—I didn't pack one for our weekend getaway. Given the circumstances, I'm happy not to be displaying the logo of an agency that no one but the chief seems to want around.

Chapter Nine

Bancroft Vacation Chalet
Miller's Grove, NY

The microwave beeps and lets me know that my coffee is warmed up. It's steaming over the rim of my cup as I take it out and bring it to the kitchen table, where I place it between a yellow legal pad and my laptop.

Taking a seat, I look out the massive windows and watch the tree branches dance gently in the late afternoon breeze. A blue jay glides by and quickly darts around the eave of the house. The view is a huge step up from my cramped desk at the Albany office. It feels strange working on a murder investigation from a place like this. After several minutes, I'm almost lulled into a trance by the beauty outside the window, but I finally shake out of it as I remind myself that I'm not on vacation. There is so much work to be done, and nearly all of it rides on my shoulders.

Scooting in my chair, I take a sip of coffee and scroll through my recent emails. Kyle has emailed the autopsy report along with his complete findings. I take my time scrolling through each document, looking for the smallest clue that could give me any further insight into the killer's twisted mind. Looking at how a crime was committed can help identify and tell why it was committed. Once I have the why, it gets easier to find the who.

The organizational level of the murder is high, as though it was clearly planned out in advance. The killer probably spent days, if not weeks, fantasizing about getting it just right. Whatever Kayla thought she was walking into, it was a death trap that she was never going to escape from. The killer was methodical and careful not to leave a trace of any kind. I'm positive that none of the DNA being analyzed by the crime scene techs will point back to the killer. Everything speaks to him possessing a very high level of intelligence; he isn't the kind of person who makes foolish mistakes.

An hour later, my second cup of coffee is empty, and I have come away with nothing new. The quiet is temporarily interrupted by Bancroft calling to tell me that the Winstons' phone records checked out. There were very few calls to or from their home phone, and all of them were to out-of-state family members. He's still waiting on a return call from Kayla's high school and promises to notify me as soon as he hears something.

"Chief," I say, "have you caught wind of any of the locals suddenly leaving town? Or anyone suspicious showing up?"

"Way ahead of you on that, Darcy. We're looking into that right now. So far, no one has popped up. But we're keeping an ear out. And you might like to know that I had a courier come through to pick up the labs from Kyle and the crime scene team. They're taking all the samples—blood, semen, hair, and the dirt beneath the fingernails—to the state lab in Albany. I know it can usually take a couple of weeks to get results back, and we can't wait that long. If you have any connections at the lab in the state capital, then now might be the time to call in any favors."

A small smile plays across my lips. "Chief, I know just the person."

"Glad to hear it. Darcy, I've always been a firm believer that it's not *what* you know, it's *who* you know."

"I couldn't agree more."

We hang up, and I navigate to my phone contacts and select a number. It's answered on the first ring.

"Well, well. If it isn't the goddess Darcy Hunt herself. If you're calling to ask me out, then I'm sorry to say that I'm already taken for the evening."

"Shucks," I chuckle. "What about tomorrow night?"

"I'm all yours."

Amy Mattson and I shared several classes during our freshman and sophomore years at college. While I was busy knocking out my basics for veterinary medicine, she was pursuing a degree in chemistry, and eventually went on to NYU, where she got her graduate degree in biochemistry. Now she works at the state lab, leading a team of laboratory scientists and technicians.

"Speaking of 'all yours'," I say, "when is Kevin going to put a ring on it? You've been dating, what, four years now?"

"Oh, you know me. Never one to be sure she wants to settle for one man for the rest of her life. Somewhere down the line, they all seem to get fat and lazy."

"You're not too far off," I muse.

"I know," Amy chirps. "So, what do you need? You're about to hurt my feelings because I'm sensing this isn't a personal call."

"Guilty as charged."

"Whatcha got?"

I spend the next few minutes filling her in, starting with my girls' weekend getting interrupted and finishing with the murder that I was sent in to help solve.

"Miller's Grove," she says. "I've never heard of it."

"It's every bit a one-horse town."

"So what do you need from me?"

"The local police chief is sending everything to your lab via courier. It should be there before you leave for the day."

"I thought you FBI folks had a world-class lab in Virginia. You're not sending everything down there?"

"I wish. Even though I'm taking the lead on the case, I'm functioning as an advisor to the town. The Bureau didn't assign me to the case. Instead, they assigned me to the town. I could have gotten everything sent to our lab, but because I'm not officially running point, it would take a few days to cut through all the red tape. And that's a few days that I don't have right now."

"So you need me to get my team to analyze these samples ASAP?"

"Would you mind?" I plead. "The information is crucial in order for me to keep the investigation moving forward."

"Sure thing. But when you close it out, you'll take me for a margarita so I can stare into your beautiful eyes."

"Thank you, Amy. You're an angel."

"I know."

As soon as we hang up, my email alerts me to a new message from the county crime scene unit. I open the secure attachment and review their preliminary findings. I quickly become disappointed as I realize that there is nothing at all in the report that will help move the case forward. All the samples they collected are being sent to Albany, which means that, at least for now, they aren't helpful. The murder weapon was not left, so we don't even have that to analyze. Most of the report's conclusions are pending the results of the lab's findings.

I have never been very good at waiting. When I was younger, my mother never failed to remind me that patience is a virtue. And maybe it is. But when I'm tracking down a killer who is likely to do it again, patience works against, not for, me.

I need answers now, something—anything—that will lead me one step closer to my objective. Kemper sent me out here because he trusts me to bring this case to a swift conclusion. I don't want to be here a week from now, having to feed him excuses as to why I haven't found the killer yet.

And then there is the clock to worry about. When it comes to a murder or a kidnapping, the clock is my absolute worst enemy. It doesn't stop when I get tired or when I've hit a brick wall. It just keeps ticking away, mocking me as the minutes and hours slide by and quickly shrink any window of opportunity I have to catch my unsub.

Opening the attached photos, I review them one by one, taking in each detail. Crime scene photos can be very helpful in that they allow investigators to see the scene from multiple angles. I pour over the photos for more than an hour, observing them with meticulous detail. But I can find nothing that helps me think in a fresh direction.

Clicking out of the photos, I return to the report and scan its contents one more time. My shoulders tense, and a chill slowly crawls down my spine as I discover a detail that I had missed on my first pass through: when Kayla's blood type was analyzed, it did not match the blood written on the counter. The blood used to scrawl out the number 16 was different and was being sent to the state lab for analysis and, if possible, identification.

I sit back and run my fingers through my hair, exhaling a long, deep breath. Was it the killer's blood, and this was his way of playing cat and mouse with us? Would he be that bold? Was it the blood of his next victim and he was giving us advanced notice? Or, if this wasn't his first killing, was it the blood from his previous victim?

A dark, foreboding cloud settles over me as I realize that I'm dealing with someone who is far more calculated than I had initially given him credit for. I'm already well behind the curve, and I can feel it.

I'm still deep in thought when a shadow grows over the glass door. I look over to see a man standing on the back porch, looking at me through the glass. I don't startle easily, but this makes me jolt in my chair. I'm just reaching for my sidearm when the man affects a charming smile and raises his hands. In an effort to show that he means no harm, he steps back from the door. I walk over and pull it open.

"Sorry to startle you," he says with an uncomfortable grin.

His eyes are a stunning hazel, his golden blond hair swept to the side. He's tall, sturdy, and wears jeans and a pair of basic cowboy boots. Even so, I don't allow his good looks to warm my chilly reply. "Can I help you with something?"

"No—I'm sorry. I didn't think anyone was here or I wouldn't have come by. Especially wouldn't have looked through the window like that."

"So why are you here?"

"My folks, well, they own the place."

I give him a puzzled look. "Your folks?"

He motions to the chalet. "You rented this from Jim Bancroft, or maybe an online booking service. But Jim Bancroft is the owner. He's my father."

I feel my muscles relax a little. "Oh. I see."

We both stand staring uncomfortably at each other. "Did you need something from inside?" I finally offer.

"No. There's nothing of mine in there." He turns slightly and points down the trail behind the house, where it disappears into the trees. "I live in a cabin about a mile that way."

"So why were you looking in?" I ask, more curious now than concerned.

"Mom said she was thinking about doing some redecorating. I was out on a walk and decided to head this way and see if she's made any progress on it."

I look out into the living room. "And has she?"

"No," he chuckles. "She hasn't done a single thing. That afghan on the back of the couch is hardly older than I am. So are the curtains. She keeps them clean, but they have good memories for her. It's not surprising that she's been sluggish in bringing the place into the modern era."

I shrug. "I like it. It's homey."

"Yeah, I guess it is."

Another moment of awkward silence opens up between us, and I realize that I could use a mental break from looking through all the case notes. If Bancroft's son is half as nice as his father, then he couldn't be that bad of a conversationalist. He might even be able to help me understand additional details about this town that could help me with the case. "I was just getting ready to put on another pot of coffee," I say. "Would you like a cup?"

He shakes his head. "I don't want to impose," he said. "Like I said, I didn't know anyone was here."

"Well, I could use a little break." I swing the door open for him to enter. "If you don't want to come in, just push the door shut as you leave." To put him at ease, I offer a welcoming smile and then turn and walk back inside. By the time I reach the coffee pot, he has stepped across the threshold and is pulling the door shut. He stuffs his hands into his pockets and looks around the space.

"I'll bet you have a ton of memories in this cabin," I say as I fill the reservoir with fresh water.

He smiles and I can see the memories piling into his eyes. "I do. Some of my best memories are here."

I recall the pictures around the living room, with Bancroft's son suddenly missing from them around the time of his middle teens. Curiosity tickles the back of my mind, but I put it to rest. Now isn't the time to come across as nosy.

"I'm Darcy," I say as I measure in fresh coffee grounds.

"Tim," he replies. "Tim Bancroft."

"I think I had the Bancroft part figured out," I smile.

"Ah, yes." He steps into the kitchen and leans back against the counter. "So how long are you here on vacation?"

I switch on the coffee pot and take down a couple of clean mugs from the cabinet. "Funny thing," I say. "I was actually on vacation when I was called out here for work. Your father asked me to come out and help him with an investigation. He was nice enough to put me up here."

"Work?" he frowns. He glances at my hip and appears to notice the gun for the first time. "You're a cop?"

"FBI, actually."

"Whoa. What did Dad need to bring in the FBI for?"

A grin plays across my lips. "You haven't been into town the last couple of days, have you?"

"No. I just got back from hunting upstate. Why?"

"There was a murder in town."

I watch as his face draws tight and his eyes widen. "A murder? Where?"

"It was a teenage girl from Pine Bluff. She was staying at the Diamond Palace Inn."

"That's terrible. This town hasn't seen a murder in a long time. Well, I guess there was Sam Calhoun gunning down Vic at his auto body shop a few months ago."

"I heard about that one."

"So what does Dad need the FBI for?" he asks.

"His investigators are out of pocket and he needed some outside help." I shrug. "I was on vacation not too far from here, so I was pegged as the closest available agent. Your father put me up here so I could work in peace."

Tim throws a glance at my laptop. "And I come as the destroyer of peace," he chuckles.

"Something like that," I wink back.

The coffee finishes and I fill both mugs and bring them to the table. I shut my computer and we take a seat. "So that trail behind the house leads to your place?" I ask.

"It does. I've been living there for about a year now. The cabin is small—nothing as nice as this—but it's just right for one person."

I take a sip of my coffee and enjoy the warm, nutty taste as it slides down my throat. "So what kind of line of work are you in?"

"I'm a hunting guide. Depending on the season, I lead hunts for deer, turkey, or small game."

"I've never been hunting. I actually don't know much about it."

"There's not a lot to it. You get in close and pull the trigger." He's grinning over the rim of his cup.

"Right," I say, "so then why do people need a guide?"

Tim wags a finger at me. "Now that's the getting in close part. I help them get on the game. The rest is up to them."

Long-held memories assert themselves in my mind. "My father used to love hunting," I say. "He and his friends would go out to the Triple R Ranch in Franklin County. If I remember right, it's a pretty popular place if you have the money."

His face brightens. "I know the Triple R very well. It's in a beautiful area. Thousands of acres. Wherever I'm out there, I feel like the only one in the world."

I nod at the bear head snarling above the fireplace in the adjoining room. "Who shot that poor guy?"

"That would be Dad. I must have been seven, maybe eight. I wanted to go on that hunt so bad, but I had broken my leg playing soccer the week before."

"Oh no," I groan.

"Yeah." He looks up at the bear. "But I was really proud of him. When they finally mounted that up there, I brought every friend I could think of to come see it. They thought my dad was the coolest guy they had ever met."

"And your dad told me that he was with the NYPD for his previous career?"

"Yeah," he nods. "He was very well-respected in the depart-ment. I was glad that he decided to move out here when he retired. And I'm glad he joined the local force. He really loves the work."

"That comes through," I say. "You can tell he feels right at home being the chief."

"So, what about you?" Tim asks. "How long have you been with the FBI?"

When Tim lays his gaze on me, I find myself struck once again by the stunning brightness of his eyes. The self-assured way he sits in the chair makes it hard not to feel a little self-conscious. I have to push away thoughts about how my hair looks or if my makeup needs touching up.

It's rare that I'm so easily taken with a man's appearance; that's more Skylar's style. My work has been my life ever since I entered Quantico, so I haven't found much time for dating since I got my badge. When I finally did make time for my previous relationship, it didn't end well at all. Skylar has forced me into several double dates with her and her boyfriend of the hour, but the man she chooses to pair me with is always too arrogant or doesn't have a clear path in life.

If I'm going to be with someone, then he will need to know what he wants out of life. So many men these days seem to think it's a badge of honor to drift and have no direction to their careers. Working as a waiter at IHOP might be the answer while they are working themselves through college, but if that's all they have their sights on, then I can't be wasting my time with them.

Skylar is completely unable to see past a well-defined jawline, a twinkling eye, or a deep, soothing voice. She's a complete sucker for a compliment and a charming smile. That may be why her boyfriends never last more than a few weeks or a couple of months at best. Eventually, she comes around to see what has been blazingly clear all along: that his good looks can't compensate for the fact that he has nothing substantial to offer and is going nowhere in life.

But Skylar doesn't mind all that much. She has her fun and then moves on to her next boy toy. I don't judge her for it. In fact, sometimes it's fun to watch things play out. She knows what she's doing and is generally the one in the driver's seat of the relationship.

I take another sip of my coffee. "Four years," I answer Tim. "As soon as I graduated from the Academy, they sent me back to Albany. It was my first choice, and I was really lucky to get it."

"Why was it your first choice? Are you from there?"

"Yes," I reply. "When I was a little girl, my father moved the family there from Southern California. For most of my life, Albany has been home."

"Do you still have family there?"

The question induces a sharp stab of pain deep inside my chest. There is no way for Tim to know that he just threw coarse salt into a still gaping wound. I feign a smile as I try to brush the pain away. "Just an uncle."

I quickly change topics. Tim is an easy conversationalist, and I soon realize how much I'm enjoying him being here. Having the unexpected interruption has been a nice break from thinking about the case. It's always been my tendency to go full force, putting all of my attention and focus on solving whatever case has been put in front of me. But if I don't find time to come up for air, then the adrenaline starts to wane and can lead to burnout, both physically and mentally. The lack of mental clarity can mean accidentally skipping over clues or failing to make important connections.

More than once, someone has had to intervene and get me to pause for a breath. That's usually a fellow agent, sometimes even Kemper, and there is usually some kind of mild threat involved. I always resist, claiming that the work needs my undivided attention. But they always end up being right. When I do take an afternoon off, or allow myself a getaway like I just had with Skylar, I always return to work with a renewed sense of clarity and focus.

I listen intently as Tim tells me about his own upbringing, filling in the contours of a childhood spent in New York City and his seasonal visits here to the cabin. "Right out this window is where I shot my first bird. A dove," he says. "Whenever our stays here came to an end, I always hated going back to the big city."

"Is your cabin on your parents' land?" I ask.

"No. This chalet sits on about thirty acres. My cabin is on five, but sits about half a mile from the back end of their lot line."

The photos in the other room come to mind once again. "Tim," I say a little reluctantly. "Can I ask you a personal question?"

He arches an eyebrow and feigns concern. "Sure? I think."

"If I'm overstepping, will you let me know?"

"Sure," he shrugs. "Would it save you a breath if I just went ahead and answered for you?"

I narrow my gaze at him. "You know what I want to ask?"

"Of course. Isn't it obvious? *Boxers*. Briefs are too constraining. You'll never find me in them."

"That's... Whew, good to know," I laugh. "Let me tell you."

"Excellent." He smiles proudly, his eyes bright with humor. "But really, what do you want to know?"

I hope that I'm not about to tread on sacred ground. After all,

Tim and I have only just met each other. But I'm enjoying my time with him so much, and my curiosity is screaming for me to ask. "When I came in last night," I begin, "I noticed the pictures of your family. The most recent one looks like it was taken close to fifteen years ago. What stood out to me was that there are recent photos of your sister on display, but none of you."

Tim's face quickly takes on a cloudy expression; it probably looks much like mine did when he brought up my own family. "Well, all that is another story within itself." He looks away, out the window, and is quiet for a long while.

Now that I am witnessing his reaction, I chastise myself for bringing it up. "I'm sorry," I say. "It's not my business."

"No. It's okay. Really." He returns his attention to me and lets out a heavy sigh. "I was a good kid when I was younger. But when I hit my teen years, I started to rebel. Dad had advanced in rank at the department, and Mom was busy working as a fashion consultant, so I had to keep myself busy. I ended up hanging out with the wrong crowd and experimented with drugs and started drinking. Nothing Mom or Dad tried could get me to stay clean. They put me into rehab, sent me away to a summer camp for teen addicts. But every time, I would relapse. It all finally came to a head one night. I was three days away from my eighteenth birthday and driving home late from a party one night. I ended up hitting a car and sending it off the road, killing the woman behind the wheel. As luck would have it, the woman was my aunt, my father's sister."

Instinctively, I gasp and my hand covers my mouth. "Oh, Tim. I am so sorry," I tell him. "I can't imagine what that did to all of you."

"It wrecked everyone," he says. "And everything. My uncle

91

wouldn't begin to entertain pressing charges against me, but the DA decided that they would. Dad was a well-respected cop on the force, but even that couldn't stop this overzealous DA who felt that she had something to prove. Thankfully, because of my age at the time of the incident, they tried me as a minor. I got seven years for it."

Hearing all that, I find that I'm speechless. I really don't know how to respond. He seems to pick up on it and smiles knowingly.

"I've had to live with my own choices," he says. "Nothing I can do will change the past. All I can do is look forward and try to mend what I can."

"So you moved back here when you got out?"

He shakes his head. "No. I made my way out to the west coast. Wandered for a little while, to tell you the truth. I've been out for a few years now and it took me a while to find my footing. Haven't touched any drugs or alcohol since my trial. But I finally remembered how much I love nature and love hunting. That helped to ground me and helped me find out who I am."

I hardly know this man, but my heart hurts for him and his family. I haven't met his mother yet, but Chief Bancroft has already gained my respect. The way that he carries himself would have never led me to believe that he had gone through something so horrific.

I suppose the same thing could be said for me, too. Just by looking at or spending a little time around me, no one would ever be able to guess that my childhood was ripped away like it was. If there is one thing I've learned in life, it is that everyone has their hidden scars. It doesn't matter if it is abuse or neglect, the death of a loved one, or broken dreams. All of us have those scars that we keep hidden under layers of artificial smiles. Some things are just too hard to talk about, too painful to dig up again, and yet still remain, no matter how much therapy and counseling you go through. The pain can ebb over time, but the scars are always there.

"I'm sure it's been nice being around your folks again," I tell him.

"That's the thing," Tim says. "Mom was glad to have me back. Over all the years, she kept in touch. Not a week went by where I didn't get a letter from her. But Dad..." Tim slowly flicks his thumb across the side of his mug. "With Dad, it's still a journey. We've had coffee a couple times since, but that's all. To be honest, I try to avoid him. I know he doesn't want to, but he harbors a lot of anger about everything I did. I was an embarrassment to him. Mom has helped him work through some of it, but what I did... It's unforgivable. Dad was really close to his sister."

The pain in Tim's eyes is evident. "I hope you can finally work it out," I offer. "You being here in Miller's Grove is the right thing."

He shrugs halfheartedly. "Maybe. At least they have had Vicki—that's my sister. She's always walked the straight and narrow. She's out in California trying her hand at acting. But she gets back over here when she can."

"You're walking the straight and narrow now," I say. "And that's what matters."

He attempts a smile. "Yeah. I guess so. This town has grown very protective of my dad, and it wasn't all that thrilled that I showed back up. In fact, I usually do all my shopping in Pine Bluff just to stay clear of the gossip and the glares."

I manage a chuckle as I try to lighten the heavy mood in the room. "The gossip is pretty bad, isn't it? If there was a Gossip Olympics, then Eleanor Riggins would steal the gold."

"You aren't joking. That lady has had a forked tongue since as far back as I can remember. She used to stop by here when I was a boy and try to get my parents to tell her news from New York City that she could feed back to the rest of the town."

He drains what's left of his coffee and then comes to his feet. "I had better get going. I'm sorry to have dumped all that on you. Not really sure how I got into all that."

"I'm good at getting people to talk," I smile. "It's part of my job. And I'm glad you told me. I don't know how long I'll be in town, but you're welcome to stop by again."

"Thanks, Darcy. It was nice meeting you." He takes a final nostalgic look around the place and then steps out onto the porch.

I follow him and stop in the doorway, watching as he crosses the deck and takes the steps down into the back yard. He pauses, and when he turns around, his face is holding a slight grimace. "I don't want this to sound wrong," he says, "but it's probably best that you don't mention me coming by. Dad might feel like I'm interfering somehow. If he has you here for an investigation, then I would rather him not think that I was being a distraction in any way."

I draw my fingers across my lips. "My lips are sealed. I won't say a thing."

"Thank you, Darcy." Tim jams his hands into his pockets and starts off on the trail. Soon he is at the edge of the woods, where he turns and raises a hand toward me. I wave back and then wait until he's out of view before going back inside.

I'm drawn back into the living room, and to the pictures. Even though Tim's hair is still blonde, matching that of his mother, it has a little more brown in it than when he was younger.

I can't imagine the pain that his accident caused his family. And I can't find a place to blame Chief Bancroft for still reeling from it all these years later. But I'm glad that Tim has moved back. Hopefully, with more time and some forgiveness, the family can finally reconcile and start laughing together once again.

Life is so fragile. You never can tell what really awaits you around the next corner. In a moment, everything can be absolutely perfect, and the next it is ripped away by a dark reaper intent on only leaving sorrow and tears in its stead. If anyone knows that, it's me.

Sighing, I turn away from the pictures and go back to the table for what I know will be a long night of work.

Chapter Ten

BEFORE

"Darcy, can't we go back now? It's getting really cold."

"Just a little farther. I think it's right up here."

Lila's next words were filled with trepidation. "Okay. But if we don't leave soon, then we won't be able to see our way back."

Darcy continued to lead the way up the rocky trail that inclined through the woods. A cold wind had started to pick up ten minutes ago and little eddies of dry leaves swirled around them. High above them, a thick cloud was whispering across the sky.

The going was hard work. The farther they went, the steeper the trail became; they had finally reached a point where they couldn't pedal anymore. At the last bend in the trail, they had finally gotten off their bicycles and started to push them.

"This had better be worth it," Lila grumbled.

"It will be, I promise. But it won't be if you start complaining."

Darcy continued to lead the way up. The higher they went, the more treacherous the trail became. Well trodden dirt gave way to loose soil with big rocks jutting out. Both of them were adventurers, and they loved the challenge. What they didn't like was the cold.

They left their campsite half an hour ago, and since then, the temperature must have dropped twenty degrees. Their father had brought the family camping for their last wilderness outing of the season before the snows came.

Finally reaching the top, Darcy set her bike down at the trail mouth and jogged up to the top of the clearing. Her heart sank. Lila ran up and stopped beside her. "You brought me all the way up here for this?"

They were standing atop a high, rocky ledge. Below them, the cliff face ran straight down to the earth five hundred feet below where the view of the valley rolled out on either side of them like a dark green carpet that had just been rolled out but not yet smoothed down.

Darcy had found her way up here yesterday and had stayed to watch the sunset. When it had finally sunk beneath the horizon, she made her way back to the family campsite by the light of dusk. All day today, she hadn't stopped begging her mother to let her take Lila up there to see it, too. Their father's bad knee was acting up again, so he couldn't go with them, and their mother wasn't much for long hikes through the woods. Finally, though, she relented and made them promise to stay on the path and to restart their return trip before the sun was gone.

But there was no sunset.

Instead, a wall of dark gray clouds blocked out a direct view of the sun entirely. It reached miles into the sky and was making its way toward them.

"Well, I didn't exactly know a storm was on its way," Darcy snapped back, slipping her frigid hands into the pockets of her jacket as she cast a worried glance toward the towering wall of gray. "Those are snow clouds," she said. "Look how fuzzy they are."

The wind was even worse up here on the ridge. Lila's teeth started to chatter. She flipped the hood of her jacket over her head, which made her look like a garden gnome. "Daddy checked the weather before we left home. He said it wasn't going to snow this weekend. He wouldn't have brought us if he thought it would."

"That was three days ago," Darcy said. "I guess the weather changed. You know how Mommy is always saying that you can't ever trust the weather report. I guess she was right."

"Can we go back now? I want to sit by the fire."

"Yeah. Okay. Let's go."

They turned away from the view, retrieved their bikes, and started down the steep, rocky trail. Within minutes, the wind picked up into brawling gusts and whistled ominously through the trees. Both girls gripped their handlebars tightly to keep from toppling over, taking care where they placed their feet. Dusk crawled across the woods and quickly yielded all remaining light to a thick cloak of darkness. A snowflake landed on Darcy's nose.

"Darcy, I'm scared."

She was, too, but she knew better than to tell her sister that. "I know the trail," she said. "We just have to keep following it. It will get us right back to the campsite. Come on, we have to move fast!"

Their bike chains and fenders clattered as they ran them over the rocky ground, trying not to fall as they hurried down the hill in the dark. They had hardly started when Darcy's shoe caught the edge of a rock and she nearly went flying. Steadying herself, she slowed her pace and took care where she placed each step.

Don't look into the woods, she silently chided herself. She couldn't remember ever being in such dark; she couldn't even see her bicycle anymore, much less her sister beside her. There was no light at all to reflect off its chrome or the shiny paint. She wanted her father to come get them. Surely he was on his way up to find them.

"Darcy?"

"I'm right here. Just stay right next to me."

More snowflakes fell. And then more. Soon enough, they found themselves in a flurry. The going was agonizingly slow. Darcy couldn't feel her nose or hands anymore.

The flurry didn't last long before it morphed into a storm and then an all-out blizzard. The wind gusted, pregnant with thick, heavy flakes of wet snow. Within minutes, the girls' jackets and shoes were soaking wet.

They kept on, yearning to get back to their parents, wanting to get into some warm clothes and huddle beneath layers of heavy blankets. But mostly, they just didn't want to be by themselves in the dark anymore.

The wind continued its menacing onslaught, slinging snow into their faces and disorienting them beyond what their senses could bear. The rocky ground finally disappeared beneath their feet, replaced by the well trodden dirt on the lower half of the trail. That allowed them to move a little faster, but not much; they kept walking into branches when the trail curved away.

They kept going, growing colder by the minute. And then the minutes stretched on, one after the other after the other. They should be back at camp by now. Darcy knew they were going slow, but camp wasn't this far away. Was it?

Suddenly, she felt sick to her stomach as a cold sliver of fear snatched her into its grip. Halfway down, there was a fork in the trail. She didn't know where the other one led off to. But she was sure now that at some point, they had turned down the fork instead of going straight. In the darkness and the disorienting nature of the snow, she hadn't noticed the trail split off.

She groaned loudly.

"Darcy? What is it?"

"We went the wrong way!" she called out above the howling wind. "We have to turn around!"

Lila shook her head fiercely. "No! I'm too tired."

Darcy was exhausted, too. But they had to keep going. "You can do this, Lila. I'm right here with you! Now stay with me and let's go!"

Lila offered no further protest. She did what she was told and turned around, reaching out every so often to make sure that her sister was still right beside her.

As they retraced their most recent movements, Darcy did everything she could to keep the most awful of the thoughts at bay. But a dark shadow in the back of her mind kept telling her that this was all her fault. She just had to show Lila the sunset, didn't she? If they didn't get back safely, then this was all her fault.

Focus, Darcy chided herself. *Just focus.*

That's when she heard Lila cry out in pain and her bike

clatter to the ground. Darcy let go of her own handlebars and quickly found her way to her little sister.

"What's wrong?" she yelled over the elements.

Lila was whimpering. Darcy had to get her to repeat her answer over the wind.

"I ran into a tree."

Darcy got down beside her, and together they found their way beneath the modest cover of a few low-hanging tree limbs. Lila was crying now, shaking violently in her jacket. Darcy drew her in close and tried to keep her warm.

Maybe if they waited for the snow to die down, then they could find their way back to the main trail more easily. They couldn't wait for sunrise; she knew that. But it couldn't hurt to take a break and rest for just a little bit.

"We'll just wait here," she said. "Maybe it will pass soon."

"O—k-k-kay."

They waited. Five minutes. Ten minutes.

Darcy lost count. It was impossible to account for the passing of time in conditions like this.

"Darcy?"

"Yeah?"

"I think I see something."

Darcy maneuvered herself up. "Really?"

"Look. Do you see it?"

And then a flash out of the corner of her eye. And then again.

"It's a flashlight," Lila exclaimed.

Darcy felt a wave of relief rush over her. She stood up and then felt for her sister's hand. "Come on."

Lila let her sister help her to her feet and looked in the direction of the light. It was growing brighter, its beams cutting across the tree branches. "Listen," she said. "The storm is dying down."

She was right. The wind, while still there, wasn't as fierce. The snow had reduced to a flurry again.

Darcy cupped her hands to her mouth. "Over here!" she yelled. "We're over here!"

At the sound of her voice, the light swiveled and held steady in their direction. As it moved closer, Darcy led her sister back to the trail. Finally, after what felt like an eternity, the light burst out of the trees and the tall shadow of her father rose up behind it.

"You girls lost?"

Darcy felt a surge of disappointment rise inside her as she realized that the voice was not that of her father. "Yes," she called out, frowning against the bright light. "Can you help us? Our parents are down at the Rickshaw Preserve campground."

There was no answer for what felt like a very long time. "Yes... I think I can help you out. That's just down the hill. Come on. The cab of my truck is full, but you both can ride in the bed. There's a camper shell on it, so you'll be safe from the weather under there." He started to walk away, taking the light with him.

"Wait!" Darcy called out. "Our bicycles. We need to take them."

He stopped and spoke over his shoulder. "I'm afraid I can't get the bikes. You'll have to come back for those later."

Lila hesitated. She had just gotten her bike as a birthday gift not two weeks prior. She'd had her eye on it for nearly an entire year. A swift elbow from Darcy punching into her coat prompted her to relent. "Okay," she sighed.

The girls huddled together as they followed the light through the trees. The man was well ahead of them now, and the snow crunched loudly beneath their feet as they hurried to catch up. Finally, they fell in step behind him.

"What are you girls doing out in a storm like this?" he asked without turning around.

"I took my sister up to the ridge to see the sunset," Darcy proclaimed. "But we didn't know there was a storm coming. It caught up to us on the way down."

"Then I'm glad I happened to run into you," he said. "They say the storm will get worse before it gets better. First snow of the year. Came a little early this year."

"What were you doing out here in the dark?" Darcy asked.

"Got some rabbit traps that I was checking on."

The trio moved off the trail and entered the woods just as the wind picked up again. The snow started to fall in thick, wet clumps again as they reached an old truck. The man yanked open the tailgate and then lifted the rear window of the camper shell. Leaving the flashlight on, he stuffed it into his pocket and held his hand out to Lila.

"Come on. Let me help you up."

Lila hesitated. "It's okay," Darcy said. "He's just taking us back to the campground."

"We'll be there in ten minutes," the man soothed.

"Okay." Lila let go of Darcy's hand and offered it to the stranger. He took it, hooked his other hand behind her arm, and lifted her up. "Watch your head now." Once Lila was safely up, he turned to Darcy. She could hardly see a thing, only a weak suffusion of light that emanated out of the man's pocket and touched on the fresh snow. She gave the man her hand, and he helped her up beside her sister.

The truck bed was empty except for a small remnant of carpet and a rusty old paint can. The small space beneath the camper shell smelled like freshly turned dirt. Darcy could feel some of it clinging to her hands.

"I'm gonna shut you both in now. I'll have you back to your folks presently. Probably want to lie down. It's gonna be a bumpy ride back down."

Darcy thanked him and snuggled up beside her sister. They heard the tailgate shut and then the glass window to the camper shell. But then Darcy heard something that gave her an uneasy feeling. A key scraped in the lock of the camper shell and turned. Lila didn't seem to notice. Maybe he wanted to make sure the latch didn't pop. After all, they were about to ride over some rough ground. Darcy pushed it to the back of her mind as they got underway.

"I still can't feel my feet," Lila grumbled.

"Mommy will get us warm. Just a few more minutes."

"Do you think she'll make us hot chocolate?"

"If Daddy can get the fire going. He might not want to in this weather."

The truck bounced off the uneven terrain, and Darcy could just make out the snow falling outside the window by the reflection of the truck's headlights. Finally, the ground leveled off and smoothed out. Darcy figured that they had reached a road of some kind.

After a while, Lila stirred. "Do you think we're almost there? It's taking longer than I thought."

"There probably isn't a direct road back to the campground," Darcy replied. "Just be patient." Her voice was steady and calm, but inside she was growing more nervous by the minute.

Suddenly, a loud, streaming hiss sounded around them. At first, Darcy thought that maybe the truck was getting a flat tire. But then she realized that the sound was coming from above them. Behind them. It was coming from the rear window of the truck's cab.

"What is that?" Lila said.

"I don't know."

"Something smells funny."

"I smell it."

"What is it?"

"I don't know." Darcy's eyelids started to feel heavy.

Beside her, Lila yawned. "I'm so sleepy."

Alarms bells were going off in Darcy's head, but she wasn't experienced enough to put the pieces together. All she knew was that she was starting to feel sleepy, too.

"Darcy?"

"Yeah?"

"What's... happen... happening?"

Before Darcy could formulate an answer, Lila was asleep beside her, her whole body relaxed now. Now it was Darcy's turn to yawn. She couldn't open her eyes anymore. Didn't want to.

The truck slowed and made a sharp, bumpy turn before picking up speed again. As Darcy closed her eyes and drifted into the blackness of sleep, it suddenly occurred to her that she had never even seen the man's face.

Chapter Eleven

Bancroft Vacation Chalet
Miller's Grove, NY

The incessant ringing of my phone rips me from the depths of a heavy, dreamless sleep. With my face still planted on my pillow, I feel blindly for the phone. My fingers finally grasp it, and I bring it toward my face, squinting against the bright glow. I don't recognize the number but decide to answer it anyway.

"Hello?" I say in a groggy voice. A glance at the clock on the bedside table shows that it's not even five in the morning.

"Mrs.—I mean, Agent Hunt?" The lady's voice is soft and quiet.

"It's Miss. And yes, this is Agent Hunt. Who am I speaking with?"

"This is Tammy Akins." There was a short silence on the line before she continued. "I was wondering if we could talk. I live here in Miller's Grove. Out past the water treatment plant."

Rubbing my eyes, I stifle a yawn. "Tammy, I would be happy

to talk with you. Daylight is still an hour or two away. Can we talk after that?"

"I know. I'm sorry to have woken you. But, well..." She drifts off.

"But what?"

"I was hoping we could meet in person before the sun comes up. I know it's a strange request, but I feel unsettled about the murder at the hotel, and I heard they had you working it."

The FBI trained me to do a lot of things, but one thing it didn't teach me was how to be someone's therapist. Kayla's murder clearly has the town shaken up. I don't blame them. Having a murderer on the loose would unsettle just about anyone. But Kemper didn't send me here to help make sure that everyone feels safe and secure. In all honesty, right now, they aren't safe. The unsub could be anyone. For all anyone knows, he could have been eating his breakfast at the diner yesterday morning, right along with everyone else.

"I understand that you feel unsettled," I say. "And that's perfectly normal. However, I'm probably not the best person to be processing that with. Is there anyone else you know who you can talk to about it?"

"Oh. I'm sorry, Agent Hunt. I'm a little nervous—I've never talked with an FBI agent before. What I meant to say is that I think I might know something that can help you."

"You mean you have information about the case?"

"That's the thing. I'm not sure," she says timidly. "Possibly."

Sitting up, I toss my legs over the bed and turn on the bedside lamp as I try to brush the cobwebs from my mind. "Okay. Go ahead."

"Is there any chance we can meet in person? I would rather

107

not discuss this over the phone. You're welcome to come here if you like. Or anywhere else that would make you more comfortable," she adds quickly. "If we could meet before the town wakes up, that would be best."

The request puts me a little on guard. "Tammy, is there a reason why we can't meet later this morning?" *When normal people are awake,* I think to myself.

"Honestly... I would rather no one know that I'm speaking with you. And word has a way of moving fast around here."

I scratch my head as I consider her request. The suggestion isn't ideal. Going to a stranger's house alone in the dark has warning signs all over it. Still, I'm intrigued and don't want to miss out on a lead that has the potential to help me solve this case.

"All right, Tammy. I'll come over."

Relief fills her voice. "Thank you, Agent Hunt. Let me give you my address. Do you have something to write it down with?"

I ask her to wait as I stand up and make my way to the kitchen table. After flipping on a light and writing it down, I say, "Tammy, just so we're clear, I'm going to send an email to my boss in Albany, letting him know exactly where I'm going and who I'm meeting with. I'm also going to provide him with this number you're calling me from."

"That's fine. I do understand that my request is probably a little concerning. I'm sorry for that. I just don't know how else to tell you what I know."

"Let me get dressed," I say. "I'll leave here in a few minutes."

As soon as we hang up, I email Kemper with Tammy's information. I know that he'll chastise me later for going alone into such a risky situation. I'm not very comfortable with it myself.

But with few leads to work on, I need to take advantage of every opportunity presented to me.

After sending the email, I type Tammy's address into my internet browser. The results put me a little more at ease when I see her name associated with the property, knowing that I won't be traipsing through the dark to some isolated or unmarked spot in the woods.

TEN MINUTES LATER, armed with a tumbler of freshly brewed coffee and a flashlight, I get in the car and take the driveway to the county road. The directions take me past a junkyard and around to the south end of town. Turning down a rural dirt road, I continue for over a mile, passing several mailboxes until finally locating the address I'm looking for on the side of a mailbox post.

I pull the car into the driveway and park beneath the branches of an overhanging tree. The house is a basic ranch style. A soft spill of light streams through the sheer fabric of the front curtains. Turning off the car, I switch on my flashlight and cautiously get out, keeping my free hand on the butt of my holstered gun as I make my way to the front door. The yard hasn't seen a lawn mower in a few weeks, and the sidewalk is cracked and in need of repair.

Reaching the door, I knock and step back to the edge of the porch, listening and watching for anything coming from behind as I chide myself into staying calm. The nearest house is a quarter of a mile back down the road, and there are no street lights. It's as quiet as a snowed-in eve. Even the peepers and crickets have gone to sleep. Finally, the front porch light blinks on and a shadow moves across the keyhole just before the lock turns and the door swings open.

A lady who looks to be in her early thirties steps into view. Her brown hair is swept into a ponytail. She's wearing cotton sweatpants and an oversized Buffalo Bills sweater.

"Tammy?" I ask.

"Agent Hunt. Thank you for coming. Please, come in."

Still wary of my surroundings, I step across the threshold and switch off the flashlight. The house smells of old timbers and faintly of freshly baked bread. I follow her into the front sitting room and take a seat on the floral print couch where I can easily see both entrances to the room.

Tammy selects a wingback chair directly across from me. "Can I get you anything to drink?" she offers.

"No, thank you." I set the flashlight beside me and notice that Tammy appears more on edge than I do. She offers me a brief, wan smile, but her eyes don't focus on anything in particular for a reasonable length of time. Her features are etched with a vague kind of simplicity. She's exhibiting all the marks of being scared. "Tammy," I say, "It might be best if you went ahead and told me what's on your mind."

"Yes. Of course." I watch as she crosses her arms over her chest and then cups her hands over her elbows. "I know it was strange, me calling you here this time of night. Or morning, really. But everyone is talking about that murder over at the Diamond Palace, you know? Do you have any leads on who might have done it?"

"I'm afraid I can't discuss those kinds of details," I tell her.

"Right—of course. Well, I just want to help if I can. And like I said over the phone, I think I might know something."

I give her a reassuring smile and wait for her to continue.

"A few days ago, I was hiking through the woods behind the house," she begins. "I like to go for a walk every day because it helps to calm my nerves. I usually turn back at the creek, but since the water was lower than it usually is, I decided to cross it and keep going. The trail stopped at the creek, but once I got to the other side, the going was still easy enough. Do you like walking in the woods, Agent Hunt?"

I haven't gone on a pleasure walk in a long time. But I have to agree with her. Going deep into the woods in this part of the country is always so calming. "I do," I tell her. "But I don't get to do it as often as I would like."

She nods and then continues her story. "I walked in a good way. It was really calming and being out there relaxed me. Even the birds were quiet. The only thing I could hear was the sound of my own breath and my feet pressing into the leaves. But then, I got frightened because I thought I heard a voice far ahead of me. So I stopped and listened, and sure enough, I heard a woman talking. She sounded upset, so I moved forward very slowly."

Tammy stops talking and stares at a fixed spot on the carpet, like she is recalling what had happened. But when she doesn't continue, I prompt her.

"Tammy?"

"Oh. Yes, I'm sorry. So I kept going and finally saw something through the trees. It was someone wearing a blue jacket. They had their back to me. After a few moments, I realized that it was the woman that I had heard earlier. And when I say a woman, I mean like a teenager. She wasn't an adult. But not a child, either."

"Okay. And then what did you see?"

"She had her back to me, but it looked like she was at a

111

makeshift campground. I could see a fire pit made out of stones. There wasn't a fire in it, but farther past it was a tent. Nothing fancy. Just some blankets thrown over a rope that was tethered to a couple of trees."

"And what did the girl look like?" I ask her. It's too early to get excited about this being a real lead on what Kayla was doing in the days leading up to her death. But I won't know until Tammy tells me everything she heard and saw.

"I only got a quick look at the side of her face. She turned at one point, and I thought she might see me, so I ducked out of view really fast. But she was pretty. Had blonde hair a little past her shoulders. And smooth skin. A little shorter than I am."

The description does match Kayla's. Still, I'll need more than that. "What was she talking about?" I asked her.

"About going to California. She was angry because whoever she was talking to hadn't taken her there yet like she was promised."

"Did you get a look at the other person?"

"No. But I'm positive that it was a man. He was on the other side of some bushes. The voice was really muffled, not clear enough to make out anything unique about it, but deep enough for me to know that it was a man.

"And then what happened?" I ask.

"She kept saying, 'but you promised... but you promised...' and then at one point, I think she started to cry. I heard some sniffles. To be honest, I felt really bad for her."

I slip my phone from my pocket and pull up the email that Kyle sent me last night. "If I show you a picture, do you think you could tell me if it's the girl you saw?"

"Maybe. I could try," she says.

"I have to warn you that it's a picture of a dead body. That's all I have right now."

"Oh." Tammy's eyes widen into dinner plates. "I've never seen a real dead body before. At least, not one that isn't made up before they display it in a coffin."

"Have you seen a TV show where they show a dead body or a cadaver?" I ask her.

"Of course. I love crime shows. But those dead bodies aren't real. They're actors with makeup on."

"You're right," I say. "So just think of it like that, okay? I'll be as quick as I can."

"Okay."

Tammy nervously rubs her elbows as I pull up the picture I want to show her. It's a photo from the hotel room, showing Kayla just as the killer left her. Zooming in on her face, I turn the phone around and extend the image toward Tammy. She leans in, squints at it, and then she bursts into tears as she nods.

I put my phone away and wait for her to collect herself, understanding just how hard it is to see something like that. Our brains are wired toward life. The finality of death makes it difficult to conceive someone that we recently saw alive as now being dead. Looking at a real dead body can sometimes feel like a punch in the face. It's unnatural and jarring and can leave anyone experiencing it reeling from cognitive dissonance.

Tammy tries to squeak out a few words.

"It's okay," I reassured her. "Just take a breath."

She reaches for a tissue from a box on the coffee table. After blotting her eyes, she gathers the tissue between her fingers and nods. "That is the girl that I saw."

Her words cause me to feel a quick surge of excitement.

Apparently, Kayla's killer hadn't factored a random hiker into his plans. This new bit of knowledge lets me know that Kayla knew her killer, assuming that whoever was with her in the woods was the one who ended her life.

As if reading my mind, Tammy suddenly says, "Oh my god. Do you think the man I heard out there with her is the one who killed her? Do you think I was that close to a murderer?"

"There is no way to know that," I say, trying my best to reassure her. "Right now, you're safe in your house. You don't have anything to worry about. If either one of them had seen you, I'm sure they would have been frightened, too. Coming across anyone unexpected in the woods can be startling. You would have known it if they had seen you."

She nods, but doesn't relax at all.

"Is there anything else that you can think of to tell me, Tammy? Are you sure you didn't catch even a glimpse of the man? A piece of clothing or the color of his hair through the bushes?"

She thinks about that for a while and I can see the cogs turning behind her eyes as she revisits the scene in her mind. "No. No, I wish I could. The blankets for the tent were just a basic gray. There were no chairs or anything else that I saw."

"How long did you stay there?"

"Not long. The girl finally said something to him that I couldn't hear. Right after that, she disappeared behind the bushes, too. And then a minute later, I heard an engine start up and they drove away."

"What kind of engine was it?" I ask. "Loud? Quiet?"

"It was really loud, actually. It growled and puttered. Maybe a truck or a sports car?"

Taking out my phone, I pull up my notes app and input the highlights of what I have just been told.

"This is very helpful," I tell her. "I'll need to tell Chief Bancroft what you've told me. Would you feel comfortable leading us to the spot in the woods where you saw them?"

Tammy's body tenses again. "No," she says quickly.

Her reaction surprises me. "Why not?" I ask.

"After the vehicle drove away, I was about to go into the campsite when I heard a twig snap somewhere. I thought maybe there was another person that I hadn't noticed. So I stayed right where I was and didn't move for almost ten minutes. The entire time, I felt like someone was watching me. My heart was beating so fast. I know it might sound crazy, but I finally found the courage to turn and run. I didn't stop until I was all the way back here at the house. I almost twisted my ankle going over the step stones in the creek."

"I'm sure that rattled you," I say. "But, Tammy, it would be very helpful if you would—"

"No!" She cuts me off. "I can't do it. I *won't* do it." She gathers her elbows into her hands again.

I offer a reassuring smile. "That's fine. The chief and I will need to go out there and look over the area. Could you draw me a map to get us in the right direction?"

Relief floods into her face as she realizes that I'm not going to make her go with me. It may end up coming down to that, and if it does, I'm sure the chief, or someone else in town, can do a better job convincing her to lead the way. For now, though, if a map can do the job, then there is no need to involve Tammy more than she needs to be.

"Here," Tammy says. She stands up, goes to a side table, and opens the drawer, quickly returning with a white blank page and a pen. Lowering herself to her knees, she lays the paper on the coffee table and runs the pen across it in a flourish of confident strokes. Before I know it, she sets the pen down and holds the paper out to me.

I can't believe what I'm seeing. The map is brilliantly sketched and detailed notes identify certain topographical markers in the woods. Tammy comes and stands beside me and gestures with her finger. "It's better if you don't start here at the house. But you can get to the trail from here. It's an empty lot on the other side of the woods, not far from here. Then you'll take the trail about a mile until you reach the creek. Here's where it gets tricky."

"And this 'X' is where you think you saw Kayla?"

"Think? No, I'm sure, Agent Hunt. I saw her. There isn't a doubt in my mind. And yes, once you cross the creek right here, then you go through these holly bushes. The way the trees stand, they almost form a path of their own. Just follow them until you get to this clearing. From there, it's maybe about a hundred yards to the south." She shrugs. "Maybe a little more. It's hard to tell when you're in the woods. And I'm not so great with distances."

I thank her and fold the paper, placing it in my lap. "You said this was a few days ago. Exactly what day was it?"

"Hang on." Tammy walks out of the room and returns a minute later. "I had to check my calendar. I had an appointment that morning. It was that afternoon that I saw her. It was three days ago. So, Friday."

"You're sure of that?" Kayla's foster parents told me that they had last seen her four days ago.

"Yes. Very sure."

"And what time?"

"Maybe two o'clock?"

I nod and thank her again. "One more thing, Tammy. Is there a reason why you needed me to come over so early?" A glance at a cuckoo clock on the wall reveals that it's just after six in the morning.

She nods. "My brother. That's why."

"Your brother?"

"Yes. Last night, I told him about what I saw in the woods. Told him everything I just told you. But then he got angry and told me not to tell anyone. He said he would look into it himself. We got into a big argument over it."

The revelation sends a chill tracking down my spine, and it takes everything in me to remain calm and to let her finish.

"He works the third shift at the semiconductor plant in Pine Bluff," Tammy continues, "and usually gets home around seven every morning—he lives here with me. I wanted to make sure that I could speak with you in person before he got back. If he saw that I went behind his back, that I would actually let you come here...." Her voice drifts off.

Alarms bells clang in my head. I'm taken aback that Tammy appears to only be concerned about her brother's anger, not the fact that he is actually trying to withhold evidence from the authorities.

"Why would he not want you to speak with me?" I ask.

"My brother," she sighs, "he has a lot of pride and likes to do things his own way. But now that I think about it, I don't really know why. He was just adamant that I keep what I saw to myself."

I pull up my notes app again. "What is his name?"

She gives me that weak, timid smile again. "Darren Malloy."

The name registers like a thunderclap. My mind immediately recalls being stopped on my way into town yesterday. Images flash of Darren, insisting that I leave town, telling me that I don't belong here. That, co-mingling with the revelation that he doesn't want his sister informing me or Bancroft what she saw in the woods, makes my hair stand on end.

I have worked countless cases where the worst crimes imaginable are committed by trusted loved ones or family members; no one would have ever thought that a brother or mother was complicit in such horrific acts. Most of the crimes that the FBI investigates are perpetrated by people with perfect smiles, 401ks, and well-cared-for pets. On the outside, the offender is pleasant, even thoughtful to family and neighbors. They don't forget birthdays and they over-tip their waiters and waitresses. But inside, they are cauldrons steaming with hate, malice, and ill-intent. As a result, when the truth comes out in an arrest or a trial, the family can't believe it.

Tammy seems to be most concerned that her brother is the controlling type. But why he doesn't want her saying anything to the authorities doesn't appear to unsettle her at all.

I can clearly see Darren's twisted, angry face in my mind, telling me to leave town and to keep my nose out of its business.

Tammy said that the unseen voice in the woods was just deep enough to determine that it was a man's. But was it so muddled that she had been unable to recognize her own brother's voice?

I take the map and my flashlight and stand up. My head is spinning. I need to speak with Bancroft right away.

"Thank you for coming, Agent Hunt," Tammy says as she

rises to her feet. She walks me to the door and opens it. I intuit that she has one more thing on her mind.

"Tammy, is there anything else you think I should know?"

She looks sad now as she answers. "I guess you should know that people around here, a lot of them think I'm crazy. And you know? Maybe I am a little. But I know what I saw. I know what I heard. It was that girl. I have no doubt in my mind."

"Why would you say that people around here think that you're crazy?"

A weak smile plays at the edges of her lips. "No. At least, not right now. If that's okay."

"Sure it is." I step over the threshold and turn back around. "Out of curiosity, how did you come by my cell number?"

"Regina Newsom gave it to me. She's the night dispatch at the police station. I told her that Darren had asked me to get it for him. She never would have given it to me if she thought I was asking. I hope that was okay?"

I wonder why Regina wouldn't have given Tammy the number. Maybe they have bad beef with each other. Whatever the reason, that's not my focus right now. So I don't ask.

"Absolutely," I tell her. "And just to make sure that we're both on the same page, neither one of us will tell Darren that I came by or that we spoke."

"Yes," she says, relief flooding her voice. "That's perfect. Thank you."

"I'll let you know if we need anything else from you or if we have trouble finding the place."

"Okay."

I hear the door shut behind me as I followed the broken sidewalk back to my car. As soon as I'm behind the wheel, I call the chief. My heart is beating wildly as he answers on the second ring.

"Bancroft."

"Chief, It's Darcy Hunt. Did I wake you?"

"Darcy. No. Not at all. Sleeping in is for the poor man. I'm glad to know that you're a member of the early risers club as well."

"Can I meet you at the station? I've discovered a new lead on Kayla's case."

"Sure thing. Let me shove these arthritic feet into a pair of boots, and I'll meet you there in fifteen minutes."

Chapter Twelve

Miller's Grove Police Station
Miller's Grove, NY

The dark cloak of night that I rode through on the way to Tammy's house is fading before a rising sun as I drive away. The country is coming alive with birds looking for their morning meal as I take the road back into town a little over the speed limit.

By the time I reach the station, Bancroft's cruiser is already sitting in his designated parking slot. I pull in beside it and hurry into the station, making a beeline for his office. He's sitting back in his chair with his ankles crossed on the desk. A cup of coffee is steaming in one hand, the other clutches the morning paper. Hearing me enter the room, he peers at me over the brim of the paper.

"Darcy. Good morning. Come on in. Shut the door."

I close the door behind me and drop into a chair across from him. A dim, yellow light on the desk provides the only light in an already dark room. A window overlooks the small bullpen, but a set of dark brown blinds is pulled down over it.

"How do you read with almost no light?" I ask him.

Bancroft slips off his reading glasses as he removes his feet from the desk. His chair creaks as he sits upright. "God gave me good eyes, I suppose. I can't get on with those bright halogens or LEDs that are so popular these days. Gives me headaches." He folds the newspaper and sets it to the side. "So, what is this lead you found?"

I begin by telling him about the unexpected phone call, my drive out of town, and the ensuing conversation, quickly jumping to the scene in the woods three days ago.

"So this lady thinks she saw Kayla?" Bancroft asks.

"Yes," I reply. "The day before she was killed."

He leans back and scratches his chin. "And who was it that told you all this? You haven't mentioned a name."

"Tammy Akins."

A deep frown settles into the chief's features. "Tammy? Ah, I wish you would have told me that at the start, Darcy."

"Why?"

He lets out a long sigh. "Tammy, well, she has a strong reputation for being the town cuckoo bird. A little off her rocker, if you catch my drift."

"I don't know that I do," I stonewall.

"Tammy has always been a little strange. I think everyone in town has been eating breakfast at Maybelle's at some point and looked out the window to see Tammy sitting at the bus stop across the street, holding a conversation with an imaginary person."

"You're kidding," I say.

"I wish I was. From the time she was little, she's not been all there in the head. It's my understanding that her bathroom cabinet is a pharmacy unto itself."

It makes sense now why Tammy said that dispatch wouldn't have given her my number if she didn't drop Darren's name, or why her brother told her not to tell anyone. It also explains her disposition; the clutching of her elbows and the simple mannerisms that she employed.

"Are you saying that she was lying to me about all this?"

"No," Bancroft says. "Not lying. Not exactly. I do believe that Tammy thinks that she saw what she did. But that it was actually rooted in reality is a different matter altogether. Darcy, last year, Tammy got the fire department out to an old campground claiming that a boy was going around starting fires everywhere. When they showed up, there was no indication of any fires whatsoever. If she wasn't on so many meds, and if we all didn't know that her heart was in the right place, she would have been in some serious trouble. If it had been anyone else, I would have arrested them for crying wolf."

A deep sense of frustration rises inside me as I pinch the bridge of my nose. The more that Bancroft speaks about Tammy, the more I can feel my hopes fade as I realize that everything she told me was most likely a figment of a prescription-fueled imagination.

"I'm sorry," Bancroft says. "If I had any inkling that Tammy was going to try and get in touch with you, then I would have warned you about her from the get-go. I think her imagination gets fired up about sensational events. Her story about the boy setting fires came a few days after some big Canadian fires across

Lake Erie blew smoke this way. The skies were unnaturally gray, and you could smell the smoke."

I reach into my pocket and unfold the map that Tammy drew for me, then hand it across the desk. Bancroft studies it for a while. "I have a general idea where this is," he says. "But there is nothing out there. No roads or anything. It doesn't make sense that she would have heard a car. It couldn't have gotten into the woods that far." He reaches out for his coffee and takes a slow sip before returning the mug to its wooden coaster. "I think it's safe to say that you've been bamboozled by the town nut. But take solace in the knowledge that you aren't the first, and you won't be the last."

I lean back in my chair and consider the proper course of action. The lab results won't be complete until later today or tomorrow. Right now, I have no other leads to pursue. Tammy may have looped me into an imaginary scenario that she believes is real, but I don't see how it would do any harm to check it out.

Quantico excels at teaching fresh agents new skills. For months, it trains them to look at cases with objectivity, pushing them to look beneath the surface to find what is not readily apparent. But for all their expertise and their technology, there is one thing that Quantico can't teach: instinct.

They can't show an agent how to manufacture that feeling deep in your gut that tells you something just isn't right, or that sensation on the back of your neck when you're staring at all the facts but know there is something you're completely missing.

But it's my instincts that have caused me to excel during my time with the Bureau. Early on in my career, I would try to ignore them. After all, no one cares about the newbie's hunch that something just isn't right. Even though I'm not a newbie any longer,

I've learned to keep my sixth sense to myself. Most agents like chasing bare empirical facts. They generally don't give any credence to feelings or intuitions. But for me, a good hunch can be the one thing between catching the unsub or them getting away with it. Scientists tell us that the subconscious mind is more powerful than we can imagine. I've learned to trust the signals it sends to my body when it screams at me to look at the information at my disposal with new eyes.

"Chief, I hear what you're saying about Tammy, but I still think we should go out there and take a look at it. The map she drew up is fairly detailed, and she even recognized Kayla from a picture I showed her."

Before the last sentence is completely out of my mouth, Bancroft is already shaking his head. "Darcy, I want to catch that girl's killer as much as you do. But I've got a meeting with the mayor in about an hour to discuss next year's budget for my department. After that, I have to interview a prospect for a new officer. I can't spend my morning going on a wild goose chase through the woods. Besides, there is nothing out there. I can promise you that."

"What if Tammy wasn't lying this time?" I say. "What if there is some truth to it?"

Bancroft removes his ball cap from his head and runs a hand through his hair before sliding the cap back on. "If there was the slightest chance that I thought she saw something, you can be sure that I would reschedule my appointment with the mayor and lead a team out there. But think of this like Tammy swearing that she saw Pennywise in the woods. Would you believe that?"

"No," I admit.

"This is no different. Take my word for it."

"Okay," I nod. "You clearly know the people in your town. If you think Tammy is lying, then I won't press the issue."

"Not lying, you understand. Just misguided." I watch as he gathers the map into his fingers and rolls it into a tight paper ball. Then he launches it over my head in a high arc. It rattles into the wastebasket near the coffee pot. "Keep at it, Darcy. You're doing a great job. I'm glad the FBI sent me someone as thorough as you. Let's just make sure we're not chasing imaginary smoke."

Chapter Thirteen

Bancroft Vacation Chalet
Miller's Grove, NY

The microwave sounds off in successive beeps, letting me know my oatmeal is finished cooking. Getting up from the table, I take out my breakfast. After adding a little brown sugar and some butter, I stir everything together and return to the table.

I've been awake for almost four hours now, and both the rumble in my stomach and my lack of energy inform me that it's past time to eat. Even though Maybelle's is just down the street from the police station, I'm not in the mood to parley with the local gossip or field any questions. What I need most is the peace and quiet that allows my mind to continue processing all the facts surrounding the case.

After leaving the station, I decided to take Tammy's account seriously. The worst thing that could happen is that I don't find anything in the woods. If that is the case, then I'll keep it quiet that I ever went out there. I don't want Bancroft thinking that I am deliberately going behind his back. I have the authority to do whatever I feel is necessary to find the answers we so desperately need. But at the same time, I respect the chief. He is a good man, and I don't want him to feel like I'm barrelling forward without any concern for his own knowledge or expertise.

Even so, I won't be able to focus on anything else until I know if Tammy is actually telling the truth. Choosing not to follow up on a lead like this is cozying up to negligence should it actually turn out to be true. This is my case, and I have the duty to do what I think is best.

I stir my oatmeal again and take a bite as I scan the satellite view of Google Maps on my laptop. After Bancroft tossed Tammy's map, there was no discreet way for me to retrieve it. For now, I will have to go off what I remember of the map, which, thanks to Tammy's excellent drawing skills, is quite clear in my mind. I compare the mental image to what I'm seeing on my computer screen and determine the best entry point into the woods.

I'm so deep in concentration that when my phone rings, it startles me. My arms give a little jerk, and I immediately feel like a fool.

"Hey," I answer. "What's up?"

"I scared you, didn't I?" Skylar asks, her voice filled with triumph. "You were in a zone."

"Yes," I reluctantly admit. "You did startle me a little."

"You always get this detached tone in your voice when you're so involved in a case. You're brilliant, and I admire you for it."

"Thanks," I say. "So, what's up?"

"Can't I just call my best friend to see how things are going over there?"

"Sure," I chuckle. "Things are... moving more slowly than I would like. If I'm honest, I don't think this victim will be the only one. I have a suspicion that there might be more murders planned. Maybe here in Miller's Grove, maybe somewhere else. This killer is very smart. He's methodical and didn't give us any clues except what he wanted us to know. The problem is, we don't know what those clues mean yet."

"Do you have any good leads?" she asks.

"Not really. And that's the most frustrating part. This killer had to have been planning this for a while. He wants to send a message, and he was highly strategic about how he did that."

"Creepy. What message?"

"I'm not sure yet. But I think I'm up against the smartest unsub I've ever chased. Something about the whole thing screams cat and mouse."

Skylar sighs into the phone. "Well, don't get so wrapped up in it all that you don't come up for air. You've told me more than once that when you stay too close to a case, then you stop being able to see the forest for the trees."

"I'm not," I promise. "In fact, the chief's son came over last night. We had a nice talk."

"Oh?" Skylar's voice takes on a conspiratorial tone. "Is he hot?"

A smile plays at the corner of my lips. "He is—but that's not the point," I quickly add.

"Of course it's the point," she remarks. "It's the only point. You don't take a man to bed if he's a toad."

"Hold your horses," I laugh. "I'm not going to bed with anyone. I'm here to do a job."

"That doesn't mean you can't have a little fun on the side."

"That's exactly what it means."

"You and I are very different people, Darcy Hunt. So very different. And how did you meet this chief's son?"

I relay how Tim showed up on the back porch peering through the window. "He just got back from a hunting trip and thought the place was empty. His mom had been talking about redecorating, and he was looking to see if she had made any progress."

"So you invited him in... then what?"

"We just had coffee. He used to vacation here when he was a kid." I tell her about his past and the tragic mistake that ended his aunt's life. "He went to jail for seven years. The chief, his dad, still doesn't have much to do with him. After all these years, they still haven't fully found their way through the tragedy."

"That's terrible."

"Yeah," I agree. "It really is. I like his dad a lot. The chief has a good head on his shoulders."

"If you ask me, Tim could probably use a good woman in his life. Even if it's just for a couple of days. If you catch my drift."

"Skylar," I sing-song. "Leave it alone. Besides, you know I'm not ready to date anyone." As soon as the words come out of my mouth, I can visualize Skylar rolling her eyes.

"Darcy," she says with a fringe of irritation, "Lucas was over a year ago. Get over him already and move on. There's an entire world of beautiful men who can rock your world if you would just let them."

"Two things," I reply. "First, I *am* over him. Second, I'm not ready to move on. My career comes first, and moving on means the distraction of a relationship that I'm not prepared to have right now. The flavor of the week works for you, just not for me."

"Ugh. I'm not telling you to get a flavor of the week. Although, I must say, it's loads of fun. All I'm saying is that a little love in your life would be a good thing."

Skylar starts into a monolog that I've heard a hundred times, yet another attempt to try to get me to change my mind about dating. After a couple of minutes, I hear her call my name.

"Darcy? Hello?"

"Hmm?"

"You're staring at your computer screen, aren't you?"

"Huh? Oh, sorry. You were saying?"

"I was saying that you need to snap out of work for a couple of minutes and give me your full attention."

"You're right." I shut my computer. "I'm sorry. You have my full and undivided attention."

Skylar chuckles through the phone. "You get back to work. Solve your case, and we'll talk about finding you a date when you get back."

"Oh, I know we will."

"It's only because I love you so much, Darcy. You're not going to be young forever. Have fun while it lasts."

We say our goodbyes, and I quickly finish my breakfast before getting ready to go. Over the last half hour, the sky has begun to cloud over, blocking out the sun and casting everything in a dreary gray light. I go into the garage and find a high-beam flashlight, then retrieve a jacket from my bedroom before heading out the front door and getting into the car.

I follow the directions in my head back toward Tammy's house and turn onto a narrow dirt road. The tall grass growing between the ruts whispers against the undercarriage as I drive farther away from civilization. I have intentionally taken a different route to where Tammy began her walk into the woods. Darren is home from work now, and while I'm not intimidated by him in the least, I'm not in the mood to have him notice me driving through his neighborhood and getting in my way.

The road terminates at a grassed-over pile of dirt. New and rusty beer cans litter the area along with cigarette butts and a couple of condom wrappers. Off to the side, among the over-grown weeds, is a moldy couch missing all its cushions, along with a burn barrel filled with ash and the blackened tips of charred wood. It looks like I've stumbled onto the town's Blue-berry Hill, where the bored and restless youth come to find their thrills.

I step out of the borrowed cruiser, shut the door, and lock the car. On the other side of the burn barrel, a narrow path leads into the woods. I step onto it and pass up more beer cans and a discarded porn mag as I make my way farther in. After thirty or so yards, the path ends and I have to make my way through the woods with no markers and nothing but my sense of direction. The trees are thin here, each of them standing several feet apart. I only have to watch out for reaching limbs or prickly vines that threaten to tear my jacket or trip me up.

After several minutes, I hear water quietly bubbling over rocks and step from the woods onto a path that takes up again on the other side of the narrow river. The stepping stones that Tammy mentioned sit sturdily in the water.

The path is mostly unused, perhaps only by Tammy herself. The lightly pressed down leaves haven't been trodden regularly enough to expose the bare dirt underneath. Crossing the river would take me away from my desired destination and lead me back to Tammy's house. Since my attention lies deeper in the woods, I turn onto the path and put the river behind me.

The sound of the water quickly fades away, and I once again find myself in the quiet. As I continue farther into the woods, the sky begins to grow darker. Even though it is now late morning, dark gray clouds swirl overhead, blocking out much of the sunlight and making it feel like dusk. A steady wind stirs the tops of the trees. Soon I feel a drizzle. Rain falls gently on the leaves and creates a relaxing symphony of sorts.

The holly bushes that Tammy spoke of are gathered together ahead of me. There is enough space between them for me to slide through without the sharply pointed leaves raking my clothes. Looking farther into the woods, I see that Tammy was right. Oddly enough, the trees almost do form a path of their own. They stand tall on either side of a cleared path several yards wide. I can't help but wonder if this is just an odd natural phenomenon or if someone many years ago had planted them this way.

Walking down what feels like a natural corridor, I continue until the woods once again take on a more familiar shape and the trees stand in uneven spaces all around me. I turn south just as the rain picks up. Fat drops now pelt the forest, and a loud crack of thunder booms overhead.

I should be getting closer now. In spite of the rain and the near dark of the woods, a strong sense of anticipation fuels my every step. I hurry ahead for several more yards before slowing to carefully take in my surroundings. I should be near the place where Tammy believes she saw Kayla.

But I don't see anything resembling a clearing. Nothing but trees and more trees. My anticipation quickly shifts into frustration as I start walking in ever-increasing circles, trying to locate an area that would easily accommodate a tent and a firepit. Recalling that Tammy said she heard a loud engine and the couple drive away in the vehicle, I see no break in the vegetation that would allow even a small car to drive in this deep.

The rain is coming harder now. I flip up the hood of my jacket and squint through the disorienting rain. The last thing I want to do is get lost out here. A glance at my phone informs me that if I do, there won't be a way to call for help; I'm completely out of service range.

For half an hour, I traipse through the forest, trying to keep my wits amid the pouring rain and the lack of light. My shoes are soaked, and I'm starting to chill when I finally throw in the towel and mutter to myself through the rain. "Well, Chief. I should have listened."

I allow myself a final look around, swiveling my head to make sure that I didn't miss what might be right in front of me. But there is nothing. Nothing but trees, bushes, and ferns. I sigh, shake my head, and start to work my way back to my origination point.

Suddenly, with no notice at all, I find myself in a small clearing. It's only about twenty square feet, and nothing but leaves cover the ground. Adrenaline floods my body as I take in the new surroundings. Moving quickly, I use the toe of my shoe to disturb the leaves, looking for any trace of a fire. But after several minutes, I find nothing. I can find no hint of ash or any disturbance that might indicate that anyone had been here over the last several years.

Tucking my hands into my jacket pockets, I shake my head

and chide myself once again. The rain is finally letting up as I leave the clearing and make my way back to the holly bushes.

Then I see it.

Another space where the trees are cleared away, this one larger than the last. Moving to it, I see a disturbance in the groundcover. My heart begins to race again as I push the wet leaves aside to reveal a pile of ash, several charred but unburned twigs protruding from it.

A renewed sense of urgency rises inside me as I carefully inspect the site. Tammy had said that the fire was encircled by stones. But there are no stones around the ash. One by one, I locate almost a dozen stones twice the size of my fist, all of them charred on one side. They had been pulled up and discarded to the perimeter of the clearing.

I also recall Tammy saying that a makeshift tent had been erected, that blankets were hung over a rope. Tree by tree, I carefully inspect the bark in the dim light, looking for any signs of wear or scuffing. I find it at the sixth tree, the bark lightly worn on the outside, just above where the trunk splits to form another branch.

My heart is racing now. Knowing that Tammy, and my belief in her, has been vindicated sends my adrenaline into overdrive. Tammy wasn't lying after all, and she hadn't imagined what she had seen. Kayla had been here, arguing with someone about a failed promise to move her to California.

Moving beyond the clearing, I search for the third and final part of what Tammy claimed to see. I find it fifty feet away, on the other side of a high growth of ferns: a narrow lane just wide enough for a car. Trees stumps litter the lane, and freshly cut saplings stand in between them. I follow the lane for a while, but when I see no end in sight, I return to the campsite.

The rain has completely stopped now. The only sound is the occasional raindrop falling from a soaked leaf. I stand here in the quiet, thinking about Kayla. Everything inside me says that she was brought here to keep her out of the way until the killer was ready to end her life, to stage her. I can't help but feel sad for her. She was just a girl wanting what everyone on this planet wants: to feel loved. She just wanted to belong, to know that someone cared enough about her to protect her and help her find her way.

A cold shiver runs down my back as I suddenly get the feeling that I'm being watched. I flip down the hood of my jacket and slowly swivel my head around, my eyes calmly searching the shadows between the trees. Even though the rain has stopped, it's still no brighter than dusk.

When I arrived in the woods, I knew that I was alone. But now I am certain that I'm not. Someone is watching. Tammy's words this morning flash through my mind: *I heard a twig snap somewhere... the entire time, I felt like someone was watching me.* My heart is racing inside my chest as I reach down at my side and slide my gun from its holster.

I feel exposed now, and a dark sense of foreboding washes over me. Whoever is out here, whoever is watching me now, they are not curious. Along with the sensation of being watched comes the heaviness of a dark evil surrounding me. It's as if I've somehow walked into a forest out of The Brothers Grimm, and some hideous monster is peering at me from behind the cover of a tree, licking its lips in expectation.

Except real monsters don't exist. Only wicked humans do,

and they take great pleasure in inflicting the worst upon their fellow beings.

I've seen what I came here to verify. It's time to leave. Another crack of thunder booms high above and rattles through the forest as I hurry back the way I came in.

I don't scare easily. It's just not in my nature. But I have learned to trust my gut. Someone is lurking back in the shadows of the forest. Even though I have my service weapon, it does nothing to dispel the sense of naked exposure that I feel. I am miles from anyone who can help, and I sense an urgent need to get out as quickly as I can.

A bush rustles behind me. I swivel around just in time to see its leaves draw still and a dark shadow move behind it. Then everything goes still. All I can hear are steady drops of rain falling from the trees and the sound of my breath.

"What do you want?" I finally call out. "Show yourself." My words sound hollow and lack any authority. I silently chide myself for exposing such a shaky voice.

Suddenly, farther away, a deep voice booms into sickening laughter. The hair curls on the back of my neck. That is not the laugh of a young boy playing games. It is the sound of black evil, the kind that takes deep pleasure inflicting the worst possible scenarios on fellow humans.

There is no doubt in my mind who is here with me. I need to leave, to get out of here. I'm not familiar with these woods like Kayla's killer is. Moving slowly, I retreat backward, keeping my weapon trained ahead and glancing down periodically to watch where I am placing my feet.

I've gone several yards when a loud scuff comes from behind me. Before I can turn to see what it is, my shoulder bumps into a tree just as a hand slides down over my shoulder. I jolt forward, swiveling around as I slide my finger over the trigger and prepare to fire.

But no one is there. Only a long tree limb dangling beside the trunk. It was the tips of the branches that grazed my shoulder. I hear the scuff again and look over to see a rabbit nibbling mindlessly on a green tuft of grass.

Cursing myself for being so skittish, I hurry back the way I came in, but no matter how fast I move, I can't shake the feeling that he is staying with me, step for step. I hear nothing, and for the briefest of moments, I think that maybe I'm the one who has gone crazy now. But I shake the thought away. I keep glancing back over my shoulder as I move from a fast walk to a focused jog. The forest begins to thin out, and for a moment, I don't know where I am. I can't get lost; these woods are too large to find my way back.

Relief floods over me as I see a familiar sight. Up ahead, the holly bushes stand just as they were when I came in. Moving through them, I finally find the path that starts near the creek. Once I'm back at the car, I get in, lock the doors, and take out my phone, which is showing several bars of service again. As quickly as my fingers allow, I dial a number.

"Darcy?"

"Chief." My chest is heaving in long, unsteady breaths. It's a struggle to form any words at all. "I found... the place in the woods Tammy told me about. I need you to come out here." I take a long look through the windshield, closely watching the treeline. "And hurry."

Chapter Fourteen

Public Land
Miller's Grove, NY

"Well, if this doesn't make me feel like a dried up cow patty."

Bancroft stands on the edge of the small clearing with his hands on his hips, shaking his head. The sky has begun to clear, and the forest is brightly lit with the early afternoon sun. "I'm sorry, Darcy. I guess I should have believed Tammy after all."

In front of us, the crime scene unit is taking pictures of the area. They have already put the ash into a large bucket to be analyzed later.

"She gave you good reason not to believe her," I say. "If I was in your shoes, I may not have either."

"You're a gracious person, Darcy. Now where was it that you said the car would have driven?"

"This way." He follows me through the brush to where the old, cut tree stumps lay. "Here it is." He walks a long way before coming back, examining the stumps. He returns to my side and places his hands on his hips.

"I didn't know this was here." He squats down and inspects the stumps, moving his fingers to feel what's left of a sapling. "From what I understand, a few years before I moved out here, a company had come in and was trying to buy up land for logging. Eventually, the proper county codes were passed to get them shut down. This must have been an early access road they made. Didn't even get a chance to get the stumps out."

"That would explain the saplings growing in between them," I say. "But it would have taken some work to cut them all down. I don't know how long this road goes back, but it has to be at least a mile. That would mean hundreds of saplings to cut."

"True," Bancroft agrees, "but a healthy man could do that in half a day with a pair of manual hedge clippers. Most of these saplings are only an inch or two in diameter. Look." He stands up and goes to the edge of what, at one time, was supposed to be the start of a road. He leans down, picks up a withered sapling, and comes back. He turns the bottom toward me. The cut that severed it from the ground is perfectly flat. "See, just a pair of hedge clippers." He runs his thumb down the side of the smooth bark as a pair of headlights appear far down the lane. The police cruiser rocks back and forth on the uneven ground as it makes its way toward us. It comes to a stop beneath the shade of a maple tree, and one of Bancroft's officers gets out.

"Goes back for nearly a mile and a half, Chief. The entrance was covered in dried tree limbs. Took me a while to pull them back out of the way. This road, if that's what we're calling it, comes out onto Ferguson Drive, out there on the northern perimeter of George Cutler's property."

Bancroft shakes his head. "That's in the middle of nowhere."

"Yeah," the officer says. "Sure is. Doubt anyone would have heard, much less seen a car heading back to the county road."

"Thanks, Duncan."

The officer returns to his cruiser, negotiates a several-point turn, and starts back the way he came in.

"This is public land then," I ask.

"Sure is. But I don't guess there is anyone who really comes out this way. All the good hunting spots start several miles north of here."

"How would the killer have known about it?"

He shrugs. "Maybe the same way Tammy did. Went for a walk and just stumbled onto it."

"Chief," I say, "can I talk with you about something that's been bothering me?"

"Of course."

"I know I'm an outsider and I don't know the people in this town like you do, but something is bothering me, and I don't want it to get ruled out just because someone might be a well-known face."

Bancroft removes his Jets hat and runs a hand across his hair before resetting the hat across his brow. "Look, I know I didn't listen to you about the Tammy thing. But, yes. Whatever you want to say, I'll try to keep an open mind about it. Whatcha got?"

I glance at the crime scene unit to make sure we can't be overheard. "Yesterday, Darren Malloy went out of his way to convince me, in a not-so-subtle manner, to find my way out of town."

"Yes. I remember."

"And then this morning, Tammy tells me that Darren didn't

want her coming to the police about what she saw out here. After you told me about Tammy's mental challenges, I chalked it up to Darren not wanting her to embarrass him. But if I'm honest, from my perspective, this is starting to not look so good for Darren."

Bancroft stares at the tips of his boots and nods his head. "I understand how you might think that." He released a slow sigh. "Listen, there's probably something you should know about Darren and Tammy."

"Okay," I say tentatively.

"A long time ago, close to twenty years ago, some bad stuff went down in this town."

My throat descends into my stomach as I brace myself for Bancroft to tell me what I already know.

"Some kids, children, they were—"

"Chief," I interrupt. "If we're done out here, can we go somewhere private where we can talk? Just the two of us?"

He frowns and gives me a curious look. "Okay. Something wrong?"

"No. I just think it would be best if we could talk in private. There's something I should probably tell you before you answer my previous question."

I surprise myself at what I'm saying, but I didn't expect Bancroft to answer my question about Darren by opening the town's closet door and showing me its many skeletons.

"Sure. We can do that." He maintains his befuddled expression. "Will my office do okay?"

"That's fine."

"Let's go then. We've seen everything we need to out here. If the crime scene unit finds anything, then they'll let us know. "

Chapter Fifteen

Miller's Grove Police Station
Miller's Grove, NY

The chief and I fill our mugs with freshly brewed coffee and take seats in his office. He is behind his desk again, but this time his feet aren't propped up. He seems to know that whatever I want to tell him, it's not about the sunny side of life.

His door is shut, and he studies me over the rim of his mug as he takes a sip of the piping hot liquid. He sets his mug down and folds his hands on his desk. "Okay, Darcy. What do you need to talk about?"

I shift uneasily in my chair. When I came to Miller's Grove two days ago, all I wanted to do was to solve the case and quickly get out of town. After all these years, the memories still hang thick, and the past taunts me. I came here not wanting to tell anyone what happened to me. No one needs to know my personal pain. That alone is for me to bear.

But as soon as Bancroft started to bring up the past, I knew I had to show my cards. I can't keep acting like I know nothing about it. Besides, Bancroft has a right to know. He is the chief of police after all. He needs to be aware that the agent investigating a crime in his town isn't a complete foreigner.

I place my mug on the edge of the desk and cross my legs, trying to find the courage to speak. My mouth and throat are dry, but I press forward anyway. "Chief," I begin, "out in the woods, you started to tell me about something that happened here in Miller's Grove nearly twenty years ago."

"That's right."

"Over the course of a single weekend, five young girls were kidnapped and taken to a place known as the Chancellery, a small stone castle in the foothills about five miles from here. Of all the girls, only one made it out alive."

Bancroft's lips draw a fine line. "That's correct. You did your research on the town, I can see. Or were we used as some test case that all the new recruits have to study at the Academy?"

"Neither," I say, and then struggle to get out the next sentence. "I was the girl who made it out alive."

Bancroft blinks as my words register slowly, as if his mind is trying to reconcile two incongruent puzzle pieces. "You?" he says slowly. I watch as his mind scans a dusty, perhaps even a buried, bank of memories. "That can't be."

"I wish it wasn't. But it is."

"But if I recall, that young girl's last name was Darcy... Lockridge." His eyes dart to the empty ring finger of my left hand. "Did you keep an ex-husband's last name or something?"

"No. I've never been married." I grab up my coffee and take another sip to coat the back of my throat as I start in on a story that I don't want to tell. "I lost my sister to the Chancellery. She and I, we were all Mom and Dad had. After I was rescued and discharged from the hospital, we went back home. But it was never the same after that. Dad started to drink a lot. Mom had to get on Zoloft and a whole cocktail of other stuff. Their marriage fell apart, and when I was thirteen, Mom moved me and her out to an apartment in Albany. Dad committed suicide a year later. Hung himself from an oak limb in the back yard. The same limb, it turns out, that Lila and I used to tire swing from. When I went off to college, I decided to change my last name. As I'm sure you know, True Crime Network had done a miniseries on what happened at the Chancellery. A lot of other networks did, too. I was tired of everyone knowing who I was. I couldn't let that weekend define my life anymore."

Bancroft stares at me for a long time as he assimilates everything I've told him. Finally, he starts to shake his head. "God in heaven, Darcy. I'm sorry. I can't imagine—"

"I didn't tell you that to gain sympathy," I interrupt. "I'm doing okay. The Bureau wouldn't have hired me if I wasn't. But since you started to bring it up in the woods, I thought you should know."

Bancroft rubs his chin for a while. "That whole thing, it scarred this town pretty good. It still isn't the same. I know you can relate to that."

I offer a small nod.

"We didn't bring the kids here on vacation for two, maybe three years after that. Everyone, town folks and vacationers alike, was full on shook up about what happened out there." Bancroft sighs deeply. "How did you and your sister get wrapped up in it? If you don't mind me asking."

"My dad loved to go camping. We all did. He brought us out to the campground north of town."

"Rickshaw Preserve campground," he says.

"Yes. Dad wanted to get in one last camping trip before it started to snow. He checked the weather before we left home and saw that we would be in the clear. A little rain was in the forecast, but that was it. But a low pressure system shot down out of Canada and brought temps and snow that no one expected. This was all before smartphones. Dad had a flip phone, but it didn't get any service after we left the city."

"So he didn't know about the change in the weather," Bancroft says.

"Right. And the day before we were... taken..." I pause. Even after all these years, my chest aches when I talk about it. "The day before we were taken," I continue, "I had ridden my bike to the top of the ridge overlooking the valley."

"Never been up there, but I've heard it's beautiful."

"Yes," I agree. "And I took Lila up there the following evening to show her the sunset. But as soon as we got to the top, we saw this huge snowstorm racing over the valley. We got caught in it on the way down. A man found us and offered us a ride back to our campsite. Only we never got there. Once we were in the bed of his truck, he gassed us. The next thing we knew we were in some high-walled stone room wearing nothing but nightgowns. We were there for two days before they selected Lila."

"I can't imagine the nightmare, Darcy."

Some days, I still can't either. For the following two evenings after our capture, Lila and I would hear ominous chanting well after dark. It was something straight out of a creepy folktale, and it was eerie; several adult voices chanting in a language we couldn't understand. Once it finally died down, we would hear a distant door open and the muffled voice of a gagged and fighting child. The chanting would begin again and the muffled screams would begin afresh as the little victim writhed alongside a frenetic chant.

Finally, the ritual would reach its crescendo, and the chanting would cease, along with the muffled cries of the victim. After that, we heard nothing else. Once a day, a plate of food was fed to us through a thin slit in the heavy metal door. We had to use the bathroom in five-gallon buckets with no way to empty them.

Late on the second night, after Lila was ripped from my arms, a fire broke out in the castle. That is the only reason I am alive today. On the north end of the Chancellery was an outdoor courtyard with a granite altar in the center. The children were sacrificed there. That night, as far as the fire marshall would later determine, a small ember drifted out of the cauldron and started a fire that lit up the night and caught the attention of the county's first responders.

The monsters who took us escaped without any trace at all. No fingerprints or hairs were left behind. Whatever evidence there had been was eaten up by the fire. The remains of four girls were identified by DNA found in a discarded pile of ash and bones just outside the courtyard. My little sister was identified only by a section of her lower jawbone that was pulled out of the cauldron.

Of all the victims, I was the only one to make it out alive. It took me years to work through the guilt of outliving Lila. It should be her who was finishing school, dating, and planning a kick-ass career. But it wasn't her. It was me. I've done my best to not take that fact for granted. I've tried to embrace life and not let the past drag me down. But guilt has a way of clinging to you like Velcro. It's not something you can easily brush aside.

"The man who took us," I tell the chief, "I never got a decent look at his face. He had a beard, but that tidbit didn't help the investigators. It was only his voice that I would remember."

What I don't tell Bancroft is that sometimes I still hear that voice in my dreams. Sometimes it's his voice on the mouth of someone else. The worst dream of them all is the recurring nightmare where I am pleading with my father in our old back yard, begging him not to hang himself. "It will get better," I promise him. "Don't leave me. It's not your time." He looks down at me from his perch on a stool and the rope snug around his neck. Then he says in the voice of my kidnapper, "All in the proper order," and then kicks his feet and begins to swing from the neck. That is the moment I always wake up, drenched in sweat and trembling all over.

Years after our abduction and my sister's murder, True Crime Network did a miniseries on the events at the Chancellery. It made for an entertaining crime story, I guess. After that, a group of committed investigators came out to examine the place again. They discovered a stone slab in the floor that served as the door to an underground tunnel. The tunnel ran over one hundred yards to a small cave in the woods. But even with fresh knowledge on how the cultish criminals escaped, no evidence was recovered in the tunnel that could move the investigation forward. If anything, it only added to the mystique surrounding it all.

That was one of the things that had brought my own father's suicide. It was enough for him to feel like he hadn't protected his daughters and that they were kidnapped on his watch. But the salt in the wound was that no one ever paid the price for it. Justice was never served.

Miller's Grove was shaken to its core amid the revelations and the national media attention it received. It wasn't hard for the news to sell a story of an ominous cult that chose an abandoned castle built by a 19th century industrialist as the place where they would murder kidnapped children.

"You know," Bancroft says, "my kids were real young when all that went down. Like I mentioned, we distanced ourselves from the town for a couple of years. Went up to Maine for vacation. Once to the Texas hill country."

Back in the woods, Bancroft had brought up Darren's name and started to tie him into the events at the Chancellery. My coffee is tepid now, but I opt for another long sip and then say, "So how does Darren factor into all of this?"

Bancroft nods. His seat creaks loudly as he leans back in it and folds his hands over his midsection. "Darren's father— Tammy's too, for that matter—was the previous chief of police. Ed was the chief when everything went down. You probably know something of him."

After my parents and I returned home without Lila, I was too busy grieving to worry about Miller's Grove. As I got older and successfully came out of years of therapy, I wanted to put it all behind me. I didn't watch any of the news specials or follow anything about Miller's Grove. I had to get on with my own life, and that meant setting my sights ahead and not in the past.

"No," I answer. "I don't know much about the case itself. My mother followed it extensively, but she died of cancer a few years ago. I never did let her talk with me about it all."

"I understand that. I probably wouldn't want to keep

lingering on it either. Anyway, Ed was the chief, and after everything at the Chancellery went down, he took it real hard. Especially since it was the job of his department to find those devils." A cloudy expression takes up residence in Bancroft's eyes. "I knew Ed. He was a friend of mine. When we would come out here on vacation, he and I would sometimes go fishing together. But he never did get over what happened up at that castle. He felt the weight of never getting anyone in cuffs over it. He died about ten years ago. Just fell over from a heart attack one night while he was working in his shed. It's my opinion that the stress and the guilt finally caught up to him."

The chief's words unsettle me. Across all these years, I've lingered long and hard on how the events of that horrible week affected me and my family. I've considered what the other families of the murdered children must have gone through. But until now, I never really thought about how the events at the Chancellery affected this town. It never crossed my mind that the chief of police would have shouldered the burden. That might be selfish of me, but I have suffered enough in my life to know that it has a way of making you nearsighted. It's hard to think of the pain of others when you are experiencing so much yourself.

"Darren grew up under the shadow of his father's sense of failure," Bancroft continues. "But for some reason, he's always held onto this belief that his father's mantle passed on to him. Ed hired him and gave him a patrol car. But after his father passed, Darren grew increasingly angry and controlling. He would pull folks over and ticket them for no good reason. Arrested a few folks that didn't need arresting. Picture a bitter and angry Barney Fife, and you're pretty well dialed in."

"Did he end up quitting the force?" I ask.

"No. There was an interim chief between Ed and me. After I came on as chief, I gave him opportunity after opportunity to turn things around. But he never did. If anything, things just kept getting worse. I finally had to let him go. It's like I told you before. He still sees himself as the town's protector. It's as if somewhere in the back of his mind, he wants to redeem the family name and show this town he's watching out for them."

The explanation about Darren helps to give some context about why he confronted me on the road. But something still doesn't feel right about it all.

"Chief," I say, "Tammy tried to tell Darren what she saw in the woods, and he shut her down. He told her not to say anything to the authorities."

He considers that for a moment. "I'm sure he just wants to look into things himself."

"She also said that whoever was with Kayla had a loud vehicle and the man's voice was too muffled to make out. Darren has a loud truck."

Bancroft picks up my thread and starts to shake his head. "Darcy, if you're thinking that Darren is our killer, if you think he could have done that to Kayla, then I'll just tell you right now, you are barking up the wrong tree."

"I don't like it, Chief. Something doesn't sit right."

"You've got to trust me on this, Darcy. Darren is not the man we're looking for. Like I told you before. He means well, even if there is much to desire with his bedside manner."

I want to believe that Bancroft is right, but right now I'm not so sure. He was the one who told me that Tammy couldn't be trusted. Deep down, I can't help but wonder if his personal relationships with the people of this town are clouding his judgment.

And I start to think that maybe his predecessor, Ed, had possibly done the same thing. What if it was just too hard to believe that the person who drank coffee two booths down from you every morning at Maybelle's was involved in abducting and murdering children? What if the former chief kept looking outside the town for answers, instead of turning their gaze closer to home? Sometimes it takes a telescope to solve a crime. But sometimes what you really need is a microscope.

"Can you at least get someone to check on Darren's alibi from the night of the murder and the afternoon that Tammy saw Kayla in the woods?"

Bancrofts features pinch into a frown. "No, Darcy. I'm not going to have my department snooping around on an innocent man. I tried to tell you why Darren is the way that he is."

So far, the chief and I have gotten along very well. But as they often do, investigations that require interagency or local LEO participation can turn into a test of will, with everyone wanting to proceed the way they think is best.

"Chief, I wouldn't ask you to do this if I didn't think it was important. You brought me in to do a job. Let me do it my way. If I'm wrong about Darren, then I'll happily admit it. I don't want to bring undue suspicion onto any of the good people in your town. But I have to be objective about everyone." There is more heat in my tone than I intend. But I'm not going to back down on this. Every lead needs to be examined, every stone upturned. A subtly hidden or overlooked detail is often the difference between solving a crime and filing it away into a cold case file.

"Darcy," Bancroft stonewalls, "I'm not going to force an inquiry into an innocent man just to fit some preconceived narrative of yours."

A hot burn of anger starts to flow through my chest. Right now, every moment is precious. We need to be looking at every angle. I'm having a hard time believing that the chief isn't with me on this.

I struggle to keep my voice calm and steady. "I'm not saying Darren did it. But I need to rule him out. That's all. I'm not working with any preconceived narrative. I just need answers. To get those, I need to figure out where to look. And where not to look." We lock eyes, and for the first time, it feels like Bancroft is my adversary instead of a partner in this investigation.

Finally, he concedes. "Okay. Have it your way. I'll have Dobbs look into Darren's whereabouts."

I feel myself relaxing into the chair. "Thank you. And there's one more thing." I field a weary look from across the desk. "Tammy said that after Kayla and the man she was with drove away, she thought someone else was watching her, that someone else was in the woods."

"She thought she was being watched by the murderer?" Bancroft deadpans. "When she had just heard him drive away in a vehicle with Kayla?"

"I know it sounds like she was being paranoid. But I thought I would throw it out there so that we're both dealing with the same information."

"Good to know," he says in a dismissive tone.

I decide not to mention that I thought the same thing. I know for a fact that I wasn't alone out there. And I'm sure that it wasn't just some teenager passing by on the way to a secret alcohol stash. Whoever was out there, peering at me from deep in the woods, was pure evil. I'm not sure what to make of that, and since it will only serve to convolute matters, for now, I keep it to myself.

Bancroft shifts in his chair, and I catch sight of something behind him that I hadn't noticed before. On a shelf sits a small picture of his family. The image is similar to those displayed in the chalet: both parents and their two teenagers with their arms around each other and a glistening lake for a background. I can only imagine Bancroft wants to remember the good times, before everything went wrong.

An unexpected twinge of guilt grabs hold of me. I'm here in Miller's Grove because their chief of police asked for help. It doesn't feel right that I've had a long conversation with his son that he doesn't know about. I've stepped across a very private and personal boundary of his without letting him know. But Tim asked me not to mention anything to his father. They both have a long way to go before things are mended between the two of them. The fact that the elder Bancroft is still unable to display any recent photos of his son is a testament to that.

He watches me as I look over his shoulder at the photo and say, "You have a beautiful family, Chief."

His features fall like a wilted flower. "Thank you, Darcy. I—"

Without even the forewarning of a courtesy knock, the office door behind me flies open and Officer Dobbs steps into the room. I turn in my seat to see his face grim and tight with concern.

"Sorry to barge in like this, Chief."

"What is it?" Bancroft asks.

"We just got a phone call. Another girl has gone missing."

Chapter Sixteen

Home of Paula Haskins
Miller's Grove, NY

"Slow down, Mrs. Haskins. Why don't you start over from the beginning?" Bancroft pulls out a chair at the kitchen table and directs the distressed mother to have a seat. He and I lean back against the counter and wait for her to begin again.

Paula Haskins is a pretty brunette with creamy skin and a slim waist. But her eyes are stained with tears and her hands tremble in her lap. Her small house smells like cats and litter boxes that have been left unattended.

"Just take a deep breath," Bancroft soothes.

She nods and takes his advice. It seems to help. Her shoulders droop a little, and the muscles in her face relax slightly.

"Now, just tell us what happened."

"I left to visit my sister in Rochester three days ago. She's been going through an ugly divorce, and I went up there to help her sort things out. Lily has been struggling with migraines, so I told her she could stay here by herself."

"And how old is she?" I ask.

"Eighteen. She graduated high school this year." Paula gives us a weak, self-conscious smile. "We're kind of dealing with a failure to launch. She hasn't gotten a job yet, and there are no plans for her to go to college anywhere."

"And what makes you think she's missing?" I ask.

All too often, parents jump to premature conclusions about their child's whereabouts. The parents arrive home to an empty house or their son or daughter fails to meet them on time at a designated place. Instead of making a few phone calls to try to locate them, they rush ahead and get the authorities involved. Most of the time, the loved one simply failed to communicate properly or didn't stick to the established timeline. When the child is found playing video games at a friend's house or eating ice cream at the local burger joint, the cops leave with the parent's apologies ringing in their ears.

But then, there are the rare situations when alarm is duly justified. A child has decided to run away from home or goes off with a boyfriend with plans never to return. And then there are the times when the worst imaginable thing has happened; the parent's worst nightmare has morphed into reality and their child has become the victim of a horrible crime. Because of the nature of my job, I usually end up dealing with only the latter.

"She would never leave without letting me know where she was going," Paula answers. "I arrived home two hours ago and Lily wasn't here. I called her phone, but it's sitting on her bedside table. That concerned me a little bit, but I didn't get paranoid right away. She never goes on walks, but I thought that maybe she decided to try one. When she wasn't here after an hour, I started calling her friends. And that's when I heard —" Paula sets her fingers over her lips and tears up again. "That's when I heard about that girl who was killed at the motel."

I pull out a chair and sit beside her at the table. I've found that when a woman is grieving or processing terrible news, it can help to have another female present to empathize with her. It allows them to feel like they have an ally that can relate to them and opens up a space for them to speak freely.

"I know this is scary for you," I tell her, "and we're going to do everything in our power to find Lily. What did her friends tell you?"

"They hadn't seen her since I left. And one of them was texting with Lily yesterday morning. But that was all."

"Where is her phone now?" Bancroft asks.

"Right here." Paula stands up and goes to a stack of magazines beside the microwave. She picks up a phone sitting on top and brings it back. Bancroft takes a latex glove from his pocket and slips it on before carefully taking the phone from her. "We'll have someone look at this," he says.

"Lily never goes anywhere without her phone," Paula says, sitting back down. "I don't know that anyone does these days."

"When did you last speak with her?" I ask.

"Around lunch yesterday. She sounded fine and said she was about to do a load of laundry."

I take a card from my pocket and set it in front of Paula. "If you don't mind, text me over some pictures of Lily."

"Of course."

I stand up and push the chair toward the table. "Paula, we're going to look around for a little bit. Let me know if you think of anything else that would be helpful."

"Of course."

"Do you have anyone you can call to come stay with you?"

She smiles weakly. "My sister is driving down from Rochester. A bit of an irony, I guess. My ex works in Alaska on the fishing boats. But I won't bother him with this until we know something more."

Bancroft and I step out of the kitchen and make our way to the living room. Officer Dobbs comes over and speaks in a quiet tone. "I've got Duncan and Sanders going down the street talking with the neighbors. So far, no one claims to have seen anything. And I can't find any evidence of a break in. All the windows are locked, and the doors don't seem to have been picked or forced open."

Bancroft gives his trademark sigh. "I really hope we're not dealing with another Kayla," he says quietly. He holds out Lily's phone. "I've got an evidence bag in my cruiser. Let me get this into one and get it to the station. Maybe IT can pull something useful off it."

After he leaves out of the front door, I slowly make my way through the house, looking for any clues that might offer a picture into Lily's disappearance. But I don't see anything unusual, nothing to indicate a struggle took place, nothing that tells me that she didn't simply walk out the front door of her own accord.

Opening the door to Lily's bedroom, I examine every inch of the space, filing all the details away in my mind. Her bed is unmade, which isn't surprising for a teenager who had no plans to go anywhere. Posters and memorabilia on the walls reveal her love for Taylor Swift, and bouquets of artificial daisies stand in vases on her dresser and windowsill.

An orange pill bottle sits on her bedside table. I pick it up and read the label: Duloxetine. The prescription is made out in Lily's name. Setting the bottle down, I finish inspecting the room and find Paula on the front porch. She's leaning against a wooden beam, waiting restlessly for the officers to return from interviewing the neighbors.

"I texted you the pictures you asked for," she says as I walk out.

"Thank you. I saw them come through."

"Did you find anything?"

"No," I say. "But the chief's officers will do a more thorough inspection when they get back."

"Okay."

"Paula, I noticed that Lily is on antidepressants."

"Yes. Since last year, when she started feeling anxious. Personally, I think it was the result of watching too much news and spending an abundance of time on social media."

"Has the medication helped?"

"It has. For the most part. She's generally a content person. Spends time with friends here and there."

"But no lapses into outright depression?"

"No. None."

I have to take Paula's assignment of Lily's mental health with a grain of salt. Teenagers can be good at hiding things from their parents. I know I was when I was in high school. My mother thought that I was a happy teenager who loved being on a cheerleading squad and playing on the volleyball team. But inside, I was a cloudy, dysfunctional mess. In spite of all the therapy I had gone through, I was still a deeply depressed teenager who became very good at hiding it.

It's not that parents don't know their children better than anyone else. Many times, they do. But they can only know what their child allows them to see, and sometimes deep depression or suicidal tendencies can go completely unnoticed. If Lily was severely depressed, her doctor most likely would have prescribed something more potent to fight it off. Still, I can't rule out the possibility that her feelings and outlook on life might be worse than anyone knows.

"Are the shoes that Lily usually wears in the house?" I ask.

She shakes her head. "No. She always leaves them just inside the door. I'm always getting after her about it because whenever I come in, I trip over them." Paula bites down hard on her lower lip. "She's all I have. I can't lose her. Oh God, I can't lose her."

I place a hand on her shoulder. "We're going to do everything we can to find Lily."

"Thank you, Agent Hunt."

As I drive away, I get that familiar feeling that I often get working cases. I'm the person they bring in when everything goes awry, when someone is missing or murdered. My job is to prevent further crimes and bring resolution to those already committed. But there are times like this one where I wish I could do something more preventative, to actually stop a crime before it happens.

Unfortunately, no one is able to do that. Evil lurks and hunts and strikes, often without any warning at all. All I can do is pick up the pieces. And while I am very good at doing that, it's times like these when it feels like it's just not good enough.

Chapter Seventeen

Miller's Grove Police Department
Miller's Grove, NY

When I arrive back at the station, Bancroft steps out of a door at the end of a corridor and waves me over.

"I've got them analyzing Lily's phone now," he tells me. "I'll be honest with you, Darcy. I don't have a good feeling about this. We don't have a lot of teenagers just turn up missing like that around here. Being that Kayla was killed just a few days ago, it's too much of a coincidence to think that Lily just forgot to tell her mother that she was going out."

"I agree. She just vanished out of thin air with no trace at all. That fits with what we know about Kayla's killer. He's smart enough not to leave any traces behind."

"I think we need to push every lever we can think of, search every nook and cranny," he says, and then motions that I should follow him through the door behind him.

The station has only one interview room. It has a typical

metal table bolted to the floor, two cameras, and a large window set with one-sided glass. Darren Malloy is sitting in one of the chairs, staring numbly at the tabletop. The chief draws up in front of the window, sticks his hands in his pockets, and observes Darren.

"I saw his truck parked at Maybelle's and decided to go in to see him. He was in a booth by himself, working down a burger. Asked him if he wouldn't mind coming across the street with me for a conversation.

I'm glad to know that, in spite of his reservations, Bancroft decided to move ahead with looking closely at Darren's alibis. Darren's hasty actions have precipitated questions that we need answers to. There is a good chance that he is just an overzealous hothead, but I won't swallow that jagged little pill without asking a lot of questions first.

"Have you been in yet?" I ask.

"No, but he's pretty anxious. I had someone go in and tell him that I had to take a phone call." The chief sets his hands on his hips. "I tell you, Darcy. I don't like this. I still don't think Darren is our man."

"Just ask the right questions," I tell him. "We just need to know where he's been and who can corroborate his story."

"I know," he chides, and then enters the room and sits across the table from Darren.

"What is this, Chief?" Darren snarls. "Did that bitch FBI lady put you up to this? You've got her behind that mirror, don't you?" Darren looks at the glass with a haughty expression and lifts his middle finger toward it. Then he raises his voice as if he's spitting venom. "You don't know me, lady. You're barking up the wrong tree, getting my town to think I'm a killer."

"Is that a threat?" Bancroft asks him.

Darren recoils a little. "No. Just an observation."

"Then help me get this cleared up. How about we start with this last Friday afternoon? Where were you?"

"Friday?" Darren shifts uncomfortably in his seat. "You know I work third shift in Pine Bluff. I leave the house around five every afternoon."

"Okay, but what were you doing before that? Say, between lunch and when you went to work?"

"I was..." Darren pauses and looks up and to his right. "...fly fishing at Beacon's Creek."

The upward glance is a clear tell that he is lying.

"Beacon's Creek, you say?"

"Yeah. Why? Is fishing a crime now, too?" He turns to the mirror. Even though he can only see his own reflection, he glares at me.

"You catch anything?"

Darren returns his attention to his chief of police. "Uh, yeah. Couple trout. That was it."

"And when did you get back home?"

"Like I said, I had to leave for work around five. So before five."

"Who else saw you fishing that afternoon? Or saw you at all. Maybe you picked up a drink at the gas station on the way out there and a clerk might remember seeing you."

Darren shook his head. "Went straight there, and straight back home."

Bancroft doesn't respond, doesn't ask another question. He only looks deadpan at Darren, who begins to fidget anxiously.

"What?" Darren asks.

"Why aren't you telling me the truth?"

"I *am* telling you the truth, old man. If you don't believe me, that's your problem."

The chief resettles his Jet's hat on his head, then folds his hands on the table. "I like you, Darren. I've always been fond of your family. Your father was a cornerstone in this town, and your sister is a lovely young lady. But I have some real concerns that you don't seem all too interested in helping me resolve."

"All my family has ever done is protect this town and watch out for it," Darren spits back. "And that counts for nothing in your eyes. You're going to drag me in here as if you really think I killed that girl in the motel? Give me a break."

"Let's move on," Bancroft says blandly. "Speaking of the motel, where were you Friday night between eight and midnight?"

"You're unbelievable. You're really going to sit there and act as if you think I killed that girl?"

"Answer the question, Darren."

"I was at work. Just like I am five nights a week. They've got me working fifty, sometimes sixty hours a week over there. I don't have time to hunt down young girls."

"But you have time to accost the FBI when I bring them into town. You have time to get in their face and threaten them."

"Threaten them," he sneers. "Is that what she told you?"

"I know you well enough to understand what happened. I don't need an interpreter."

Darren gives an indifferent shrug. "We don't need the FBI around here. You know that as well as I do."

"Actually, I don't. I brought her here for a reason."

164

"Look, I gotta leave for work in a little while. Are we about done?"

The door behind me opens, and a wide shaft of light falls on me as Officer Dobbs steps into the dark room. He shuts the door, comes over to me, and speaks in a low voice.

"We just got a call from Francis Pettis. She's one of the town's few homeless people. She remembers seeing Darren's truck at the back of the Diamond Palace the night of the murder."

My eyes widen in surprise. "Is she sure?"

"She is. His truck has that Predator symbol on the back window."

"Why is she just now telling us this?"

"She didn't think anything of it at first. No one around here would have thought that Darren could do something like what happened with Kayla. But since there haven't been any arrests yet, she thought we should know. She said there were several cars in front, but other than the night clerk's car, Darren's truck was the only vehicle in the back."

I recall that the motel's rooms are only along the front of the building. The rear backs up to the woods and is probably only used for storing the garbage dumpster.

I press the call button for the interview room. On the chief's side, a yellow light blinks on and turns off when I let go of the button. "Excuse me a minute," he says to Darren, and then takes his leave of the room.

"What is it?" he asks me, and I nod to Dobbs. Dobbs relays the details of Francis Pettis' phone call. The longer he speaks, the higher Bancroft's brows rise.

"Call over to the factory in Pine Bluff," the chief tells him. "See if he was at work on Friday night. He couldn't be in two places at once. Either he was at work, or he was at the motel." Dobbs nods his understanding and exits the room. Bancroft looks through the glass at Darren. "I knew he was lying to me. He's not acting like himself."

"How long can you keep him here?" I ask.

"If his alibi for the night of the murder doesn't check out, then that will give me enough to arrest him. We have a witness who says she saw his truck there. If he's lying about being in Pine Bluff that night, then I won't need anything else."

I set my hands on my hips and chew on my bottom lip.

"What are you thinking?" he asks me.

"I need to make a phone call and head out for a while."

"Okay. Where are you going?"

"Chief, you brought me in here to help. I hope in the short time I've been here that I've earned your trust."

He thinks about that for a second. "Yeah. I guess you have."

"No matter what, just hold Darren until I get back."

He frowns slightly but nods his agreement. "Okay."

"And don't ask him about Lily yet. If he's got her somewhere, then we'll need as much leverage as we can to get him to tell us where she is."

I cross the room and open the door, squinting against the bright halogens in the hallway as I make my way back to my cruiser in the parking lot. Once I'm behind the wheel, I pull up my priority contacts and dial Kemper, my SAC at the Albany office.

"Darcy," he answers, "how's it going out there?"

"Slow," I admit. "But we're making some headway. Listen, I need a favor from you."

"You and everyone else," he quips lightly. "What do you need?"

I quickly relay my request. "And I need it ASAP," I tell him. "Like in less than half an hour. Sooner if you can."

"Half an hour? I don't know, Darcy. If the judge is in court, then we're out of luck. Either way, half an hour would be a world record."

"I know it's a slim chance, but I need you to try. A world record is what I need right now."

"Let me see what I can do. If I can get it, I'll email it over." He pauses and then says, "You don't need me to send anyone out there to help you, do you? I don't think Simmons is busy with anything." There is a thread of humor in his tone.

"Trust me, I'm fine," I say.

Special Agent Daryl Simmons is my office nemesis. Besides donuts and Hot Pockets, I'm convinced that his single reason for waking up each morning is to make my life a living hell. He's always standing over my shoulder, criticizing my work. As for himself, Simmons hasn't closed out a case in months and spends most of his time in the office heckling me and the other agents who are focused on doing good work.

Kemper has tried time and time again to get Simmons transferred to another office. But his attempts are never successful; Simmons is the lieutenant governor's nephew. All it takes is a quick call to his uncle, and he can leverage all the political clout he needs to get his way.

I don't understand why someone would want to join the FBI just to sit around and take up space. Maybe he is so insecure that just being able to tell people that he's an FBI agent gets his rocks off. Whatever the reason, I think the entire office will have a huge party should the day come that he finally decides to transfer.

"You're sure about this?" Kemper asks. "You know I don't like asking the judge for favors like this unless it's absolutely necessary."

"And you know I wouldn't ask you if it wasn't," I reply.

"Okay. Give me half an hour."

Chapter Eighteen

Home of Darren Malloy
Miller's Grove, NY

After failing to receive an answer, I knock on the door again, but louder this time, then take a couple of steps back and wait some more. Still, no sound comes from inside. Since the doorbell isn't working, I knock again.

"Tammy?" I call out. When Darren's sister doesn't respond, I go down the front steps and cross through the front yard to the side of the house. The back yard is hemmed in by a low, rusted chain link fence with tall weeds intertwined through the lower links. The handle to the gate is unlocked. I lift it and swing the gate open as far as it will go before the weeds catch it.

Kemper has just emailed me the search warrant signed by Judge Richard Forrester. Kemper has built a strong rapport with the judge and doesn't get asked many questions when he puts in a request for one. But he won't ever use that clout haphazardly, knowing that there is a limit to how many favors you can ask of a sitting judge.

I didn't tell Bancroft what I was going to do because I know Darren might wonder why he is being held at the station for so long. If he starts to suspect something and asks the chief about it, the chief can honestly say that we do not have a warrant. That's also why I've come alone. In a typical scenario, I would be accompanied by several officers, and we would take our time combing every inch of the place. Sometimes, we will even cordon off the home and require anyone living there to find alternate living arrangements until we're done, which can take up to a few days, depending on the size of the house.

While Darren doesn't strike me as the brightest bulb in the pack, I have learned that the smartest criminals can easily hide behind a false exterior. It's a mask they put on to divert attention and to keep investigators looking the other direction. Something tells me that Darren is smarter than the rest of this town gives him credit for.

Tall, uncut grass swishes against my pants as I negotiate my way to the back door. Beer cans and discarded chip bags litter the back porch, which could use a good power washing. A narrow path cuts through the yard and moves out toward a thick treeline thirty yards away. I step up to the back door and knock loudly, calling out Tammy's name again. When I get no response, I try again.

I recall Tammy saying that she hardly ever leaves home. Did Darren threaten her not to speak with the authorities again? An unsettling feeling rolls through my stomach, and I reach out and grab the handle. Surprisingly, it turns in my hand and the door opens. The cruiser has a lock pick set in the glove box. Over the years, I've gotten good at picking doors. Even so, I'm always glad when I don't have to.

"Tammy?" I call out.

I step inside. It's dark. No lights are on. "Tammy? It's Agent Hunt with the FBI. We spoke this morning."

Silence.

I locate a light switch along the wall and flip it on. A soft yellow light bathes the room, and I call for Tammy again as I quickly make my way through the house. The last thing I want to do is scare her if she thinks she's alone in the house. After a cursory perusal, I discover that I'm the only one here.

Working quickly, I don a pair of gloves and begin searching each room, starting with the kitchen and searching the drawers, cabinets, and pantry, then getting down on my back to look underneath the sink.

In my haste, I left the flashlight I took from the chalet's garage in the cruiser. Rather than go back out and get it, I locate one in a drawer and take it with me into the living room. After I do a thorough search of everything there and then in the dining room, I make my way down the hall. The first bedroom I come to is sparsely furnished. A pressboard dresser stands against one wall, and a twin bed sits in a corner with only a bare mattress on top. The closet is filled with plastic bins bulging with Christmas decorations. I pry each one open, quickly sift through them, and find nothing but what might have looked like Christmas spirit thirty years ago.

I finish with the room and move to the end of the hallway while continuing to listen for the front door to open. I know that

Tammy will see my cruiser in the driveway if she returns home while I'm still here, but I would rather not scare her with my unexpected presence in her home.

I stand in the doorway of Darren's room for a moment to get my bearings. The room is immaculate. Everything is in its proper place. The bed is perfectly made. There is not an article of clothing on the floor, and every item on the dresser is perfectly positioned and spaced against the item next to it. It's unexpected and a little disorienting given the state of his yard and what I've come to see in his rash behavior and angry demeanor.

The room is a perfect reflection of self-discipline and order that would make any boot camp drill sergeant proud. It is exactly what I would expect from the man who killed Kayla. The man who met her in that hotel was precise and smart, leaving no traces and a decisive, albeit cryptic, message that we had yet to understand.

My heart beats faster as I search the room, looking under the bed and through his desk and nightstand. Other than two Playboy magazines, I find nothing but well-folded clothing in his dresser. I open the closet's accordion doors to see each hanger perfectly spaced and Darren's shoes lined up in neat pairs. Crossing the small room, I carefully stand on top of the desk and shine the light into the air vent. It's empty.

I feel pressed for time as I continue my search. I hope that Bancroft has already verified Darren's alibi. If not, then I may not have much time left. The chief will need more than a reported sighting of Darren's truck to keep him at the station.

Bracing a hand on the wall, I carefully step down off the desk and find my footing as I hear a soft thump behind me. I turn to see what it is and freeze. Tammy is standing in the doorway, her eyes wild and angry. Her hands are clutching a .38 revolver. And it's pointed right at my heart.

Chapter Nineteen

Home of Darren Malloy
Miller's Grove, NY

Tammy's hands are trembling as I meet her gaze from the other side of the gun. The dark, cavernous barrel stares at me like a sinister evil eye.

"What are you doing here?" she demands.

"Easy," I say slowly. "I have a search warrant to look around the house and the property."

Her brows knit together. "Search warrant? For what?"

"Chief Bancroft is questioning Darren over at the station. We're looking into... an angle." Even though I have a gun trained on me, I still don't want to give away the details of my search.

"An angle? What angle?"

"Tammy, would you mind lowering the gun? I'm not here to hurt you."

Her hardened gaze stays on me, but it slowly begins to soften.

To my relief, she lowers the weapon. Tears fill her eyes. "I thought you were him," she said softly.

"Darren?"

"No. Kayla's... killer."

It doesn't surprise me that she hasn't considered her brother's possible complicity in the murder.

"I was on a walk—I didn't go deep into the woods like last time. Seeing Kayla out there really upset me. But when I came in the back door, I heard something in the back of the house."

"You didn't think it was Darren?" I ask.

She shakes her head. "Darren said he was going to get something to eat at Maybelle's and then wasn't going to be gone until tomorrow afternoon sometime."

That's new information. I recall Darren telling the chief that he had to leave for work soon. "Did he say where he was going?"

"He never tells me those kinds of things. It used to be that he would just go to work and mostly hole up in the house until his next shift, but lately, he's been gone a lot more." Tammy frowns as she focuses on me standing in her brother's room. "You said you had a search warrant. Did Darren do something wrong?"

"I can't talk about the details. But I can show you the search warrant if you would like."

She thinks about that for a moment. "That's okay. I trust you. And Chief Bancroft," she adds. "Darren isn't in any serious trouble, is he?"

"The chief just wants to be thorough," I reply. "Do you mind if I ask where you got the gun?" While I wasn't exhaustive in my search of the rooms, everything I had examined so far had been done with a careful eye. I hadn't come across any guns, and Darren strikes me as the kind of man who would have plenty.

"This was one of my father's guns," she says. "He gave it to me just before he died. I keep it in my nightstand drawer. Never really had a reason to take it out until now."

"I'm sorry for frightening you," I tell her. "Did you not see my car out front?"

"I finished my walk out behind the house. I didn't look out front."

"I need to finish my search," I tell her. "Would you mind waiting in the front of the house?"

"Okay." She pauses and looks thoroughly around the room. "What are you looking for exactly? Did Darren do something wrong?"

I offer a disarming smile and my best attempt at reassuring her. "No. Not as far as I know. The chief just asked me to come over here and see if there is anything that sticks out."

"Okay." She frowns as though she's trying to make sense of it all. Hopefully, my answer is cryptic enough to quell any more anxiety on her part.

"Tammy, would you mind waiting in the living room while I finish? I shouldn't be too much longer."

"Okay."

"And I'll need to check your bedroom as well."

"That's fine," she shrugs. "I don't know what you're hoping to find, but I have nothing to hide."

"I'll need your gun," I tell her. "I can return it to you when I leave."

She flips it in her fingers and hands it to me with the butt facing forward. After I take it, she starts out the door. "Tammy?" She stops and turns around. "Do you or Darren own any more guns?"

Even though a gun did not feature in Kayla's murder, I would still feel better knowing where all of Darren's firearms are. I'm also carrying out a search warrant with a family member on the premises. Not that I don't trust Tammy; she is clearly an innocent bystander. Still, I don't want to leave anything to chance. I'll feel much safer if I can account for all the guns as I continue my search.

Tammy nods toward her brother's nightstand, something I have yet to search. "He keeps his 9mm in the drawer there. All his other ones are in the barn out back."

"A barn?" I hadn't noticed one when I went through the back yard.

"It's more like a large shed. But we've always called it the barn. It used to be my father's. When Darren and I were younger, Dad used the space to make custom picture frames as a hobby."

"Would you mind walking me out there when I'm done in the house?"

"Sure. I'll be in the living room."

I thank her and continue my search of Darren's room. His handgun is exactly where Tammy said it would be, along with the most recent edition of Sports Illustrated. The gun is loaded. I remove the hot round from the chamber and slip out the magazine, then relieve the .38 of its six rounds, too. Leaving the magazine and the ammunition on his desk, I slip the weapons into the back seam of my jeans, freeing my hands once more.

Ten minutes later, I've completed my search of the house and have found nothing of consequence. Even the attic presents me with nothing rewarding, and a thread of anxiety runs through my stomach as I make my way back down the hall. I was hoping to find something that would implicate Darren. So far, I haven't had any luck.

When I return to the living room, Tammy is sitting on the couch with her hands folded in her lap. A crease forms just above the bridge of her nose. "Darren isn't in any trouble, is he? Does this have anything to do with Kayla?"

I give her a warm smile. "I can't talk about the details," I say. "But you don't have anything to worry about." It's a borderline lie, and I feel bad about saying it, but I don't know how she might react if I tell her that her brother is my primary suspect in Kayla's murder. For now, I need to keep my suspicions quiet. That will help to ensure that people's emotions or opinions don't get in the way.

"I'm going to step outside and make a quick phone call," I tell Tammy. "After that, can you point out the shed to me?"

"Yes. I can."

I step out the back door and call the chief. His phone rings several times before going to voicemail. After trying again with no luck, I call the station, and assuming that the chief is still interviewing Darren, I ask for Dobbs.

"Darcy?" he answers. "What's up?"

"Is Darren still there?" I ask him, and I find that I'm praying a silent prayer that he is.

"Yeah. For now." My shoulders relax, and I take a deep breath. "But not for long, I don't think."

"What do you mean?"

"The chief can't get Darren's workplace on the phone. They aren't answering. As you can imagine, Darren is getting tired of the chief's questions. I think he's about to cut bait. Without confirmation that his alibi is bogus, we don't have any way to hold him. Where did you run off to anyway?"

"I'm at Darren's place looking around. Listen, I need you to get the chief to hold him as long as he can."

"Darren's place? Darcy, you know as well as I do that you need a warrant to make anything come of that."

"I've already got one."

"Oh."

"Just make sure Darren stays right where he is," I say. "Whatever you do, do not let him leave."

"All right, Darcy. I'll tell the chief."

We hang up, and I feel a renewed sense of urgency to find something quickly. Opening the back door, I stick my head in. "Tammy? I'm ready."

She comes around the corner and joins me on the porch. I follow her down the trail that leads through the back yard. It finally forks in the tall grass. One direction leads out to the woods and another to a thick stand of trees and bushes in the corner of the property.

Tammy stops and points to the corner. "It's out there. On the other side of the trees. It's hard to miss once you get over there."

"Aren't you coming with me?"

"No," she says with a quick shake of her head. "I went out there a couple of weeks ago to look for the hedge trimmers. Since Darren has neglected the yard, I decided to do some work myself. But he came in before I even had a chance to find the trimmers, got up in my face, and threatened me for being in there. He really scared me, Agent Hunt. I've never seen him like that." Tammy lowers her head and looks soberly at the grass. "Darren has changed a lot this last year. He's angry all the time these days. I hardly recognize him anymore." She lifts her head and looks in the direction of the shed. "I'll never go in there again."

"Is it unlocked?"

"Probably. But I don't have the key if it isn't."

"Go ahead and head back to the house," I tell her. "I'll go check it out."

We part ways, and I move quickly along the path to the corner of the lot, passing between a large stand of trees before approaching the large shed. The pine plank siding was painted dark green at some point in the distant past, but most of it has been chipped away by the elements. The wood underneath is sun bleached and stained gray with mildew. A small window unit fills in a cutout in the wall, rattling loudly as it cools the air inside. If this is where Darren keeps his guns, then the small air conditioner was a smart decision. Leaving guns and ammo in a warm, humid room can initiate corrosion very quickly.

I step to the door to find a rusty padlock hanging from the eyelet of an old hasp lock. When I give it a hard yank, it does nothing but throttle the inside of my hand. Wincing, I look around for anything that might help me break it. There is an old wheelbarrow on the side of the shed, along with a pile of rotting lumber and a rusted truck axle.

After shuffling through the grass, I finally discover a large rock. Picking it up, I carry it back to the door, heave it above my head, and then slam it down on the lock, stepping to the side to avoid it falling on my feet.

The lock doesn't budge. I scramble back to the rock and pick it up again. Getting in the shed could be the difference between Darren getting off scot-free or finding the evidence to charge him with Kayla's murder.

As an investigator, my job is to furnish the U.S. attorney with as much evidence as possible. The attorney's office won't move the case to trial unless they're sure they can get a conviction. I've seen far too many investigations never go to trial because enough evidence wasn't obtained before or after an arrest. The prosecuting attorney wants us to give them a watertight case, and part of my job is making sure I give them everything they need to put the right person away for good.

I raise the rock above my head again, and as I heave it down, the padlock gives a discernible pop and swings out at a lopsided angle. Moving quickly, I slip the padlock from the eyelet and toss it to the side. The door squeaks loudly on rusted hinges as I pull open the door and take a step inside. It smells heavily of mildew and rotting wood. I locate a light switch on the inside wall and flip it on.

The shed resembles nothing of the orderliness of Darren's bedroom. There is a large worktable in the center, the top stained and nicked from years of hard use. Tools and old wood trimmings are strewn across it.

I step deeper inside and pause to get my bearings. The exposed rafters over my head hold long strips of wood, metal piping, and rusting lawn tools, all of it coated in a layer of dust and disintegrating cobwebs. One corner of the floor is stacked with paint cans, another with dirty rags. On the back wall is a large gun safe. I go to it and pull the handle. It doesn't budge; the door is locked.

Given that the house has an unused bedroom, it's strange that Darren would choose to keep his guns out here in the shed. Even with the air conditioner mitigating against the corrosive heat and moisture, it still isn't the most ideal place to store a cache of personal weapons.

But it isn't the guns that hold my curiosity, however. It's whatever else Darren might have inside the safe. I'll finish my cursory search through the shed; if Darren's alibi doesn't check out, then the chief can get a locksmith out there to break into the safe in the event that Darren fails to give up the code and key.

I work my way deeper into the shed, concentrating my flashlight on areas that the naked bulb above me casts in shadow. I peer behind a wood lathe, a bandsaw, and a planer before training my light on a pile of lawn tools.

Across the room are wooden cubbies that serve as shelves for all kinds of knickknacks and tools. I go to them and carefully search each shelf, rummaging all the way to the back, opening toolboxes and tackle boxes with no success.

When it comes to disposing of evidence, criminals vary in how they go about it. If the murder is unmeditated and occurs in the heat of the moment, the murder weapon is often left behind or found not far from the scene. But the man who killed Kayla was precise and had probably been planning it for a very long time. In those kinds of crimes, the evidence is often kept, hidden away so the killer can take it out and use it as a mental aid to relive the pleasure he experienced during the murder. If the evidence is disposed of, it's usually done so no one will ever find it: sent to the bottom of a lake, burned, or buried in a place far away from the scene of the crime.

Disappointment rolls over me as I work my way back to the door of the shed. The evidence could be anywhere; it was a long shot that I would find anything out here. When I return to the station, I'll get the chief to send a search team back out here to turn everything upside down. If Darren hid anything out here, we'll find it. His truck will need to be searched as well.

I need something—anything—that can help me get this resolved. A bogus alibi and someone who sighted Darren's truck at the motel might work for an arrest. But it's still too thin to get a jury to convict. My job is to get criminals locked up for good. To do that, I need tangible proof that links the suspect to the murder. Once I have that, I can leverage it to make Darren give up Lily. Once she is home safe and sound, then my work here will be done; I can go home and once again try to forget that this town even exists.

I stand in the open door and take a final glance around the shed. I had come out here full of optimism, hoping that I would find the needle in the haystack that I so desperately need. Now I will have to return to the station empty-handed.

Frustrated, I kick at the pile of rags on my way out. The toe of my shoe slams into something hard, causing me to wince. Curious to know what I hit, I dig through the rags and push them to the side. Behind them is a metal toolbox coated with a grimy layer of grease and dirt. I kneel down and fidget with the latches. They are snapped down tight, and it takes me over a minute to pry both of them up. They finally give way, and I lower myself into a squat and pull the lid up.

No sooner have I glanced into the tray than my veins surge with adrenaline. Staring up at me is a coil of braided steel rope. Kyle had said that Kayla had been strangled with a one-sixteenth-inch rope. This one matches the description. Even more telling is the thin stack of paper bags sitting beside the rope, the exact kind that had been placed over Kayla's hands.

I stand and pull out my phone, then quickly dial Bancroft,

hoping that he has the foresight to answer this time. When he answers on the fourth ring, his greeting is hardly out of his mouth when I speak without the formality of a preamble.

"Chief, I'm over here at Darren's. I found the murder weapon." My voice is charged with nervous energy.

"The murder weapon?" he asks. "You mean the steel rope?"

"Yes. And the bags that were over Kayla's hands. Darren has them hidden in a toolbox in his shed. I need you to get him to tell us where Lily is. He was probably planning the same thing for her." A dead silence fills the call. "Chief?"

"Darcy, I had to let Darren go."

His words hit me like a baseball bat across the shoulders. I pinch my eyes shut and tighten my grip on the phone. "You what?"

"No one answered at the semiconductor plant. Darren was getting especially irritated and demanded to be let out. I didn't have enough to arrest him."

"How long ago?"

"Maybe five minutes. I'll get every available officer out there looking for him."

"Chief, Darren killed Kayla. There's no doubt that he has Lily, too."

"Ah, shit." It's quiet for a few moments as he considers what to do next. Finally, "Stay there until I can get a team out to you. They'll need to cordon off the property and send Tammy somewhere else until we've released it."

"I'll wait until they get here," I tell him.

"Good work, Darcy. I really didn't think Darren had it in him. I guess it goes to show that you can never be sure about anyone."

We hang up, and I anxiously wait for Bancroft's team to arrive. Skylar never tires of reminding me that patience is not my strong point. More than once, she's been at the back of a long line with me at the grocery store and whispers in her best Inigo Montoya impression, "I hate waiting."

I know that it's catchy to say that patience is a virtue. Maybe it is, but it's not a virtue that was passed down to me. I hate waiting in traffic, hate waiting in line, and I wholly despise having to hang around for my number to come up at the DMV or my name to be called at the doctor's office.

Even more, when I'm waiting on feedback from Quantico's profiling team or results on a file transfer from another office, my cortisol spikes and I start feeling anxious. Working as an agent for the FBI means that being successful at my job requires that everything gets done quickly and efficiently. When they don't, investigations can stall, perhaps even giving an unsub the distance they need to get away with their crime for good.

So I've always tried to take my negative traits and make them work for the good of the job. My inability to wait means that my mind can't turn off. I'm constantly looking for new angles and connections, using the time to go back over all the data and pursuing hunches that I had not yet had time to consider.

Walking back to the worktable, I slip Darren's 9mm and Tammy's .38 from their place at my lower back and set them on it. Then I exit the shed, leaving the toolbox exactly as I found it, and use a weathered tree stump a little ways away for a seat.

I have half a mind to go back to the front of the house and move my cruiser farther down the street. Surely Darren is feeling the pressure that we're on to him. He might be racing back here to his house this very second to retrieve the evidence. If he is, I don't want him to see the cruiser.

But I decide against moving from my present position. In the event that he takes an alternate route here, like through the woods at the back of the property, I don't want to risk him snatching away the evidence while I'm moving the car.

A thread of anxiety flickers through me as I rub the tops of my thighs with the palms of my hands, and wait.

Chapter Twenty

"Any word yet?" I ask.

"No. Not yet. But I expect to hear something soon."

Bancroft and I are sitting in his office. I've just returned from Darren's, and I'm ready to charge ahead. On the other side of the wall, the entire bullpen is a frenzy of action, everyone in the station employed in some way with finding Darren. After being released, he never returned home and didn't go to work.

"I put out a BOLO on his truck and called the county sheriff," Bancroft says. "He's putting up blockades on all the roads leading in and out of Miller's Grove. His cell phone is not issuing a signal, which means that he most likely took out the battery and removed the SIM card."

It's been almost two hours since Darren walked out of the station. Since then, no one has heard from him or seen him. Word will spread fast in this town that Darren is the one who put all of them into such a fright these last two days. If anyone even catches a sniff of him, we'll certainly be the first to know.

"Tammy is going to stay with a friend," I say. "She's pretty shook up about it."

After Bancroft's team arrived, I spent half an hour at Tammy's kitchen table interviewing her. Unless she's a world-class liar, she was completely stunned by what I told her about Darren. When I left her house, she was still rubbing tears off her cheeks.

"To tell you the truth, Darcy, we're all pretty shook up. I know I didn't believe you about Tammy seeing anyone in the woods. Or when you told me that I needed to take a closer look at Darren. I suppose an apology is in order."

"No need. Let's just find him and get Lily back. I want to make sure everything is watertight against Darren. We'll need to get Francis Pettis on the record that she saw Darren's truck at the Diamond Palace the night of the murder."

"I already have an officer looking for her," he says. "She's usually in one of a few places. Spends most of her time at the underpass at County Road 98. As soon as we locate her, I'll question her myself."

I let out an exasperated breath. "Chief, I need to know more about Darren. You said that he grew angrier and angrier as the years went on, that you finally had to fire him from your department. Was there no one at all who thought Darren was heading toward a cliff like this one?"

"I don't know, Darcy. You know well enough that small towns aren't always sweet tea. Sometimes they're as bitter as under-cooked collard greens. Everyone gets real good at putting on a happy face and saying hello. But some of them would stab a neighbor in the back the first chance they got. I don't think anyone considered Darren capable of something like this. Yes, he's grown angrier, but I think we all chalked that up to him living in his father's shadow and not matching up to the person he has always thought himself to be." The chief reaches back and rubs the back of his neck, his face pinching into a grimace. "If I'm honest, I was hoping that Kayla's killer wasn't one of our own. I was crossing my fingers that we were dealing with a psychopath who happened to randomly pick our town."

I feel a real sense of satisfaction that we've found Kayla's killer. That feeling doesn't go as deep as I would like, however. Lily is still out there somewhere, and Darren isn't locked behind bars. If we don't move quickly, don't get a break somehow, then we might be looking at the murder of yet another innocent girl.

"Chief, we need a list of anyone who crosses paths with Darren on a regular basis. His barber, favorite waitress, any friends that he might throw down some beers with. And someone needs to go out to Pine Bluff and speak with his boss and his coworkers. They might be able to tell us something we don't know."

Bancroft leans forward and lays a finger onto a button on his phone. The line utters a loud beep, and a lady answers.

"Yes, Chief."

"Kathy, I need you to get Vera to assemble a list of anyone who comes into regular contact with Darren Malloy. If anyone has even glanced at him in the last two weeks, I want to know who they are."

"I'll get her started on it right now."

As soon as he ends the call, my phone rings. I glance at the screen to see Amy Mattson's name. Hopefully, her lab has come up with some results I can use.

"Amy," I answer. "Whatcha got?"

"Not much, I'm afraid. The hairs and semen samples are all a no-go. None of them are in my system except for one hair sample. It belongs to a former convict who served six years for assault and battery. But he died in an auto accident in Virginia two months ago."

That the motel still hasn't been cleaned well enough to remove a hair from two months ago gives me the creeps. That, and the numerous semen samples discovered on the already filthy floor. Seedy motels are cheap for a reason.

"What about the blood sample?" I ask. "And the dirt from under her fingernails?"

"The dirt is taking a little longer, but I hope to have something for you before lunch tomorrow. And the blood, it's not in any of my systems." Amy's tone is apologetic. "I was really hoping to get you something more concrete by now. But this is the best I can do. I have a national database that I ran it through, but nothing turned up there either. I'm sending the blood off to Quantico after all. They might be able to run it against a deeper level of the CODIS database." And then, as if reading my mind, she says, "I know you hate waiting. I'm sorry, I'm working as fast as I can."

"Don't fret it," I tell her. "We just identified the killer, but he's still on the loose. I have a suspicion that the clues he left for us are the key to what he's thinking next."

"I'll call you as soon as I have something."

"Thanks," I tell her, and we hang up. I'm glad that I have Amy in my corner. With her looking at labs, I know that results won't be delayed and that detailed analysis is ensured. It's one less thing that I have to think about as we try to find Darren and bring everything to a close.

"I'm hoping the search team will turn up something at Darren's place that will steer us to where he's keeping Lily," Bancroft says as he shakes his head. "I just can't believe Ed's son would have turned out like this."

The desk phone beeps, and his secretary's voice comes through the speaker. "Chief, the semiconductor plant in Pine Bluff is on line three, returning your call."

The chief and I exchange glances. "Thank you, Kathy. Put them on." A soft click issues through the phone. "This is Chief Bancroft."

The voice on the other end is gruff and tinged with slight impatience. "Chief. This is Walt Kilgore with LMI in Pine Bluff. I have a message here that I need to call you."

"Yes, Walt. Thank you for returning my call." Bancroft then relays his need to verify Darren's recent work schedule.

"Okay. Give me a minute," Walt says. "I need to pull up our payroll program and see what hours he's logged." The line is silent for a while with only the soft peck of computer keys floating through the phone. "What dates were you needing again?"

Bancroft tells him, and we both seem to hold our breath as we wait for a reply.

"Let's see," Walt muses. "Friday night... nope, Darren wasn't here. Got marked absent."

"You're sure about that?" Bancroft asks. "He wouldn't have come to work and forgot to punch in or out?"

"No. That's not how it works here. Because our largest client is the Department of Defense, we have to abide by certain contractor agreements and account for every person on the floor. You can't access it without your badge—can't even get through security and into the parking lot without it. We would have had a record of him coming into the facility and then on the floor itself. Not only that, if you don't scan your badge, you don't get paid. That's how we keep track of hours."

"Does Darren generally miss shifts?" Bancroft asks.

"No. Up until recently, he's been a diligent employee. Stays pretty much to himself. But looking over this time card, I'm seeing an unusual pattern of absences this last month. Hey, is everything okay with him? It's not every day a chief of police calls about one of your employees. Should I be concerned about anything?"

"I can't offer any details right now. But I would ask that if he comes into work at all that you contact me immediately. Please pass that on to all the shift managers and security as well."

"Okay." Walt's voice is strained now, but he doesn't press for more details. The chief thanks him and the call disconnects.

Bancroft rubs his palms into his eye sockets and blinks hard as he pulls them away. "Darcy, I need to find out which friend Tammy went to stay with. I want to have a talk with her. Maybe I can help her think of somewhere Darren likes to frequent. She would tell me if she knew."

"She was really shook up when I left her earlier," I say. "She seems like a sweet girl."

Bancroft leans back and studies his fingernails for a while. When he looks back at me, his face is drawn and pensive. "Darcy, what made you get into this gig? Chasing down the worst that humanity has to offer isn't exactly a top pick on high school career day."

The question catches me off guard. I never have liked talking about myself. Not unless it's with my closest friends and confidants. Even then, I would prefer something else to be the topic of conversation. I learned a long time ago, and even more recently, that the more you let people in, the greater chance that you're going to walk away with scars. I know that if I didn't already have so many wounds, then I wouldn't be so skittish about sharing more of myself with others. Bancroft's question forces me to gauge just how honest I want to be with my answer. He seems to sense this.

"If I'm opening a closed door, then forget I asked," he says. "I don't want to pry."

"No. It's all right." I take a deep breath and decide to feed a few coins into the honesty meter. "Maybe because of what I went through at the Chancellery, I was destined to do this," I begin. "It took me a long time to find out how to live on the other side of it. I guess they say that people like me either go into law enforcement or become a shrink. I'm too ADD to sit in a chair for hours on end listening to people's problems." I shrug. "So after trying to fight the fates with a good run at veterinary school, I decided that I wanted to help bring closure to families. There isn't a greater torture than not knowing who harmed a loved one."

Bancroft studies me quietly. I can see that he wants to ask a probing question, but he holds back.

"Besides," I say, "there is something incredibly satisfying when you finally catch the unsub. Knowing that you had a direct hand in putting them behind bars. It's an adrenaline rush like no other."

"So you're an adrenaline junkie?" he muses out loud.

"You bet I am," I laugh. "In my line of work, the next rush is always right around the corner. There's really nothing like it."

And it's better than sex, I think to myself. At least any sex I've had in a very long time.

I can hear Skylar's words echo in my ears, telling me how I need to get my work/life balance in order. She's an exceptional agent herself and has somehow managed to have a solid social life outside of work. Juggling friends while being an incredible mother and styling hair... In a lot of ways, I envy her ability to squeeze the most out of life.

Bancroft nods thoughtfully. "I know what you mean. Back when I was with NYPD, there was never a dull moment. I spent too many decades running off adrenaline and coffee. But I'm too old for all that now. It's one of the reasons I moved out here after I left the force. Thought it was about time I started running off fresh country air and country fried steak instead."

A rueful grin plays at the corners of my mouth. "But I see you haven't completely left the city behind. I've gotta say, Chief, you don't meet that many Jets fans these days."

"What's that?" he frowns.

I motion to the hat.

"Oh. No. I hate them. I'm a Patriots fan all the way. Although, I've got to say, it's not the same without Tom Brady."

"Hate them?" My forehead crinkles into a curious frown. "Then why wear a hat with their logo?"

He slips the hat from his head, turns it around, and examines the logo, his eyes channeling a far off look as he answers. "Three years ago, a man came into town, all the way from Portland. He had decided that he wanted to get back into his son's life. His wife had moved all the way out here to Miller's Grove a year earlier to get her and the boy away from the father—Ted Parker was his name. Won't ever forget it. About a week after he showed up, she came by the station and spoke with one of my officers. Told him she was scared that Ted was going to hurt them. We couldn't do much about it since he hadn't done anything to them yet. Legally, they were still married, so we couldn't just tell the man to make tracks. When she came back the next day, she asked to see me personally. Sat in that chair you're in right now and one of my officers kept the boy busy in the bullpen while we talked. I'll tell you, Darcy, Norah was just outright scared. I offered to put her up in a hotel in Pine Bluff, but she thought he would find them. So I went over to her place to have a talk with Ted. He was as sweet and genteel as a Confederate gentleman. But I could see the malice hidden deep inside his eyes. Later that night, I was roused out of bed by dispatch who got a call from one of the Parkers' neighbors. Turns out that Ted had turned a gun on his wife and killed her. The boy—Simon—he hid away under the front porch steps. By the time we got there, Ted had turned the gun on himself, too. When social services came to get Simon, he came over to me, removed this hat from his head, and handed it to me. 'Thanks for trying,' he said, and then left with the caseworker." Bancroft nestles the hat back onto his head. "That boy had the hat snaps on the tightest notch, and it was still too big on him. But he wore it nonetheless."

"And you wear it to remind you?" I ask.

"I do. I could have done more for that family: tried harder to convince her to leave, dug around to find some kind of dirt on Ted so I could have thrown him in a cell for a few days. Maybe that would have given her a chance to make some decisions. The hat reminds me every day I wake up to give this job everything I have, and not to cut corners."

"Where is the boy now?" I ask.

"He was placed with an aunt somewhere in New England."

I can't help but respect Bancroft's commitment to getting things right. Too many in the higher echelons of law enforcement are on personal power trips, busy forging alliances that will only serve to further their careers or get more acclaim from their communities. I know this is a second career for Bancroft, but over the last few years, I've met far too many small town LEOs who care more about advancing their egos than upholding the rule of law.

"The way I see it," he says, "we all have regrets or wounds of some sort. Every last one of us. The difference is whether we let them stall our way forward or whether we press on ahead in spite of them. You don't serve with the NYPD for as long as I did and you don't go through something like I did with Ted and Norah Parker with getting some regret stuck on you." He shrugs as if it has all been decided. "The only thing to do is to press ahead. We're the good guys, Darcy. We don't get the luxury of riding into the sunset without any scars."

I couldn't have said it nearly as poetically, but he's absolutely right. I'm only a few years into my career with the FBI, and I already have enough nicks and scratches on my heart from where things just didn't turn out the way everyone hoped.

Bancroft's chair slides back as he rises to his feet. "I'm going to head on over and see about having a talk with Tammy. It's been a long day for you. Why don't you take the night off? I'll let you know if anything surfaces."

"I'm fine, Chief. Really. I won't be able to sleep anyway."

He hitches up his gun belt and comes around the desk. "Darcy, I need you running on a full tank. Go back to the chalet and kick your feet up. You won't do me any good if you're worn out and muddle-headed."

I can see the prudence in his words. I don't like the idea of kicking my feet up, but it might help to clear my mind so I can continue to give my best to bring this across the finish line, closing out this case.

I concede with a weary nod.

"Good. We'll talk soon," he says, and exits his office with a focused and determined gait.

Chapter Twenty-One

Bancroft Vacation Chalet
Miller's Grove, NY

My mind is awhirl and running at warp speed. It feels like a week has passed since Tammy's phone call woke me well before dawn and she told me she had something important to tell me. The subsequent events of the day have left me exhausted; my feet ache and my shoulders feel like blocks of knotted wood. Everything in me wants to fall onto the bed fully clothed and just close my eyes for a few minutes. But if I do that, I know I won't wake until tomorrow. Right now I don't have the luxury of sleeping for twelve hours.

Lily is out there somewhere. But just where exactly is anyone's guess. I can only hope that Darren will accidentally tip his hand or that someone might witness suspicious activity that might lead us to her. Until then, the only thing I can do is to continue compiling data, trying to forge fresh connections and clues using the information that I already have.

I know that Bancroft is right. I need to stay clearheaded. If I don't, then I run the risk of missing important links or crucial details altogether. It's not easy for me to relax. Doing so feels counterintuitive, like I'm wasting time or being selfish. But I know that's not true. Finding time to recharge will allow me to continue working at maximum efficiency.

With that in mind, I go into the bathroom and fill the bath with hot water. After a little searching, I locate a bottle of bubble bath and a small basket with several bath bombs beneath the sink. I toss in a bomb and it begins to fizz beneath the water. After pouring in a generous amount of bubbles, I slip out of my clothes, pull my hair up in a clip, and slide into the water.

Immediately, I can feel the tension in my muscles melting away. My eyes close and I relish the warmth and the way my body responds to the scents of lavender and passionflower steaming gently from the water. I lay there for a long time, letting my body unwind from the last two days. But my mind finally traces its way back to the events of the day. I don't resist, as doing so will help me sort out all the details and keep them organized.

I think back over my conversation with Tammy, walking into the woods, Bancroft's interrogation of Darren, exploring Lily's room, and finding the murder weapon under the rags in Darren's shed.

In all of it, there is one thing that bothers me most; the one thing I can't shake. When I was alone in the woods, standing where Tammy claimed to have seen Kayla, a heavy, disparaging feeling had taken hold of me, stemming from the close proximity of someone who is the embodiment of absolute evil. That deep, sinister laugh that resonated through the woods booms in my ears once again, forcing me to make my body relax beneath the water.

That sense of abject evil doesn't fit what I know about Darren. I know for a fact that it wasn't a prankster. But the worst among us often wear their masks with absolute precision. Ted Bundy was a well-educated, handsome, charming man. To everyone who knew him, he appeared to be the archetypical American man. Darren has deceived everyone in this town for far too long about his true nature. Now that he has been exposed, I wonder if the mask will finally come off, if he will allow those who know him best to see who he really is underneath.

The water cascades off my body as I stand up and reach for a towel. I flick away some of the larger patches of bubbles still clinging to my skin and then step out of the tub and towel myself dry. I return to my bedroom and slip into a pair of leggings and a sweater before going into the kitchen and making myself a chicken salad sandwich along with a cup of chamomile tea. Then I sit down at the table and watch a couple of squirrels chase each other through the trees as I eat. The sun is descending below the treetops, stretching the shadows across the ground.

As I dig into my meal, I realize just how famished I am, and the food quickly disappears from my plate. Finished, I rinse the plate off in the sink and grab my laptop. With a bath and a meal behind me, I feel rested and energized, ready to continue working on the case.

I sit down at my laptop and begin to catalog everything that I know so far, noting every detail, person, and location involved. Frustration builds inside me again as I conclude that I just don't have enough information to move on. Lily could be anywhere. Darren has all night to do something with her, and there is nothing I can do about it. This is one of the hardest parts of my job, knowing that people are counting on me to provide answers and direction and to be completely stumped and facing a brick wall.

Skylar's voice asserts itself in my head, bringing a balanced perspective to my own chastening conscience: *"You can only work with what you have, Darcy. You can't work magic every time."*

Every part of me wants to work magic, to find answers in spite of the lack of direction. But I can't. I'll have to wait and see what tomorrow brings. Until more details surface, until a clue appears that can send me down a fresh path, I'm glued in place.

I take another sip of my tea and frown at the tepid liquid. I didn't realize just how long I've been sitting here deep in thought. I stand up to get the circulation going in my legs again and am jolted by the loud buzz of the front doorbell. I normally wouldn't startle like that, but the events of the day have set my nerves on edge. Even with a relaxing bath behind me, the tension of the day isn't completely gone.

I make my way down the hallway to the front door and am relieved to see a familiar face when I look through the peephole. I quickly tousle my hair and use my fingers to comb it back before grabbing the door handle and swinging it open.

"Tim. Hi," I say.

He's wearing blue jeans and a dark green Henley that shows the curvature of his muscles. A youthful grin plays at the corners of his lips. "Hey, Darcy. I hope I'm not interrupting your work."

"No," I say. "Not at all. As a matter of fact, I was just wrapping up for the day. Well, not completely," I add quickly. "I'll probably be up late working on something." I don't know why I feel the need to justify my work ethic to him, but that's how it comes out. Maybe it's because I know he's the chief's son. Deep inside, I probably want him to know that I am committed to this case, that I'm not slacking off. I finally stop psychoanalyzing myself long enough to ask him what he needs.

"I came by to drop these off," he says. "They're homemade cookies. Mom made them for me and I thought I'd pass some along." He's holding a ceramic plate covered in plastic wrap. His face drops a little, and his cheeks take on a fresh color. "And now that I'm here, I feel like a middle-aged woman bringing a freshly baked treat to the new neighbor."

An easy chuckle escapes my lips, and I accept the plate from him. The sun is well below the trees now, and the sky has taken on bright orange and purples. The air is crisp but not cold. "I think I'll sit on the front porch and watch the light disappear from the sky. Would you like to join me?"

A rueful smile touches his lips. "Sure. In that case, Dad has some beer in the garage refrigerator," he says. "Do you want to have one?"

"I don't want to drink your father's beer, Tim."

He waves me off. "It's fine. Mom is the one who usually buys it for him. He won't miss any of them. Because I'll replace them myself after you leave."

I twist up my lips as I consider it. A beer does sound good. Technically, I'm on the case until I bring it to a conclusion. But a beer to take the edge off a long day wouldn't hurt. "Sure," I concede.

"Be right back."

I settle into a rocking chair and unwrap the plate, selecting a cookie from the top. Tim returns with two beers, the caps already popped off. He hands me one, and I ask if he wants a cookie.

"Better not. I already had two on the way here." He settles

into the rocking chair beside me and takes a long pull on his beer. "So, how was your day?"

"Tiring, if I'm being honest. Here's hoping tomorrow is better." I take a pull on my bottle and relish the coolness of the lager sliding down my throat. I'm glad when Tim doesn't press for more details. I don't want to cloud our time together by talking about work.

Looking out over the driveway, I notice that my car is the only one there. "You didn't drive here?" I ask. "Why did you come to the front door?"

He gives me a knowing grin. "If you remember, when I came by the other night, you were prepared to shoot me. Or jump out of your skin. Or both. When I stepped off the trail behind the cabin a few minutes ago, I saw you working at the table again. Thought things might fare better if I rang the doorbell like a normal person."

I decide not to tell him that even the doorbell made me jump a little. I don't know why I'm so edgy out here. It must be the fact that I'm back in Miller's Grove again after all these years. "That was probably a good idea," I laugh and take another pull on my beer.

Chapter Twenty-Two

I quietly make my way through the trees, closely watching every step so as not to bring my foot down on a decaying branch or dry twig that might give away my presence. The forest is thick around me and makes the going slow, but I am not in a hurry.

Ducking my head around a protruding limb, I step past a wide, moss-covered boulder and continue my progress. Up ahead, I see a break in the trees, which tells me that I've finally arrived at my destination. Moving around an evergreen tree, I crouch down and inch forward until I'm right beside the dirt driveway. I reach out and carefully push away the nearest branch.

I see her.

My heart beats faster. She is sitting on the front porch, deep in conversation, laughing at something that the man next to her said.

I'll have to be especially careful now. The police have brought her in to solve Kayla's murder. She is an excellent agent and clearly knows what she's doing. She has already been to both Kayla's house and Lily's house and continues to ask all the right questions.

I watch her as she rocks back and forth in the chair, oblivious to my presence as she listens to him talk. I watch them for a long time, relishing the scene as adrenaline courses through me.

It has been such a long wait. So very long. But when everything has been said and done, the wait will have been worth it. A man can hold out forever if he knows that he will see his desire fulfilled at the end of it all. Hope is one of the most powerful motivators in the world and is what has kept me so patient all this time; the knowledge that one day I would get what was taken from me.

He says something that makes her laugh again, and she looks over at him like she is enjoying his company. They can laugh and relax tonight. They can sit there and talk and enjoy the sight of the setting sun. Soon enough, I'll disrupt everyone's world again. It has already begun. But I have something more in store for them all, and this town deserves everything I have planned.

My entire body tingles with the thrill of anticipation. All the years that have gone by, all the years of waiting and then waiting some more, they are finally over. Kayla will always have a special place in my heart. She was the one who got things started for me, this scheme that I have waited so long to unfold. Kayla didn't know it, of course, but that doesn't really matter. She was the first domino to fall.

The rest will follow soon.

Chapter Twenty-Three

Bancroft Vacation Chalet
Miller's Grove, NY

Tim is talking about a hunting trip he has planned when my concentration is pulled away by the sense that we're being watched. It's the same feeling I had in the woods earlier today, as though some demonic presence is leering at me from the shadows. I stand up and step to the edge of the porch. Nothing moves: no tree limbs, no scuff of leaves, no snap of a dry branch. Just a crisp, gentle breeze stealing across the yard.

And then it's gone. Whoever was there has vanished.

"Darcy?" Tim calling my name snaps me back. "Something wrong?"

I return to my chair, still deep in thought. "I'm not sure."

"Did you see something?"

"I guess not." I don't want Tim to think that I'm losing my mind. "I thought I might have seen a deer."

"You probably did this time of night." In my peripheral vision, I see him eyeing me. "You sure you're okay?"

"Yes. Fine." I take another long sip of my beer. "You were telling me about an elk you got last year."

"Yeah. Well, that was about it. Took a couple hours to pack up the meat. Thankfully, we had a snowmobile parked not far away."

"What did you do with it?" I ask him.

"Donated that one to a local Indian reservation. A lot of the folks there don't have much." Tim scratches at his beard stubble and rocks back in his chair. "So how about you? What do you do for fun?"

"Work," I smile, and then raise a defensive hand when I see the frown emerge across his face. "I know, I know. I need to get a hobby. I hear it all the time. But I really do love my work. If it was drudgery, then I'm sure I would take up tennis again. Or hiking."

"So only work can hold your interest?"

I know that answering that in the negative would only make me seem one-dimensional. "I like movies. And reading history. Especially from the Roman era."

"Movies? What kind? I'm a Spaghetti Western guy, myself."

"Action," I say. "I'm not really a rom-com kinda girl. So Die Hard, James Bond, Fast and Furious. Well, a few of those. And I do enjoy the occasional Western."

His eyes brighten at my answer. "No rom-coms? Then, in that case, you just went up a few notches in my book."

"A few notches? I was already that low?" I laugh. He shoots me a wink, and I feel an unexpected flutter in my stomach.

"Everyone starts in the middle," Tim says. "Then things either go up or down from there."

"So I'm going up then?"

"Yeah. I think so." He grins.

We sit in companionable silence for a couple of minutes and watch the color drain from the sky as we work down what is left of our beers. My thoughts naturally drift back to the case, and I find myself musing out loud. "What is the message?"

"What's that?" Tim asks.

"Oh, sorry. I didn't realize that didn't stay in my head," I chuckle. "The motel the other night—the way the things were staged in the room were clearly intended to send a message. But it was too cryptic to make sense of. I just don't have the right pieces to solve it. Unless I'm completely missing something."

Tim nods. "Whatever it is, I'm sure you'll get it," he says. "Sometimes it just takes time or maybe seeing things from a fresh angle."

"Yeah," I agree. "I guess you're right."

I'm glad when Tim doesn't press for more details. I really shouldn't be talking about the case at all, especially the particular details. Limiting the details of a case to law enforcement is important. It limits false information getting passed around and can keep the unsub in the dark, keeping him from knowing what progress law enforcement might be making on the case. It keeps us in the driver's seat. Although, I am beginning to think that I am not the one behind the wheel at all. Whatever Darren wants us to know with the way he staged the motel room was completely lost on me. And now he had taken someone else.

My mind races back through the details: the bagged hands, the number written on the counter inside a triangle, the blood that apparently did not belong to Kayla. It just wasn't enough to move on. Like having one chapter of a book and being expected to see the entire story.

Bancroft has already put out the word about Darren. I'm sure every soul in town has heard by now and are keeping their eyes and ears peeled for his whereabouts. The more people who know that we're looking for Darren, the better.

As if detecting my growing frustration, Tim says, "Darcy, your office sent you here to help Dad because you're good at what you do. Just stay the course. You'll figure it out."

"Thanks," I say, but I struggle to share the same optimism he has. Finally, he rocks forward and comes to his feet. "I guess I'd better get going."

Even though the case caught back up to me, the mental break and the companionship has been nice. "Thank you again for the cookies," I tell him. "Make sure to tell your mother they're delicious."

"Will do. You uh, you think you'll still be around for a couple more days?"

"I'm sure I will. There's still a lot to be done."

"I'm glad Dad called you in to help. In a way that has nothing to do with the case." A mild flirtation edges his voice.

I feel my face flush. "I am, too. See you soon?"

"You bet. Maybe when you get things wrapped up, you can come over to my place before you head back home. I make a mean turkey chili."

"That sounds nice. I love chili." I walk with him down the steps and into the yard. "Do you need a flashlight to get back? It's nearly full dark."

"I could walk the route back in my sleep. Won't take but fifteen minutes." He eyes me, and for a moment we're both stuck.

Finally, he breaks the tension with a knowing smile and turns to leave. "Goodnight, Darcy."

"Goodnight, Tim."

As he rounds the house and disappears from view, I find that I'm smiling a little too much. It's been a long time since I've enjoyed the company of a man like that. I wasted a full year dating Lucas, who ended up being nothing but a self-centered, cheating weasel. Tim is kind and self-assured, brimming with quiet confidence. A meal at his place sounds like something I could certainly get behind.

I gather the bottles off the porch, and when I go back inside, my laptop stares at me from the table, as if luring me back in. Resisting the pull, I decide to call it a night. If I turn in now and get a good night's rest, then I'll be ready to take on tomorrow, whatever it might bring.

I have a feeling that it's going to require every ounce of training and focus I can give it.

Chapter Twenty-Four

"This is bullshit, Ronny. Completely unacceptable. Get some answers and call me back."

Bancroft is fuming when he slams the receiver back in its cradle. It's the next morning, and I'm sitting in his office nursing a mug of coffee while he calls every person with influence in the town. Up until now, I've only seen him maintain a professional and polite demeanor. He was firm with Darren in the interview room yesterday, and that was absolutely called for. This is definitely a side of him that I haven't experienced yet.

In a way, I'm glad to see him like this, glad he is taking the case so seriously. He is the chief of police in Miller's Grove, which means that keeping everyone safe ultimately falls on his shoulders. With Lily missing, I'm sure he's taking it personally. I like Bancroft, and I hate to see this falling on him, but that might be exactly what we need to get this case solved and to get Lily home safe and sound.

He gives an indignant shake of his head and looks across the desk at me. "No one knows a thing," he says. "Can't say where Darren might be or where he might have taken that girl. One of Darren's old friends called me last night and told us to check Willow Crossing. It's an old picnic area that was closed down maybe fifteen, twenty years ago. Darren's friend said they used to go there and drink when they were teenagers, even took their girlfriends out there. I had Dobbs and a few other officers check it out. But there's no sign anyone has been out there in years. He could have that girl anywhere. Could be five states over by now."

"Chief," I say, "I think she is being held in town somewhere. Wherever Darren has Lily, it's very close."

His brows furrow. "What do you mean?"

"Think about it. Darren was trying to send us a message with the way he killed Kayla. I know you put the word out all over town, but if Darren ditched his phone after you released him, then he still may not know that we have the murder weapon. He's going to keep her close. He'll want to send a second message."

"We don't even know what the first message means, Darcy. What in the hell is he trying to say?"

The frustration on Bancroft's face matches precisely how I feel myself. "I don't know."

"How is it that I've got two people missing in my town, and all of a sudden, no one knows a single thing? All the gossip corners are silent. Absolute crickets. If someone jaywalked on Main Street, someone would call dispatch to rat them out. But when a madman, who is known to just about every one of us, goes missing, then no one has a single thing to say. Absolutely nothing."

I take another sip of my coffee as my mind works overtime to make the right connections. "We'll get to the bottom of this, Chief. I promise." Two dark circles hang like used tea bags beneath his eyes. I know this is wearing on him as much as it is on me. "Did you get any sleep last night?"

He shakes his head. "I laid in bed until about 1 AM. Finally just got up and spent time between our kitchen table, love seat, and the front porch, trying to think of anything we might have missed. The mayor called me—late—nearly midnight. You know that bastard is more concerned about winning reelection later this year. His concern over Lily was clearly underwritten by his worries about his polling numbers if this case doesn't get buttoned up. I despise men like him, Darcy. He's supposed to be a public servant. I can't believe people can't see through him."

"They do eventually," I say. "Sometimes it just takes a challenging candidate to expose people like that for what they are."

He nods. "Yeah. So what about you? You get any sleep?"

"A little. I got up before dawn to review all my notes. If we're going to close this case, then I need to find a pattern. Something that can tell me what he's planning next, and where. But right now, we just don't have enough to go on."

I leave out the details from my time with Tim last night. I feel a little disingenuous not telling him that I have been talking to his son. But I don't want to break Tim's trust. Whatever happened between the two of them really isn't any of my business, and bringing it up now might only serve to distract the chief from this investigation. "How did the conversation go with Tammy last night?" I ask.

He gives a rueful shake of his head. "Not great. She cried a lot. I've always liked that girl. I believed her when she said she had no idea where Darren might be."

"Did you ask her about the man in the woods with Kayla? I know his voice was muffled, but does she think it could have been Darren's?"

"She's not sure. But she thought there was a chance. Darren has a deep voice. The man in the woods with Kayla did too, according to her."

I hear a scuffle in the hall behind me, and an officer barks out an order. The door to Bancroft's office bangs open and Paula Haskins bursts in. Like Bancroft, she looks like she hasn't slept a wink.

"Where's my daughter?" she cries. "Where is Lily?"

I place my mug on the edge of Bancroft's desk and stand up, moving toward the hurting mother. I go to set a comforting hand on her shoulder, but she quickly swats it away. Behind her, Officer Dobbs is giving his boss a distressed look. Bancroft gives him a knowing nod and dismisses him with a quick wave of his hand.

"Mrs. Haskins," Bancroft says, "Let me assure you that we're doing everything we can to find your daughter. We—"

"I don't need your assurances," she bites back. "I need you to *find* her." She glances at the chair I was just sitting in and then at my mug. "Not sitting around sipping coffee and shooting the breeze." She raises her arm and points in the direction of the station's front door. "You should be out *there* looking for her." Before either of us can respond, her body softens and she raises her hands to her face and starts to sob.

Putting myself in Paula's shoes, I understand how the optics look. But right now, we just don't have enough to go on. Everything in me wants to be out there, beating the streets and knocking on doors, asking if anyone has seen Lily. But that method rarely, if ever, yields any results. It can help psychologically, but not tactically. If people are moving—doing—then they feel like they are somehow in control, exhibiting just how much they care for the person who has gone missing. But right now, I need to make myself available for when something more actionable does come in. When it does, I'll need to be in a position to move on it immediately.

Paula doesn't resist now as I place my hand on her upper back. "Paula, I know it looks like we're shooting the breeze, but I promise you that we're not."

The distraught mother regains a measure of control and wipes at the tears streaming down her face. "They're saying that Darren Malloy took my daughter. Is that right?"

"Yes, ma'am," Bancroft replies. "We've put the word out all over town, and we've issued a tri-state alert. We've already scouted out half a dozen places he is known to frequent, and I have officers stationed at strategic points in town. We're watching to see if his cell phone shows a signal again, and we're keeping an eye on his credit card usage. If we get any kind of ping, then we're prepared to move quickly."

"I just can't believe this," Paula sobs. "It's such a nightmare. Lily has never hurt anyone. She's just a normal girl." I snatch a couple of tissues from a box on Bancroft's desk and hand them to her. "Thank you." We wait as she blows her nose and blots her eyes. "I'm sorry for bursting in like this. I just don't know what else to do."

Bancroft stands up and comes around his desk. "It's all right, Mrs. Haskins. I know this is a very difficult time."

"I saw that monster at the grocery store last week. He was in line in front of me. I could have never imagined..." She trails off as Bancroft shoots me a glance.

"Mrs. Haskins, why don't I help you back to the front?" he says. "I think Officer Robbins is at her desk. I'm sure she would be happy to sit with you for a while."

Paula nods. "Okay. Thank you." Bancroft shepherds her down the hallway toward the administrative wing. He returns a couple of minutes later and shuts the door before going back around the desk and dropping into his chair. "Darcy, it's days like this that I really hate my job. Feels like *I'm* the one wearing the cuffs, shackled until I have more to go on."

Even though I feel the same way, I don't say anything to Bancroft. He brought me here to help him stop a killer, and while I am at a temporary standstill until something else surfaces, I still need to project confidence in the outcome. If I allow myself to fall into a cauldron of negativity, then it will wear off on Bancroft and his entire department. It's important that morale stays high. Of all people, I do not have the luxury of becoming despondent or pessimistic.

"We're going to get him, Chief," I reassure him. "It's just a matter of time."

He nods and echoes my silent sentiment. "I just want to grab him before he does something to Lily."

Behind him, on the wall, is a small wood-framed picture that I hadn't noticed until now. A slightly younger looking Bancroft is standing beside a sturdy man who looks to have a few more years on him. The other man has closely cropped gray hair and a strong jawline. He's handsome and smiling, but I detect a weariness in his eyes. I nod at the wall. "Who is that in the picture with you?"

Bancroft swivels in his chair and looks up. "That there would be Ed. Tammy and Darren's father. That picture was taken, oh, a few years before Ed died, before Linda and I moved out here for good. We had come out here for the town's Fall Festival. Ed and I were in charge of getting all the meat cooked. That man, he could grill a chicken thigh to absolute perfection." Bancroft swivels back toward his desk and shakes his head. "Ed has got to be rolling over in his grave right about now. Shows that you just never know how people are going to turn out. I wish I would have known what has been brewing inside Darren all this time."

"Don't do that," I reproach him. "Neither one of us has X-ray vision into people's hearts and motives. The law can't stop bad people from breaking it. It's only there to let the good people know where the boundaries are. You should feel responsible for your town, Chief. But if you're not careful, something like this could send you to an early grave like it did to Ed."

Bancroft rubs his hands over his face. "You're right. We just need to stay the course."

"I know your officers have interviewed all Darren's known friends or associates," I say. "But what about any ex-girlfriends or romantic interests?"

He huffs and shakes his head. "The last woman Darren dated was three or four years ago. She broke up with him after he started getting paranoid about her possibly seeing other men behind his back. She wasn't, as far as I could tell. But Darren still slashed all four of her tires when she was at work one day. As you can imagine, he has never been so great with people."

A knock rattles the door behind me, and Bancroft tells

whoever is on the other side to enter. Kathy, his secretary, steps through the door and nods a hello to me before placing a file on Bancroft's desk.

"Chief, here are the additional details you requested. I've printed off the last two months of call records from Darren Malloy's phone, as well as two months of transactions from his debit card and credit cards."

"Thank you, Kathy."

She hesitates. A worried expression is etched across her face. "Chief, do you think Lily is going to be all right?" She works up a stunted smile. "She and my Sarah used to be on the same soccer team when they were younger. I just can't believe this is happening. After everything that happened with the Chancellery all those years ago, I never thought we would see murders like this again."

"You know I can't give you any promises, Kathy. As much as I would like to. We all want to find that girl more than anything. How is Paula holding up out there?"

"She just left. Officer Robbins and I spent a few minutes with her. We reassured her the best we could, but there isn't exactly a thick sense of optimism running through the building."

Bancroft taps the top of the file with a couple of fingers. "Hopefully what's in here will help." Kathy leaves with a tenuous nod, and Bancroft pushes the file toward me. "See if you can make heads or tails of anything in here. I have to go over to City Hall. Have a meeting with the mayor. He wants an update on our progress. I'll tell you what, Darcy. It's days like this that I wish I was a sheriff. If I was an appointed official, then I wouldn't have to think twice about shoving my boot all the way up the mayor's ass."

"Better you than me," I laugh. "Good luck."

Chapter Twenty-Five

Miller's Grove Police Station
Miller's Grove, NY

I spend the rest of the morning in a secluded cubicle within the station's administrative area, meticulously culling through all the data in Darren's phone and bank statements. I've marked them thoroughly with three different highlighters and a pen, utilizing a system that has served me well for years. When I'm dealing with large amounts of data, it's crucial to sift out the irrelevant information and find patterns that might direct my attention to any angle that I've been blind to.

Bancroft still hasn't returned to the station. I can just imagine the fun he's having with the mayor. He doesn't strike me as the kind of man who enjoys politicking. But making nice with the mayor goes hand in hand with his job. As for me, I prefer to remain a relatively unknown agent who quietly does her job. All the baby kissing, ass kissing, and handshaking isn't for me. Even the thought of it makes my stomach twitch. I don't have a thread of politician's DNA in my body. The fake smiles, hollow promises, and shifting alliances made to help you stay in power have no appeal to me whatsoever. I suppose it's all a necessary evil and someone has to do it, but that person will never be me. The years have taught me that the best life is the authentic life. Learning to be myself, to live with honesty and integrity, those are the best rewards.

Bancroft's ability to do the bidding of the town's leadership is admirable. He's clearly not the kind of man who wants to play the game either, but I know he does it because his job requires it. When the mayor is your boss, sometimes you just have to suck it up and play nice.

I go to take another sip of my coffee but then stop when my fingers tremble across the handle of my mug. Since Bancroft left, I've consumed three cups of coffee and as many donuts. The stress of finding Lily has caused me to break my commitment to watching what I put in my body. There is something psychologically pleasing about going to the coffee pot while your mind churns. Maybe it's the passive effort that gets your body out of a sedentary position. Whatever it is, I draw my hand back and decide that I have more than enough jazz pumping through my system.

Most of Darren's banking transactions are typical grocery store purchases, gas station fill-ups, and utilities. But three transactions, in particular, stand out. One of them is from an online adult entertainment boutique that specializes in toys and lingerie. The other is a flower shop in Pine Bluff, and the third is a jewelry store in Buffalo. Each transaction on its own doesn't pose any red flags, but the fact that all three occur within one week of each other does.

There was no jewelry on Kayla's body, no flowers in the motel room, and yet I shudder to think that he might have used them to woo her closer to him in his own twisted way.

Nothing stands out in Darren's call logs from the last month, and I don't yet have access to his text messages; Bancroft promised that he would have them to me by this afternoon. I tap my pen on the desk and think, frustration building inside me with every tick of the wall clock. I was hoping that I would be able to excavate something more from the data, something that might lead me to where he is now. But even in that, I come up short.

The coffee has me completely on edge now. My insides are jittery and my fingers feel like they're vibrating. Staring at all these line items and numbers for the last few hours has my thoughts all muddled. I need to clear my mind. Standing up, I shut the file and cross the room.

Dobbs is at his desk, staring at his computer screen. Like everyone else in this building, his face is drawn tight with worry. "Agent Hunt?" I stop in front of his desk and turn to face him. "I want to thank you for coming out here and helping us. I know your office probably didn't give you much of a choice in the matter, but we're all glad you're here. Most agents, I expect, would grumble their whole way through. You haven't done that." He makes a weak attempt at a smile. "I think what I'm trying to say is, thanks for your commitment to figuring this out."

A smile forms across my lips. "Of course," I tell him. "When we finally get all this wrapped up, I get to leave and go back home. But Miller's Grove will be stuck facing another run of horrible crimes. If I can, I want to make sure that you all have to suffer as little as possible. That really matters to me."

"That comes through. We really won the lottery with you."

"I don't know about that," I laugh and slip my keys from my pocket. "I'm going to get some fresh air. When the chief returns, tell him I'll be back soon."

"You got it."

I push through the double doors at the front of the station and step outside. The town is eerily quiet, as though holding its breath for what might come next. I get into my cruiser and drive slowly down Main Street with the windows down, letting the cool midday breeze stream through the car. I suck in a deep breath of the fresh, piney air and exhale a lungful of pent-up frustration.

Something about this case isn't sitting right. It hasn't since I woke up this morning. The problem is that I don't know exactly what it is. But it's silently poking at the back of my mind, as though telling me that there is something else I need to be looking at.

We've got Darren pegged. We have the murder weapon. So what else is there? I can't help but feel like I'm missing something that is staring me right in the face, but for some reason, I can't pinpoint what it is.

This is one of those rare times when I wish Kemper would have sent someone else in. For all the ballyhoo that Officer Dobbs just heaped on me, this might be one of those cases when another agent could have seen what I'm missing.

I don't feel like this very often. Even when hitting a brick wall, I always press through and keep my own emotions out of it. But this town is counting on me and I'm coming up short. Another precious life is at stake. I sigh again and drum my fingers across the steering wheel as I continue the drive through town. The few faces I see on the sidewalks are drawn, heavy with anxiety, renewing a commitment inside me to bring this ordeal to a swift end.

My phone rings and I slow to a stop at a red light before taking it out. "Hunt," I answer.

"Darcy?" It's the chief. His voice is filled with urgency. "Where are you right now?"

I glance out my windshield and scan the buildings slowly moving past me. I'm not familiar with the cross streets. "There's a Happy Smiles Dentist and a Kute Kurls Hair Salon. Why? What's wrong?"

"Someone just called in to the station. She swore to have seen Darren's truck heading east toward town."

A rush of adrenaline spikes through my veins. "Where exactly?" I asked.

"Just past the city limit sign on Route 80. My nearest officer is ten minutes away. If you're over by Kute Kurls, then you're just down the road from where she saw him. He may have turned off somewhere in between."

"I'll look for him," I say.

"Be careful, Darcy. I know we found a lot of Darren's guns at his place yesterday, but there's a good chance he has something on him. The rest of us are on the way."

"I will." We hang up and I scan the street outside the windshield as I ease back down the road. "Where are you?" I mutter. "And what's making you risk a trip into town?"

I slow the cruiser's speed to less than twenty-five miles an hour, ten less than the posted limit. I don't want to go so slow as to draw attention, but not so fast that I miss spotting Darren. My cruiser is unmarked, so it shouldn't draw any unnecessary attention. My heart is beating hard behind my ribs as I swipe my gaze right and left.

Soon enough, the town begins to thin out, with more land stretching out between buildings, and the businesses becoming fewer and fewer. Crossing the last intersection, I keep my eyes peeled for anything that looks like a functional road cutting through the trees. I'm about to turn around and head back to Miller's Grove when I spot a sign up ahead, partially obscured by the trees: *Gas 'N' Go*. Continuing on a little more, the shapes of two vehicles parked at the pumps emerge.

One is a silver Camry.

The other is Darren's truck.

The black, late model Dodge Ram has a lifted suspension which reveals a muddy undercarriage. It's facing away from me, and seeing the Predator sticker in the center of the back window causes me to draw my gun, which I keep near my thigh as I casually pull into the station and park at the pump behind the truck. Darren is nowhere to be seen.

What is he doing showing himself in the middle of the day? If he needed gas, why hadn't he done it in Pine Bluff, where there was less of a chance that someone would notice him? The decision to come here was either brazen or stupid, probably a little of both.

Placing a hand on the door handle, I slowly open the door and step out of the car. The gas nozzle is still set in the mouth of the truck's gas tank, but no gas is running through it. Droplets of sweat break out across my forehead as I slowly make my way past the tailgate and move toward the front door. I come up quickly to the front window and point my gun toward the cab. It's empty. A glance shows no one in the back either.

My view of the convenience store is blocked by a large panel truck. Slowly moving around the front of Darren's truck, I shift around the next set of pumps and freeze when the front door of the building rattles open. Footsteps scuff across the pavement, and a thin shadow falls across it just before Darren Malloy steps into view ten feet from me.

"Darren!" I yell, and train my gun on him. "Freeze!"

As soon as his head whips in my direction, his eyes nearly bulge from their sockets.

"Get on the ground! Now!" He freezes but hesitates to obey the rest of my order, like he's mentally flipping through a Rolodex of options. When his eyes meet mine again, I know exactly what he's going to do. Before I can repeat my command, he releases the two bottles of Dr. Pepper and the bag of chips he had just purchased and bolts away, charging toward the side of the building. Cursing, I run after him as I slip my finger off the trigger.

I have to give him credit. Discharging a weapon near open gas pumps is a fool's errand. Clearly, Darren knows this and decided to call my bluff.

I reach the corner of the building just in time to see him disappear around the back. My feet crunch over gravel and glass from broken beer bottles as I pump my legs as fast as I can and shoot past a stack of empty pallets and a pile of old tires. Reaching the corner, I turn to see Darren struggling up a thinly wooded hill behind the station. After shouting out another order for him to cease, I start up the hill after him.

The soil is loose and finding purchase is difficult. I have to holster my gun in order to free both my hands, then use tufts of Timothy grass to stabilize my path upward. Above me, I hear Darren curse loudly. Rocks and pebbles spill down the hill, and a moment later he emerges from the trees face first, his feet reaching over the back of his head as he tumbles down the hill in a loose tangle of arms and legs. The large stone that he lost his footing on dislodges and follows him down as I quickly and carefully pick my way down.

Darren makes a final revolution before landing with a hard thud beside the dumpster behind the station. Scrambling toward him, I almost lose my own footing as the loose soil slides out from under my feet. Reaching out, my fingers latch onto a jutting rock just in time to interrupt a precarious fall. I find my footing again on a firm patch of grass and cautiously trust my weight to it.

Below me, Darren lays motionless on his back. I scramble down the last few feet of the hill and bring out my pistol as I reach him. His flannel shirt is covered in dozens of small tears, his face with tiny nicks and smudged in dirt. His head swivels toward me. In spite of the pain I know he is experiencing, all his hate for me clearly hasn't ebbed.

"You bitch," he growls and tries to get up.

I place my free hand on his shoulder and shove it back to the ground. Then I place the business end of my gun between his eyebrows.

"What do you want already?" he bites off. "I haven't done anything."

"Then why did you run?"

"Because ever since you showed up, the chief has decided he doesn't trust me. I wasn't in the mood to deal with you again."

"No. That's not it. Where is she?" I demand. "Where is Lily?"

"Lady, what are you talking about?" He tries to move an arm but moans from the pain.

"So this is how you're going to play it? You know, I don't play by the same rules as the rest of this town."

"Is this about me telling you to shove off the other day? I hurt your pride and you get the chief to question me and now you threaten me?"

"I haven't threatened you, Darren. Not yet. But you had better believe it's on the agenda." I press the muzzle of my gun so hard into his forehead that he starts to scream.

Behind me, I hear the squeal of tires as a vehicle slides to a stop across the pavement. A car door flies open. Hurried footsteps draw around the building, and I hear Bancroft's voice over my shoulder. "Darcy! Darcy, what are you doing?"

"Getting him to talk, Chief."

He stands beside me and assesses Darren. "What happened?"

"Fell down the hill," I say. "He tried to escape up the hill into those woods."

He squats down beside me. "Where is Lily, Darren?"

"You both are insane, you know that? What's your problem?"

"You know damn well what the problem is, young man. Why don't you just come clean?"

"I'm not saying anything," he snaps back. "Not until you get that gun out of my face and I get checked out."

Bancroft sucks on a tooth as he considers the demand. "Fine." I pull back my gun as he grabs Darren by the collar and hauls him to his feet. Then he sets his large hands on Darren's shoulders, pivots on his heels, and slams him into the back wall of the gas station. Darren howls in pain as Bancroft grabs his wrists and cuffs him. "Let's go."

Chapter Twenty-Six

Miller's Grove Police Station
Miller's Grove, NY

In spite of his rough tumble down the hill, Darren doesn't appear to have any broken bones. At least, nothing severe. His right forearm and left shoulder are sensitive to the touch, possibly indicating a hairline fracture, and when I lead him out of the cruiser and into the station, he's favoring his left leg. But he is the only one concerned with that right now.

Since neither Bancroft nor I was able to get Darren to talk back at the gas station, we brought him back to an interview room. Given the desperate nature of the case, Bancroft decided that Darren was in good enough shape to answer our questions before allowing a doctor to examine his injuries.

Now we're standing in the anteroom watching him through the one-way mirror. "I'll go in with you," Bancroft says, "but I want you to take the lead on this."

I nod and step inside the room. Bancroft follows me in, shuts the door, and takes a seat beside me at the table. I place his file on the table and fold my hands over it while giving Darren a frigid stare. "I hope you're ready to talk because my patience has expired. Now, where is Lily?"

The right side of Darren's face is bright red from the road rash he got when landing beside the dumpster. A large gash runs over his right eye, and blood has run and dried down his cheek. He huffs and shakes his head disdainfully. "Who in the hell is Lily?"

"No," I say. "This is not how this is going to go."

"I thought you folks at the FBI got some kind of special training?" he smirks. "At Quacko or someplace, right?"

"Quantico," Bancroft corrects him.

"Whatever. I think I'll stick with Quacko. Because you, lady, are a quack." Darren stares me down with such vitriol that I get the image of lasers coming out of his eyes. Ignoring him, I get right to the point. "We already have you for Kayla. Now where is Lily?"

"You keep using that name," he says. "What makes you think I know? She go missing or something?"

Bancroft clears his throat. "Darren, this will go a lot easier if you just cut the bullshit and come clean. You're in a heap of trouble as it is. We found the wire in your shed."

Darren blinks hard. His brows furrow. "Wait. Wire? What wire? What are you two talking about?"

I unfold my hands and flip open the file. Inside is a clear evidence bag with the braided wire inside. I hold it up and watch his expression. "You didn't find that in my shed. I've never seen that—wait." His eyes widen with fear. "You still think I killed that girl in the motel?"

We don't give him the pleasure of a response.

"You're—you're outta your damn mind." His voice takes on a higher pitch. "Chief, you've known me for years. You really think I would do something like that?"

"It's not a matter of what I think, Darren. This wire right here is what was used to kill that girl in the motel."

"I haven't seen that in my life!" Panic spreads across Darren's face, and his body, which had been slouched in his chair, is now rigid and bolt upright. "God, Chief, I didn't kill no one. And I didn't take some girl named Lily, either."

"Okay, fine," I say. "Then why don't you tell us where you really were last Friday night? Your alibi didn't check out. Your supervisor said you didn't show up for work like you told us."

He shifts uncomfortably in his chair again and looks down at the table as he mumbles to himself.

"What's that?" I ask.

He curses and shakes his head. "It's my private life. I shouldn't have to tell anyone that."

I nod. "Then I hope you can afford a good lawyer. Because you're going to spend the rest of your life in prison. Do you know what they do to arrogant, insecure men like you in prison, Darren? On your first day, they—"

"Rita!" he blurts out. "I was with Rita, okay?"

"Rita?" I ask. "Who is that?"

Bancroft frowns in Darren's direction. "Davis? You're saying you were with Rita Davis?"

"Yeah."

"Doing what?"

Half of Darren's face is red with dried blood. But now the entire thing blooms brightly with what seems to be a combination

231

of anger and embarrassment. "Chief, look, you can't say anything about this to anyone. If you do, then—"

"Doing what?" Bancroft repeated, his voice booming with an impatient authority.

Darren sighs deeply and shakes his head. "We're, uh. We're kind of seeing each other."

The chief's mouth falls open, and he uses both hands to rub his brows. "You expect me to believe that you're sleeping with Rita Davis? Come on, Darren, you'll have to do better than that."

"It's true. Ask her."

"Oh, we will," I ask, and then look at Bancroft. "Who is Rita Davis?"

"What's the lingo these days? A... cougar? That's it. Rita is a cougar. Worth over a hundred million dollars. She lives in a mansion way out of town. Up in the hills." Bancroft leans forward again and fixes his stare on the man in front of him. "And you know what else she is? Married. That's what. Rita Davis is married to Mr. Davis. And he is going to kick your ass from here to Niagara when he gets wind of this."

"No! No, Chief, look. You can't tell him. If you—"

Bancroft slams a fist on the table, which stops Darren mid-sentence. "I don't give a rat's ass about your relationships. Especially one that would entail a magnificent scandal once it gets out of the bag." He reaches out and snatches the photos from the top of the file, then lays them out facing Darren. He jams his finger into the first one. "Maybe you already know this, but this is Kayla Hanover. That picture was taken by a friend earlier this year. When she was alive and well. This one"—he jams his finger onto another one—"is from Saturday afternoon."

When Darren turns his attention toward the second photo, the color drains out of his features. He gags and turns away.

"That mark around her neck," Bancroft continues, "matches precisely the wire that we found in your shed yesterday."

"*No*. No-no-no-I did *not* kill that girl. Are you kidding me? Chief, come on."

I pull out his bank statements that I was combing through this morning. "In the last week, you ordered flowers, jewelry, and made a purchase at an online adult boutique."

Darren's apparent shame at sleeping with Rita Davis now appears to be overridden by the realization that we have him in our crosshairs for a heinous murder and a second kidnapping. "All that was for Rita, okay? I was trying to show her how much she meant to me. And you know, have some fun."

I study him closely as I pose my next question. "Why has your cell phone been off since you left the station yesterday, and intermittently over the last few weeks?"

"Because, Rita, she's skittish about getting caught. She made me promise that before I start heading toward her place, I'll take out the SIM card and the battery. Her husband owns some big tech firm in New York City. If he starts getting suspicious, then she doesn't want my phone to show anything."

That feeling that I started to get earlier swarms over me again. The feeling that I was missing something, that one of the pieces just wasn't fitting. Now I'm starting to think I see why. "You're obviously in a very different economic strata than Rita is. How did the two of you even meet?"

Darren sucks on a tooth and looks away. "Sometimes I hang sheetrock on the side. Rita is remodeling a wing of their house.

One of her contractors brought me in as a sub to help. I was there working late by myself one night, and well, you know."

"Why did I not see any recent deposits on your bank statements other than the semiconductor plant?" I ask.

"The contractor, he pays sixty days out. I've got the W-9 in the glove box of my truck if you want to see it."

The chief is having Darren's truck towed back to the station. Once it gets here, a team will go through the contents. I tug a picture of Lily from the paperwork and set it over one of the crime scene photos, carefully watching his expression. There is no recognition in his eyes.

"Who's this?"

"You tell us," the chief replies.

"Is this the other girl you said went missing?" Then he huffs, and his upper lip curls into a hateful snarl as his eyes bore into mine. "You're a real piece of shit, you know that?"

"Where is Lily?" I demand.

"You asked that back there at the gas station when you were assaulting me." He looks up at the camera mounted in the corner and says again, this time with more emphasis, "Assaulting me." Then he turns his attention back to me. "My lawyer is going to have a field day with you, lady. As for some Lily, you're barking up the wrong tree. Ask anyone in this town. They've known me since I was a little kid. I'm no kidnapper."

Ignoring him, I ask, "Where were you on Friday night? We have a witness that has your truck parked behind the Diamond Palace."

Darren slicks a hand down his face and sighs. "This is just great. Of all the weeks for something like this to happen in this town."

"Why were you at the Diamond Palace?" Bancroft asks, his tone edged with irritation.

"Rita, all she's ever known is the high life. She wanted to do something a little crazy. So she got a room at the Diamond Palace. I guess there was something about doing it in a seedy motel that made her feel excited. So I drove us there, and she went in and got the key, paid cash, and scribbled a fake name on the registry. She made me park in the back for obvious reasons. We were only there for a couple of hours."

Bancroft looks toward the one-way mirror and said, "Dobbs, send someone to get Rita Davis and bring her here. Tell them they're not allowed to take no for an answer." He turns back to Darren. "Son, I don't know if you understand my level of irritation with you right now. This town has experienced a terrible murder that I am currently unable to handle on my own. So I brought in the FBI to help. For some reason, you thought it would be a good idea to harass the agent they sent me and tell her she's not wanted. Then you give me hell yesterday when I question you. Even now your attitude is the pits." He jams his forefinger onto Lily's picture. "Now this young lady has gone missing and all you can do is think about yourself. And you know, it's crap like this that caused me to let you go from this department all those years ago. You could have been as good as any officer I've ever hired. In fact, you could have been your father's equal. But for some reason, you're too damn focused on yourself to be of any worth in this community."

Upon hearing that he could have been his father's equal, Darren's eyes rim with tears and he hangs his head. As he takes the brunt of Bancroft's words, it begins to dawn on me that for the last twenty-four hours, I have, in all probability, been focused on finding the wrong man. I was working off the information that I had at the time, but the feeling that the real offender has outsmarted me and caused me to waste precious time on a diversion makes me want to scream. Like he told Darren, the chief brought me in to help, to bring all of this to a swift conclusion. Instead, I've only served to drag things out. I allowed myself to get blinded. Sure, the wire at Darren's shed was a good indication of his complicity, but if the Rita angle checks out, it looks like the wire and the paper bags were actually planted in the shed, placed there for the sole purpose of providing misdirection.

And I fell for it. Hook, line, and sinker.

My phone buzzes on the table, pulling me from a rare moment of self-pity. I excuse myself and step from the interview room as I answer the call.

"Amy, tell me you have something."

"I certainly do," she sing-songs. "Ready for it?"

"More than you know," I mutter. "Whatcha got?"

"Okay. The material beneath Kayla Hanover's fingernails is actually a naturally occurring collection of minerals. What you thought was dirt has the molecular makeup of dolomitic limestone. And I found traces of carnallite and sylvite present as well."

I wait for her to continue, but get nothing else. "Amy, I slept my way through college chemistry. You'll have to help me out."

"Oh, right. Sorry. All these minerals are something you would expect to see around a salt mine."

My heart starts to thump wildly in my chest. "A salt mine?"

"I don't know what it all means, but that is what these results are telling me."

"Amy, you're the best. I owe you dinner and drinks."

"Don't I know it? But right now, go get your unsub."

We hang up and I return to the interview room, approaching the table and scooping up the file. I ask Bancroft to join me on the other side of the door. When we're alone in the anteroom, I ask, "Is there a salt mine anywhere near Miller's Grove?"

His brows knit together. "Sure. The Franklin-Dorsey mine. It shut down back, well, I guess back in the late eighties. It's about ten miles outside of town. Why?"

"Because that is where Kayla's killer wants us to go."

Chapter Twenty-Seven

Wild Spruce Nature Trail
Miller's Grove, NY

Shelby Campbell followed the curve in the road and pulled her Taurus into a space beside the picnic pavilion. She sang along to her favorite Adele song and waited for it to finish before turning the car off. Then she rolled down the driver's side window a few inches, slipped her phone and keys into the center console, and stepped out into the sunshine.

It was the perfect day. Not too hot, not yet chilly. The quiet chirping in the treetops attested to the birds' approval as well. Shelby stepped to the mouth of the paved walking trail and spent several minutes stretching her muscles, taking extra time with her lower back. This last week she had started to feel some tightness there and the last thing she wanted was to injure it on her run.

Finished stretching, she started down the trail at a brisk walk and glanced at her Fitbit. In half a mile, she would move into a slow jog and then accelerate into a run at the one-mile mark.

She had only recently started running. At first, she hated it, but as she continued to push herself to go a little bit farther and then a little more, the endorphins finally kicked in and she experienced what the initiated called the "runner's high." There really was nothing else like it. A deep sense of calm would overtake her, and all her stress would melt away. Once she got past the initial burn in her muscles, Shelby discovered that she could run for miles and miles. When she downshifted into her cooldown, any anxiety she had brought with her would be gone, and her entire outlook on life felt more positive.

Sometimes, like today, she would leave her phone in the car. Other times, she would strap it to her upper arm and listen to a playlist as she cut across the trail. But today she wanted to enjoy the quiet sounds of nature and clear her thoughts. Life had been far too busy lately, and the circuitry between her ears felt like a jumbled mess.

Work had been a challenge, her online college classes were proving to be more difficult than she had anticipated, and her boyfriend of two years had decided to break up with her. And the icing on the cake was that her mother had just been diagnosed with stage 4 lung cancer. Through it all, Shelby had somehow managed to keep it all together. She hadn't fallen apart yet. *Yet.* But she could feel it bubbling beneath the surface, a simmering pot ready to explode.

The soles of her shoes scuffed quietly on the pavement as she followed the trail. A rabbit leaped off the path in front of her, and she crossed a small bridge that took her over a gently flowing creek. The sun laced shadows on the ground and a gentle breeze stirred the tops of the trees.

Half an hour in, Shelby raised her wrist and checked her

Fitbit: just over three miles. One more to go and she would turn around and start making her way back. As she continued on, her thoughts turned toward her mother. Last week, the doctors had given her only four months to live. Five if she was lucky. Her mother was everything to her, and the thought of having to go on without her was almost unbearable.

She forced the thought from her mind and turned her thoughts toward more pleasant things. Her best friend's birthday was coming up, and she quickly got lost pondering what kind of party she should plan. Soon enough, she had reached the four-mile mark and turned around. Her body was on autopilot now, her legs warm and loose, the blood rushing to provide oxygen to her muscles. She retraced her route down the trail, crossed the creek, and downshifted into a walk a mile from the parking lot.

Her hands tingled a little, and her mind was completely clear of any brain fog whatsoever. It was an exhilarating feeling, and she couldn't wait to get back out here tomorrow and do it all over again.

In the corner of her eye, the sunlight glinted off something in the dirt just off the trail. Shelby slowed to take a closer look. It was a cell phone. Frowning, she picked it up, brushed it off, and examined it. The home screen was locked, but the background image showed a snowy mountain range. The device looked to be in good shape.

Shelby continued on, and as she cleared a wide bend, she cast her attention farther down the trail and saw a man with his back toward her. He was hunched down a little, his gaze sweeping right and left across the trail. As Shelby drew closer, her shoe scuffed loudly on the pavement, and the man wheeled around, apparently a little on edge. Shelby offered a quiet hello and started past him.

"Excuse me," he said. "Did you happen to see a cell phone along the path? I think I may have dropped mine on the way back to the parking lot."

Shelby held up the phone triumphantly. "Is this it?"

He studied it for a moment and then broke out in a smile. "Yes. Thank you." She held it out to him and he took it, examining it for scratches before slipping it into the front pocket of his jeans. "You're a lifesaver," he said. "There's no way I can afford another phone right now. I must have dropped it when I was feeding the rabbit."

"Feeding a rabbit?" Shelby said with a grin. "They let you get close enough?"

"Sometimes," he shrugged. "Squirrels are easier, but every now and then I can get a rabbit to munch on the end of a long carrot."

"Very cool," she said. "I'll have to come out here and try it sometime."

"Do you come out here often?"

The man seemed harmless enough, but in some small corner of her mind, alarm bells started to go off. The question had an edge about it that she didn't like. He had a pleasant smile on his face, but somehow his expression looked as though he was looking right through her. Like maybe he was seeing something else entirely. She didn't bother to answer his question, but started past him without saying anything else. Her heart was racing now, and adrenaline flooded her veins as an inner voice screamed for her to run.

Without looking back, she hurried forward just as two strong hands gripped her shoulders from behind and prevented her from going any farther. As she went to scream out, a hand snaked across her mouth and clamped down. She struggled, but only for a moment. With a single heaving breath, the chloroform made its way into her nostrils and then her lungs. Her body slackened, and as she sucked in more of the tainted air, the darkness enfolded around her and she slipped from consciousness.

The man glanced down the trail to make sure they were still alone and then stood grinning over her body. "Thank you again for the phone," he chuckled. "I'm going to have a lot of fun with you. A *lot* of fun." He leaned down, hooked his arms beneath her armpits, and quickly backed Shelby into the treeline, her feet dragging limply out in front of her.

Chapter Twenty-Eight

Franklin-Dorsey Salt Mine
Cascade County, NY

"She's sure it's from a salt mine?" Bancroft asks. He slows his cruiser off the county road and turns down an unmarked dirt lane.

"Yes," I reply. "She said the minerals are a match."

He grips the wheel tightly and shakes his head. "I don't like this, Darcy. It all feels like a game of cat and mouse. And I'm starting to think that we're the mice."

"Chief, whoever is behind all this has been planning it for a long time. These are not crimes of passion. They have been methodically planned and carried out with detailed precision. Now that it appears that Darren isn't our man, we have to go back to the drawing board and look at everything in a fresh light. We'll get him. We just need to stay the course."

"I like your optimism, Darcy." The car grows quiet for a while before the chief speaks again. "I don't know that it really matters to the case," he says, "but I'm glad that Darren doesn't seem to be our guy. I think that would have completely ruined Tammy. That woman has been through enough."

Tall grasses whisper loudly against the cruiser's undercarriage, and before long, small bushes and saplings start to pop up in the long-neglected road. The chief slowly negotiates a bend and is forced to stop in front of an adolescent tree growing right in the middle of the road. There's not enough room to navigate around it.

"We'll have to walk from here," he says. "If memory serves, I don't think it's more than a quarter of a mile."

We take out our sidearms and step out of the cruiser. Bancroft goes around to the trunk, bringing out a set of bolt cutters. "The county put up a fence a while back as a deterrent against curious visitors and adventurous kids."

As we start down the road on foot, I push away thoughts of what we might find here. "Why did the mine shut down?" I ask.

"Not exactly sure. I think it may have had to do with larger and more accessible salt deposits up around Lake Ontario. Miller's Grove grew substantially back in the sixties and seventies because of the support economy the salt mine brought with it. But when it shut down, a lot of the younger families went on to find work elsewhere. But a lot of the folks who were at retirement age decided to stay. And now a good deal of their kids have stayed. The semiconductor plant came into Pine Bluff about ten years ago and opened up a lot of new job opportunities."

"And the mine has been shut off from the public ever since?"

"Yes. The mouth of the mine was sealed with concrete and the railroad ties pulled up. It's my understanding that afterward it used to be a place the high schoolers would come to have fun.

About twenty years ago, the fence was put up and I think it worked well enough. As long as I've been chief, my department hasn't had to respond to any calls out this way. As you can see, it's not something you can easily gain access to anymore."

We step around a maple sapling and come face-to-face with a chain link fence. It stands eight feet high and has a single thread of barbed wire running across the top. A thick chain is threaded around the gate. Bancroft slings the bolt cutters up, and a minute later the chain pops loose, slides off the gate, and falls to the ground. Setting the bolt cutters down, he swings the door open, and I pass through behind him. We take out our sidearms and keep our heads on a swivel.

"What are we supposed to find out here, Darcy? Why would he want us to come here?"

"I'm not sure, Chief. But I think we'll know when we find it."

"You think he might be walking us into a trap of some kind?"

I shake my head. "No. He's created his own game of Connect the Dots. Watching us connect one dot with the next gives him supreme satisfaction. Right now, he is enjoying the feeling of being in control. He won't be quick to let go of something that gives him so much pleasure."

The road terminates suddenly on a thick stand of hemlock and mountain laurel. We push into them, careful not to let the branches scratch our faces. We don't seem to be going anywhere in particular when we step out of the trees into a large open area covering multiple acres. It's dotted with tufts of wild grass and saplings several feet high. Bancroft lifts an arm and points to the left. "Over that way is the entrance to the tunnel."

We start in that direction and pause at a bare patch of sand and rocks a couple of feet below us. Years of rain runoff have cut into the limestone and formed the appearance of a dry riverbed. We jump down and follow it toward the mine, our feet crunching over loose pebbles and rock.

As we go on, my heart starts to pump faster, and I feel a nervous prickle across the back of my neck. Both of us are on high alert now, scanning the treeline, and surveying the vacant property as we periodically glance behind us.

I'm well aware that we're not the ones in the driver's seat. We're playing into a well-executed scheme that has been orchestrated by a psychotic monster. I have to trust that my training, experience, and intuition are enough to work things out from there.

The dry bed of sand and pebbles start to rise at an easy incline. We move up it, and twenty yards later we're back on level footing on the east side of the clearing. In the distance, a shadowy circle sits against a rising hillside at the treeline. Bancroft motions toward it. "That's the entrance of the mine over there. If he wanted us out here for something, I guess we might find it over there."

We start toward it. The infill of concrete is layered with weather-worn graffiti, probably made from bored teens who used to come out here to have a good time far away from the inquisitive eyes of their parents.

We pass a fallen tree and a large boulder before Bancroft says, "Over there."

Something is lying near the mouth of the mine. With my sidearm clutched in a double grip, I hurry forward and scan my surroundings, finally letting out a deep groan as I draw closer and drop to my knees beside Lily's body.

Her lips are blue, her skin pale. But unlike Kayla, who was

strangled with a wire, Lily has a railroad spike through her heart. The top of it stops an inch above her chest, and blood has congealed around it. I touch her forearm with the back of my hand as Bancroft comes up beside me and releases a weary sigh.

"Damn this," he growls. "Just, damn this."

As with Kayla, Lily is perfectly displayed. Her hands are bagged, and she lies on a thin black sheet in a burgundy, knee-length dress.

"She's still in pallor mortis," I tell him. Her skin, while not holding the natural warmth of a live body, is not yet cold. "She hasn't been dead for any more than forty-five minutes. Probably less."

He jerks his hat off his head and whisks it to the ground as he curses loudly. "You're telling me that if we had had those lab results an hour ago, we could have saved her?"

"No," I reply. "I don't think that at all."

He gives a confused frown as he bends down and picks up his hat, brushing it off before he puts it back on. "What do you mean?"

"I mean that whoever is behind this must have had a basic idea as to how long it would take to get the results back from the lab. And that means he has some kind of working knowledge of how the system works. He wants us to feel like we're trailing just a few inches behind. But the truth is that he was going to kill her regardless of how quickly we got the results back. Like you said earlier, this is a cat and mouse game. He never intended to give us a chance to rescue Lily. He gets his rocks off by watching us reach for the carrot."

"So he's watching us then."

"Yes." A chill threads its way up my spine. "He is."

Bancroft gets on his phone and calls for his team to respond to the scene. "And bring a chainsaw," I hear him say. "You'll need to cut down some trees to get the vehicles back in here."

He hangs up and we take our time examining the scene in front of us. Like Kayla, Lily's arms are crossed peacefully across her chest, her toenails are perfectly polished. Sitting beside her head is a large flat rock. Instead of one triangle painted in blood, now there are two, both of them overlapping. In their center is a number: **17**.

"Why start at sixteen?" I wonder out loud.

"What's that?"

"Kayla was the first victim. Our attention was supposed to be drawn to the number sixteen. Not only was she killed in a room with that number, but it was also written on the counter in someone else's blood. Now he has added another triangle and called attention to the next number in the sequence. I want to know why he started at sixteen."

Bancroft scratches his chin. "Good question. But why lay out numbers at all? What's the point?"

"He wants us to figure it out."

"Why?"

"Because it makes him feel smart. He's stuck inside his head. But he believes himself to be incredibly smart and resourceful. By laying the murders out the way he does, he is giving us a tiny window into his mind, showing us how smart he is. These clues are a subtle way of showing us what drives him and why he does this."

I spend the next few minutes visually assessing the body. "Chief," I finally say. "I need your team to go back through everything they can find on Lily over the last few weeks. Her victimology is different. It's not like Kayla's."

"How so?"

"With Kayla, the unsub clearly had a relationship with her. Tammy saw them together back in the woods, arguing. Then she apparently drove off with him and later met him at the motel of her own volition. We could have missed something with Lily. If she knew him too and willingly went with him, then that would match his previous MO. If not, then he's changing it. If that's the case, then it means that it will be more difficult to pin him down."

Most predators have an ideal victim that they prey on. In this case, it's young and vulnerable girls. If he is going to spend his time carefully wooing the first one, then I would expect him to do the same with the following. There is obviously a method, a pattern to his madness, one that he is trying to get us to see. But how he is selecting his victims is not yet clear.

"What do you think is under her nails this time?" Bancroft asks me, wearing a pained expression.

"I couldn't begin to guess. But whatever it is, it's where he wants us to go next. Which means that there will be another girl."

"So I've got a serial killer on my hands," he murmurs to himself.

Technically, I can't label our unsub a serial killer until I have three bodies. But I don't correct the chief. If I can't get my head around all this and find a way to stop what is happening, then I have no doubt that a serial killer is exactly what we're dealing with.

"If she's been dead less than an hour, then Darren couldn't have done this," Bancroft adds. "He was fifteen miles from here.

And heading into town from the opposite direction, not driving away from here."

"You're right."

Before we left to come out here, the chief directed an officer to place Darren in a holding cell until Rita could verify his alibis and we were absolutely sure that he had nothing to do with any of this. It looks like the only thing he's been guilty of is being a jerk and making a cuckold out of Rita Davis' husband.

Far in the distance, a bright twinkle of light catches my attention. I squint toward it, toward the top of a cliff that overlooks the wide valley we're standing in. My heart suddenly skips a beat, and as the image settles into my mind, my knees lose their strength. Forcing myself to stay upright, I struggle over to a small boulder and sit down on it. A sharp pain slices through my chest as the memories surface.

"Darcy? What's wrong?"

I focus on my breathing as tiny stars dance across my vision and the salt mine swirls around me. "He's watching us."

"Watching us? Who?"

"The unsub. He's up there on that cliff." A few more deep breaths and my head clears, but not before leaving a pounding headache in its wake.

Bancroft spins and uses his hand as a visor. "How can you see that far?"

"I saw a twinkle. Like you would get reflected off a scope or a pair of binoculars."

"Well, that could have been anyone then."

"Didn't you tell me Rickshaw Preserve campground was shut down for the season while they made upgrades?"

"Yes, but it could be a worker or a tourist who violated the perimeter warning."

"It's not. He wants to watch us. It gives him a sense of control. I'm sure it's him." I push off the rock and find my footing again as I look back toward the cliff. I know his eyes are watching me, taking in our movements and facial expressions as we survey what he has left for us.

"Are you all right? I know seeing Lily like this isn't easy."

"Thank you," I tell him. "It is hard. But it's not that." I nod toward the cliff. "Up there, right where he's watching us, that was where I took my sister to show her the view the night we were taken."

Bancroft groans but doesn't say anything.

"As soon as we pushed our bikes up there, we saw the storm hurling toward us. We turned around and got caught up in it a minute later. That was the last time I had a normal moment with my sister. The snow came, then the darkness, and soon after that, we were taken by some man who posed as if he wanted to help us. Two days later, she was dead."

"I'm sorry, Darcy." The chief's tone is soft and kind, and I can tell that he is being completely sincere. "Everything inside me right now wants to lift my hand and give him the bird," he says. "But I don't guess that would help anything."

"It wouldn't," I agree. "It would only give him more pleasure." And with that, we return our attention to the body.

Bancroft takes out his phone again. "I guess I'll let Marty know. As soon as my team gets here, I should probably go meet him."

"Who's Marty?" I ask him.

"He's our volunteer chaplain. He's better with the whole

251

breaking-the-news-to-relatives thing than I am. I'll go with him, but he's better at the talking part."

"Let Mrs. Haskins know that she can call me if she needs to. Sometimes having another woman to talk to can help."

"Certainly will."

"And do you think you could get the county sheriff to send you some deputies to help search these woods before it gets dark? There has got to be something out there. Even a boot or shoe print. Anything we can find would be helpful at this point. And if my weather app is right, then it looks like we're in for a doozy of a rainstorm tonight. Anything we can't find tonight will be erased."

"I'm on it." With that, he dials a number and steps away as I continue to stare at the body of a girl I couldn't save.

Chapter Twenty-Nine

I readjust the field glasses over my eyes and take in the scene far below me, watching as she halts suddenly and looks out in my direction. From her position down at the old salt mine, she is far too distant to make out anything this way. But I can see her perfectly; every facial muscle, every memory deep in her eyes, the hoard of emotions that scroll hauntingly across her face. For a moment she looks lost and confused, and I watch her stumble toward a large rock and use it to rest on as she struggles to get a hold of herself. He walks over to her, and they begin to talk.

The girl's body lies before them, perfectly displayed, just like the succulent offering that she is. Everything is coming together. Just as I have dreamed of for all these years.

The waiting has been agonizing. So much so that there were times that I thought I wouldn't be able to endure such a dry period of time. But my commitment to doing what is right has kept me steady, helping me take the long view instead of giving in when the road seemed too long. For many long years, I have waited—planning, calculating, making sure no detail was overlooked.

I never would have imagined that I would be capable of waiting for such a long candle wick to burn down. There were times when I almost broke my vows and moved ahead on my own timeline. But I resisted and learned to count down each day, knowing that the wait would be worth it. That is what emboldened me toward the finish line. I am so close now, and when I cross it, an entirely new game will begin.

The very thought of it excites me to my very core. I will be released from the commitments that were laid on me all those years ago and finally be free to do as I please. With all my secrets out in the open, I will finally be whole.

What I am witnessing is the stuff of dreams; dreams becoming reality. Seeing the girl's body lying down there, motionless, the color drained from her skin and her chest motionless in death—it creates a euphoria deep inside me that is almost overbearing.

I will never understand how people live their lives as they do. It's a mystery to me how they carry on each and every day without a longing for the taste of another person's blood. They all walk around as if they deserve to be here, as though their lives are their own and they can do whatever they please. But nothing could be more false. Some lives were created strictly to be a sacrifice. This world does not yet understand that. But through my faithfulness and the faithfulness of others who will be raised up after me, the world may finally come to see.

I am the chosen.

I am also the chooser.

Being a faithful servant means properly discerning who must be laid upon the altar. I am one of the lucky ones who have been tasked with this sacred trust. At times, the responsibility feels overwhelming. But other times, times like this, when I can look upon the fruits of my patience, I feel completely alive again. Knowing that, because of me, people have perished.

It is the way it should be. I answered the call, the one that came to me in my dreams all those years ago. I have been faithful to do what I was told.

And I will continue to be. All the way to the beautiful end.

Chapter Thirty

Bancroft Vacation Chalet
Millers Grove, NY

Kyle now has Lily's body in the morgue, and Bancroft and his officers are still trekking through the woods around the salt mine with assistance from the sheriff's department. Rather than searching the woods looking for something I know we probably won't find, I opted to come back here to the chalet and spend time reconsidering everything I know about the case.

Over the last twenty-four hours, I had started to look at everything through the lens of Darren's complicity. Now that I can write him off as misdirection, the facts are disorienting. It's like looking at a picture of a sunset before the photographer informs you that it's actually a sunrise. They may look similar, but they're just not the same. And in my line of work, perspective is everything. The angle, the viewpoint, and the way data is interpreted is the difference between success and failure; bare facts don't mean anything unless they're set into a meaningful framework.

Now that my framework has shifted, I have to look at everything I know afresh. The unsub has a specific script in his mind, and he's sharing some of it with me, baiting me, wanting me to get on his wavelength.

The key will be to do it faster than he thinks I can. If I can beat him at his own game, then I might have a chance at stopping him. If not, this could go on indefinitely, or until he makes a mistake. Somehow though, I don't see him missing a beat.

After making a quick bowl of fettuccine for dinner, I sit down at the table and spread out all my notes across the surface, along with the crime scene photos. Since I won't have the photos from the scene at the salt mine until tomorrow, I pull up the pictures I took with my phone.

Except for the means of death, the two crimes are identical. It's the violent way that Lily was murdered that clearly sets this one apart. Instead of using a wire, the unsub chose to end her life in a more gruesome maneuver. Did he get angry and his sudden passion suddenly caused him to alter the way he wanted to kill her? That is the most logical answer.

And yet it contradicts the serene way that her body is staged. Like Kayla, she was displayed in a peaceful manner. A furious murderer would not have gone through the trouble. He would have wanted her to outwardly display the fury he felt inside—we would have found her in a bloody, broken heap. And then there is the dress. Did he force her to put it on or did she know him and hope to please him by wearing it?

Shifting my attention from the body, I focus on the scrawl made in blood. In the motel room, there was one triangle and the number in the center. Now there are two. It's clear now that the notch in the triangle was actually a space to join in another one.

257

And now the second has a notch as well, which tells me that there are plans for another.

Reaching for a pen, I sketch out three interlocking triangles and then stare at the image for a while. Symbols function as visual depositories of meaning. That's all that letters and words are. They are symbols that serve as individual bearers of meaning. But other than a vague association with heavy metal rock bands, I don't know what this one means.

I slide my laptop in front of me and type a search query into the browser. Scrolling through the results, I click on a link, which leads me to a page discussing the various meanings of the three interlocked triangles. The most common agreed upon interpretation refers to the symbol as a valknut, which was used by ancient Germanic peoples and Norse Pagans in the context of various death rituals.

"Death rituals?" I say out loud. "Is that what this is? A religious rite?"

I click into several more links to fully understand the valknut and to make sure I'm not missing anything else. A dive down the rabbit hole of pagan death rituals yields results that are far too cryptic and variegated to help narrow down what the unsub might be thinking. After a while, I shut the computer, stand up, and pace around the living room as I think.

Is the unsub trying to tell me what he's doing, without revealing why? Are these girls fodder for an ancient ritual? Or offerings of some kind? This whole thing is starting to feel like trying to complete a 500 piece puzzle with only seven pieces. There is no way for me to fill in the gaps without more details. I can only hope to sketch a path forward without someone else dying first. I can almost feel this town hold its collective breath as it waits for me to make sense of it all and stop the madman who has draped a cold blanket of fear across its streets.

My phone rings, jolting me out of a deep, contemplative stupor.

"Hey!" Skylar is as chipper as ever. It's one of the things I love most about her. While I keep up a skeptical lens at all times, Skylar is an eternal optimist, always one to testify to the sunny side of life.

"Tell me I can do this," I answer.

"Do this? Girl, of course you can. Are you kidding me? You're Darcy effing Hunt. The best damn FBI agent I know."

"I made a wrong move, Sky. And now another girl is dead because of it."

A heavy silence takes up the line. When she speaks again, she sounds more like a chastising mother than a best friend. "Darcy, you didn't kill those girls. Just because your guy is hiding deep in the shadows doesn't mean you're not doing your job right. You want me to come out there and lend you some fresh eyes?"

I ponder that for a while. "No," I finally tell her. "I just need to regroup. The truth is, I haven't felt this inept since the Coldwater case two years ago."

"Okay. I get that. But how did that case turn out?"

"I put him away for the rest of his life."

"Exactly."

"But not until he drowned six girls and two of the boyfriends."

"And agents across four different field offices tried to find him for three months. Not only was it you who stopped him, but you did it just five days after they let you start working the case."

I nod and absently twirl a lock of hair around my finger. "Do you know what a valknut is?"

"A valknut? Yeah, sure. Remember Jordy, that bass player from Steelthunder I dated a few years back?"

"Sure," I grin. "I never saw you. You were always at his place."

"And what a gorgeous place he had, too. And his body... mmm, that wasn't so bad either." She releases a long, nostalgic sigh into the phone.

"Skylar...."

"Oh, right. Anyway, he had a valknut tattooed on his forearm. It's the three triangles, right?"

"Yeah. Somehow it plays a role in all of this. I just don't know how."

"Isn't it like some Viking death symbol?"

"Something like that. I just can't understand what he's wanting me to see. And I'll be honest, I feel like I should be able to see it."

Skylar huffs into the phone. "That's what they do, Darcy. The worst of them try to get under our skin. It's all a mind game. But you're not inept. Well, maybe at choosing the right man to date you are. Other than that, you're the best of us."

"Thanks," I say. "I guess I needed this phone call more than I realized."

"Trust your gut. It hasn't failed you yet. You're going to get him, Darcy. If I know anything, I know that."

My phone beeps, notifying me of another call coming in. I glance at the display. "I need to go," I say. "The ME is calling in."

"You've got this," she says a final time, and then I switch lines. "Hey, Kyle."

"Darcy. You have a minute?"

"Of course. Fire away."

"Okay. Well, as you can imagine, the cause of Lily Haskins' death was due to a massive puncture wound to her heart. It sliced into her right ventricle and nicked a hole in the wall of the aorta. She would have died within moments. No indication of sexual trauma. Which again, I have to say is strange given the nature of the crimes. With most female kidnappings that end with a violent death, I would expect to see some bruising around the thighs or vaginal trauma."

"Any idea what's under her nails?" I ask.

"This stuff is darker. Sand or dirt, perhaps. But I can't be sure."

"Kyle, that may be our only solid link to a location that the killer intends to visit. How quickly can you get it to the lab? I can have my colleague in Albany standing by."

"The chief is going to send a courier to Albany first thing in the morning. This storm is about to roll in, and it looks like it's going to be a mammoth. The weather center said it's creating a lot of wind shear that will make it ripe for tornadoes."

Outside, the clouds have already blocked out the sun and continue to grow darker, casting everything in a dingy gray.

"And everything else is the same as it was with Kayla?" I ask.

"Actually, there is one thing that's different. There's a symbol carved into Lily's back."

His words make the hair on my neck stand at attention. "What is it?"

"I can't say for certain. It looks like some kind of ancient symbol. I'm not sure what they're called. A rune?" he mutters to himself. "I think they call it a rune. But I'll let you decide that for yourself."

"Can you text me a photo?"

"Sure."

We hang up and I wait impatiently for the photo to arrive. Five minutes later, I'm about to call Kyle back when my phone dings with a text. The large carving takes up most of Lily's back and looks like interlocked greater than and less than signs.

I sit down at my laptop again and search for runes, which lands me on a page with a Norse rune alphabet. The meaning of each one is noted beside its associated symbol. My eyes scan the legend until they locate the symbol. It's called *Jera*. The description indicates that this is the rune of harvest and reward for patient actions within a cyclical process. I dig deeper, searching for more definitions across multiple sites, even looking for additional clues to a possible meaning outside of the Norse tradition.

But a strong consensus emerges. This rune speaks to a continual process—cycles—which require great patience and which are finally rewarded with abundance.

Are these girls the unsub's harvest? Is this what he has been patient for, and has he been planning this for a long time? What kind of repeating cycle is he working with? Frustration builds inside my chest as more questions lead to fewer answers. The unsub is taunting us with these clues, dangling them in front of us without providing enough to truly move on.

My phone rings. It's the chief, and he sounds weary, if not altogether sad. "I just got back from telling Paula Haskins that her daughter isn't coming home. I sure do hate this part of my job, Darcy."

"I'm sorry you had to do that," I tell him, and then push that thought as far back as I can. Sometimes it's almost too much to think that good, innocent people are dying on my watch.

"Did Kyle get you his findings yet?" he asks.

"He did. And Chief, I think we're dealing with religiously motivated killings."

"How so?"

The first drops of rain ping on the deck outside as the wind continues to toss the tree branches. "Lily had a Norse rune carved into her back. And the incomplete triangles at both scenes appear to be moving toward a valknut."

"A what-noot?"

"A valknut. It's an ancient symbol used by Norse Scandinavian pagans and Germanic peoples."

"So... witchcraft stuff?"

"No. It's an ancient religion that was holistically adopted by an entire culture. A valknut is three interlocking triangles. And right now—"

"We only have two," he finishes for me.

"Right. Which would seem to point to a death ritual. I don't think it's too far of a stretch to say that the girls are sacrifices of some kind. And the killer carved a rune into Lily's back."

The line goes quiet, and Bancroft does not respond.

"Chief?"

"Sorry, Darcy... listen, I need to run back to the station for something before this storm opens up on us. Why don't I stop by the chalet in the morning and we can put our heads together on all this?"

"Sure. Everything all right?"

"Yes, fine. Just need to go look into something is all. I'll see you in the morning. Make sure to stay indoors. I heard this storm is mighty angry." And without another word, he hangs up.

Having to inform a mother that her daughter has been murdered on your watch is a difficult house call to make. I know the lingering effects of that are resting heavily on the chief right now. But his sudden mental absence wasn't because of his visit with Paula Haskins. It was more than that. Whatever I said about the religious nature of the murders sent his thoughts elsewhere.

I don't really like the idea of him not sharing what he might be thinking. After all, he did ask me to come to Miller's Grove to help, and I won't be able to do that unless he's willing to share everything he knows with me.

Thunder cracks loudly overhead, shaking the windows as the clouds finally open up and send down heavy torrents of rain. Whatever Bancroft might be thinking, I'll have to wait until the morning to find out just what it is.

Chapter Thirty-One

The wind continues to lash the woods outside the cabin. The sun set an hour ago, and it is now darker than a coal mine out there. The storm's assault has been brutal; I can't remember the last time I experienced one this ferocious. Wind howls around the eaves like a mournful coyote as lightning flashes like a strobe light, briefly illuminating the glistening leaves of the trees as their branches are violently tossed back and forth.

Above me, the rafters creak against the onslaught. Tree branches scratch loudly along the west side of the chalet, giving me a mental image of dark, reaching fingers trying to get inside. I chasten my imagination and put my focus back on my work.

The longer I study the religious connection to the murders, the more probable it seems. My unsub is framing his monstrous actions here in Miller's Grove by some vague religious senti-ments. But too many questions still remain. Is he atoning for his own sins or punishing those he believes to be sinful? But then maybe sin doesn't even factor into it at all. It could be that this is all a means of showing fidelity to a god or gods. Are his actions penance or duty? The symbols point toward some kind of cycle of time. But is this the beginning of a cycle or the middle of one?

A quick search through the Bureau's database reveals no similar murders over the last few years. The only case bearing any similarities was a string of murders in Ohio. Using a green permanent marker, the killer marked each girl with a cross on her right cheekbone. But that was five years ago, and the perp is currently serving a life term.

The key to solving this case will be to get as deep into the mind of the killer as possible. Right now, I know precisely what he wants me to know. It's my job to extrapolate those details, to look into them to find out the *why* of the murders. Once I have the why, it will be easier to find the who.

I'm scribbling a note across my pad when suddenly, the lights flash across the house, wink again, and then blink out entirely. The quiet hum of the refrigerator winds down, and other than the glow emanating from the screen of my laptop, I'm left in complete darkness. I sigh, set my pen down, and slap the lid to my laptop closed so I can conserve the battery. If the power doesn't come back on tonight, then I don't want to be stuck without the ability to conduct deeper research. But then I think that the internet will probably be out as well.

As my eyes adjust to the darkness, the chalet begins to feel much larger than it did when the lights were on. The vaulted ceiling seems to rise into a high peak that is so dark my eyes cannot penetrate. Pushing back from the table, I rise to my feet and step over toward the large windows overlooking the rear deck.

Somewhere in the darkness, I hear the muffled snap of a tree branch as the wind continues to howl across the eaves. A sheet of wind blows across the windows and spreads out across the deck before rolling off into the woods. Then another shock of thunder booms overhead, rattling the windows and a vase on the counter. The chief wasn't kidding; this storm is incredibly angry.

Another strobe of lightning flashes across the treeline, illuminating everything in a momentary flicker of glistening silver. Then all of a sudden, the rain lets up a bit. It's still pouring out there, but not enough to make me think that I'm on the edge of a hurricane.

And that's when a familiar sensation crawls over me, enveloping me like a wicked fog. The room feels heavier, and a cold jolt of fear ripples through my body, almost paralyzing me with a sense of dread that I cannot shake. A ripple of goosebumps breaks out along my arms.

I hug myself tightly and brave a glance behind me into the darkness, feeling foolish for the sense of foreboding that has suddenly swallowed me up. Peering out through the windows again, my veins turn to ice as another flash of lightning illuminates the outline of a man standing at the edge of the treeline. I blink and look closer, making sure that my eyes aren't playing tricks on me.

But he's real. Still there, clothed in a full length raincoat with the hood pulled up. Even so, there's no mistaking the bushy gray beard protruding from under the hood. The rest of his face is shrouded in darkness.

I stand there, frozen, my chest rising and falling in nervous, hitching gasps. Even with my sidearm on my hip, I can't shake the sense that he can see into my soul. His very presence is penetrating, as if he has X-ray vision and sees whatever he wants to, from my past to my present fears.

"Get it together, Darcy," I order myself out loud. "He's right there. He came to *you*. You can stop this right now." And as if they have a mind of their own, my hands release their grip on my elbows. My right hand goes for my gun as my left goes for the door bolt. Flipping it back, I rush out the back door, a cold shower of hard rain shocking me as I cross the deck into the absolute blackness and try not to lose my footing on the slick surface.

Another flash of lightning offers me a merciful and momentary strobe of light.

The man is gone.

It wouldn't have taken but a couple of steps for him to back up into the treeline so that I couldn't see him anymore. Cursing myself for my rash behavior, I quickly move left against the deck railing, finally crouching down beside the grill in hopes that I might get another glimpse of him. I have never been one to get intimidated easily, but this move on my part wasn't made with a cool head.

I wait for more lightning.

And wait some more.

In spite of the storm's overwhelming chaos, I can still feel him near, a storm more violent than the one above me teeming inside him. A nascent roll of thunder crackles overhead before releasing a deafening boom that shakes the grill and sends a shockwave through my chest. It's so overwhelming that I have to bite down on my lip to keep from screaming.

The rain is freezing, pelting me with hundreds of angry

drops. I'm soaked to the skin as I close my eyes and try to think. If he came here to hurt me, he would have done it already. He wouldn't have shown himself like that. Instead, he's taunting me, dangling that carrot of his right in front of me. And I fell right into it, doing exactly what he expected I would.

He doesn't want to hurt me. Not yet, anyway. If he did, he would have done so already. He's enjoying the thrill of staying a step ahead of me, of intimidating me.

When the lightning flashes again, I slick a hand down my face, rise to my feet, and call out: "Show yourself, you bastard!" But my words are whisked away by the rushing wind the second they pass through my lips. I can't even hear them myself.

Frustrated and defeated, I cross the deck and feel my way back to the door. Flinging it open, I step inside just before the wind slams it shut behind me. Then I freeze, overcome with a sense of panic. Could he have come in through the back door without me seeing?

With my service pistol at the ready, I feel my way to the table, locate my phone, and switch on the flashlight, panning it around the floor. Other than the water I just tracked in, the rest of the floor is dry. Releasing a tense breath that I didn't realize I was holding, I bolt the door and stand beside the table dripping like a half-drowned cat, feeling a little foolish for running out there the way that I did.

I'm shivering, my teeth chattering as my body shakes beneath my soaked clothing. I need to get out of them quickly before I end up catching the flu. Then I'll be no good to this case whatsoever.

Phone flashlights were not designed to penetrate the darkness, and mine doesn't function much better than a few candles. But even though the weak light isn't bright enough to dispel the shadows in the corner of the living room, it does assist me in making it to the front of the house without bumping into anything.

I've worked a lot of cases in my four years with the FBI. This is the first time an unsub has been bold enough to personally taunt me, basically getting right into my face and letting me know that he sees me. It's yet another reason to believe that I'm dealing with a special kind of monster that I've never faced before. He's made his crimes into a game of sorts and wants me to play along.

As I make my way into the front entryway, the light reflects off a series of small puddles near the front door, causing me to freeze in my tracks as my heart drops into my stomach. I raise my gun and swallow back a cold rush of terror. The misshapen patches of water lead from the front door and into my room, which is directly off the wide hallway.

I know beyond a shadow of a doubt that I locked the front door when I arrived back here from the salt mine. After all, I'm out here by myself, several miles outside of a small town where a killer is prowling. I distinctly remember coming in and locking the door.

He could be anywhere in the cabin. All he had to do was remove his raincoat and boots and he would leave no trace of his whereabouts. My heart is pounding in my ears, and by sheer force of will, I propel myself into action. Moving quickly, I swipe off the phone's light and move to the side of the hallway, setting my back firmly against the wood paneling. Unless the unsub is using some form of night vision, then he's at the same disadvantage as I am in terms of seeing anything at all; I can't even see the end of my nose.

Silently slipping my phone into a pocket, I clutch my sidearm in a two-handed hold while listening intently for any sound passing for something other than the patter of rain or gusting wind: a creak of a floorboard, the rustle of clothing, a whisper of breath.

I swallow hard on a parched throat, expecting at any moment for a hand to shoot through the darkness and grab me.

And then the unexpected happens. The room is suddenly filled with light, causing me to flinch as my eyes start to adjust. From across the house, I hear the refrigerator hum and the microwave clock beep as it comes back to life. The power is back on.

After waiting for my eyes to fully adjust, I step away from the wall and move toward the doorway of my bedroom near the front door, all the while maintaining a high level of alertness around me. With my gun at the ready, I slip around the threshold and quickly take in the room. No one here. Only the wet outline of footprints that stop beside my bed. That's it. I quickly check the bathroom and the closet, then drop to my knees and look under the bed, which only contains several dust bunnies and a forgotten sock.

I rise to my feet and face the door as I study the wet tracks. It's as if he came and stood by my bed and then vanished from the spot. No footprints or water are tracing a way out of the room. The pattern makes no sense whatsoever. My eyes scan the room a final time, and I check to make sure the window is locked before my eyes fall on a folded piece of paper lying on my pillow.

Allowing duty to command my curiosity, I leave the paper there and begin a thorough sweep of the house, carefully checking each and every room. I locate the attic access in the garage and find it locked from the outside with a heavy padlock, so I know he can't be hiding up there. And the front door is locked too—both the handle and the deadbolt—exactly as I had left it.

After checking all the windows, I am completely mystified. He clearly entered through the locked front door, came and stood by my bed, and seemingly vanished from the spot.

The storm is starting to abate now. The wind has died down a little and the rain, while still coming down hard, is not as violent and fearsome as it was earlier. The branches have stopped scratching on the side of the house. But that offers no relief now that I know my unsub was standing right here in the house just minutes ago.

On one hand, I'm furious at myself for taking his bait and running recklessly into the darkness after him. On the other hand, I can't believe he came into this house and then snuck away. In doing so, he's confirmed the psychological profile that I offered to Bancroft. The unsub wants me to know that he's in control, that he can get as close as he desires and still get away scot-free. He wants me to know he is the one calling the shots.

In some way, I have to admit that he's right, and that causes intense and unexpected feelings of inadequacy to rise up inside me. What if I am unable to track him down? What if he proves too elusive for me? Then Bancroft will have asked for my agency's help for nothing. I'll have let everyone down: Bancroft's department, this entire town, and the families of the victims, to say nothing of the victims themselves.

Because I've always been extremely confident in my abilities as an FBI agent, this newfound distrust in myself is a completely foreign feeling. There have been plenty of cases over the last few years that had me pulling my hair out and burning the midnight oil trying to get them solved. But other than the Coldwater case, they never made me doubt myself, never caused me to wonder if I was skilled enough to actually bring them to a successful conclusion.

Don't get me wrong, my personal open-unsolved rate is well below the Bureau's national average of 63%, but it's not perfect. There are still unsolved case files that haunt me to this day, their very presence mocking my commitment to finding answers at any cost.

The symbols are a start in the right direction, but they will only get me so far. Since the unsub is the one dangling them in front of me, I can only take them with a grain of salt. They might help me understand why he does what he does, but I don't expect them to serve me very well when it comes to actually finding him. The runes aren't going to spell out his home address so I can just walk up his front steps and arrest him.

This entire case is starting to feel like all the answers I need are lying deep beneath a glacier, and the only tool I have to work with is a blowtorch. With Darren, I took the bait and wasted an entire day focusing on him. And now, even though the monster I am looking for was standing right here only five minutes ago, I still have no way to truly pursue him.

The sensation of being completely behind the eight ball is starting to wear on me. But I know that if I capitulate to how I feel, then I'm just playing into his hand, doing exactly what he wants me to do. I think about calling Skylar and taking her up on her offer to help. I decide against it though. I don't have the time to get her up to speed. All my energy needs to be focused elsewhere.

As the initial surge of adrenaline starts to wear off, a chill crawls down my spine as it dawns on me that my rashness put me in a position where the unsub could have easily killed me if he had wanted to. Had I stayed inside, then I would have heard him come in through the front door. Unless it was a disguise to throw me off, his beard puts him over fifty years old, and maybe over sixty. Even though the lightning allowed me a brief look at him, he was still half-cloaked in shadow. Because of the hood slung over his head, it's not easy to nail down how tall he might be, but a rough guess would put him at five-nine or five-ten. He appeared well-set, with broad shoulders framing out a moderately stocky build. I'll make note of that in the file I'm creating, but the description is too generic to help; there are probably half a million men in this state that fit a vague description like that.

I decide not to call Bancroft about the intruder. It's over now, and there won't be anything he can do about it. If this storm has another band coming our way, then I don't want him getting caught up in it.

Returning to the kitchen, I open a drawer and take out a pair of metal salad tongs, then select a fork from the drawer beside it before making my way to the bedroom. Whenever I travel for work, I always bring my designated work backpack with me. Not only do I keep my laptop in it, but essentials like a couple of changes of field clothes, basic surveillance equipment, evidence bags, and a box of nitrile gloves. Since Kemper handed me this assignment while I was on vacation, I wasn't able to bring the bag with me. That means that I don't have the gloves that would come in handy right now.

I know agents who follow their training advice and keep a go-bag in their cars. That way, when they're unexpectedly called into the field, they don't find themselves in the position that I'm currently in. It looks like the better part of prudence would be keeping my bag in the trunk of my car, too.

The tiny puddles of water have almost completely evaporated off the floor when I re-enter the bedroom. Approaching the bed, I grab the cream-colored paper with the tongs, remove it off the pillow, and lay it on the bedspread in front of me. Using the fork, I push back a side so that it lays flat. My heart is racing, my hands cold with sweat, as the paper folds away and its contents are revealed to me.

It's another rune. This time a vertical line with two right-facing barbs on either end, making me think of a bent or broken staple.

My laptop is still on the kitchen table, but surprisingly, I have no desire to look up its meaning. For one reason: I know he wants my curiosity to control me. But if I do that, he is still in the driver's seat, a place I have no interest for him to remain. If he is still in the woods, watching to see what I will do, then running down the hall to grab my computer will be exactly what he wants.

Instead, with the note still clamped in the mouth of the salad tongs, I take it back to the kitchen, place it in a zippered freezer bag, and then set it on the table along with all my papers. What-ever it means, my analysis can wait until morning.

For now, though, I'm exhausted, the events of the last half hour having wreaked havoc on my energy levels. I return to the bedroom and lock the door, then slip out of my clothes and get into the shower, letting the warm water wash away the tension residing deep in my muscles. I close my eyes and stand directly beneath the flow of water, relishing the sensation as my mind tries to make sense of what happened here tonight.

By the time the bathroom is all fogged up and the hot water is running out, I've decided that I won't allow him to get inside my head. I won't give him the satisfaction. That's the least I can take from him. He wants me to think that he is some special kind of monster, and use that image to intimidate me into fear. But the truth is that he is just a man, a man with a warped sense of reality, who grabs and murders young women for pleasure. The way he displays the bodies and uses the symbols, along with the way he entered and left the chalet tonight, adds a certain level of mystique to the case. And yet he puts his pants on one leg at a time, same as I do. He has to eat and drink the same as I do. Even though he vanished from my bedroom without leaving any discernible trace, at the end of the day, he is just a man. If I don't keep that front and center in my thinking, then I'll elevate him to a status that will blur how I see things. And that is precisely what he wants.

The shower knobs squeak as I turn them off. After toweling dry, I open the bathroom door and step into the bedroom, relishing the cooler air on my skin as it whisks the heat away from my body. After getting dressed for bed, I brush my teeth and slide under the sheets, deciding not to return to the kitchen table. It's been a long few days, and there really is nothing else to do tonight. A good night's rest will prime me to keep my mind in high gear tomorrow, to continue to explore the threads that asserted themselves today.

As I lie in the dark and my eyes stare blankly at the ceiling, there is still one thing that keeps me from drifting off. I can't make sense of Bancroft's reaction when I told him about the rune. It was as if he mentally hung up the phone and chased his thoughts elsewhere. If mentioning the rune made him think of something that connects to this case, then why wouldn't he say something? Why just brush my inquiry off and act as if everything was normal?

Tomorrow will come soon enough, and hopefully, answers to all the questions rolling around in my head.

Chapter Thirty-Two

Bancroft Vacation Chalet
Miller's Grove, NY

I never dream. Well, that's not exactly true. Psychologists are quick to inform us that everyone dreams, three to six times every night in fact, and only during the REM stage of sleep. It's really just a matter of whether we remember them.

So I suppose that I do dream, but it's rare that I can actually recall one after I wake up. When I was younger, I had a recurring nightmare of Lila being snatched off a swing at the playground. My feet were buried deep in the sand, and I couldn't move them. I would scream and struggle and plead for the man to bring her back, but all in vain. Every time I would wake up in a cold sweat with my worried mother kneeling beside my bed and stroking the hair back from my forehead. When I was awake enough to realize that I had been dreaming, I would burst into tears, knowing that a much worse version had already happened in real life. But as the years ticked by and my waking hours found me focused on moving on with my life, the nightmare faded until it finally vanished altogether.

Now, even though I am fast asleep, I feel as if I'm swimming, drifting in the murky waters of some deep and dark body of water. My limbs feel weightless, and my hair fans out across my face as a sound from far away reaches my ears. It's rhythmic and hollow, drifting through the water but sounding as if it didn't originate there. When I hear it again, I can feel my body start to rise up from the murky depths and move toward the glistening surface of the water just above. The thumping sound grows louder the closer I get to the surface, and it's not until I break through it that I realize my lungs have been starved for oxygen. My mouth opens wide as my lungs suck in hungry gasps of air.

It is only when my eyes flick open that I realize I have been asleep. I'm sitting up in bed, my palms braced against the mattress, with my chest still hungrily heaving for oxygen. The knocking sounds persist, however, and are no longer muffled like they were when I was under the water. The sound seems to have followed me out of my dream. Then I realize that I am looking at things the wrong way. The knocking sound did not follow me out of my dream, but entered into it. Someone is knocking at the front door.

Throwing back the sheets, I swing my legs off the bed and place my feet on the floor. I squint at the lambent tendrils of light escaping the edges of the curtain. A glance at the digital clock beside the bed tells me that it's almost eight o'clock in the morning, and that unexpected knowledge jolts me awake. I had planned on getting up at six-thirty. Have I really overslept the alarm by that much? From the front porch, I hear someone call my name before knocking loudly again.

"Okay, okay," I mutter as I stand up. "I'm coming." Unlocking the bedroom door, I step into the entryway and look through the front door's peephole. My tired eye tries to make sense of what it's seeing. Once it focuses on the person standing on the porch, I unlock the door and swing it open, squinting against the bright onslaught of the sunrise.

"You had me worried there for a minute," Bancroft says. After he takes a long look at me, I think I see a smile tug at his lips. "Not to be rude or anything, but you look like you had a fight with a big bottle of Benadryl, and lost."

I take a step back. "Come on in."

"Party a little too hard last night?" he asks as he steps inside.

I shake my head. "No. I don't typically drink while I'm working in the field." As I shut the door behind him, I can feel my cheeks flush with embarrassment. I never sleep in like this. Especially when there is so much urgent work to be done.

"Here," he says, nodding toward a white box in his hand, "I got us some donuts. Figured you probably weren't much of a junk food kind of person, but I brought them anyway. I'll meet you in the kitchen with these. If you... uh..." Words fail him as he looks at me in the cotton shorts and spaghetti strap tank top that serve as my pajamas.

I struggle to suppress a grin as I turn on my heels and say over my shoulder, "Be right back."

I can hear the relief in his voice as he speaks his next words. "Good deal."

FIVE MINUTES LATER, I step into the hallway dressed and groomed. After leaning over the bathroom sink and splashing some cold water onto my face, I feel alert, although the lingering effects of the dream still cling to my mind.

I find Bancroft standing beside the table eating a chocolate glazed donut from one hand while observing the note I placed inside the plastic zipper bag in the other. "What's this?" he asks around a mouthful.

"Long story," I mutter, and then notice that he was kind enough to get a pot of coffee going. I pull two mugs from the cabinet and place them beside the pot. It's not finished brewing, so I turn around and lean against the counter. "I'm sorry for sleeping in," I tell him. "That's not like me at all."

He waves me off. "You don't owe me an explanation, Darcy. Cases like this can wear on us in ways we can't see. At least, that's what my wife has always told me. And I think she's on to something."

Without even giving enough time for the devil and angel on my shoulders to start debating about whether I should have a donut, I move to the table and pick through the remaining five that are there. My hand comes away with a Boston cream, and I pop the edge into my mouth and bite down. The taste of the fried dough, along with the chocolate icing and the soft cream, causes me to moan out loud. I would normally avoid these like the plague, but the chief's wife is right: this case is wearing on me. A little comfort food couldn't hurt at a time like this.

The coffee pot gurgles behind me, letting me know that the coffee is finished brewing. Going back to it, I grab a mug and fill it. "I think I drank all the half-and-half," I tell the chief. "I hope that's okay."

"Black is fine." A chair scrapes across the floor, and he takes a seat at the table.

After filling both mugs, I set them on the table and take a seat. I don't talk while I finish my donut and sip my coffee, and Bancroft doesn't cut into the silence, although I can easily tell that something is weighing heavily on his mind. After plucking a napkin from the box, I wipe my mouth and take another sip of coffee before giving him my full attention. "I take it that everyone made it through the storm safe and sound?"

"For the most part, yes. A few folks had some downed trees and broken windows. Ernest Kent had a heart attack when the thunder erupted right over his house. Unfortunately, EMS wasn't able to respond in time. But he lived a good, long life. It's going to be hard on Jean though. And cell towers all over the region are out, but I'm expecting them to be back up later this morning." He looks around the inside of his chalet and cuts his eyes out the windows. "Looks like everything out here fared all right."

"Except for the power outage, the storm doesn't seem to have affected anything," I tell him.

His brows lower as he frowns. "The power went out? For how long?"

"Maybe ten minutes? Why? Didn't parts of town lose power, too?"

He shakes his head. "No. No outage reports. All the lines and transformers held steady."

That makes a slight chill run down my spine.

"You said they went out for ten minutes?" he asks.

"Roughly. Yes."

"Hmm, I'll take a look at the breaker box before I leave."

I understand now just why the power went off. It wasn't the lightning or the wind that did it; it was the man standing in the storm. By shutting off the power, he ensured that I would look outside and see him there. I'll tell Bancroft the details of last night, but first I want to hear what has him so thoughtful.

I take another sip of my coffee. Thankfully, the caffeine has started to clear away the cobwebs strung between my thoughts. "Chief, you got off the phone with me pretty quickly last night after I mentioned the valknut and the symbol on Lily's back. What's on your mind?"

He offers a tight, pensive smile and rubs a thumb down the handle of his coffee cup. "Nothing gets past you, Darcy." He sighs and slowly rubs his chin. His next sentence is completely unexpected and feels like a right hook across my cheek. "What all do you know about your kidnapping case here in Miller's Grove all those years ago?"

I blanch and feel a cold sensation track down the back of my neck. "Why? What do you mean?"

"Well, you're FBI, so I'm sure you've spent plenty of personal time looking into the details of your kidnapping and your sister's death."

The donut suddenly feels sour in my stomach. "I haven't—not really. But what does any of that have to do with our case?"

"I don't know. That's why I brought it up. When you mentioned the rune last night, it took me back to what happened at the Chancellery all those years ago.

"Chief, what are you talking about?" I bristle.

"You really aren't familiar with the details?" His question borders on accusation, though I know he doesn't mean it that way.

"No, Chief. I was ten years old when it happened. Like I told you before, it drove my father to suicide. My mother drew back from life and isolated herself. My teen years were filled with therapy and then more therapy. By the time I was old enough to look into everything, I didn't want to. Not even after I joined the Bureau. It wasn't going to bring my sister or my father back from the dead. It wouldn't restore everything I had lost."

"I understand," he nods. "Then you need to know that with your and your sister's kidnappings at the Chancellery, there were runes involved as well."

His last sentence is so unexpected that I just stare at him, unblinking. "You're saying that what is happening in Miller's Grove right now is connected to my kidnapping almost twenty years ago?"

"No," he says quickly. "I'm not saying that. Just that there are certain similarities."

"What kind of similarities?" I ask, my tone almost demanding.

"Way back then, the detectives found runes etched into some of the stones that made up the Chancellery castle. You might know that when the authorities responded to the fire, it had already consumed most everything. Your sister's remains were identified by the Miller's Grove medical examiner at the time. But it wasn't easy. He didn't have a lot to work with. Just a part of her jawbone, I believe."

"Yes," I nod. "I do know that."

"So one of the few things the detectives had to work with were the runes," Bancroft says. "There just wasn't much left. Any fingerprints or DNA were wiped out by the fire."

"How do you know all this?" I ask him. "Weren't you still with the NYPD when it happened?"

"I was. But when I became chief seven years ago, I pulled out the files so I could have a better understanding."

"You looked at the case yourself?"

"Yes," he nods. "Glanced through the files anyway. It was the biggest thing to ever hit this town. Since I was going to be the chief of police, I wanted to make sure I had a working knowledge of the details."

"So how do you think it all ties into what we're dealing with right now?" I ask. "Everyone who was involved with our kidnapping and Lila's murder died nearly a decade ago."

His face shows genuine surprise. "So you heard about that?"

"Of course. I never would have stayed away from the case had I thought the monsters were still out there somewhere. If I thought for a second that my sister's killers weren't dead or in jail, I would have given everything I had to find them. FBI career or no FBI career. But once I heard that they were all dead, I was able to start my process of moving on. Nothing was going to bring Lila back. I know other agents who entered the FBI because they wanted to help families get the kind of answers that they never did. But that wasn't me. And maybe it means that I don't care as much. But staying chained to the darkness of my past would only serve to cripple my future."

My answer causes a small smile to form across his lips. "Glad to hear that," he says as he pushes back in his chair and stands up. "Follow me outside for a second. I could use some help bringing in a few things."

The sun has nearly burned all the dew off the grass as we trek down the front steps and into the driveway. The air holds that cool, crisp sensation that comes the morning after a storm. Birds chirp happily deep in the woods and a couple of squirrels chase each other across the yard. I follow the chief to the rear of his cruiser, and when he pops the trunk lid, I look down to see three banker boxes huddled together.

"What are these?" I ask.

He eyes me as if looking to gauge my reaction. "These are the files from the Chancellery case."

My throat suddenly runs dry as it dawns on me that I'm going to have to plumb the horrors of my own past to try to solve my current case. I close my eyes and take in a slow, steady breath.

Somewhere in the distance, I hear Bancroft's voice. "Are you up for it?" he is asking. "I know this is a surprise. If it's too painful, or if you—"

"No," I interrupt, my eyes flicking open. "I'll be fine. If you think there is something in these boxes that can help us solve this, then I'll go through them."

"I'm sorry it had to be you, Darcy, but I do think it might be worth looking at them." He reaches down and grabs a box, then asks me to place one of the other, lighter boxes on top of it. As he steadily makes his way back to the front door, I grab the last one and balance it on my leg as I shut the trunk.

A minute later, we have all three boxes on the table. I feel some kind of cognitive dissonance as I read "Chancellery" on the side of two boxes, scrawled in black permanent marker that has started to fade with age. "Give me a minute," I say.

"Sure thing. I'll be right here."

With my mind spinning, I open the back door and step onto the deck. Crossing it, I take the steps down to the grass and walk over toward the trail that leads back into the woods. As if my mind is trying to prepare for what might be in those old case files, images start to swirl around me, images that I haven't seen in so very long: Lila and I playing on the swingset in our back yard; her kindergarten play, where she acted out the part of Tinkerbell; walking up the hill with our bikes and getting caught in the snowstorm; her being ripped from my arms just before she was murdered.

"All in the proper order."

My head whips around toward the sound of the voice, my hair flinging out around me. The deep, gravelly voice was clear as day, originating from right behind me, right here on the trail's entrance. But no one is here. There wouldn't have been enough time for someone to speak so close to me and then vanish.

"Get a grip, Darcy," I mutter, feeling a little foolish.

I know why I heard it. My mind is drawing nearly two decades of suppressed memories to the surface, things that I have not thought of in a very, very long time. A bench sits a few yards from me, nestled into the treeline and hedged with a bed of red perennials. I go to it and sit down as tears start to flow freely down my cheeks.

That voice, it was the same one that Lila and I had heard that night in the snowstorm, that of the man who led us to his truck and then kidnapped us. And it belonged to the cloaked man who ripped Lila from my arms that cold night when we huddled together on the cold stone floor. Over the years, everything had started to blur together for me, to get fuzzy around the edges so that the details became muddled.

But now the precise words run through my head as clear as a bell. *All in the proper order.* What did that mean? What order? Did they take Lila first because they were operating under a precise code, and taking me before her would have disrupted that? I won't know until I start digging through the boxes Bancroft brought over. But then, maybe I'll never know.

Brushing the tears off my face, I stand up and return to the chalet. Bancroft is in the living room, staring regretfully at a picture of his family. When he hears the door shut, he turns from the picture and approaches the table.

"Darcy, I'm sorry," he says. "I'm serious. If we need to figure out another way to go about this, then I'm happy to try."

"No. I need to do this. I just had to get through the shock of it all. I really did not expect that I would have to sift through my old case files again."

"And you don't think it will be a conflict of interest? I mean, emotionally, anyway?"

"It probably is," I admit, and offer him a weak smile. "But I'm good at compartmentalizing. I'm not about to let my personal feelings get in the way."

"All right," he nods and pulls out a chair. "Where should we start?"

Chapter Thirty-Three

Unspecified Location

The room smelled musty. It was thick with smells of damp and well-nourished earth.

She slowly opened her eyes and blinked, but could see nothing at all. Only darkness. She lay perfectly still as her mind took a few minutes to catch up and recall her most recent memories. As the images slowly materialized, a cold jolt of fear coursed through her body. She had been running on the nature trail. She found a phone. A man on the path had said it was his. And then... then what?

Shelby Campbell sat up. Far away, a narrow shaft of light cut mercifully into the darkness. While it did nothing to illuminate her immediate surroundings, it did serve to orient her a little.

Her left wrist was throbbing, aching something fierce. She couldn't move her jaw; it was fixed in place. And something was stuffed in her mouth. Another streak of panic ran through her as she realized that she was wearing a ball gag. The leather straps cut hard into her cheeks and fastened behind her head. She lifted her right hand to reach behind her head but was stopped short by a sharp tug inside her wrist, followed by a shock of searing pain running through it and up into her forearm. She screamed painfully against the ball stuffed in her mouth as she tried to suck in enough air through her nose to keep from passing out.

Once the pain started to diminish, she used her free hand to feel along her wounded wrist. Horror descended on her as her fingers found a braided wire that went down into her wrist, past her tendons and bone, through the muscles, and threaded out to the other side.

Her left hand flew to her mouth as tears stung her eyes. "Oh, my god," she thought, and struggled not to pass out. Frantically, she reached back with her left hand and felt along the clasp of the ball gag. The straps were hooked hard around the bottom of her jaw, making it impossible to loosen them. At the very back, a tiny lock held the clasp firmly in place.

Later—she had no idea how long—she heard a muted clang, and the narrow shaft of light grew into a burst of sunlight as a door was opened and then shut again. Her abductor coughed. His footsteps padded toward her and stopped several feet away. All she could hear was him breathing heavily from his nose. She remembered now what he looked like when she met him on the trail. Try as she may, Shelby couldn't even make out the outline of his physical frame.

"I will take that contraption off your face if you promise not to scream," he finally said, his voice smooth and reassuring. Shelby tried to speak through the ball, but it only caused her to gag and her throat to spasm reflexively. Her captor chuckled and stepped toward her. "I'll take that as a yes." Leaning close to her, he bedded his nose into her hair and drew in a deep breath, taking in her scent. "Ah, feminine beauty and fear. My two favorite smells in the world. If only they could find a way to bottle it. I'd buy up everything they had."

Shelby shuddered with repulsion as the lock gave way with a small click and her captor slid it out of the hasp. With a few more maneuvers, the leather straps released their tight hold on her jaw. Reaching up with her free hand, she grabbed the gag and yanked it from her mouth, slinging it wildly into the darkness and sucking in deep lungfuls of welcome air.

"Did you kill those other two girls in town?" she finally managed to ask.

"Do you really want to know the answer to that?"

She decided that she couldn't bear to hear him say that he had.

"Why? Why me?"

"That... is complicated. And I don't have time for such a drawn out explanation. However, you are needed. The time has come."

"The time?" she shrieked. "What time?"

"The fullness of time. The calendar pages, they have all been flipped."

"*Please*. Let me go. I just—just want to go home."

"Your home is here now. This is where you belong. Until the moment is right."

"Oh god," she choked. "But I didn't do anything to you. Please, I promise not—"

"You promise not to tell," he broke in. "Yes. I've heard it all before. All of you are so predictable." His voice grew firmer and irritated. "And that makes it all quite boring. It used to be fun and invigorating. But every one of you is the same, making promises we know you never intend to keep."

In the inky darkness, Shelby started to sob.

"Yes... cry." He uttered a dry, guttural laugh. "It will all be over soon."

With that, he padded across the dirt floor and made his way back to the door. A brilliance of daylight temporarily blinded her as the door was flung open. As soon as it slammed shut, Shelby fell back onto the vinyl mat that served as a mattress, her body shaking as she wept uncontrollable sobs of grief.

Chapter Thirty-Four

Bancroft Vacation Chalet
Miller's Grove, NY

I sit at the table, staring at the stacks of paperwork spread out before me. Right now, I have to force the professional in me to preside over the personal. In a more ideal scenario, I would have had time to prepare myself for digging through everything. The information in all these files represents nothing but pain to me. My life was forever altered by what happened here in Miller's Grove. It was hard enough getting the call to come out here to help the chief. But now, having to go back and excavate information from the files of my own case... It is more than a little unnerving.

Bancroft seems to pick up on the storm brewing inside me. "We just need something that might help us find a connection into the killer's mind, Darcy. Once we have that, we can get all this back into the storage locker. And hopefully leave it there for good this time."

I nod. "I know. But since our unsub is a copycat, he'll put his own spin on things. The ancient symbols meant one thing to The Four. But they could mean something else to our guy."

"And speaking of The Four." Bancroft grabs a thick file from one of the boxes and places it on the table in front of me. "Here is most everything we have on them."

I flip the cover back and examine the paperwork. Buried inside are four 8 ½ x 11 photos. I unconsciously hold my breath as I study them. It's been nearly ten years since I've seen these, and it's no less easy right now than it was back then.

Nine years ago, exactly nine years after my sister's murder, four men from the surrounding area committed collective suicide by ingesting suicide capsules. They were all dressed in oversized cult robes and laid down around a large bonfire after swallowing the capsules. Their bodies were found two days later by an unlucky hiker.

I was a senior in high school at the time and arrived home after classes one afternoon to change out for soccer practice. My mother was on the couch in the parlor—a room she didn't frequent often—and asked me to come sit beside her. Her eyes were damp, and her hand tightly clutched a tissue. She told me about the suicides and said that we had to go downtown to the Albany police station; they had copies of the photos of the men. Since I was the only one still alive who had had any contact with someone from the Chancellery, the authorities needed me to try to identify which of the men had kidnapped me.

But I had been unable to identify anyone. When the man appeared in the snowstorm and offered us a ride in his truck, it was too dark. And the night that Lila was killed, I hadn't been able to make out his features, either. I had only heard his voice.

294

Strangely enough, no recordings of their voices were ever recovered.

I struggle to keep my emotions intact as I study their faces once again. Gary Shaw: bulging hazel eyes and a high, sloping forehead; Hugh Parkman: tawny skin and broad cheekbones; James Glanz: pockmarked skin and a buzz cut head; Elijah Burch: a bushy brown beard and thoughtful, piercing eyes. The media, always in search of a juicy true crime story, had dubbed them The Four.

What really shook the community was that each of these men lived among them and were not only well known, but liked as well. Shaw was a longtime clerk at the post office; Parkman and Glanz worked for the utility company in Pine Bluff; for over two decades, Burch had owned a popular barbershop here in Miller's Grove. All of them were lifelong bachelors.

One of these men kidnapped me and tore my sister from my arms. But I'll never have the satisfaction of knowing which one.

"How do we know their deaths weren't forced or coerced?" I ask Bancroft.

"Here, let me see that." He's looking toward the file, so I push it over to him. After rummaging through it, he comes out with a wrinkled piece of paper that is smudged and dirty. "This was left under a rock several feet from the fire's ashes." He hands me the letter, and I read it out loud:

We have fulfilled our duty. Faithfulness has been our mission. Now the time has come for us to be free. We have been chosen to escape the day of doom which is coming for all. Our faithfulness

has granted us entrance into the halls of the here-
after. We lie now in peace and give thanks for the
lives we took in order to secure us our place in
the Great Hall. Glory to the eternal gods, to
whom we now offer ourselves and journey now to
meet.

I read the note again, silently this time, focusing on each and every word, as well as the single, ancient symbol drawn below the words. "Whose handwriting is this?" I ask.

"Elijah Burch wrote it. His fingerprints were found on it."

"I wonder why there are no names on this," I say out loud. "Why wasn't it signed?" The note does not appear to have been written hastily or to have been created under duress.

"I don't know the answer to that, but forensic handwriting analysis matched it to extant papers with Burch's handwriting on it." He frowns and then says, "The events of the Chancellery were around this time of year."

"Yes," I nod. "The anniversary is in three days, in fact."

"Could that be a coincidence?"

"At this point, I'm not sure. The murders at the Chancellery occurred over two nights. The deaths of The Four in one single night. The murders we're dealing with now have been strung out over a few days."

"So if we're dealing with a copycat, then he could be taking what they did and putting his own spin on it."

"Exactly," I agree. "If that is what we're dealing with, then it could be a form of syncretism."

"Syncretism?"

"Yes. Think of a mixing bowl. You pour in whatever religions you want, stir, and bake for a few years. When it's all said and done, you have your own religion. The ancient aspects might be what gives him his sense of authority and purpose. The rest of it is his own concoction."

"And yet with The Four, all the men were somehow on the same page with it," Bancroft says. "So much so that they were willing to kill others and finally kill themselves for it."

"One of them would have had the dominant personality," I say. "And my guess would be Burch, being that he wrote the letter. What did a search of their homes turn up?"

Bancroft fingers the paperwork in front of him again and slips out more pictures. "Here. There are a lot more of these, but this will give you a general idea. Each of the men had a dedicated bedroom like this in his house. All four men were lifetime bachelors—none of them ever married. I guess these were sanctums of some kind."

The pictures he lays in front of me make my bones shiver. In each room, the walls are painted black, and various sized runes, crosses, and valknuts are painted across them in crimson. Black and red candles stand on large silver candelabras. In the center of the room is a three-tiered shrine for burning incense.

"And no one ever knew or suspected them?" I ask the chief.

He shakes his head. "They were experts at compartmentalization. It's one of the reasons their suicides hit the town so hard. Not one person around here suspected that something was wrong with them. Parkman and Glantz met at Maybelle's every Thursday morning and had breakfast with a large group of men. By every account, they were perfectly normal."

I shake my head and run my fingers through my hair. "I had

no idea. My mother tried to revisit it with me just before I joined the FBI, just before she died of cancer. But I still didn't want to hear about it."

It really is a lot to take in. I know my sister's killer is dead, but sitting here looking at all this makes my skin crawl and opens up a barrage of fresh questions that I know I'll never get answers to. Of course, this really isn't about me or Lila anymore. It's about a new sequence of murders possibly inspired by those almost two decades ago.

"Who had access to these files?" I ask. "In order for our copycat to do what he's doing, he must have some kind of direct knowledge of The Four."

Bancroft shrugs. "The details of The Four's case were sealed by a judge. The media only got enough details to label the case what they did and then infer as many details as they could. But in the hands of the media, the case became more fantasy than fact. I think that's the only reason it isn't a top story in the true crime archives. It's so unique that the public would have just eaten it up. But these files aren't for public consumption."

"Why did the judge seal it?"

"You have to remember that this was around the time of the Whiskey Run murders." His brows knit together. "You familiar with that one?"

"Of course. It was on every front page in the country. People's mouths were sewn shut while they were still alive, then they were tortured until they screamed so hard their lips tore."

He nods. "You might also remember that three months later, the killer was apprehended, but then the killings started again. In two different regions of the country no less. It inspired at least two copycats. Because The Four had so many unique elements and the case quickly gained so much national attention, the interim chief didn't want someone trying to copy it. So he got a judge to put it under seal."

"I suppose a decade wasn't long enough to keep someone from being inspired by both The Four and the Chancellery," I say, looking down at all the paperwork spread across the table. "If that is what is happening, then I'll need to pinpoint some kind of connection to what is happening now. If I can find some clue in all of this as to what our current unsub might be thinking, then we might stand a chance of getting a step ahead of him. Assuming, that is, he isn't done."

The chief's phone rings loudly in his pocket. He draws it out and answers. "This is Bancroft." As he listens to the person on the other end, his face darkens and he quickly rises to his feet. "I'll be there in ten minutes. And, Dobbs. Keep a tight lid on this. This town is on edge enough as it is." He hangs up and gives me a weary, pointed look. "Another girl has been reported missing."

I utter a deep groan as I stand up. "Who?"

"Shelby Campbell. Her roommate called up to the station and said she didn't come home last night. Her car was found at the entrance to the Wild Spruce Nature Trail where her roommate said she likes to run." His keys jingle as he takes them out of his pocket.

"Should I come with you?"

"No, stay here. Me and my officers can handle this. I need you to find a pattern, Darcy. Figure out what we're supposed to be seeing that we're blind to right now. That's something I can't do."

"Okay," I tell him. "I will. Let me know if you find anything I need to be aware of."

He stares out the window behind me as he processes the phone call. When he speaks again, his voice is laden with worry. He clearly feels a tremendous weight of responsibility for each and every soul in his town. "I need us to get this guy, Darcy. We have to stop him."

"We will, Chief. We will."

After he leaves, I sit back down and return to the stacks of information in front of me. I know now that in order to go forward, I have to go back. But I still can't shake the feeling that I'm looking at exactly what the unsub wants me to be looking at. The clues that he has dangled in front of me have led me back to files of the Chancellery and The Four.

I can't help but wonder if I'll find the answers I need in time to save Shelby Campbell. It will take every ounce of focus I can muster to not only see what the killer wants me to see, but to then get one step ahead of him.

It's difficult to believe that just a few days ago I was on vacation with my best friend, and now I am facing the most complicated and personal case of my entire career. Actual lives are at stake, and I can't help but feel a sense of overwhelming responsibility to get this one right. I don't know Shelby Campbell. But I do know one thing: I need to get her home safe and sound.

Chapter Thirty-Five

Cascade County
Miller's Grove, NY

The midday air is crisp and refreshing as I slowly wander down the narrow trail behind the chalet. The maples and oaks have shed most of their leaves, and firs stand tall and green. Up ahead, the bushes rustle and a raccoon scampers into view several yards in front of me. He stops in the middle of the path, rises onto his hind legs, and sniffs the air, then turns his face in my direction. After eyeing me for several moments, he scurries back into the woods.

After three hours of meticulously combing through faded and yellowing paperwork, I needed to take a mental break. My thoughts are a web of interconnected details from both cases. If I'm going to make sense of it all, I'll need to step back far enough to see subtle patterns and associations in the data. Right now, my mind and eyes are weary. If I'm going to continue to assimilate the data at such a rapid pace, then taking a short break from time to time will be critical. I stuff my hands into the pockets of my jacket and take in a deep breath as I continue to negotiate the twists and turns of the trail, soggy leaves still wet from the storm squishing beneath my feet.

After I've gone close to a mile, I hear a hollow, rhythmic sound through the trees. It's loud and thumping, coming every ten seconds or so. The farther I go, the louder it gets until it's just on the other side of a stand of laurel. The trail finally ends on a large, open clearing, where a small cabin sits. A thin trail of smoke drifts upward from the stone chimney.

Tim stands beside a large pile of sectioned logs, splitting them on a tree stump one at a time. He's wearing a green and gray checkered flannel shirt, along with dark blue jeans pulled down over a pair of cowboy boots. I watch as he splits a log and sets another one in its place.

Thump. The log splits and falls away.

I start toward him and clear my throat so as not to startle him. He turns, and as his hazel eyes meet mine, they gleam with recognition. His blond locks are dark with sweat and finger-combed away from his face. A smile breaks out across his face.

"Darcy, what brings you out here?"

"I don't know," I shrug. "I guess I just needed a break."

"I'll bet. You've been working non-stop since you got to Miller's Grove. Do you want some coffee or something? I can make a pot."

"No. Thanks," I smile. "I should be getting back soon. How did you fare through the storm last night?"

"Just fine. The place doesn't have electricity. Just a fireplace and an old fashioned water pump."

"Seriously? You haven't brought it out of the stone age yet?"

"No," he chuckles. "But when a big storm like we had last night comes through, I don't have to worry about things I rely on going out of commission. I like it. It's quiet. Simple. I go into town a couple times a week to check email and voicemails. Don't even get cell service out here. Dad's chalet is right at the limit of the closest cell tower range."

"You know," I tease out, "Your dad was just at the chalet with me, working on the case."

A smile tugs at the edges of his mouth as he shakes his head. "I see what you're doing there, Darcy."

I feign innocence and hold back a grin that is trying to break out. "What do you mean?"

"You want me to talk with him."

"Could it hurt?" I ask gently. "I saw him looking at your family pictures. You couldn't miss the pain in his eyes."

Tim heaves the ax handle across his shoulders and fixes his attention down toward his feet. He shuffles them uncomfortably. "Dad has got to be willing to let some things go," Tim says. "And as best as I can tell, he isn't there yet. I hope he will be soon. I do miss him." Facing the stump, he gets a sturdy grip on the ax handle and swings the iron head down, cleanly splitting the log. The pieces fall away from each other and tumble off the stump onto the ground.

There is something wildly attractive about a man who likes to hunt and split his own wood. The fact that he lives in a cabin without electricity doesn't hurt either. Tim is obviously adept and skilled in so many areas, which only serves to raise the needle on my attraction meter.

Bringing up his father has clearly made Tim uncomfortable,

so I move to change the topic. "Do you ever make it out to Albany?"

"No. Not in a long time. But I probably could if I had the right reason to." He sets the ax down and leans the handle against the stump, then walks over and stands right in front of me. Scents of musky sweat and wood smoke drift off of him. He leans in and before I know what is happening, his lips are on mine, soft and warm. He lingers for several moments and then pulls back.

"What was that for?" I ask, waves of heat radiating off my cheeks.

He shrugs. "Not sure. Except that you're beautiful and I thought that warranted a kiss." He takes a step back and eyes me with a coy grin on his lips. "You want to come inside? I have a fire going and can get another pot of coffee going."

My first reaction is to say yes, but it's overrun by the urgency of my current responsibilities. "Thanks, but I'd better be getting back. I have a lot of work to do. This case isn't going to solve itself."

"I understand," he nods. "What would you think about grabbing some dinner tomorrow night? Somewhere in town?"

"Sure," I say, trying hard to tamper my enthusiasm while still recovering from the kiss. "I'd like that. What time?"

"Seven? How about I pick you up at the chalet and we'll drive into town together?" Then he quickly adds, "Or I can meet you there. Whatever you're comfortable with."

"No, you can pick me up," I smile. "Are you thinking something extra fancy like Maybelle's?"

"As fancy as Maybelle's is, I think you might like The Cattle Cooker a little better. If you like steak, that is."

"Like steak?" I say. "I respect all vegetarians and vegans. And

I even get along with a few pescatarians. But I'm a carnivore at heart. I've never been able to say no to a medium rare ribeye."

"Then steak it is." His gaze lingers on mine for a while, and I feel like a silly schoolgirl as my knees turn to water.

"I'd better get back," I say quietly, trying not to trip over my words.

His smile is infectious. "Tomorrow night then."

Chapter Thirty-Six

"She's an incredible girl. A real ray of sunshine, if you ask me."

After speaking with Tim, I returned to the chalet and sorted through the most crucial documents from both cases, then stuffed them into a box and brought them down to the station, where I started working at the cubicle where I was yesterday.

The peace and quiet of the chalet allowed me the freedom to be alone as I processed what I was seeing. It was heart-wrenching at first, digging up old wounds and haunting memories that have lurked in the back of my mind since I was a child. I felt like being around other people and wanted to be in close proximity to the chief should I have any further questions.

Officer Dobbs has stopped by my cubicle to brief me on their search of the area around the Wild Spruce Nature Trail. There was a thin break in the tree line not far from the front trail entrance. But after a while, it faded out and didn't lead to anything helpful. For all practical purposes, Shelby Campbell has simply vanished.

Dobbs is clearly bothered by her disappearance on a personal level. "I can't think of a nicer young lady," he continues. "In fact, just a few months ago, at the summer carnival, she did all the face painting for the youngsters. She's even babysat my niece a few times." He looks down at the pages scattered across the surface of my desk area. "Any idea what we're dealing with yet?"

"No," I reply. "But I think all this will get me closer. It's an extensive puzzle that I have to put together. Pieces from three separate cases that span almost twenty years."

My attempt at optimism doesn't erase the hopeless concern from his face. "Why do you think he's doing this?"

"I wish I knew," I tell him. "The first two cases were unbiased and religiously motivated. But I haven't been able to get into the head of the current killer. Is he also a religious zealot or did something about the previous cases connect with him so he wanted to copy off of them? I just don't know yet."

"Yeah," Dobbs nods. "Well, I won't keep you any more. All of us around the department are getting pretty anxious. If we can help you in any way, let us know."

"I will. And thanks for the offer." He walks away, leaving me to my work.

Part of me wants to get as many eyes on this as I can. Most of the time, that is the best thing that can happen for a case. I even have half a mind to call Kemper and request that he send me a couple of agents to parse out the data with me. It would certainly save precious time. But something tells me that isn't the way I should play this. It needs to be one person looking at everything, taking in every detail in order to form a composite whole. If I bring in more agents or officers, then I run the risk of atomizing the data so that no one can make a larger picture out of it. So for the time being, I return my attention to the Chancellery case and focus my efforts there.

Lila and I had been two of five girls kidnapped that weekend. At the time, we knew that we weren't completely alone, even though we were locked away in a room far from anyone else. An hour before Lila was taken, we heard the pleading, high-pitched screams of another girl, the echoes of which haunt me to this very day. The subsequent investigation discovered the charred remains of four girls, including those of my sister. On the north end of the Chancellery was an outdoor courtyard with a granite altar in the center. Atop the altar was an iron grate, and the cauldron beneath held what little was left of their remains.

The fire department determined that an ember from the altar had been whisked inside by the wind and had set the wooden rafters aflame. Everything else in the castle had been destroyed. Even the robes I saw my captor wearing were not accounted for. All DNA evidence had been destroyed by the fire, and the monsters involved got away scot-free and without a trace. It was as if they had never even been there. As for myself, I was only minutes away from being consumed by the fire; the first responders had arrived just in time.

I turn to a picture of my sister's remains with a fusion of fury and grief stirring inside me. Her lower jaw was all that was recovered, and only identified by dental records that the Miller's Grove medical examiner had secured from her pediatric dentist in Albany. The other girls' remains were more easily identifiable.

Looking at the old notes drawn up by the case detective, he

concluded that the girls were an offering of sorts—that they had been sacrificed in some kind of religious ceremony. This was deduced primarily through the carving of the runes as well as my recollection of the cultish robes, as well as the chanting I heard in the castle prior to the fire.

I locate the pictures of the runes taken at the Chancellery. In total there are four symbols, and the detective's notes regarding them are extensive, providing historical definitions as well as his own attempt at interpreting what they meant to those at the Chancellery.

I spend the next hour focused on this part of the investigation, as this is where the past seems to connect most with the present. But when I finally lean back in my chair and rub my eyes, I don't feel any further along than I did earlier this morning. It's nerve-wracking and frustrating. The runic symbols that were carved into the stones speak to sacrifice, birth, and joy. The single rune drawn on the note left by The Four implies, ironically, life or living.

Most religiously motivated violence can be tied back in some way to a passage of scripture or religious text. That makes it much easier to discern motivations and intent. But the runes are far more mysterious and enigmatic, the Scandinavian version of what Egypt had with their hieroglyphics. Their meanings have a wide range, and could be far wider than we realize if I'm right: if The Four were operating within a syncretic religion where they put their own meaningful twists on things, then we may never know just what they were thinking. That means that my current unsub is probably putting his own spin on something whose meaning is already very elastic.

My eyes find the detective's notes from my interview and

where he had hastily copied my account of the man's words who took Lila from me. *All in the proper order.* The detective's notes—Rodgers was his name—reveal that he had put forth a tremendous amount of thought working through this phrase. What order were they dealing with? Youngest to oldest? And what was so important about this order? What was its basis? The detective's questions end with no apparent answers.

And then there are the runes that apply directly to my case. The one carved into Lily's back, the *Jera*, speaks to an abundant reward for those who are patient within a cyclical process.

The symbol left on my pillow last night is a *Perthro*. For whatever reason, this one couldn't wait to be discovered with his next victim. The unsub wants my attention on it now. But why? Is this a game of cat and mouse and he is challenging me to stop him? Does he want to see if I'm capable enough to stop the fullness of his plans from being completed?

The *Perthro's* meaning is hotly debated. But there is enough consensus to conclude that it points to the bringing forth of a great burst of knowledge that has been hidden from view. If I didn't know better, the unsub is getting ready to accomplish what he believes to be a big reveal, a great uncloaking. There isn't much I can do with that, but I finally decide that trying to understand the symbol carved into Lily's back would be worth the effort.

There is a fixed pattern—a cycle—that is clear to him. If I'm correct in that, then it means that I should be able to see it too, if I'm taking in all the relevant information and parsing it correctly. Either a cycle is coming to a close or one is beginning. Perhaps both. A cycle would point toward a specific number laid out in a discernible pattern.

Flipping the pages back on my notepad, I start with a fresh piece of paper and begin to scribble down my thoughts. That fatal night at the Chancellery, four girls were murdered. Nine years later their four killers willingly poisoned themselves. And now it's—I glance up at the department calendar hanging on the side wall of the cubicle—nine years since that event.

In three days it will be exactly nine years since The Four killed themselves. Is that the pattern? Nine-year intervals, each with four victims? Is that what my unsub is trying to copy? All this time I hadn't made a connection because I have been personally dreading the twentieth anniversary of Lila's death a couple of years from now. When it comes to remembering an event, our minds naturally think in terms of five- or ten-year increments. The twentieth anniversary of 9/11 was a major event across this country. But not the eighteenth anniversary. Every October that goes by is another reminder that I no longer have my sister. But the twentieth one will have a meaning all its own.

But were these men working from a cycle of nine years? With four victims or offerings each time? The Four clearly saw themselves as offerings. I pick up the note they left behind and read the last part out loud: *"Glory to the eternal gods, whom we now offer ourselves and journey now to meet."* Four offerings each time.

I freeze. No, that's not right. There weren't four victims when I was a girl. There were five. And I was the fifth. The cauldron fire blazing out of control was the only thing that saved me. Based on that, did they modify their number of offerings nine years later? Or were there still...?

My stomach sours and adrenaline rushes into my bloodstream as the thought pulses through my mind. Were there only four? In my case, there were five victims. But one did not end up being offered. With The Four, did the same thing apply? Were there actually five, but one was held back or did not enter into the offerings? Is that why the note was not signed and they did not affix their names? Because there was one still left? One who would keep the cycle going?

Is that who is doing all this now, nine years later? The fifth man? The questions make my blood curdle.

My fingers scramble for the crime scene photos of The Four. Their bodies lay perfectly proportioned out around the fire; there isn't room for a fifth. Going back to Detective Rodger's notes on the case, a hard lump forms in my throat as I find a single note hurriedly scratched into the margins several pages in. "*Five?*" it reads. On the next page, my eyes land on something they had passed over the first time through. "*Is there another?*"

Jumping to my feet, I rush across the floor and hurry down the hall to Bancroft's office. His door is open and as I rush in without knocking, he looks up from his computer monitor. I shut the door and quickly take a seat.

"Darcy, what bee crawled up your bonnet?"

"Chief, tell me about Detective Rodgers. He worked on both of the previous cases, right?" Even though I'm in good physical shape, I feel almost out of breath.

Bancroft frowns and folds his hand on the desk. "He did. Why?"

"When did he leave the department? I need to find a way to speak with him."

"Harry left the department a few years after The Four died. Retired down to the Florida Keys. Must have been the year after I moved here and became Chief."

"Do you have a phone number for him?"

"Why? You have all his notes. What can he tell you that's not in there?"

"I do have all his notes. But I think that Detective Rodgers had a hunch that he couldn't prove. One that I don't think he had much evidence for. It would really help me if I could speak with him."

The chief lets out a long sigh and shakes his head. "Then I hate to be the one to tell you. He was diagnosed with Alzheimer's a couple years back. His wife is still friends with a lot of folks around here. I got word two, maybe three, weeks ago that they were bringing in hospice. Even if he hasn't passed yet, Harry still won't be in any position to talk or remember."

I slump into the chair as another dead end hits me right in the face.

"But you know, Ed's death really took a toll on Rodgers, too. He felt somewhat responsible for his chief's death since he was the one tasked with finding answers." Bancroft leans into his forearms and looks at me across the desk. "Tell me more about this hunch you say he might have had."

"All this time they've been called The Four. The note they left was written by Elijah Burch, so he was clearly involved. And there is no reason to think that the other three weren't as well. But Chief, what if there was a fifth one? And what if that one continues to lurk among us just like The Four had done?"

His eyes widen briefly as the weight of my words hits him. "That seems like a pretty big leap. Is there any evidence that would suggest that?"

"Nothing solid," I reply. "Only circumstantial. But I've only had the case files for a few hours. That's why I wanted to speak with Rodgers about it. He spent years looking at everything, and there are some indications in his files that he might have pondered a fifth man. I didn't find anything to suggest that he seriously pursued that line of inquiry, or what made him think that it was a possibility in the first place, but I'll never know. What I do know is that it could work."

The chief nods and thoughtfully scratches his cheek. "What about you, Darcy? What has you thinking all of a sudden that there might have been another?"

"We're obviously dealing with people being used as offerings. Eighteen years ago, I was supposed to be the fifth one. But because of the fire, I got away. Nine years later, four men are used as offerings. The Four killed themselves on the anniversary of the Chancellery burning down. In three days, it will be another nine years."

"So you're saying that whoever is running around my town is planning on snatching up a total of four girls?"

I nod. "Possibly."

"Then if your theory is correct, there would need to be another fifth girl somewhere. Someone who gets off the hook, as it were."

In my haste, I hadn't worked that far ahead. "I guess so," I admit. "I don't have it all sorted out yet. There are a lot of threads to weave together. But this could be something."

"I'm not sure, Darcy."

A bristle inside at his lack of enthusiasm. "Chief, at the very least, our guy is copying aspects of murders that this town has witnessed before. And keeping to the same cycle of years. True, some facts got out before The Four's case was sealed, and he could simply be a copycat, tossing out random pagan symbols just for fun."

"But?" he presses.

"But I don't know if I believe that. It's all too tight, too perfect. And there is just no evidence to suggest it's true. Whoever he is, he has a finely tuned plan and is pure evil, not someone who is simply getting kicks and laughs loosely copying something from the past."

The Bureau works hard to remind its agents not to get hyper-focused on one theory. If it turns out to be wrong, then precious time has been wasted racing toward a dead end. Ideally, an agent can hold multiple and even competing theories in their minds while running new facts against each theory. I very well could be staring down another false trail, but in the event that I'm right, I can't just toss it to the wind.

Bancroft still doesn't seem convinced, and I guess I can't blame him. But he asks me what I need him to do.

"What about Detective Rodger's wife?" I ask. "If he held on to the cases for as long as he did, then surely he vented any frustrations or theories to his wife. Am I wrong in thinking that?"

The chief rubs his chin and nods. "Yeah. You could be on to something there. Lord knows I've gone home and talked with Linda about any number of things weighing on me. But I really hate the idea of reaching out to Valerie at a time like this."

"Do you think she would really mind if she thought it could save lives?" I ask him.

"I suppose not." He drums his fingers on the desk. "But even if there is a fifth man who's been out there all these years, how are we going to find out who it is?"

"Assuming that I'm on the right track, I think he wants us to know who he is. Or at the very least, that he was a part of their group. That's why he is directing our attention back to these cases."

"Now why in the world would he do something foolhardy like that?"

"I won't presume to know at this stage," I admit. "But some killers can start to crave public notoriety. In their narcissism, they think that they are exceptionally brilliant. Eventually, they want others to share in that knowledge as well. It's a source of their sense of social power. They start to offer clues to see if the authorities are smart enough to get on their wavelength. But for whatever reason, they feel insulated enough from being caught in the event that their puzzle is solved. Both the Son of Sam and the Night Stalker would fit such a profile."

"Okay," Bancroft nods. "I can buy that." Then he gives a rueful shake of his head. "So a cycle of nine years and then another cycle. When does it end?"

"Cycle," I mutter out loud.

"What?"

"Cycle," I repeat, this time with a little more enthusiasm. I still haven't gotten around to telling Bancroft about the unsub coming into his chalet last night. And now still isn't the right time. It will only prompt him to worry on my behalf, and right now, we don't have time for that. "One of the runes has to do with a cycle," I tell him. "It points to continual processes—cycles—which require a great deal of patience. Eventually, some kind of reward comes in abundance. In my opinion, waiting nine years to act, and then another nine years, would require a tremendous amount of patience."

"Yes," he nods, "I assume it would. But then what is the reward?"

I shrug. "Eternal life? The Four's note said something about meeting up with the gods. They could see themselves as agents of their god or gods, doing their work here on earth."

"I think you could be on to something here, Darcy. Even so, you should know that I put in a call to the Federal Bureau of Prisons and requested a list of all convicted murderers who have served their time and have been released from prison over the last twelve months."

A frown grows across my face. "Why would you do that?"

"Because right now we're chasing a ghost. A very real ghost, but a ghost nonetheless. The details of the Chancellery case were a field day for the press. You know that. It's why you changed your name. Our guy could have been sitting in his cell and been inspired by those details. It could be that we're dealing with a repeat offender. He could have planned all this for when he got out.

"That's actually not a bad idea," I concede, although it feels too distant. Our unsub is moving and acting as if this whole concoction is an extremely personal and intimate thing to him.

"I gave them your email. They'll send it to you once the list is complete. It might not yield anything, but at this point, I'm turning over every rock I can find. And to be honest with you, I sure hope that's what it turns out to be. Or something like it, anyway. A fifth person connected to the original four would mean that our guy could be someone else we all know around here. Hell, it could be Jimmy Crowley at the hardware store or Eugene Snider at the lumber yard."

"Yeah," I agree, the word drifting soberly off my lips. The

chief is right. It could be anyone in this town, still living among them all these years later. Or he could absolutely be right. It could be that someone in prison was inspired by what he read and saw on TV about Miller's Grove. Maybe he waited to get out to plan something around a pattern of years that he saw.

Bancroft straightens his posture as if he's ready to keep moving. "Okay then. I hate to bother her at a time like this, but let me see if I can get Harry's wife on the phone. Both of those cases were his bane. He never could solve them. There were times I thought he might follow in Ed's footsteps and end up having a heart attack over it all."

I can easily recall the two meetings I had with Detective Rodgers eighteen years ago. The first one was when I was still in the hospital, where the doctors had wanted to keep me for observation for a couple of days. I remember Rodgers being very gentle and kind in his questions as he tried to prompt my memory for any details that might help his investigation. After I was discharged, my parents took me to the Creamy Cow ice cream shop in town so that Rodgers could interview me a final time. He thought it would be best if we could talk away from the station, which could be intimidating for a young child.

Over a double scooped ice cream cone, I told him everything I remembered, but I couldn't give him any specific details that he so desperately needed. My kidnappers had been too careful, never letting me see their faces. All I had was the man's voice, but that didn't help much.

As I remember, Rodgers was a kind man. And going through his meticulous notes, it's easy to see that he was fully committed to both cases. He must have retired feeling like he had let his town down. Like an Olympic athlete who trains all his life but walks off for the final time having never medaled.

A knock on the door prompts the chief to tell whoever is there to enter. Dobbs doesn't bother to step in, just leans forward and pokes his head across the threshold. "Chief, Darren is making a pretty big racket in holding. He's yelling and hollering about suing you and the entire department if we don't let him go."

That gets a snicker from Bancroft. "You tell him he can just settle his ass down. I'm convinced that he doesn't have anything to do with this. But because I found a murder weapon on his property, I have to keep him for good measure. You tell him I can either keep him here on my own accord or I can actually arrest him, get him in front of a judge, and then he can post the half million in bail, or whatever high number the judge will think best to set the number at. His choice."

A wide grin forms across Dobbs' face. "You got it, Boss." Then he leaves, shutting the door quietly behind him.

Bancroft taps a single finger on his deck and then looks at me with a flummoxed expression. "Darcy, I think we might have forgotten to see past our own noses on this one."

"What do you mean?" I ask.

"How is it that *you* ended up on this case? Have you thought of that yet? Why, of all the FBI agents in the state, are *you* the one working this case? The case that has a direct tie to your own kidnapping and your sister's death?"

His questions are unanticipated and turn my veins to ice so quickly that I am unable to suppress a shudder. He's exactly right. I hadn't looked past my own nose. I had been so busy assimilating data and trying to find where it cohered that I had missed the odd fact that I am the one working on it. Kind of like missing the tree for the forest, you might say.

"Yes," I nod slowly, "what are the odds?"

"Can't be a coincidence, if you ask me."

"But *you* asked me here," I tell him.

His face folds into a deep frown as he thinks back to his reasons for doing so. "Yes. I did," he muses.

"When my boss called me to come here, he said you needed me because one of your detectives is in ICU from a car accident and the other is on an Alaskan cruise."

"Yes," he nods. "That's right."

Considering that the chief just finished noting that our killer could still be anybody here in town, I'm not willing to rule anyone out. "Who is the detective on the cruise?" I ask.

"Gordon Lutz."

"Are you sure he's actually on it?"

Bancroft's eyes spark with understanding. "Holy geez. I see where you're going with that." He thinks for a moment and then says, "It's not Gordon. Just yesterday he texted some of us here at the station pictures of him and his wife on the ship with the mountains in the background. I can show them to you if you like, but I don't think the photos are altered in any way."

"No. That's okay."

"And I hired him just three years ago. He moved out here from Chicago. Wanted to get away from the big city life."

"So that leaves us with your detective in the car accident."

"Yes. Rhonda Higgins. I got a call this morning that she's been moved into the Step Down Unit."

"What was the nature of her accident?" I ask.

"We're not entirely sure yet. They had her intubated for a

few days, and she wasn't able to speak. But I know it was out in Cortland County, in the middle of nowhere. She was on her way to visit her brother and his family in Syracuse. The sheriff up there thinks it was a hit and run. Said the side of her car is swiped with gray paint from another car, and there was no sign of another vehicle at the scene. A mother and her kids came across the wreck some time after it happened. Found Rhonda unconscious in the front seat and the airbag deflated in her lap."

I can see the concern on his face for his detective. "I'm sorry that happened," I offer. "And I'm glad to hear that she's on the mend."

"Me too. Sounds like she'll have some physical therapy to get through, but hopefully we'll see her back to work here at the station in a few months."

I know all of this is working hell on the chief's emotions, even though he would never tell me that outright. Even so, I try to temper my next words. "Chief, do you think our unsub is the one who caused Rhonda's accident? To keep her away? Then you would have to call for help?"

He gives a slow, thoughtful nod. "Now that we're connecting a few of the dots, it does seem like a strong possibility. You say you were attending a bike race in Delfax County? Surely our guy couldn't have orchestrated you being there?"

"No," I admit. "He couldn't have. And yet he did make sure that you would have to call for outside help."

I certainly don't understand it all right now. But there is no doubt in my mind that the unsub made sure that I would be the one to respond to Bancroft's call for help. He wanted *me* to be the one to work on this case and to tread through the old case files. It feels like with every step I take forward, I'm moving deeper and deeper into his perfectly engineered web. So far, I have yet to take a step forward without him knowing it well before it happens. Every move I have made has been exactly what he wanted me to do. I've been little more than a marionette.

My brain feels like it's about to explode. Eighteen years, three cases, all tied together. It's all a lot to unravel. Feeling overwhelmed, I push out of the chair and rise to my feet. "Chief, I need to clear my head for a while."

"Of course you do," he smiles. "It's a lot to process." I reach the door and open it. "Darcy." When I turn around, I notice the flinty resolve in his face. "We're going to stop him," he says in a low, determined voice. "And you're just the one to do it."

I nod pensively, wanting so desperately to believe that he is right. Then I take my leave of his office and start back down the hall.

Chapter Thirty-Seven

Main Street
Miller's Grove, NY

A cloud drifting overhead temporarily bathes me in shadow as I make my way down the sidewalk that runs down Main Street. Here and there, residents are popping in and out of quaint little shops as cars slowly drift by.

I've always loved sleepy small towns. There is a simplicity to them that you just can't find in the city. In a place like this, you eventually get to know everyone, whether you want to or not. I chuckle to myself as I recall what Bilbo Baggins said to his fellow hobbits on the eve of his eleventieth birthday: *"I don't know half of you half as well as I should like; and I like less than half of you half as well as you deserve."* To me, that perfectly sums up a small town. You like some people, want to know others better, and some you wish you had never met at all. But you still know a little something about just about everyone.

I pass the florist and wave through the glass as he arranges a bouquet of roses in a vase at the counter. The owner of a small bookstore is sweeping a fresh drift of leaves off his doorstep and tips his hat to me as I walk by. I continue, lost in my thoughts when, without any warning, the bakery's glass door swings open and nearly punches me in the face. A small lady emerges and shuffles out. As she does, the delectable smells of pastries, cookies, pies, and freshly baked bread drift into my nose, causing my stomach to rumble.

"Oh," the lady says as she turns and sees me. "I'm so sor— Why, hello, Agent Hunt. How are you?" Eleanor Riggins' features quickly shift from surprise to outright conspiracy. I have to give it to her. She's a true chameleon, able to throw the switch from sweet old lady to gossip extraordinaire in less than a second.

"I'm fine, Eleanor. How are you?" Her cheeks are over-rouged and her cotton ball hair is so perfectly rounded. She glances furtively down the street to ensure that we're not being overheard. "I'm fine. Just fine. Thank you for asking—you know, the word around town is that Darren might not be who you're looking for? Is that right?"

"I'm sorry," I say, "but I can't comment on an active case."

"Of course you can't, sweetheart. Of course not. But you know, this whole thing has just got all of us around here so stirred up. This town has gone through so much over the years, one could start to get the idea that it's cursed. Is it true they found the murder weapon at Darren's place?"

"Eleanor, I—"

She goes on as if she hasn't heard me. "He never did find his path in life." She shakes her head as she leans closer to me. "That man just hasn't been right in a long time. A shame, really, because he showed so much promise when he was a boy. Ed is probably looking down on his son with such disappointment. Darren just fell so far from that tree." She lays a hand on my forearm. "Has anyone told you yet what Miller's Grove has been through over the years? Horrible, just horrible. It all started at that old castle outside of the town. And do you know that..." Her voice drifts away as her eyes find mine, and for the first time, she seems to really see my face. Now she is looking at me with a straight, blank stare. To be honest, it's a little bizarre.

"Eleanor?"

She blinks, and her eyes widen. "Oh, my dear Lord in heaven. You're the girl."

The way she says that last part leaves no doubt as to her meaning. I groan inside but am careful not to register anything on my face, deciding to play it off if she'll have it. Somehow though, I don't think there is a way to get past this one. She's just too good. "What girl, Eleanor?"

"The girl from the Chancellery. Oh, my Lord. Is it really you?"

I can almost hear my soul groan as I look into her eyes and see revelation sparking in them. This elderly lady, with her loose tongue, is the absolute last person around here I would want to know my true identity. She steps up closer, raises a hand, and starts to pinch at my cheeks as she continues to study my eyes and my features. I take a step back as gracefully as I can to extricate myself from her pawing.

"It *is* you," she says with some wonder in her voice. "My Lord." I just shrug, not really in any mood to confirm it. Eleanor looks away for several moments as she processes this new bit of insight. When she brings her attention back to me, her eyes are filled with far too many questions. Before I can excuse myself, she starts up again. "But that girl. Her name was... well, now, let's see. Ah! Lockridge. It was Darcy Lockridge, if I recall. But yours is Hunt." She taps a finger on her thin bottom lip before dipping her head and looking down at my left hand, searching for a ring on my finger. "Did you get married? Is that why you changed your name?"

"Eleanor, I'm sorry. That's not something I really want to discuss." I do my best not to look irritated, but this whole exchange is really starting to get under my skin.

"I just can't believe it's you. What a twist of fate that you are the one who got assigned to these new murders. Or maybe you asked to be assigned to this case." Her eyes brighten with a fresh memory. "Did you know, after what happened to you and those other children, that Dateline show came out here? They did a whole program on you and what happened up at the Chancellery. Interviewed your parents for the show, too, if I recall correctly. Your picture, it was all over the newspapers and television. I could never forget it." A genuine smile tugs at the corners of her lips. "I always wondered what happened to you. After something like that happens to a child, you just never do know how they might turn out. My neighbor's niece, why she...."

I find myself tuning her out as she continues to wag her tongue. This lady could surely write the book on every bright spot and dark corner of this town. She's been here a very long time and has seen people come and go, most of them stay, and probably knows things about their lives that they think no one else in the world is privy to. So as much as I would like to continue my walk down the street in silence and put as much distance between myself and Eleanor Riggins, it occurs to me that she might be able to help me with something. I really do hate politics, but maybe a little diplomacy couldn't hurt.

"Eleanor, can I ask you a question?"

She stops her rambling mid-sentence and offers a delighted smile. "Of course, dear. What would you like to know?"

"Did you personally know any of the four men who took their own lives nine years ago? The men who were responsible for what happened at the castle?"

Her face takes on a shadowed expression, and for the first time since I met her, I feel like I'm seeing the real Eleanor. She looks hurt and wounded. "I did," she says softly. "All four of them, in fact. Gary Shaw stamped my mail for years and sent all my Christmas packages. Elijah"—she turns and points to a store-front a few doors down—"he used to run a barbershop right over there. I lost track of how many times he and I would stand outside his shop and talk. When they died like they did, and it came out that they were the ones who were responsible for every-thing up at the castle, we just could not believe it. And then for some reason, the case was sealed, and no one was able to get all the details of what took place. That made it all the harder for us to swallow." She clasps her hands together and seems to wilt as she thinks about the past. "You have to understand, Agent Hunt. These men were our friends. We laughed with them and played bingo and horseshoes with them. They attended residents' funerals and weddings, volunteered at festivals, and donated to local causes."

I half expect her to ask me more about what really happened the day they committed suicide, but to my surprise, she doesn't. I can see that what those men did still looms darkly over this town, and how the recent murders are causing old wounds to surface all over again.

Eleanor's voice becomes weaker, almost timid, with her next question. "You don't think it's happening all over again, do you?"

I sigh and choose my words carefully. "To be honest, the chief and I are doing our best to get to the bottom of it. It's important to both of us that everyone in Miller's Grove feels safe and protected. We're doing everything we can."

"I know you are, dear. And not that you need it, but if you want my two cents about the whole matter, I never have been convinced that those four men were the only ones."

Her statement makes my skin prickle. "How do you mean?"

"Who's to say that there weren't others? Those four killed themselves, but no one was ever arrested for their involvement at the Chancellery. There is nothing to say that they were the only ones."

I'm intrigued to hear her talk like this, especially since the chief and I were just discussing this very possibility.

"Did you ever speak with anyone about that?" I inquire. "Did you ever bring it up to Detective Rodgers?"

She huffs and shakes her head. "Harry? No. He was far smarter than myself. I'm just an old woman. And it has only been a gut feeling. There isn't anything the authorities can do with a nosy old woman's feelings."

I'm actually a little impressed with her self-awareness. Eleanor might have her nose across every domestic threshold in town, but that doesn't mean she has no boundaries or discernment at all.

"If you ask me, if there is another, then it wouldn't surprise me to find out one day that he was close to the investigation."

"What do you mean?" I ask, my curiosity piqued.

"These were high profile cases, Agent Hunt. And with yours in particular, because it wasn't sealed off, it garnered national attention. For there to have been no leads on a case like that for nine years, I always had a suspicion that there was someone close to it all who could manipulate facts or details to their advantage. Hide their tracks, as it were." She huffs and then shakes her head. "But then maybe I've just watched too many crime shows over the years." Her head sags and all of a sudden she seems even smaller, like she shrunk somehow. Bringing up the past seems to have stolen all of her energy. She pats my arm a final time and nods to herself. "Well, Agent Hunt. I think I'll head on home now. Good luck with the case. I'm rooting for you, dear." Then without waiting for a reply, she turns and walks away. I start back down the sidewalk.

"She wasn't always that way, you know."

I look over to see the owner of the bookstore wiping down the windowsill with a rag.

"How do you mean?" I ask him.

"Eleanor was never nosy until everything started to happen back then. I think she felt out of control like we all did, and she wanted to do what she could to protect her town. Since then, her getting into everyone's business has morphed into a hobby of sorts. Maybe even an addiction," he grins. "But when she started it, her heart was in the right place." A customer comes up behind him and enters the shop. He offers me a curt nod and then follows the woman inside.

It really is unnerving to think that absolutely anyone in this town could be the one we're searching for. The cook at

Maybelle's or the florist who waved at me earlier. Or even the bookstore owner.

I know that the only way I'm going to stop this madman is to get one step ahead of him. That means I have to get further into his head to draw the right pieces together so I can see what he sees. Only then will I be able to beat him to his next move and finally give this town the peace that it deserves.

Chapter Thirty-Eight

It's early the next morning, and I feel the case starting to wear on me. Dark circles cling to the space beneath my eyes, and I feel completely spent. The relaxing time that I was having with Skylar before I got the call to come to Miller's Grove feels like it was months ago. My neck and shoulders are knotted up, and the urgent need to find Shelby Campbell in time weighs heavily on me. I'm doing my best not to feel demoralized and beat down.

There is also the fact that I'm still in the very town that took everything from me. Adding pain to pain, I now understand that the recent murders and kidnappings actually tie back to my own past. The entire case is tearing open old scars inside me, making me miss my sister, and renewing old guilt over being unable to save her.

Getting this case right is about so much more than me and my feelings. I'm doing everything in my power not to make it personal, even though it absolutely is. Once I allow my personal feelings to override my reason and intuition, then the only proper thing to do is to call Kemper and tell him to send in another agent to assist. But as it is right now, I have far too many hours wrapping my mind around every detail and clue to easily transfer it to another agent. It would take far too long to bring them up to speed, and time is something I don't have enough of.

I know I'm on the right track with this case, that I'm looking in the right direction. I know my unsub won't stop with Shelby; she is only the third one. If the runes tell me anything at all, it's that there is at least one more girl that he is going to murder. To stop this madness, I'll have to beat him at his own game, to get ahead of him and somehow predict his next move. It won't be easy, and the sheer hubris that he has shown in leading us every step of the way tells me that he doesn't expect me to beat him.

Sleep didn't come easily last night. The thread that came up with both Bancroft and Eleanor kept weaving its way deeper into my mind as I tossed and turned. While there is no objective proof yet that there was a fifth man, I have no doubt now that that is precisely what we're dealing with. For two decades he has been lurking around this town, watching its residents suffer and mourn at his hands. And yet he walks among them as if he is a trusted friend.

I've gone through Detective Rodgers' notes several times now. His research in the runes and Nordic mythology is extensive, showing his personal dedication to finding answers for those families who were ravaged by the actions of several wicked men.

Looking through his notes, I can see that Rodgers concluded

that both sets of events were part of a Scandinavian ritual sacrifice called a *blót*. The *blót* was an exchange in which sacrifices were offered to the gods for the sake of getting something back in return, like fair weather or a good harvest.

But I see several discrepancies in Rodgers' theory. From what I have learned through my own research, a *blót* is usually performed during a solstice or an equinox, and that doesn't match the October date of the Miller's Grove murders. Rodgers also wrote out half a page of notes on a cultic center in Denmark over a thousand years ago, where they gathered every nine years to sacrifice people and animals.

Everything that I see seems to confirm my own theory that we're dealing with a syncretic religion, not ritual purists who are concerned with keeping the letter of their religion. Instead, they are an incorporation of beliefs from one religion, tacking on pieces of another, and finishing with their own personal flair or twist.

And this is what is making it so difficult to get inside my unsub's head. While there appears to be a general consensus on what each rune could mean, it might mean something completely different to him. Whoever he is, he is highly intelligent, perhaps even a sinister genius. While I can't prove it, I'm starting to think that he could have been controlling The Four all along, probably spending many years slowly poisoning their minds and hearts to get them to believe in the unique variant of his religion.

In the late '70s, Jim Jones convinced hundreds of people to take cyanide capsules and commit collective suicide. Those who didn't want to were forced to ingest them at gunpoint, but most everyone under his sway took them uncompelled and of their own free will. They even gave them willingly to their own children. Jones was a lot of things, but above all, he was a master manipulator.

I lean back in my chair and tap the tip of my pencil on the desk. What Eleanor said to me yesterday continues to ring in my ears as good sense. It would make sense if the fifth man was somehow close to those trying to solve the case, someone who would know how LEOs think, how quickly they respond, as well as their investigative tactics. That could also be a good explanation for how they got away with absolutely no trace at all the night of the Chancellery fire.

A thin shot of adrenaline rushes through me as I start to feel like I'm finally turning a corner. But first I need to be absolutely clear on who doesn't fit the bill for being the man behind it all. The deceit in this town has run too deep, and I can't start off this leg of my investigation by assuming anything at all, no matter how much I might want to.

Scooting my chair back in, I snatch up the desk phone and put in a call to the AFO. The phone on the other end is answered almost immediately. "Propellerhead extraordinaire, here to solve all your technical woes. To whom do I have the pleasure of speaking?"

"Cheetah, It's Darcy Hunt. You have a minute?"

"Darcy! Of course. For you, I have all the minutes you need. At least, until three o'clock this afternoon. I have to cut out early today to take my mother to her doctor's appointment."

Cheetah is the AFO's IT whiz. In Albany, his suite of computers and monitors are on the floor below mine, but I find myself down there several times a week asking for help with something or other. His nickname stems from his inordinate love for Cheetos. I've never seen him without the tips of his fingers bright orange from them. Even at the work Christmas party last year. I know it's kind of gross, but it's something we all overlook because of how much of an asset he is to our work.

"Awesome," I tell him, then keeping my voice low, I provide him with the details of what I need. He asks a few clarifying questions and then promises to get back to me ASAP. I spend the next fifteen minutes stretching my legs, topping off my coffee cup, and making idle chat with the desk sergeant. Finally, the phone rings and I hurry over and snatch it up.

"Darcy," I answer.

"Okay, here's what I've got," Cheetah says without preamble. "He's clear, as far as I'm concerned."

"You're one-hundred percent sure? It's a big deal that you're not wrong."

"Positive."

"Go on."

"On the night in question, in October 2003, Jim Bancroft was at an NYPD awards ceremony. I'm looking at a picture of him there that was in the next day's newspaper. Exactly nine years later, he was in Rome with his wife. His passport was stamped the day of. I didn't see any social media accounts from any kind of family. That would have made it easier. But I think this should be enough for your purposes."

"Thank you, Cheetah. You're a genius. I would have never figured out how to find all that by myself."

"I know," he says with an air of pride. "That's what I'm here for. Hit me up if you need anything else."

"You got it." We hang up and I sigh with relief. I hate to have gone behind the chief's back like that. I haven't suspected him for a minute, but at this point, I can't rule anybody out unless I first have proof. Every single step I take from now on will have to be done with absolute certainty.

I PLOP into the chair in front of Bancroft's desk and wait for him to hang up the phone. I notice that he looks exactly how I feel, exhausted and thinned out. I'm starting to understand how Darren's father died of a heart attack after not finding any answers and staring day after day into the face of pure evil.

The chief hangs up and looks at me with his jaw set resolutely. "That was Harry's wife. She confirmed his hunch that there was a fifth one, but he never pursued the angle because he had nothing to go on." He shakes his head and sighs heavily. "We have to find this guy, Darcy. At this point, I don't care what we have to do. This has to end. Now."

His tenacity is nothing short of energizing and is exactly the sort of attitude that I need him to have right now. "Here's how I want to run this going forward," I say. "We're going to look at any and everyone who was in some kind of public service position from at least the nine-year span between the Chancellery murders and the deaths of The Four. We need to look at all crime techs, police officers, and support staff. Everyone."

"All right," Bancroft nods. "I have no problem with that. But what is your reasoning?"

"We're not going to get anywhere by just drumming our

fingers. Lily was killed less than an hour before we got to her, which may indicate that our guy is familiar with state lab processes and timelines. I'm convinced that somehow our unsub understands the inner workings of the system. So we need to start by looking at everyone in the LEO ecosystem and move out from there."

Bancroft nods vacantly, but I'm still not sure he's convinced. So I continue. "Yesterday, you said that this was starting to feel like a game of cat and mouse. And you know what? You're right. It is. Which means that the only way to win is to anticipate the next move and beat him to the punch. He gets pleasure from feeling like he's smarter than us and staying one step ahead." I think back to when I was alone in the woods the other day. He was close. Very close. And his laughter was maniacal. "He gets off on the feeling of power that that brings him," I continue. "Chief, if he is the fifth man, then he stood around for years and watched this town try to navigate the chaos and fear that he created. What better way to watch it than to be right in the middle of those working hardest to solve it?"

He taps his index finger on his desk and then offers a slow and thoughtful nod. "I do see your point. You might be onto something. So how do you want to proceed?"

Now that I know that I won't have to wrestle with him to keep this investigation heading in the right direction, I feel a tangible sense of relief. "Like I said, I need your help compiling a list of any and everyone who was in a public service position from at least the nine-year span between the Chancellery murders and deaths of The Four, starting with those closest to the case itself. It's important that we don't skip over a single person."

"Then I'll need to get Vera to assist with that. She's worked in this building for nearly thirty years and can help me parse out who was working here way back then." He catches the look in my eye and quickly picks up on what I'm thinking. "And I can vouch for her, Darcy. Her niece was one of the girls who died that weekend. Messed her up pretty bad. And she's been divorced for years. So it's not as if she's unknowingly in a relationship with our guy."

"Okay," I nod. "I just want to make sure that Vera knows that she has to keep this close to the chest. She can't tell anyone what we're doing. Whoever we're looking for is probably trusted by everyone, obviously someone no one has suspected after all this time."

"I understand, Darcy. Mum's the word."

"After I have a list, we can start to narrow it down from there," I continue. "I think it's safe to say that anyone under thirty-five can be ruled out. At least, initially. I'll rule out our unsub being a teenager when all this started." Last night, before I left the station, I finally got around to telling the chief about my unwelcome visitor at the chalet the other night. Now I recall the brief glimpse I got of his bushy gray beard. "Most likely, we're dealing with someone over the age of fifty."

He jots some notes on the pad in front of him. "Have you heard back from your friend in the lab in Albany yet?"

I nod. "Amy called me on my way to the station this morning. She promised that the specimens we sent over are her top priority. Still, it might be until the end of the day or tomorrow before she can tell us what it is. If so, it will be too late."

"How do you figure?"

"There is a four day time span between Kayla's and Lily's

murders. Late this afternoon will be two days since Lily was murdered at the salt mine. Would I be reaching if I suggested our copycat might be planning his grand finale on the anniversary of the Chancellery murders? If that's the case, and if our guy is planning on killing a total of four girls, then we have two days to figure this out."

The corners of Bancroft's mouth turn up into a smile as he shakes his head. "I have to say, Darcy. I'm impressed with your ability to string everything together and make sense out of it. I guess they do teach you agents something at the Academy after all." He tosses me a wink, which serves to lighten the heavy mood in the room. He looks down at his notes and scribbles something else. "So we either find a guy we've been trying to catch for nearly twenty years in the next six to eight hours, or we find out what was under Lily's fingernails in time to beat him to the location."

"Yes," I shrug, and hearing him put it in those terms makes me see just how daunting it is. Still, I'm going to give it everything I've got. "I asked Kyle to find someone who can analyze the specimens under Lily's fingernails on this end, in the event that Amy can't come through in time."

His brows furrowed into a frown. "We don't have a decent lab like that in the entire tri-county area. How would we pull that off?"

"Kyle knows a guy who teaches chemistry at the high school in Pine Bluff. It's more of a way for him to stay busy after retirement. He spent thirty years at DuPont as a chemical engineer. He doesn't have all the diagnostic tools like a lab would have, but he's going to make do with some of his own equipment. It's a long shot, but right now, we need to work every angle we possibly can."

The chief doesn't look convinced, but then I guess I'm not either.

I start to get up but then stop myself. "Oh, and one more thing," I add. "It might be a wise move to put a team of officers up at the Chancellery. It's still two days from the anniversary, but that might be where he wants to get back to."

"That would be pretty risky on his part," the chief says. "He has to know that, of all the places around here, that would be our first guess. Which means that, for him, it would be the last place he would want to kill someone."

"I agree. Even so, it might be a good idea for you to station some officers out there and get them to find a good place to hole up and hide. If our guy is planning on returning there, I don't want him to see them and get scared off. Just make sure we vet your men first."

"Okay. I'll get a few men to post up out there."

A question has been rolling around in my head for the last few days, but I haven't really wanted to ask it. I was hoping that I would be out of this town by now. Since I'm not, and since it's clear that these recent murders tie into the horrors of the past, I find myself asking it now. "Chief, whatever happened to the Chancellery after the fire?"

"Half the castle burned down. Once the case became above-the-fold news all across the country, a lot of folks came out here to see it. But no one around here liked that all too much. The heiress who owned the deed to it finally sold the property to the state, and then the state razed what was left of the structure to the ground. Pulled up the foundation and planted elms and oaks. As far as I know, anyone walking by these days would think they were just in the middle of the woods."

Somehow, knowing that the castle isn't there anymore is strangely comforting. I will never be able to forget the bitter cold of that stone room that Lila and I huddled in as the snow flurried in from the glassless window above us. The sounds, the shadows, and the feelings of that night will never leave me.

Early on in my career, when I was fresh out of the Academy, Kemper taught me how to trust my intuition. New agents are often quick to dismiss their gut instincts, not wanting to be wrong because they are dealing with incomplete information and can't point to anything objective to justify their actions. But Kemper helped me to hone those instincts and I've learned to go with them, even if sometimes I end up being wrong.

And now, all these years later, now that the pieces are falling into place, there is not a doubt in my mind that I am hunting the very individual who stole my sister from me and took the lives of three other precious girls that night. And it is equally clear that he wants me to be the one to find him. It seems likely that Rhonda Higgins, the chief's only available investigator, was run off the road so that someone else would be put on the case. My sister's killer didn't just want the FBI to look at this. Somehow, he made certain that it would be me.

He got what he wanted. I don't know how long he has been watching me or keeping tabs on my life. But it doesn't really matter. In spite of everything he might think he knows about me, he doesn't. He's not inside my head, and he doesn't know how I tick. By bringing me back to Miller's Grove, back to where it all started, he has made a grave miscalculation. He might be steps ahead of me. He might have been planning all of this for years, brooding on it all until the calendar finally caught up with his freshly hatched fantasies.

But all that doesn't matter to me. I didn't come back to Miller's Grove only to return home empty-handed. I'm going to stop him. I'm going to expose him. And then I will make certain that he pays for every bit of the wrong he has done.

Chapter Thirty-Nine

Unspecified Location

S he blinked, but she may as well have had her eyes closed. She couldn't see anything at all. Even the thin shaft of light that had cut around the edge of the door earlier was gone now. When he left the last time, he had shut the door so firmly that it left her in complete and utter darkness.

The smell of musty earth was her most dominant sensation. That, and the pain throbbing in her wrist. The earthy smell reminded her of her grandmother's root cellar up in Michigan. Shelby hadn't bothered to scream for help after he left the first time. All this dirt was taking his side, not hers. It absorbed even the smallest hint of sound and echoed nothing back. Even if her voice could manage to trail through the tunnel and out the door, he would only come and slip the ball gag back on her head. And she couldn't bear the thought of that. It made her feel the worst kind of claustrophobia while making her focus completely on resisting the urge to gag.

How much time had passed? A day? Two days? He had given her a bottle of water, but no food. But she had wasted the water when he had stepped closer and started to cup her breast in his hand. She had instinctively smacked him with the bottle on the side of the head. He had only laughed, picked up the bottle, and left.

Her wrist was swollen now, hot to the touch. She knew it was infected. She could feel some of the dirt that had gotten into the wound where the wire threaded through her wrist. Now even the slightest movement made her feel like someone was setting a blowtorch to it.

Another bug crawled across the back of her neck. Shelby jerked, and with her good hand she smacked it, then rubbed the flat of her hand along the dirt to wipe the guts off her skin.

She sat back against the wall of dirt and thought back through her life, wondering how things had ended up like this. She had been on a run. That was all. Just an innocent, everyday run down her favorite nature trail.

Her chest trembled as she struggled to suppress the onslaught of another panic attack. Tears slipped from her eyes and ran hot down her cheeks. Shelby watched as her dreams and plans for her future streamed across her vision as clearly as if she were watching them in high definition television. It wasn't supposed to be like this. How could anyone get pleasure from doing this to another human being?

Her breath became more ragged as her mind turned toward the worst. What did this man plan on doing with her? What lay ahead? The possibilities that streamed through her mind prompted a heavy groan to escape her lips. "Why?" she whispered weakly to herself. "Oh, god. Why?"

Shelby flinched as a loud clang sounded at the other end of the tunnel. The door swung open and light streamed in. After closing the door, he seemed to take his time making his way toward her. He stopped several feet in front of her and for a long time said nothing. Had it not been for the sour smell of his sweat and the soft whistle of air through his nostrils, she would have thought she was alone again.

"I'm finishing up the last of the preparations," he finally said. "We will be leaving soon."

Her lips were trembling so hard she could barely form a sentence. "Leaving? Where?"

"We are going on a hike. You like to run for exercise. Surely you enjoy going on hikes as well, Shelby."

Hearing her name cross his lips sent a shudder through her entire body. "I just want to go home," she replied softly.

"Of course you do. But, Shelby, you are not thinking about what I want."

"You're a monster," she sobbed.

"Yes. I suppose so." He was quiet for some time again, the only sounds that of her soft sobs which were quickly absorbed by the surrounding soil. "Soon," he continued, "It won't be long now." Then he started back toward the door.

"Please..." she begged. "I'll do anything. Anything at all."

"And I would let you. Oh yes, how I would let you. But, I have my orders. And I cannot overstep them."

Shelby did not understand what he meant, and decided that she didn't want to. He left, and she gritted her teeth as another deep groan rose up from deep within her.

"I don't want to die," she cried into the darkness. "Please. I don't want to die."

Chapter Forty

Medical Examiner's Office
Police Station - East Wing
Miller's Grove, NY

"Are you sure you don't want me to come out there? My ASAC has me going blind reading through all these cold case files. I could be out there in three hours. You just give the word."

"Thanks," I tell Skylar. "I think we have it covered for now. Stay where you are and if I do need help, I promise to let you know."

A disappointed sigh radiates through the phone. "Are you sure you're okay? I can't imagine what this is doing to you."

"To be honest, I don't have the luxury of thinking about myself right now. My emotions don't get a say so in the matter. Maybe when all this is over, I'll fall apart over a bottle of wine."

I haven't given Skylar all the details of the case, especially the part where the unsub singled me out to be here, and that he is toying with me, leading along a path that he has already laid out. But I have told her enough. She knows Miller's Grove is where everything happened when I was a girl. She's a great agent, and I know that if we had a few more days to comb through these names, then I would absolutely take her up on her offer. But as it is, we're basically down to the wire now.

"When it's all over, I'm treating you to a girl's weekend at the spa. No interruptions this time."

"That sounds amazing, Sky. I will completely take you up on that."

"Go get him, Darcy. You can do this."

We hang up and I run my fingers through my hair, trying to ease some of the tension that is slowly creeping up the back of my head.

It's past noon now. The sun has already reached its zenith and is slowly beginning its trek into the west. I'm keenly aware that every second that ticks by is one last second that Shelby Campbell has to live.

Something tells me that we're on the right track, that we're much closer than we were yesterday. Even so, I still feel like I'm driving blindfolded down a winding mountain road in the middle of the night.

"All right, hun. I think this is everything." Using two hands, Vera picks up a stack of personnel files and moves them to the front edge of the desk.

We're using Kyle's office as we run our inquiries into everyone who worked in some proximity to the local law enforcement in Miller's Grove and Pine Bluff at the time of the Chancellery murders, and at least a decade beyond them. Vera and Bancroft quickly eliminated a large number of names, removing people from the pile who went through career changes a long time ago or passed on. Looking at the stack of files makes me realize just how long of a shot this is. But I can almost hear Kemper in my ear repeating his oft-heard refrain: *Possibility-based thinking, Darcy. You don't always have to see the whole. Just trust what you see in the parts.*

Vera stands up and moves toward the door. "Let me know if you need anything else. I really do hope this works."

Bancroft nods his thanks. "Certainly will, Vera." After she leaves, Kyle, Bancroft, and I sit at a folding table that Kyle set up specifically for our purposes, then begin the process of whittling down the names. The process is slow going, and over the next couple of hours, we throw out dozens of names, eliminating them through their whereabouts over the last week, utilizing several state and local databases that the Bureau gives me access to, and even social media. Some of these men have moved away from Miller's Grove over the years and we're looking to verify their locations and movements over this past week. When we locate financial transactions and phone records that place them far away from the area, then they go into a different pile. That's not to say that they couldn't have covered their tracks and made it look like they were spending money in Missouri when they were really here, but that's a stretch and right now I don't have the time to dig past any such smokescreens.

The stack continues to dwindle, and I can feel myself getting nervous when I finally look across the table to see only three files left. These are the only ones that tightly match our search criteria. Kyle picks up the first one and flips it open. "Harvey

Nicholes," he begins. "Age sixty-two. Resides off Center Street on the north end of town. He was Chief Ed's sergeant for many years until retiring five years ago."

Bancroft nods. "He worked for me for a while. Saw him at Maybelle's the other morning when you and I were there, Darcy."

"How well do you know him?" I ask.

He shrugs. "We haven't kept up since he retired. He's one of the quiet ones but always did his job well. Never had any complaints about him."

"Is he healthy?"

Bancroft nods, picking up on my drift. Our killer is strong and mobile, someone who was able to walk a long distance through the woods to the salt mine. He was also strong enough to drag Shelby Campbell away from the nature trail. "He is."

"Let's look at these other two," I say, "and then we can decide how to move ahead from there."

Kyle flips open the next file. "Marvin Hess. He was the ME for twenty-five years. After my internship and fellowship at NYU, Miller's Grove offered me this job. I was his replacement."

"And you've been here two years now?"

"Yes. A couple months over that."

"What is your take on him?"

He shrugs in response. "To be honest, it's strange to see his name on your list. He was nice. Pleasant. Very good at this job. He even taught me several tricks of the trade I hadn't learned in school."

"Marvin moved farther out to the country when he retired," Bancroft interjects. "Lives about an hour from here. I think I've only seen him once since he handed the reins over to Kyle. At the July 4th celebrations, I think it was."

"And what about this last one?" I say, nodding to the final folder on Kyle's side of the table.

"Let's see," Kyle says, picking it up. "Aaron Gardner. He was a paramedic for seventeen years. Worked out of the fire department annex. I see him around sometimes. He has a husky that he likes to walk up and down Main Street."

I turn toward the chief. "What else can you add to that?"

"Nothing. I've not personally met him. But we can probably ask around."

The room is quiet for a few minutes while I peruse the contents of the files again. "None of these men ever married," I tell them. "That fits the profile of what we saw with The Four. Do any of them have beards?"

"Hess and Gardner," the chief replies. "The department doesn't allow its officers to grow beards, so Nicholes never had one. Gardner was technically an employee of the county and they let their EMTs keep short ones."

I nod, thinking through all the details that we've just been over. "Chief, can you send some officers to these men's homes and see if they are willing to be brought in for questioning? If they aren't there or aren't willing to, I want to be told immediately. And can you have Pam locate some photos? I would like to have them for reference."

"Certainly. Hess' place is out of jurisdiction, so maybe you and I should ride out there together."

"Okay."

He stands with a groan and slowly stretches out his limbs. "I'm starting to think that I'm not built to do anything more than sit in a fishing boat or an easy chair all day. You two youngins are lucky not to be dealing with aching bones and swollen joints."

That draws a laugh from me. "If I keep getting cases like this one, I'm sure my body will be protesting soon enough."

"Give me a few minutes," he says. "I'll have Vera see about getting some photos and Dobbs getting some cruisers over to Nicholes' and Gardner's places."

After he leaves, I look over at Kyle, who looks like a deer in the headlights. "You okay?"

"Yeah," he blinks. "I'm just usually on the back end of all this. It's a little strange seeing the process at work. Especially having to look through all these files of people that I see in town all the time. People I've come to trust, you know?"

"I do. I appreciate your help with it all and for letting us use your office. It's away from all the hubbub of the admin wing. Since I don't know who we can trust, it was necessary to go through these files away from inquisitive eyes and ears."

He nods, but still seems a little shaken by it all. It's a little humorous to me that a man who spends his days sawing open chest cavities and weighing organs can be shaken by anything. But we all have our pressure points, I guess.

"Have you gotten any word from your friend who is analyzing the specimens you gave him?"

"Not yet," he replies. "He's in the back working on it now. I don't think he'll be able to be as detailed as the lab since we don't have all the compounds and chemicals they have at their disposal. Let me go back and see how he's getting along."

"Okay," I say. "Just keep me updated with even the smallest guess or development." After he leaves, I slick a hand down my face and shake my head. Part of me wants to perform the ritual I have done so many times in the past. I want to close my eyes and promise Shelby Campbell that I'm going to save her. But I find that I can't do it right now. I wasn't able to get to Lily in time. I wasn't able to keep the promise that I made to her outside of room 16 and I'm starting to weary of making promises that I am unable to keep.

Chapter Forty-One

"They just don't make music like this anymore, do they?"
Bancroft and I have been on the road for close to an hour now. The Eagles' "Tequila Sunrise" streams through the cruiser's speakers as we wind our way deeper into central New York. With every minute that ticks by, I can feel my stomach tighten just a little more. My mind is telling me that I'm completely chasing the wrong angle, that what I'm looking for is back in Miller's Grove somewhere. And maybe it is, but I decided on a specific course of action earlier this morning, and before I completely give it up, I need to see it through. Even so, it's been a long drive out to Marvin Hess' place and the day isn't getting any longer, just the shadows as the afternoon continues to drag on.

I do agree with the opinion of the music though. I don't peg the chief for the kind of man who appreciates the grungy talents of Pearl Jam and Kings of Leon like I do, but Skylar never tires of labeling me an old soul. My tastes in music are wide and varied, and I really do enjoy the sheer genius and talent of bands like The Beatles, The Rolling Stones, and even The Everly Brothers.

"This song always makes me wish I was on a Caribbean beach with a drink in my hand," I agree. Even so, a relaxing vacation is the furthest thing from my mind right now. "I know you moved to Miller's Grove only seven years ago," I say, "but did you personally know any of The Four? Did you ever cross paths with any of them during your vacations?"

He nods as he carefully takes a sharp turn in the road. "I did. Two of them, anyway. Elijah Burch cut my hair several times. Had a witty sense of humor. While I don't think I ever made my way into the post office, Shaw and I did exchange pleasantries from time to time at the Taproot. He typically sat at the far end of the bar nursing a glass of Scotch."

A sign up ahead makes us aware of an upcoming crossroad. Bancroft slows the cruiser and turns onto it, punching off the music as he does so. "Next turn will be on the right," I tell him, looking down at the maps app on my phone.

Country houses drift by, most of them set back off the road a little ways. They all have long driveways and are set about twenty yards apart. Tall, wild grasses line both sides of the road, and fir and pine trees stand tall overhead. After Bancroft takes the next turn, we find the mailbox with Hess' house number on it. Gravel crunches under the tires as we turn into the driveway and take it to the front of the house, which is a brick ranch-style, painted white. The shutters are an earthy green, as is the trim around the eves. The yard is dotted with trees, and low-trimmed bushes run along the front of the house. Everything is plain and unadorned; there are no flowers, no bursts of color anywhere.

We step out of the cruiser and make our way down the front walk, taking the three steps up to the porch. I notice immediately that the windows are dusty, as are the entire porch and the two wicker chairs sitting in front of the casement window.

"Here we go," Bancroft mutters, and presses the doorbell. We wait for half a minute before he tries again, following the doorbell with a hearty knock. "Marvin? It's Jim Bancroft. You have a minute?"

No answer, and no apparent movement inside. The blinds are closed over the windows, so there is no way for us to peek inside. After knocking a final time, we step off the porch and regroup by the cruiser.

"You want to try around back?" I ask. "I hate the idea of coming out here for nothing." He's about to answer when the side door to the neighbor's house creaks open and a wide lady with her gray hair in curlers steps onto her driveway. Her brows are drawn low over her eyes in what might be the deepest frown I've ever seen. "Can I help you?" she calls out.

"Yes, ma'am," Bancroft says, taking a few steps in her direction. "We're looking for Marvin Hess. Have you seen him around lately?"

By some incredible contortion of her face, her frown grows even deeper. "Marvin? Why I ain't seen that man for, I don't know, coming up on two years, I suppose."

The chief and I exchange glances. "This is the only address we have for him," he says. "Are you sure he hasn't been around?"

"Sure of it? Of course I'm sure," she spits. "My grandson comes over and mows Marvin's yard every two weeks. He has a landscaping business." She says that last part with a sudden gust of pride. "He makes sure that the place stays looking nice."

"Do you have a way to contact Mr. Hess?" I ask her. "A phone number or another address?"

"No. Why would I?"

"Fair point," I mutter under my breath. "So he left two years ago and pays your grandson to keep the grass down?"

"That's about the sum of it. What is it that you need him for?"

"I'm afraid it's personal," the chief answers. "How does he pay for the grass?"

"Beats me. I never bothered to ask."

The chief turns back to me. "Looks like a dead end. I'll need to go back to the office and see if we missed another residence under his name. Or maybe he's staying with a relative."

"I don't remember seeing anything about a relative," I say. "Hold on." Returning to the cruiser, I slip Hess' file off the dash and flip it open. Under family associations, the only names listed are a mother and a father, both of whom have passed. As for this residence, Hess purchased it two years and three months ago. And yet the neighbor just told us that she hasn't seen him in nearly that long.

Pulling out my phone, I call Cheetah and tell him what I need. "You got it," he says in his typical cheerful demeanor. "Hang on the line." I hear the rapid-fire click of his keyboard as he works on my request. "Okay, here we are. I only have one phone number listed in his name. It's a landline registered to the address you're at now."

"No cell phone?" I ask him.

"Nope. As for the monthly house payment, it's set up on auto pay from a trust Hess created a couple of years ago. Same thing for what looks like a monthly payment to a local landscape company, residential electricity, and annual property taxes."

"So then where is he?" I ask.

"Beats me. I see absolutely nothing on my end. No debit or credit card transactions, no gas stations or hotel purchases that would indicate that he's traveling."

I return the file to the dash and start back toward the chief. "What about a vehicle?"

"Let's see... He has a 2015 Buick LaCrosse. The trust has paid the renewal on the registration. All pretty weird, if you ask me," Cheetah says. "People do this kind of thing all the time, but they don't just vanish. They move to Florida or visit Europe for a period of time. They still use their cards to purchase things and cell phones to call people. Who is this guy, anyway?"

"I can't get into it now. I really appreciate your help, Cheetah. I'll call you if I need anything else."

"You got it."

My heart is beating a little faster now as I walk back to Bancroft and fill him in on what I just learned. "What do you think it all means?" he asks.

"Honestly, I have no idea. But we need to get into that house and look around."

He adjusts his hat and looks back to the front door. "We don't have a warrant. I can't just walk right into his house, Darcy."

"Chief, Hess has everything on autopay and didn't have any close ties to anyone when he retired. He could have died inside the house. He wouldn't be the first to go missing for that long without anyone noticing. At the very least, he could have died two years ago and his carcass is lying on his couch. At worst, there is something else going on. We just don't have time for a warrant." I can see the wheels turning in his head as he considers my request. I don't want to butt heads with him on this, but one way or another I'm getting into that house within the next five minutes. "If we find something, then we back out and get a warrant," I add. "I'm not looking to arrest someone right now as much as I'm trying to save a young lady's life. To do that, I have to be able to cross names off my list."

To my relief, he finally nods. "All right. Let's do it your way. I have a Halligan bar in the trunk of the cruiser."

"Thank you," I tell him, trying to cloak my relief. We need to thoroughly examine every angle we are presented with, and leaving without searching the house would, to me, be nothing short of indolent.

He removes the Halligan bar from the trunk, and under the watchful eye of the neighbor next door, we make our way to the side of the house. A padlock is hanging from the drop latch attached to the chain link fence. Thankfully, the shank isn't secured into the locking mechanism. The chief threads it out and hooks it on a fence link before lifting the latch and pushing the gate open. Even though we're in a quiet neighborhood in the country, going in through the back door will minimize attention from any passersby. We can also gain a full view of the entire property.

The back yard is mostly empty. A covered grill sits on a concrete pad near the back door, and a burn barrel rests in the back corner, the top expertly threaded with spiderwebs. Next to the back door is a plastic bin made for storing play toys or back-yard equipment. I lift the lid to find bundles of envelopes and flyers stacked on top of each other. "It's the mail," I shrug. "I guess the lawn guy is putting it in here."

I shut the lid as the chief knocks loudly on the back door. After receiving no response, he works the bar into the door jamb and works surprisingly quickly. He has the door open within a minute. I lead the way in, making our presence known as we cross the threshold with our weapons drawn. "Marvin Hess, FBI. We're coming in!"

"Marvin? It's Chief Bancroft. You in here? If you are, you need to show yourself."

The house has a dry, musty smell to it. All the lights are off, and the sunlight filtering through the blinds creates a hazy yellow atmosphere. We quickly clear the kitchen and living room, then start down the hallway. Everything is covered with a thin sheet of dust, including the hardwood floors, which our feet leave prints in as we traipse over them. We clear the bedrooms, closets, and bathrooms one by one. Each room is furnished as if someone lives here. The glaring discrepancy is the dust and the appearance of not being lived in at all. That, and no personal pictures of any kind. The mirror and sinks have no water spots. There are no discarded clothes or towels anywhere, yet the master closet is stocked with everything you would expect in a man's closet: shoes, suits, shirts, and a cigar box with several watches in it.

Except for the dust, everything looks normal. Well, that and no Marvin Hess.

We return to the kitchen. There's nothing whatsoever in the refrigerator, although it is humming quietly and cold inside. Other than some cans of tuna and green beans, the pantry is bare. No dishes in the sink or dishwasher. The garage is mostly empty, but organized.

"This is pretty damn peculiar," the chief murmurs.

I holster my sidearm and nod. "Downright creepy, if you ask me. No one has been inside this house for a very long time."

"Why would he just drop off the face of the earth, but keep everything running here?"

"I don't know," I reply. "But it certainly doesn't add up."

"I'll put in a call to the station and see if they can find anyone who has kept in touch with him over the last two years," he says. "And have your people see if they can track any close relationship ties to him. An out of state girlfriend or something like that."

"Yeah. Okay." We're both staring into the living room. Everything is as it should be. Even the television remote is sitting next to a coaster on the end table.

"I'll get someone out here to fix the door," he sighs. "Let's head on back to town."

Chapter Forty-Two

Pebbleroad Cafe
Cascade County, NY

"I don't know what I was hoping to find. Maybe a room with runes and candles, just like the homes belonging to each of The Four."

We're sitting in a booth at the Pebbleroad Cafe, a few miles outside of Miller's Grove. It took him a while, but the chief finally convinced me to stop and get something to eat. "Running on fumes never helped anyone cross the finish line," he said more than once. Technically, that may not be quite factual, but I didn't press him on it. Now he's swirling a spoon in his coffee as I look blankly out the window and hear the seconds ticking in my head with no more actionable leads to move on.

"I think I was hoping for the same thing, Darcy. I just don't know what to make of it."

"It can only be two things," I offer. "Either he intentionally vanished or he has gone to live with someone else for an extended period of time. The thing that really gets me is no cell phone and no banking transactions. That all smacks of someone who wants to be completely off the radar, not someone who just slipped off it."

He sighs and takes a sip of his coffee. "I don't know. It's all a little strange, to be sure. But for all we know, he had a late-life crisis and is off shacking up with a sugar lady with every intention to return."

"For two years, Chief?" I ask, a layer of incredulousness lacing my tone. "I'll grant your premise, but not for two years. Nobody just goes around without owning a cell phone anymore. No one. Something is off with Hess' entire situation."

"So why keep the place going?" he pushes back. "Why not just sell it and get everything out of his name?"

"Optics?" I shrug. "If someone was sniffing in his direction, then he would be made aware of it without us being able to verify anything credible. Everything about this is suspicious. Solid evidence or not, I'm starting to think Hess is our guy."

He answers with a vigorous shake of his head. "No. An empty house isn't enough to stab a finger at someone." His phone rings, bringing our conversation to a halt. As he answers, I look back out the window as I try to quell the frustration rising inside me. A minute later, his phone call has ended.

"Nicholes and Gardner both came willingly into the station for questioning. Nicholes has a sturdy alibi for the nights in question. Dobbs is working to verify Gardner's."

"Okay," I nod.

The chief takes another sip of his coffee and sighs. "Darcy, look. I don't want to be at odds with you on this. I brought you in to help me. But saying that you're willing to point the finger at

Hess with such little evidence seems a little trigger-happy to me. Remember, you did end up following a false trail with Darren."

"Chief," I fire back, "Darren had the murder weapon in his shed! And whoever the actual perp is, he's incredibly smart. He plans well in advance and for every outcome. And what I saw at Hess' place back there fits the bill."

A few of the other patrons in the restaurant turn to look at us as I raise my voice. The space between the chief and me grows uncomfortably quiet as we each ponder the case from our own points of view. "I'll tell you what," he finally says. "Let's get some food in our stomachs and head on back to the station. Between now and then we can decide how to move forward from here."

I give him a silent nod in reply.

"I'm going to use the little boy's room. If they bring my food before I get back, can you make sure they bring ketchup with it?"

"Sure thing."

After he disappears into the restroom, my phone dings with a text from Skylar. She's checking in to see how things are going. I send off a reply, telling her that I think we're getting closer.

I know the chief isn't completely wrong. It is still too early to tell if Marvin Hess is the man we're looking for, and if he is the one who took Lila and me all those years ago. Maybe the personal part of me is starting to get the upper hand over the professional, something I swore I would never let happen. Maybe I want so badly to find my sister's killer that I'm willing to see things that just aren't there.

I'm still texting when a chill drifts over me. A shudder runs down my spine, as if a frigid breeze just rolled through the front door. The cook comes around the half wall beside me and places our food on the table as I finish typing off another reply to Skylar.

Without looking up, I glance over at the plate with the chief's burger on it. "Thank you," I say. "And can I get a side of ketchup for the fries, please?"

The cook leaves and walks back around the half wall. As he disappears into the kitchen, my body freezes like a stone monolith at his reply: "All in the proper order."

My eyes dart toward the kitchen door just in time to catch a glimpse of the back of his head before the door swings shut. He's burly and thick-necked, his gray hair is slicked back into an oily sheen, and broad shoulders are exposed out of a sleeveless T-shirt, peppered with hairs. My heart is thumping so hard I think it might break my sternum. As much as I want to dart from the booth and go after him, I find that I can't move. It's as if his words had some dark power to immobilize me.

Those words. They were the same ones spoken over me the night my sister was taken. But even more than that, I sit here trembling in horror because not only were those the very words I heard so long ago, they were also spoken by the very same voice.

I look down at my trembling hands and clench my jaw as I force my limbs to move, silently screaming at myself to get up and move. It works, and as I bound from my seat, I turn and run straight into the chief.

"Darcy, what in the—"

"Chief, he's here," I pant, and move around him.

"What? Who?"

"It's Hess. I'm sure it's him. He spoke—the voice—just go out front and keep an eye out for him. And don't let any vehicles leave the area. None at all.

"Darcy, I don't..."

But I'm already gone, pushing through the swivel door and

running back into the kitchen as I sweep my gaze around the room. A short, olive-skinned man stands at the stove attending to a country fried steak. He's certainly not the man I saw. But I don't see anyone else. Moving as quickly as I can, I dart around the stainless steel island and scan the room. "A man," I tell the cook, who is looking at me like I'm crazy. "A man just came through here. Gray hair? Stocky?" He just looks at me and shrugs indifferently, a cigarette tilting from the corner of his mouth. "He just delivered food to—" I stop mid-sentence, realizing how futile this is and how much time I'm wasting. My eyes find the rear door of the building, and I fly past shelves stocked with pots and pans and commercial-sized cans of shortening, beans, and gravy.

Reaching the back door, I slam my hands into the crossbar and burst into the sunlight. The hard packed ground is strewn with gravel and terminates at a grassy pasture fifty feet away. Not far beyond that is a dark treeline.

No one is out here. Moving away from the cafe, I scan out toward the treeline again before quickly checking both sides of the building, along with the inside of the dumpster. Then I run into the grass toward the trees and keep my eyes peeled for anything out of the ordinary. After a while, I stand still, listening for any sounds of movement through the grass or in the woods. There is nothing but the whispering of wind through the tops of the trees.

My heart is still beating a hundred miles an hour as my fingers curl into angry fists by my side. Before I know it, I'm growling out loud. "Where the hell are you?"

THE BRIGHT BLUES and reds of the cruisers' lights pulse against the front of the Pebbleroad Cafe as Bancroft and his officers interview the last of the employees. A massive search was made of the surrounding area, but nothing turned up. As seems to be his custom, our guy just vanished into thin air.

I'm still reeling over the fact that my sister's killer just spoke to me. He was within a single foot of me, and I didn't even know it until it was too late. For the last nine years, I've lived my life with the belief that Lila's killers were dead. Because of that, I have never taken the time to dig into the past or to really examine everything that happened surrounding The Four.

So now that the truth is starting to reveal itself, I feel crippled with guilt and indecision. Too many emotions are rolling around inside me and vying for the top position: fear, regret, guilt, doubt, and hopelessness. I'm sure each emotion will eventually try to dominate at some point, but right now, it's a blazing hot anger that is winning by a wide margin.

The man who ran Rhonda Higgins off the road to make sure I came back here, the man who entered the chalet the other night and put the note on my pillow, the man who has been killing innocent girls again; he is the very same man who snatched my sister from my arms.

Part of me wants to ask why he would start killing again. There won't be a rational answer to that; men like him are too far gone into their own heads. But I can wonder why he saw fit to drag me back into all this. Why me? Why not just let me go and live my own life? Is it because I'm the one who got away?

Up until now, I could only guess that the man we were chasing was Marvin Hess. Now I know for certain. The chief, however, isn't fully convinced of that yet. While we waited for his officers to respond, I could tell that he was contemplating whether I had completely lost my mind. None of the employees recalled seeing a man who matched the description I gave them. The cook remembers seeing someone come through the kitchen just before I burst through. But he only saw them out of his periphery and didn't bother to look up, thinking it was a waitress. Thankfully, a customer sitting at a table in the far corner of the cafe recalled seeing the back of the man who delivered our food to the table, and I think that is the only thing that's keeping Bancroft from thinking that I've completely fallen off my rocker. That, and the fact that none of the employees claim to have delivered the food to our table.

I'm also angry that I froze and didn't react sufficiently. He was right there, right at my elbow, and I completely choked at the opportunity. This time it didn't take me charging off into a dark rainy night to try to nab him. Considering that a young girl's life is at stake, and probably another after her, that mistake is almost unforgivable.

"He's toying with you, Darcy. Don't let him into your head."

I turn around in the front parking lot to see the chief standing in front of me. He looks as weary as I feel.

"I know," I say with a slight nod.

"I know that you know. But you need to hear it. I'm not convinced that it's Hess we're dealing with. But I believe you when you say it's the same man who kidnapped you and your sister. I can also see how he manipulated everything to get you here on this case. That little stunt he pulled at my chalet the other night, and what he did just now, he's trying to show you that you're no match for him. I want to know if you believe that?"

I look away, toward an afternoon sun that is rapidly working its way down toward the tops of the trees. "I don't know what to believe anymore."

"Then he's won."

I shake my head and kick at a small rock near my feet. "He was right there, Chief. Right there."

"I can't imagine what you're going through right now, Darcy. But we're not going to find him by you letting him get the best of you. He doesn't think you can stop him."

"Yeah. Well, maybe I can't."

"Hey!" Bancroft's tone is fierce and commanding. I look up at him and see a stony, determined expression etched into his face. He looks like a completely different man. "Snap out of it. You moping like this, doubting yourself. That is exactly what he wants you to do. He's no smarter than you are, Darcy. I know he wounded you in one of the worst possible ways, but that still doesn't give you the luxury of doubting yourself. This entire investigation you've been two or three steps ahead of me. You're smart and capable, and I'm not about to stand here and watch you fall apart. Not while he is still out there."

I'm stunned by his response. And grateful, too. His words are exactly what I need to hear right now. Everything inside me wants to revert to how Hess made me feel two decades ago. But I'm not that girl. I'm an adult with a badge from the Federal Bureau of Investigation.

I nod and clench my jaw. I can't remember the last time someone went all drill sergeant on me, but I'm glad he did. "Thank you."

Behind him, Bancroft's team are making their way back to their cruisers. Once again, Hess has completely vanished, giving us nothing that we can work with to follow him.

"Let's get back to the station and regroup. Whether or not it's Hess that we're really dealing with, if we don't get to the bottom of this soon, then Kyle is going to have another body to keep him busy over the next couple of days. And I try to do my best to make sure that Kyle is bored out of his mind, if you catch my drift."

"Yes, I..." I trail off as his words spark something in the back of my mind. A fresh swell of confidence rises inside me and I look back at him. "I think I have an idea. We need to go back to the station. *Now*."

Chapter Forty-Three

Unknown Location

She had read once that people who know they are dying become deeply nostalgic and reflective. It made sense. Shelby had fallen into doing that very thing over the last few hours. She had been thinking of everything she wanted to accomplish but would never be allowed to do: visiting London, skiing the German Alps, hiking the AT. In a big way, she knew she was mourning her own death, grieving over everything that this monster was snatching from her.

It didn't seem fair how someone could be allowed to take the life of another human just because they wanted to. Steal a car? Rob a bank? Even kidnap someone for ransom. Fine, she supposed. But to have the power to murder another person? It just wasn't fair.

She had given up hope that she might be dreaming. She knew that she wasn't. This was really happening, and it was the stuff of every woman's darkest nightmare.

"Why me?" she whispered to the darkness. "What did I ever do?"

A loud clang sounded from the end of the tunnel, and the door was pulled open. The light hurt her eyes and she turned away from it as he started in her direction. When he stopped in front of her, she didn't look at him, and she knew what he was going to say before he said it.

"It's time to go."

"Where?"

"Away."

Shelby could detect a note of pleasure, if not excitement, in his voice. Her lips were trembling, but somehow she still managed to speak. "Do you enjoy killing people?"

"Yes. Very much."

"Why?"

"Why do you like mustard on your cheeseburgers and prefer honey on your pancakes instead of syrup?"

A shudder passed through her stomach as she realized that this man knew far more about her than she had thought. He must have been stalking her for a while. Watching her. "I just do," she replied.

"Because it gives you pleasure, Shelby. That's why you prefer honey on your pancakes. And that is why I kill."

For some strange reason, she didn't feel like pleading anymore. It wouldn't work, and she wanted to die with her dignity intact. That was her plan for now, anyway. She just hoped that she could keep it. She didn't want to die a coward.

"You probably want to get out of those clothes, don't you?"

She did, but she knew that he had a different meaning behind that statement than she did, so she didn't reply.

"I have a dress for you in the truck. It's burgundy. Quite beautiful. And nail polish that I know you will like."

"Nail polish?"

"I'll paint them for you after we get there. You are going to look beautiful, Shelby." He leaned down and picked up the gag.

"Please, don't put that thing back over my face. I promise, I won't scream."

He chuckled happily. "You don't like the gag, do you?" She didn't answer. "Okay, then. You do not have to wear it. There won't be anyone to hear you, anyway." He paused. "I have to unlock your wrist. It's going to hurt. I need you not to scream. Can you do that for me?"

Shelby swallowed hard. If she had to, she would bite off her tongue to keep from having to wear that gag again. "Yes," she nodded.

"Turn around."

She did as she was told. He wasted no time stepping up behind her and nudging his nose into her hair. Then he took a deep breath and sighed contentedly. Shelby closed her eyes tightly and shuddered against the fear and repulsion that it sent coursing through her body. He finally stepped to the side and took her wrist in his hand. Tears rolled down her cheeks as spasms of fire shot through her wrist and up her arm. As he worked a tool onto the cable, she bit down hard on the inside of her cheek. She was unable to keep back a loud whimper and thought that she might pass out. Finally though, she heard a snip and the cable slipped out of her wrist.

"There," he said. "Are you ready to go?"

She felt glued in place, too scared to respond.

"Go, then." He nudged her forward, and Shelby started for the door at the other end of the tunnel.

One foot in front of the other, she thought. *Just one foot in front of the other.*

They finally reached the door, and he placed his hand on the back of her neck and squeezed so hard it nearly made her cry out. "Not a sound. You hear me? Not a sound." Then he pushed open the door and led her back outside.

For several moments Shelby could see nothing at all, temporarily blinded by the light of a late-evening sun. She focused on placing one foot in front of the other as she frantically tried to think of a way to keep this monster from leading her to her death.

Chapter Forty-Four

Medical Examiner's Office
Police Station - East Wing
Miller's Grove, NY

"What do you mean there are no recordings?"

"I mean, there is nothing," Kyle replies. "Not anywhere, in any of the files. I've searched them all at least twice."

"What format were they recorded in?" I ask.

"Hess was old school. For nearly his entire tenure here, he did his autopsy recordings on those little micro-cassettes. When he was done, he placed them in the patient's file. And they're all there, there's just nothing on them. It's like they were scrubbed or something."

Of course they were. He's thought of everything.

"He never moved over to digital at all?" I ask.

Kyle nods. "He did, actually. From 2016 on, he kept them on the local server."

"I remember that," Bancroft adds. "Right after I came into this job, the department ungraded most of its systems. Hess griped for a little while about having to change the way he did things."

"So let's look at those files," I say.

Kyle shakes his head. "I don't think you're getting it, Darcy. I'm telling you, everything is gone. The tapes have been scrubbed, probably by a powerful magnet, and all of Hess' audio files are gone from the server."

The chief growls beside me. "Why would he have erased it all?"

"It's the same thing with the house," I explain. "He didn't want to leave sufficient evidence for us to peg him with any certainty. He wanted me personally on this case. But he also knows that I am the only one who can recognize him by his voice, which would tie him back to the Chancellery."

"He retired over two years ago," Bancroft replies. "So if it is him, then he's been planning this for that long?"

"Longer, if you're asking me. Think about it. The runes speak to a long cycle. This entire thing has spanned almost twenty years. Two cycles of nine years." I look back to Kyle. "You never noticed that all his recordings were missing?"

He shakes his head. "I never had any reason to check. None of the autopsies he did had to be revisited or looked back up. Most of them were pretty straightforward."

The door opens and Vera steps into the room. "Here is the picture you requested, Agent Hunt. I found one in a stack of photos from the summer festival a few years back." After she leaves, I turn it over and study it.

"Right there," Kyle says as he looks over my shoulder. "That's

Hess on the left. He was volunteering as a parking lot attendant that particular year."

The image has three men in it. All three are wearing matching red shirts. Hess has a full gray beard and beady eyes set beneath strong brows. He's stocky with wide shoulders and thick forearms. Unlike the other two men, Hess isn't smiling. Stoic is the word that comes to mind.

Studying the image, I feel equal parts revulsion and disappointment. Revulsion because I have no doubt that this is the man I saw at the cafe an hour ago. The disappointment stems from not having seen his face in the snowstorm, or when he came to take Lila all those years ago. I wish I could match what I see in the picture with a clear face in my memory.

"What do you think?" Bancroft asks.

"It's him. I never got a look at his face at the cafe, but I just know it's him. He has the same build. And the beard."

The room goes silent as all three of us stare at the photo. I know that each of the men with me is warring with his own feelings right now, not wanting to believe that this man that they knew and trusted is the man we're looking for.

I have to give it to him. Hess truly is a brilliant man. Demon from hell or not, he has outsmarted us at every turn. All this time and no one even suspected that it was him. Not only is he part of the chaos that repeatedly strikes this town, he is the mastermind behind it all.

I can't help but marvel at the thoroughness of his planning. But then out of the blue something strikes me like a lightning bolt, bringing me back to the urgency of the present.

"You're not as smart as you think," I mutter.

"What's that?" the chief asks.

"I think I can prove it. Who handles all the IT for the station?"

"Jerry does."

"Where is his office?"

"On the other side of the building. The hallway past my office. First office on the right. Why?"

I hand Kyle the photo and go to the door. "Give me a few minutes. I have an idea."

FOR THE NEXT TWENTY MINUTES, I pace back and forth down the narrow hallway as I wait for Cheetah to do his magic. The wait is excruciating. If this doesn't work out, then I will never be able to conclusively prove to anyone else that Marvin Hess is my kidnapper. There is so much hanging on this, and as I pace, tiny beads of sweat break out across my forehead.

Finally, Jerry emerges from his office wearing a consternated expression. "Well?" I ask, not wanting to wait a second more than I have to.

His round face breaks into a smile, and he lifts up a thumb drive. "Got it."

A fresh hit of adrenaline buzzes through my veins. "Thank God."

He hands me the thumb drive. "I don't know how your guy in Albany—Cheetah? Is that his name?—I don't know how he did it, but he managed to locate some digital crumbs from the deleted files on the server and reassemble a few of them. I'm pretty good at what I do, but I never would have been able to do that."

"Jerry, thank you!" I blurt, and then hurry back to Kyle's

office with my prize. Bancroft and Kyle are browsing through old personnel files on Marvin Hess when I charge into the room and hold up the thumb drive like it's an Olympic trophy. "Got it!" I announce triumphantly.

"Got what?" the chief frowns.

"My IT guy found a way to get some of Hess' audio files off the server."

Kyle's eyes bug out. "You're joking."

"No. Here." I hand him the drive, and the chief and I assemble around him as he takes a seat behind his desk and plugs the device into his laptop. My heart is thumping like a paranoid rabbit as he navigates to the file menu and hovers the mouse pointer over it.

"Ready?"

I close my eyes and prepare myself. "Yes."

Kyle double taps the file, and his speakers fill with a wash of white noise. After a few seconds, a soft rhythmic clicking in the file gives way to a deep, rough voice. "...portal triaditis in the liver, which indicates acute narcotism. Swelling of the lymph nodes in the portal region..."

My entire body tenses as I listen. I don't realize that my breathing has quickened until the chief sets a reassuring hand on my shoulder, causing me to flinch and open my eyes. "It's him," I gasp, and move out from behind the desk.

"Holy god," Bancroft says.

Kyle pauses the recording. He looks terrified. It doesn't take much imagination to understand why. Hess spent months training Kyle before handing the reins over to him. Now he has to come to terms with the knowledge that he personally knew one of the most vicious criminals this state has ever known.

"It's him," I repeat. "The man from the cafe. The man who... who offered to take Lila and me back to the campground."

Bancroft curses loudly. "That bastard was right under everyone's noses the whole damn time!"

"I... I can't believe it," Kyle says softly.

The room lapses into silence as we individually process what we've just confirmed.

"This town is going to melt down over this," the chief says. "It's been almost a decade since The Four. And now they'll have to learn that there was another. And Marvin, no less." He shakes his head soberly.

Everything in me wants to walk down to the supermarket on Main Street, buy a couple of bottles of wine, and take them back to the chalet. I can feel myself starting to crack around the edges —looking down at my hands, I can't stop my fingers from trembling. But I don't have the luxury of checking out right now.

"Kyle," I say, trying to steady my voice. "What kind of progress is your guy making on materials you found underneath Lily's nails?"

"I just spoke with him while you were down at Jerry's office. He said he's making progress, but that he doesn't have anything conclusive yet."

"I don't need something conclusive, Kyle. We're out of time. *Shelby* is out of time. Whatever he has, I need it, and I need it right now."

"All right. Hang on. He's down the hall. Let me go talk with him."

The next couple of minutes pass agonizingly slowly. No words pass between the chief and me as we fill the time trying to make sense of all of this in our own way. Kyle finally comes back looking none too enthused and returns to the chair behind his desk.

"Well?" I prod.

He shakes his head. "He doesn't really have anything. Tried using a few chemical compounds he has, but couldn't get anything conclusive."

"But what does he have?" I ask, trying to cloak my impatience.

"Two substances. One he is positive is granite limestone."

I look at the chief. "What around this area is made of granite limestone?"

"Hell, what isn't? The boulders in the woods, the upper layers of the hills and foothills themselves. Hess may as well have left us with a sample of air."

"But he presented us with it because he thinks we can figure out where he is going to kill Shelby," I protest. "Kyle, you said there was a second substance?"

"Yes. He said it was mixed in with the granite. He had to spend a lot of time looking at it under a microscope, but on the molecular level, it appears to be a leaf from the mulberry family. So something like a jackfruit, ficus, or fig tree. Most of those don't even grow up here. But those are his best guesses."

"I don't think I've ever seen one of those around here," Bancroft frowns. "Kyle, do you know anyone who has those on their property?"

He shakes his head. "No. I'm not sure I even know what a jackfruit or fig tree looks like."

"Darcy? You okay?" Bancrofts asks.

I blink. "I know where we're supposed to go."

"You do? How?"

"The night before Lila and I were taken, I went on a bike ride up the hill alone. At the top, I saw a tree with broad leaves and strange fruits laying on the ground around it. I took one back to the campsite and asked my dad what it was. He said it was a fig."

"Whoa," Kyle says. "So where is this tree exactly?"

I look at the chief. "Rickshaw Preserve campground. At the top of the cliff, which is what the granite is. And the tree is on the right side as you face the valley. It's where Hess was watching us from when we were at the salt mine the other day. It must still be there."

Bancroft's eyes widen as the connections start to form. "You're sure?"

"Chief, I'm more than sure. This case has been nothing more than Hess drawing me back into his orbit. He counted on me never being able to get ahead of him. This is him toying with me. There is no doubt in my mind that he's taking Shelby up to the lookout at the top of the cliff."

Bancroft nods and starts toward the door. "I'll get every available officer up to Rickshaw Preserve right now."

"No."

My commanding tone stops his forward momentum. He turns back around. "Why?"

"Even though he'll think the chances are slim, Hess will be watching to see if we have it figured out. In the event that we do, he will be expecting your entire cavalry to descend on the base of the Preserve. Our only window of opportunity is to get up there without him detecting us. We can't do it with your entire force charging up there. He'll kill Shelby and disappear before we're within half a mile of him."

"I can't let you go up there alone, Darcy."

381

"I don't want to go alone. You're coming with me. Have your officers come in behind us at intervals, and approach from alternate points of the compass. Tell them to arrive in silence, park further out, and arrive twenty minutes behind us. Any ideas as to where we can enter the preserve without tipping him off? Going through the front gate isn't an option."

"I know," Kyle pipes up. "I like walking out there. On the south slope of the Preserve is a service entrance for the park rangers. I don't think they use it all that much. It seems like Hess might know every square inch of this county, but if he really isn't expecting you, then that's the place to go in at. Unless, of course, that's the trail he uses to get in there."

When I look at the chief for confirmation, he shakes his head. "I don't know that area very well. If Kyle says that's the place to enter, then I have no qualms with that."

"Okay," I say, and feel the adrenaline kick in. "Chief, can you brief your team in under five minutes? Shelby doesn't have long to live."

He adjusts his hat over his brow, and a stony, determined look enters his eyes. "I can do it in three."

Chapter Forty-Five

County Road 98
Delfax County, NY

The trees fly by like blurry phantoms as the chief speeds his cruiser away from Miller's Grove. I'm amazed at his ability to handle every sharp turn with a set of skills that would match the practiced expertise of any NASCAR driver. My GPS shows that at our current pace, we'll be at the Preserve in eight minutes.

Bancroft's phone is perched on the dash cradle, and he is speaking with the county sheriff, explaining his need for backup and their assistance in cutting off any means of escape. "Establish roadblocks at every junction within five miles of the Preserve," he says. "And send anyone you can into the valley to keep an eye on the river and the old pass at Eagle Run."

The sun is below the treetops now which means that we have less than thirty minutes of any kind of light remaining before we have to hike up in the dark. Flashlights won't be an option as Hess would see us coming from a mile away. I can only hope that we'll get to Shelby in time. By this time of day, Lily was already lying dead at the salt mine. I now have a keen awareness of my service pistol on my hip. It feels weightier all of a sudden, like it is begging for me to take it out.

As a teenager, I would often lie in bed at night fantasizing about confronting and killing my sister's killer. I wanted to be the one to find him and make him pay for what he did to my family. But after The Four were discovered, that dream died with them. It was yet another thing that they stole from me. Now, as Bancroft slows for another turn, I feel the old fantasies rising from their tombs.

For two-thirds of my life, I was haunted by a man who was absolute evil, who had no face and no name. But now the phantom has a shape, a face, and a name. He is tangible and real now. And somehow makes me want to see him dead even more.

As a law enforcement officer representing the federal government, I don't have the luxury of getting revenge, but I also know that if I come face to face with Hess, I won't hesitate to blow his brains to kingdom come.

Bancroft ends his phone call with the sheriff and, as if reading my thoughts, says, "Darcy, if we find Hess up there, if he stands down, then you'll have to do the right thing." His words fall between us like a hammer. "Will you be able to do that?"

I don't answer, just stare numbly through the windshield.

"Darcy, if it were me, everything inside me would want to do it. But if you do, he wins. You've come this far. You've done what he didn't expect you to do: you outsmarted him. Not only by verifying his identity but by determining his next location faster than he must have accounted for. You can't kill him in cold blood."

"I know" is all I say.

"I know that you know. But I need to hear you say that you're not going to execute him. If you can't, then I can't let you march up that hill with me."

Rage boils inside me. "Okay," I say dutifully. "I won't kill him unless he gives me good reason." But I don't know if I really believe that.

"Good." He nods. "That's good to hear."

A small billboard badly in need of paint slides by outside my window, reminding folks to eat at The Cattle Cooker next time they're back in town. It reminds me that I have dinner plans with Tim tonight. I move to text him to let him know that I won't be able to make it tonight when a pain of guilt stabs at my chest.

I can't shake the knowledge that in some way I have been lying to the chief. Tim asked me not to say anything to his father about him stopping by to see me. I honored that for a few days. But now it just doesn't seem right. A glance at the GPS tells me that we still have several minutes until we arrive at the south end of the Preserve.

"Chief, can I get something off my chest?"

"Of course. It would probably be better than me sitting here thinking of all the times I could have throttled Hess while he was at the station."

"You should probably know that the night I arrived at your chalet, Tim happened to stop by." I watch the chief's brows furrow and his face pinch tightly. "We've had a few conversations and were planning on having dinner at The Cattle Cooker tonight. I'm sorry I didn't tell you sooner. I know the two of you are somewhat at odds right now."

His jaw clenches tightly as he shakes his head. I'm half expecting a burst of steam to shoot from his ears. "Darcy, what are you talking about? What do you mean that you've had a few conversations with him?"

I expected him to be upset, but not like this. "Like I said, I was working at the table when Tim happened by the chalet the other day. We got to talking, and he mentioned how the two of you aren't on the same page right now."

With no warning at all, Bancroft slams on the brakes as he jerks the wheel. The cruiser skids to a stop along the shoulder, sliding to a halt. Bancroft takes his hand off the wheel and turns to face me. "You're telling me that you talked to my son?"

"Well, yes. And to be honest, I didn't expect you would be this upset about it."

He huffs out a breath, and I see a storm of emotions in his eyes. "Darcy, I don't know where you are getting your information from. But I don't have a son. My only son—Timmy—he was taken from us in a car crash when he was seventeen. He's dead."

Chapter Forty-Six

Rickshaw Preserve
Delfax County, NY

A vicious chill skitters up my arms and settles on the back of my neck. "Dead?" And then, without thinking, I ask, "Are you sure?"

"Of course I'm sure!" Bancroft booms. "You think I would joke with you about something like that? Timmy was on his way back from a friend's house one night when he got T-boned by a delivery truck. He died on his way to the hospital. Who is this person posing as my boy?"

I'm struggling to make sense of what he's telling me. Tim told me that he killed his aunt in a car accident when he was seventeen. But now I'm hearing that the real Tim actually died at that age.

"Your sister... Tim didn't accidentally kill her in a traffic accident?"

A muscle twitches in Bancroft's jaw as fire burns in his eyes. "I don't know who is feeding you this information, Darcy. My only sister is in good health and lives in Nashville."

"But he said—he said that he recently moved back to Miller's Grove. That he lives in a cabin back in the woods behind yours. I've been out there and spoken with him."

"Darcy, the nearest cabin to mine is Charlie Langford's place. The trail behind the chalet takes you to it a mile back. But Charlie lives in Georgia and only comes up during the summers."

"Then if the man I've been talking to isn't your son, then... who is he?"

"How in the hell would I know? I don't understand why someone would pull such a stunt. We have some pranksters in town, but no one who would stoop this low."

The inside of the cruiser is quiet for a few moments while we both process what we've just learned. It doesn't make sense. The man that I know as Tim is kind and charming. Why would he lie to me like that?

Whoever he is, and whatever it is about, we're not going to figure it out right now. I finally motion down the road. "You'd better keep going. We can sort all this out later."

As the chief pulls off the shoulder and starts to accelerate, my cell phone buzzes with an email. I open it to find the dossier of the recent prison releases that Bancroft had requested to be sent to me.

"Guess we don't need this," I mumble.

"What's that?"

"Nevermind. It's not important." I feel deflated and confused and have to fight with myself to get my focus back on Shelby.

A handful of miles ahead of us, the foothills that make up Rickshaw Preserve rise high, thickly blanketed with firs and pines. Up on top, on the other side, just out of view, is a place I never wanted to see again, much less visit. I steel myself for what's ahead.

"What else did that man tell you?" the chief finally asks. A hurricane of old pain and fresh anger flares across his face.

"He fed me this entire backstory of his life. He said that he accidentally killed his aunt in a car accident when he was seventeen and that you were still struggling to forgive him for it. So he asked me not to mention to you that he stopped by or that we talked. It kind of made sense because your family photos didn't have Tim—Timmy," I correct, "in them after a certain age." I leave out the part where he brought me freshly baked cookies ostensibly made by the chief's wife.

He growls again and I pass the next couple of minutes by mindlessly scrolling through the profiles in the dossier, my finger sliding across the glass in intervals.

"Oh my god," I gasp.

"What is it?"

"Oh my god," I choke out again.

"Darcy, dammit. Would you tell me what's wrong?"

I slowly raise my phone so he can see the photo. "What am I looking at, Darcy?"

I bring the phone back and examine the name. "Chester Rollins. It's the man posing as your son."

"Where did you find that?"

It takes every ounce of strength my mind can muster to stay focused on answering his question. Nothing makes sense right now. "I—it's the dossier from the Bureau of Prisons that you asked for. All the convicted murderers who have been released from prison over the last twelve months."

Bancroft curses and shakes his head. "Give me his details."

There is no doubt that it is the same man. His eyes are the same hazel, but instead of manifesting the soft and kind expression that I'm used to seeing, they're filled with hate and malice. His golden blond hair is slicked back and nearly pasted to his head. "Chester is twenty-nine years old. Spent twelve years in an upstate prison for murdering a sixteen-year-old girl. It looks like they were dating and he killed her because she wouldn't move across the country with him. He was tried as a minor and released two months ago. After his trial, the DA found new evidence that pointed to his complicity in four other murders. But they couldn't present enough evidence for a conviction."

The chief slows the cruiser and turns left onto an unnamed dirt road. A posted sign notifies motorists that it is to be used for official state and county business only.

"We'll have to worry about Rollins later," Bancroft says. "Let's keep our focus where it needs to be for now."

"Look," I say. "Up there."

Twenty yards ahead, a brown truck is parked in the grass. The chief slows the cruiser to a stop and turns off the engine. "Here's hoping we're right about all this," he says, and quietly opens his door. We step out of the cruiser with our service pistols at the ready and slowly approach the truck, me on the right, Bancroft on the left. A quick peek in the bed shows nothing but a coil of braided wire; inside the cab is empty as well.

We stand there for a moment listening to the breeze in the trees, hoping to catch the sound of someone moving through the woods. But there is nothing. Sliding around to the front of the truck, I lay the flat of my hand on the hood. "It's still warm," I whisper. Very warm, in fact. If the truck is any indication, then I was right about Hess taking her to the lookout. But are they one hundred yards up the hill or have they already reached the top of the cliff?

The main entrance to the campground is a mile farther down the county road. From this side of the Preserve, the only way up to the lookout is via the side of a steep hill that flanks our current position. The way Bancroft is looking, I can tell that he is bracing himself for the climb. He isn't as young as he used to be, and the light is fading fast, which will make it more difficult to navigate. He nods toward the hill, and I follow behind him, my heart beating as if in tune with the questions pounding through my head.

Will we get to Shelby in time? If so, will I be able to keep myself from murdering Hess in cold blood? And why did Chester Rollins deceive me like he did? What was his angle and how does he factor into all of this? Concentrating on questions that I don't have an answer to at the moment is a meaningless waste of focus and energy, so I relegate them to the back of my mind as we pick our way upward.

The soil isn't much better than it was on the hill that Darren Malloy tried to ascend behind the gas station. It's loose and studded with rocks large and small. Every chance I get, I reach out and find a tree trunk to keep me stabilized. The chief stays just in front of me and sets a steady pace, stopping briefly every few yards to pause and listen for any kind of sound above.

The going is slower than I want, but any faster and we risk our feet slipping out from under us. The higher we climb, the deeper we get into the woods, which buffers the pale light from the setting sun and cloaks us in a dingy yellow light.

The chief is panting by the time we reach a rock face that rises up high above our heads. A thin ledge runs along its base and angles around to the top, serving as the only viable way around. We exchange uneasy glances, and he finds a handhold on the rock face, then hugs it as he shuffles his way up. Directly below us, the hill runs downward at a sharp forty-five-degree angle. His boots scatter a handful of pebbles, and they bounce off a bed of dry pine needles before careening down the hill.

I slide in beside him and nudge myself against the rock face, carefully matching his pace and stepping over a jutting protrusion of granite just as a blood curdling scream pierces the quiet forest high above us.

"Dear god," Bancrofts says.

She's here. Shelby's here. Relief pours through me, but it's tempered with the realization that we're probably too late.

Fueled by pure adrenaline and the need to save Shelby Campbell, Bancroft shuffles his feet faster up the inclining ridge. Nearing the top, he reaches for an exposed tree root and heaves himself up. Only the root isn't rigid enough to sustain his weight. The root pops a foot out of the soil, causing the chief to careen backward. He grabs on tighter to the root for balance, but it's rotten and snaps off. Before I can do anything about it, he's slipped off the ridge and is falling backward in midair.

He lands on his back with a loud grunt at the base of a tree twenty feet below me. It's everything I can do to look back at him without falling off the ledge myself. I can't call out to him for fear of betraying our presence here. I watch helplessly as his lips part and emit a soft groan as he tries to say something. He struggles fo a moment, seems to think better of it, and then, slowly raising a hand, he waves me onward. I hesitate, not wanting to leave him here alone. For all I know, his back or leg is broken. But I know I don't have a choice. He might need to be carried out of here on a stretcher, but his life, unlike Shelby's, is not in imminent danger. I offer him a solemn nod and turn back up the hill.

Chapter Forty-Seven

Rickshaw Preserve Campground
Delfax County, NY

I finally manage to make my way up the ledge without suffering the same fate as the chief. Once I'm on solid footing on top of the rock formation, I turn and give him a final glance. His eyes are closed and he's not moving. But his chest is rising and falling; a good enough sign, I suppose.

Turning my attention upward, I continue up the slope. After another thirty feet, it slowly begins to taper and I find that I'm able to make much better progress. As I angle my way toward the peak, I don't stop to listen for anything—there is just no time. But I keep my breathing steady and quiet so I can detect any sounds that don't belong. The fall air is crisp and cool up here, and my breath starts to mark the air in the fading light.

A trail emerges on my right and I step onto it, following it around a thick stand of trees and up toward the peak. The scream had to have come from this general vicinity. But I don't see anything. Shelby must have screamed as Hess was dragging her up the hill because they aren't anywhere to be seen.

The trail begins to curve northward, and as I pass a fallen tree on my right, I freeze. My mind begins to hurl memories at me, filling my head with visions and voices from a buried past:

"We went the wrong way! We have to turn around!"

"No! I'm too tired."

"You can do this, Lila. I'm right here with you! Now stay with me and let's go!"

I'm standing at the fork in the trail. The very one we missed in the darkness of the snowstorm. If I hadn't led Lila onto the trail I'm on right now, if I would have turned at the fork, then we would have never fallen into the hands of Marvin Hess and the four men that he controlled.

A second scream from higher up causes my past to disintegrate like smoke. I snap my gaze up the hill and hurry on again. It's not far now, and my senses are on high alert, my gun out and at the ready as I take care not to step on anything that might give away my presence. Another fifty yards and I slow my advance as I hear voices up ahead. I slip off the trail and into cover.

"Shut up!" I peek through a clump of bushes to see Hess leaned over Shelby Campbell. The flat, rocky surface of the lookout is not fifteen feet beyond them. His back is toward me and Shelby's eyes are two black saucers of fear. "I should have left that damn gag on you." A backpack is sitting at his feet, and with one hand he's searching for something inside it. His other hand is around Shelby's throat. A burgundy dress is spread out beside her.

Slowly, I step out of cover and move toward him. From her place on the ground, Shelby catches a glimpse of me. Just as I raise a finger up to motion for her to stay silent, Hess catches her gaze and whips his head around.

Only it's not Hess at all.

It's the man I came to know as Tim.

Chester Rollins.

His eyes are red, crazed with bloodlust. As my mouth opens to order him to get his hands up, he moves swifter than a demon. He flies off of Shelby and darts behind a boulder to his right. Shelby responds by starting to sit up, but before she can do more than raise her head, Rollins' hand shoots out from behind the boulder, grabs a clump of her hair, and drags her out of my sight.

I quicken my pace and stride toward the boulder, swinging to my right so I can have a better angle from which to get him in my sights. His next words nail me in place.

"You come a step closer and she dies, Darcy!"

For some time, the only sound is the wind in the treetops and Shelby's soft whimpers.

His voice finally rocks the hilltop again. "You've been following me? How did you find me up here?"

I ignore the question. "Why are you doing this?"

His eerie laugh booms off the cliff. "Why am I doing this? Do you know how long I've waited for something like this?"

Even though the question is rhetorical, I still have an answer ready. "Twelve years, Chester. That's how long."

It grows quiet on the other side of the boulder. "You know my name?"

"Yes." And in that moment, I decide how I want to play this. "I've known the entire time, Chester. I've just been waiting to catch you in the act."

"You lie!"

I slowly start to inch my way up the hill so I can at least get my eyes on Shelby again. "Why Miller's Grove?" I ask. "Why now?"

"Because he told me to."

"Who, Chester? Who told you to?" The pieces are starting to fall into place for me now. Not all of them, but enough. I know who told him. But right now, I just need him to keep talking while I think of a plan.

"I don't know his name."

"Give me a break," I call back. "Someone convinces you to kill for him and you don't even learn his name?"

"I'm not killing for *him*!" he screams. "It's for *me*."

"Why? What did these girls ever do to you?"

"You don't get it. You can never get it." I can hear Shelby whimpering in fear. "Shut up!" he screams at her. "Darcy, I'll ask you again. How did you find me up here?"

"I followed the clues you left under their nails, Chester. How else do you think?"

"Under their nails?" he mutters to himself. "Wait... you're telling me that the stuff he told me to put under her nails was to clue you in where I would be next?"

"Yes. To the next location he was going to send you," I say with an air of indifference.

He curses loudly. "Why would he do that?"

"Because you are nothing but his puppet, Chester. He's using you to do what he wants. And he doesn't care if you live or die."

"Oh, I'm not dying. That's for damn sure."

"You kill Shelby and you're not making it off this hillside alive."

I hear Shelby cry out in pain and then a brief scuffle ensues.

A moment later the two of them reemerge, Chester using Shelby as a human shield. He has a small revolver pointed at her temple and starts leading her up the hill toward the cliff as they continue to face me.

I keep my gun trained on him and match their pace as I follow them up. I keep my gun trained on him, but I don't have a clean shot. From this distance, I could just as easily hit her. I need to keep him talking. It could be my only chance to get him to make a mistake.

"So this guy," I begin, "he set all this up and promised to let you do the killings?"

"Yes. He started sending me letters a few months before I got out of prison. They were vague, but hinted at it. When I got out, he directed me to a secluded place upstate where he had left some cash and a long letter spelling out what he wanted me to do." Chester finally reaches the flat slab of granite that serves as the lookout. I keep inching to my right as I slowly ascend, trying to keep the right amount of distance so as not to frighten him into a rash move.

"What's in it for you? Why not just go off on your own?"

"Why?" he growls. "Because I've been sitting in a prison cell for over a decade. This was a ready-made fantasy just waiting for me to reach out and take it. And because he wanted me to get inside your head. And the head of the chief. That sounded like a lot of fun. It *was* a lot of fun."

"So the materials you've been placing under the girls' nails. He provided you with those?" I bump backward against something. A glance behind me lets me know that I've backed up into the fig tree.

"Yes." I watch him move a little closer to the edge. The sun has set over the mountain on the other side of the valley, leaving the sky streaked with purple and orange. "Everything. The dresses, the instructions on how to kill them, and what to leave behind."

He inches closer to the edge of the cliff. All this time Shelby has dutifully moved along with him. But now she freezes. "Let's go!" he screams in her ear.

"No! You're going to throw me over."

"No," he growls. "I am not. But if you don't do what I say, I'm going to put a bullet in your head."

She looks at me with a helpless expression, her eyes pleading for me to do something.

Chester inches closer to the edge, and I can see his wheels turning as he considers how he wants to play this. Whatever arrangements he had with Hess are thrown out the window now. Every move he makes from here on will be calculated to save his own skin. I'm now just ten feet away from him.

"You need to put your gun down, Darcy."

"I can't do that, Chester."

"You're here to save this girl's life. If you don't put that gun down, then she dies."

"The way I see it, she dies either way." That elicits another desperate whimper from Shelby. "The question is whether or not you make it out alive."

He stops several feet from the edge and looks around, getting a quick lay of the hilltop. When a cunning smile begins to tug at the corners of his lips, I know exactly what he's going to do.

"Oh, I'm making it out alive, all right. You want to save the girl, then fine. Save her."

As Chester dips his head behind Shelby and completely

disappears from view, everything moves in slow motion. Shelby cries out as Chester thrusts her violently toward the edge of the cliff. Her feet lift off the ground as she hurls into the air and flies face first toward her doom. Chester turns from her and starts for the cover of a tree and, ultimately, his escape down the hill.

In a move that takes only microseconds and is more instinct than decision, I take aim at the back of his head and squeeze off a single round before dropping my gun and bursting toward Shelby. She lands with a hard thump and slides off the ledge. With her screams filling my ears, I lunge out, my chest punching hard into the granite as I reach out and grab her ankle just as she slips completely off the ledge.

Her momentum carries both of us forward and is too much for me to overcome. As we slide forward, Shelby moves farther down the cliff face and I slide farther and farther toward the edge. We finally ease to a stop with my head and shoulders hanging over. Shelby is dangling face down; the only thing keeping her from plunging to a sure death five hundred feet below is the tenuous grip I have on her ankle. "Don't move!" I scream down at her.

Gravity inches my torso closer and closer to the edge as a hot bolt of panic shoots through me. I try using the toes of my shoes to find some kind of purchase on the granite behind me. But it's no use. There is nothing to stop us, not even any protruding branches growing along the cliff that I can grab hold of.

My veins turn to ice as I feel two hands grip my torso, and prepare to be helped the rest of the way to my death.

"Hold still and relax. I've got you."

I nearly burst into tears as I hear the chief's voice in my ears. "Oh, thank god. Shelby, honey. Hold on. We're going up."

Bancroft heaves me back, and I move up several inches. With a loud, focused groan, he finally pulls me all the way back to safety, then grabs Shelby's other ankle and carefully draws her up as well.

She's screaming hysterically when she finally collapses beside me.

"It's okay," Bancroft soothes. "It's okay. You're safe now." She quiets down and reduces her screams to soft sobs. I give her a reassuring smile as I sit with my chest heaving as I try to catch my breath.

"Chester," I pant. "Where is he?"

A small smile forms on the chief's lips as he dips his head to my right. I look over to see Chester Rollins' body sprawled in the pine needles, half his forehead missing from where my hollow point exited his skull.

"A hell of a shot if you ask me," Bancroft says.

"You fell," I say. "Are you all right?"

"Might have fractured a bone in my leg."

"And you made it the rest of the way up?"

"We can do crazy things hyped up on adrenaline."

"Yeah," I nod. "Thanks for saving me back there."

"Thank you for saving Shelby."

I slowly push off the rock face and rise to my feet, then help Shelby to hers. She's terribly shaken. I can't imagine what these last two days have done to her. I wrap a gentle arm around her and offer her a comforting smile. "Come on. Let's get you out of here."

Chapter Forty-Eight

Maybelle's Diner
Miller's Grove, NY

The chief and I are standing in Maybelle's parking lot after enjoying a hearty breakfast inside. He's leaning on his crutches and trying to figure out how to position his leg. After the doctor found a hairline fracture in his right femur, they wrapped the entire leg in a cast. All the doctors and nurses tried to convince him to use a wheelchair for the first couple of weeks but he wouldn't hear of it.

"You sure you don't want me to give you a lift back to the station?" I ask him.

"I'm sure. Linda will be here any minute. She wants us to get out of town for a few days. Said I need to take some time off. And you know, I can't say that I disagree."

"You deserve it," I tell him.

"And so do you." He adjusted the crutch pad under his armpit. "Listen, Darcy. I don't think there is another soul on earth who would have taken this case had they been in your shoes. After everything you went through out here as a child, you still didn't reject the case when it was assigned to you. And I know that going up to the Preserve wasn't easy. I'm sure it brought up all kinds of memories with you and Lila."

Even now, hearing her name out loud leaves a dull ache behind my ribs.

"I think what I'm trying to say is that you have my utmost respect."

"Thank you, Chief. It was an honor to work alongside you. And I'm sorry that Hess tried to get to you with the whole angle with Timmy."

"It's all right. I just wish I would have known all along that it was Hess."

"Don't do that, Chief. No regrets."

He nods. "Yes. That's good."

After rescuing Shelby Campbell, I decided to stay in town through the anniversary of the Chancellery and The Four. To the town's collective relief, yesterday came and went without incident. No kidnappings, murders, or cryptic signs left behind. It seems that when we took down Chester Rollins, we disrupted any further plans Hess may have made.

Hess' vacant house was raided the night that we rescued Shelby. So far, the search has yielded nothing as to his actual whereabouts. But he's out there somewhere, and I can't shake the feeling that he will still be watching me from a distance.

But he won't get to continue his hellish plans forever. Now that I know he's out there, I won't rest until he's six feet under or rotting in a jail cell. I don't care what I have to do, I'm going to find him.

There are still a great many questions that we may never get answers to. Like why did Hess have Chester write out a number inside the valknut he was slowly creating? It started with the number 16. The best I can come up with is that Hess is letting us know how many kills he has under his belt. But if we include the murders from the Chancellery and those of The Four, that only brings us to eight.

My office and a team at Quantico are scrambling to connect Hess to any other murders over the last twenty or thirty years. So far, they haven't come up with anything, but looking into something like that and discovering the proper connections can take a great deal of time.

And then there is the blood that Chester used to write out the triangles and the numbers. The lab is still trying to identify who it belongs to. As much as I'm glad that I put a bullet into Chester's head, I would have liked the opportunity to question him further. Somehow though, I'm not sure if he would have truly had many of the answers himself.

A search of the cabin that Chester was using didn't turn up much. A typewritten letter with instructions for Shelby was found under the bedroom mattress. But it was unsigned and only had Chester's fingerprints on it.

In the low hillside behind the cabin, a tunnel was discovered along with a braided wire used to keep Shelby hostage. I shudder to think that Shelby was less than thirty yards from me the day took a walk out to the cabin and saw "Tim" chopping firewood.

I take out my keys now, and the chief walks me to my car with assistance from the crutches. "We'll never know who he had chosen as his next victim, Darcy. But whoever she is, you saved her."

"No, Chief. We. *We* saved her."

He shakes his head. "Nope. I was behind you every step of the way, doubting every move you wanted to make. Anyhow, you go on now." He extends a hand, and we shake fondly. "You're welcome to come visit anytime. Although, I can imagine that this is probably the last town on earth that you would want to return to."

"Thanks, Chief. Come see me in Albany sometime. I mean that."

"You can bet your britches I will."

I give him a final smile and get into the cruiser, lifting my hand to wave at him as I pull out of the parking lot and onto Main Street. I'm not sure I could ever visit Miller's Grove again. If Hess starts up here again, the case will certainly be slotted to another agent with no personal attachments to it. But I do hope that Bancroft will come see me in Albany. That is one of the things I love most about my job. While you do meet your fair share of morons scrambling to advance their careers at any cost, you also meet some good people as well. People who are kind and committed to finding justice at any cost.

As Main Street turns into the county road, Miller's Grove slowly slips away in my rearview. I set my sights ahead and point the car toward home.

Epilogue

The old television gives off a dingy gray glow as Lucy and Ricky Ricardo argue over a camping trip. But I'm not really paying attention to their antics. My mind is elsewhere.

Chester Rollins failed me. I should have known he would. I employed Chester's services simply as a means to insulate myself. I needed to be free to move about and cast my shadow over everything I was trying to do.

But even more than his failure, I cannot shake the knowledge that she got ahead of me. I underestimated her. She beat me at my own game. Somehow Darcy outsmarted me. The very thought makes me burn hot inside. I can feel the hateful ember glowing deep in my soul, making me want to scream. I don't know how she did it, but she won't have the opportunity to do it again.

I'm making new plans now. Plans that will not take nine years to come to fruition. I was faithful with what I was supposed to do. It was not my fault that I could not offer the last girl.

Down the hallway, the toilet flushes and a door opens. She walks into the living room and drops into the easy chair beside mine. I turn and look at her. Her blonde hair falls loosely down her back, and she's wearing a black tank top, which exposes the valknut tattoo on her shoulder. I reach out and touch it, lightly run the pad of my thumb over it.

She watches the television show with great disinterest. There are times that I see a spark of light in those eyes, and it makes me wonder if she's still deep down in there somewhere. Looking at her now, I can't help but chuckle inside. She'll never know that she was to be the fourth girl. Her blonde hair would have looked so beautiful against the darkness of her burgundy dress.

But all is not lost.

A new cycle begins, one of my own making. Soon enough, I will have to offer her up.

In the meantime, one more surprise awaits Darcy Lockridge —that's how I'll always think of her. Not Hunt. As I think of how she will respond, a laugh rises from deep inside my chest. I tilt my head back and open my mouth, letting the laughter boom out of me.

No, all is not lost indeed.

'M DRIVING along to the relaxing sounds of the Eagles when I hear my phone ring. I pass a sign informing me that it's only fifty more miles to Albany. I have to stop by the office and start filling out paperwork. But I am so looking forward to being home. A nice soak in a hot bath with a glass of wine is absolutely on the agenda.

I turn the music down and answer the phone through the car's Bluetooth.

"Darcy," Kemper says, "are you on your way back yet?"

"I am. Still about an hour out. Why?"

"I have to run upstate to manage a personal crisis. I won't be here when you get back." There is a brief silence before he continues. "What I'm trying to say is that I wanted to speak with you in person."

"Is something wrong?"

"Well..."

I've never known Kemper to be indecisive about anything. So the way he is acting right now gives me pause. "What is it?"

"I know Amy, your friend in the state lab, had to send the blood samples from your case to the lab at Quantico."

"Right. She did."

"And because hospitals have updated their records systems over the years, it took Quantico a while to find a match."

A buzz of excitement runs through me. I've been more than curious to find out what Hess was thinking with the blood samples. "So they did find a match?"

"Yes, and Darcy... well..."

"What, Boss? Out with it already."

A heavy tremor rolls through me and my world narrows a Kemper speaks his next words.

"The blood is an exact match to your sister, Darcy. I thin she's still alive."

THE END

Don't miss the next book in the Darcy Hunt series, *Her Final Wish*, available on Amazon now!

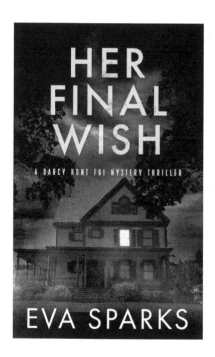

Note from the Author

Dearest Reader,

Thank you for taking the time to read *The Girl in Room 16*. As a writer, I understand that every book holds an unspoken promise to you. That promise is that you will enjoy the story. I hope that you feel I kept my end of the bargain and that you thoroughly enjoyed your time with Darcy.

I will always do my best to make sure that each and every book I write is as thrilling and captivating as it can be.

If you enjoyed spending time in Darcy's world, would you be so kind as to leave a brief review about what you liked most? As a self-published author, positive reviews can go a long way to getting my books in front of other readers, and I'm working hard to write stories that you will continue to enjoy. And feel free to recommend the book to other mystery lovers as well.

I'm so excited to continue this series, and I promise to release each one as quickly as possible. As a reader myself, I can't stand having to wait months for the next installment.

I'm off to work on Darcy's next thrilling investigation, which will be out very soon!

Love,
Eva Sparks

P.S. If there are areas of improvement that you would like to suggest, or if you noticed any typos, would you email me directly and let me know? I reply directly to each and every email I receive: evasparksbooks@gmail.com.

Made in the USA
Middletown, DE
20 January 2025